THE
MIDNIGHT FRONT

THE MIDNIGHT FRONT

A DARK ARTS NOVEL

DAVID MACK

TOR

A TOM DOHERTY ASSOCIATES BOOK
NEW YORK

THE MIDNIGHT FRONT

Copyright © 2018 by David Mack

A Tor Book
Published by Tom Doherty Associates
175 Fifth Avenue
New York, NY 10010

www.tor-forge.com

Tor® is a registered trademark of Macmillan Publishing Group, LLC.

Library of Congress Cataloging-in-Publication Data

Names: Mack, David, 1969– author.
Title: The Midnight Front / David Mack.
Description: First edition. | New York : TOR, a Tom Doherty Associates Book, 2018.
Identifiers: LCCN 2017039667 (print) | LCCN 2017044578 (ebook) | ISBN 9781466890848
   (ebook) | ISBN 9780765383204 (hardcover : acid-free paper) | ISBN 9780765383198
   (softcover : acid-free paper) | ISBN 9781466890848 (ebook)
Subjects: LCSH: World War, 1939–1945—Fiction. | Wizards—Fiction. | Magic—Fiction. |
   Paranormal fiction. | GSAFD: Alternative histories (Fiction) | Fantasy fiction. |
   Occult fiction. | War stories.
Classification: LCC PS3613.A272545 (ebook) | LCC PS3613.A272545 M53 2018 (print) |
   DDC 813/.6—dc23
LC record available at https://lccn.loc.gov/2017039667

Our books may be purchased in bulk for promotional, educational, or business use. Please contact your local bookseller or the Macmillan Corporate and Premium Sales Department at 1-800-221-7945, extension 5442, or by email at MacmillanSpecialMarkets@macmillan.com.

First Edition: January 2018

Printed in the United States of America

0 9 8 7 6 5 4 3 2 1

for those who were silenced,
and those still struggling to be heard

There are both heroes of evil and heroes of good.

—François de La Rochefoucauld, *Maxims*

1939

AUGUST

The night reeked of demons.

Their stench haunted every direction as Nando Cabral fled through wooded hills south of Lemberg, Germany, less than five miles from the French border. He lurched like a drunkard, one hand clamped over the gunshot wound in his left flank. Shafts of moonlight pierced the trees' canopy. Blood pulsed against his palm with each step he took.

He glanced at his pursuers. Blurs of motion, twenty yards away and getting closer.

It was too dark to see their faces, but the young Spaniard knew who they were. He didn't know how they'd found him, but it didn't matter now. Only a handful of spirits were yoked to his bidding, just enough to afflict him with a constant headache. He didn't have the minor legion he'd need to fight one fellow karcist, never mind two. All he could do now was run.

A spectral whip cracked, spitting green fire as it ripped bark from the trees to his left. The enemy was upon him. All hope of reaching France abandoned, Nando turned and steeled himself for battle. His foes moved like wraiths, over a dozen meters apart.

To split my focus, Nando reasoned. With a thought he dispatched two demons normally tasked with divination to be his sentries. Then he used another spirit's gifts to make himself invisible—a delaying tactic at best, but every second mattered in magickal warfare.

His enemies were nowhere to be found—whispers lurking in the dark.

He silenced his steps with the talent of ARIS, one of the Descending Hierarchy's patrons of thievery. Though the ground was littered with dry twigs and debris, he skulked across it without leaving a trace or making a sound.

They must have seen me trailing their courier. Other than one moment on the streets of Stuttgart, he had been careful to stay out of sight and under the concealment of warding glyphs. Breaking cover to track the Thule Society's messenger to his final destination had been a calculated risk—one that had earned Nando a bullet in his gut and the attention of the two enemies his master Adair had warned him to avoid at all costs.

He searched the night as he flanked his foes. They had caught him less than prepared for battle, but he wasn't defenseless. The strongest spirit he held in yoke was BELETH, a king of Hell renowned for its love of destruction. Nando felt the fallen angel's wings as if they were his own. He beat them twice, unleashing strokes of thunder that rent tree trunks into splinters. Shock waves coursed through the broken forest, churning up dust—

Twin bolts of violet lightning arced through the haze and struck Nando's chest. They hit like a charging bull, launching him backward. He tumbled over roots and sharp rocks.

A sharp freezing pain in his chest stripped away his invisibility as he lost his mental hold on GLASYA, which returned to the Abyss, the letter of its duty discharged. Nando pawed at the maggot-covered wound in his torso and realized he had been felled by the spear of SAVNOK, a marquis of Hell that delighted in spreading pestilence.

Movement, on his right. He lashed out with a demonic blade against which no armor could stand, only to see it deflected.

A darting form on his left. Nando made the trees his soldiers. Their limbs lashed out to seize a red-haired young woman. Within seconds she was snared, an oaken branch coiled around her throat and clamped over her mouth.

Nando commanded the trees, *Tear her*—

A fireball swallowed him whole.

It was a strike from a demon's firebrand. Nando filled the air with screams, but he couldn't hear them over the roaring of hellfire.

When the last lick of flame died, he lay supine before his enemies. The woman, now free of the trees, stood tall. She radiated contempt, her copper mane so tousled as to look almost feral. If not for the malice in her blue eyes, Nando would have found her beautiful beyond compare.

Equally striking was her companion, a fair-haired man with chiseled features. Even after waging a duel in the forest, he looked immaculate. His shoes betrayed not a scuff, his tailored suit admitted not one wrinkle. If the warnings Nando had heard from his master Adair were true, the man before him had to be the Nazis' top sorcerer, Kein Engel.

Kein regarded Nando with weary regret. "So much potential. What a waste."

The woman made a fist of her right hand. "Let me finish him."

"No, Briet. It needs to be me." From beneath his black trench coat, which bore a swastika on its lapel, Kein drew an athamé, a black-handled knife used in ceremonial magick. He kneeled over Nando, whose ravaged body was racked with tremors. Leaning close, Kein dropped his voice to a confidential volume and spoke in perfect Spanish. "Training you and the other *nikraim* as karcists was clever. Your master Adair never used to exhibit such foresight."

Nando wanted to spit in the dark magician's face, but his mouth was as dry as cinders, and it took all his strength to speak. "You won't beat us all."

"I have already killed Adair's other five like you. And when I find the last of your kind, the one that was hidden, this war will be over"—he stabbed the blade into Nando's heart with a savage twist—"and a better future can begin."

SEPTEMBER

The silver Austin Ten slowed to a halt in front of the Royal Army recruiting office. Outside, rain slashed up St. Giles' Street, scouring the façades of Oxford town houses. Thunder rattled the chauffered car's windows as Cade Martin grasped the rear door's handle.

His father, Blake Martin, grasped Cade's arm. "We're late, son. Be quick."

"I'll be back before you can say 'Chamberlain's a knob.'"

Cade's mother Valerie leaned forward to speak past her husband. "Cade, we're serious. The storm's washing out the roads. We can't afford to miss the boat, it's—"

"—the last one home to America. I know, Mom." He opened the door. Rain drenched him as he paused to tell his father's English driver, "Don't let 'em leave me behind."

"No promises, Master Cade."

"You're a peach, Sutton. Never change." Cade dashed through the squall. After all the years he had lived in England—first at a boarding school in London from the time he was fourteen, and then at Oxford's Exeter College for the last two years—he had come to admire the dryness of British wit, and to delight in skewering its pretensions whenever possible.

The predawn hours in Oxford were always dark, but the storm made this morning doubly so. In spite of the downpour, wind, and gloom, a line of men stretched down the street from the recruiting office, all waiting to enlist in the war Germany had sparked by invading Poland two days earlier. Most of the men looked like locals, but Cade recognized a few from various Oxford colleges. He went to the only one he knew by name. "Claydon! Have you seen Miles?"

The gangly student winced as the wind shifted and stung his face with rain. "He's inside. Crazy blighter was at the head of the queue."

"Shit." Cade shook his head, annoyed at himself. *Knowing Miles, he stood out here all night to make sure he was the first one in.* "Thanks, Claydon." He hurried up the steps and shouldered past the queue. His passage was tracked by frowns, but he paid them no mind. *They're all just dead men walking.*

He pushed open the door at the top of the stairs and strode inside. The foyer was spare, lacking chairs, sofas, or other comforts. Small tables sported hand-bills extolling the virtues and rewards of national service. Minding it all was a cherub-faced corporal who nearly fumbled his clipboard as he intercepted Cade. "Sir, you need to wait your—"

"Relax, I'm not dumb enough to enlist. I'm just looking for someone who is." The corporal stammered as Cade hurried past him and down a corridor. Drawn by Miles's rich baritone, Cade passed portraits of military officers whose mustaches were likely older than he was. At the hall's open last doorway, he stopped and leaned in.

Miles Franklin, his best friend and fellow Oxford undergraduate, sat in front of a desk lorded over by a sergeant whose every pen, paper clip, and sheet of paper had been placed parallel or at a perfect right angle to one another, as if his stationery and office supplies had been mustered into a parade formation. Disapproval drew a frown beneath the man's trimmed mustache when he saw Cade. "And you are . . . ?"

The question prompted Miles to turn toward Cade and beam at the sight of him.

"Cade! Come to your senses, old boy?"

"No, I came to watch you take leave of yours." To the sergeant, Cade added with mock excitement, "I never saw a man throw away his whole life before."

Miles got up. "Forgive me, Sergeant, but could my friend and I have the room for a moment?"

The sergeant stood and retrieved his hat from a rack in the corner. "Very well, Mr. Franklin. One minute." He left the room, pausing only to scrunch his eyebrows at Cade, who answered the sergeant's disdain with an irrever-ent smile.

Miles towered over Cade. "What are you playing at?"

Cade mused that they must seem to others like a pair of mismatched socks. Cade wore the suits and ties expected of Oxford undergraduates, yet on him they looked like bad disguises, whereas Miles had a knack for fashion. By the same token, Cade was pale and ordinary-looking, while Miles was ebony-skinned with regal features. Even their voices were a study in contrast. Cade was convinced his American accent sounded doltish next to Miles's English baritone. "Dammit, Miles. I can't believe you'd leave Oxford with half a degree just to join the army."

"Believe it." Mischief sparkled in Miles's eyes. "You can do it, too."

"It's not my war."

"That's your father talking." He set his hand on Cade's shoulder. "Come with me! The army's happy to sign up Yanks."

"Yeah, but they don't take gents like *you*."

"Like me?" He held up a brown hand. "Sons of Africa?"

"You know what I mean." He checked over his shoulder to make sure the sergeant had not returned. "Poofters."

Miles laughed. "The army frowns upon categories of *behavior,* not categories of *person.* I'll be fine."

"You're just gonna live a lie for the duration of the war?"

"I won't have to." He poked Cade. "Unlike you, I know how to control my appetites."

His teasing made Cade recall the many nights they had haunted the pubs of Oxford, telling tales, singing songs, and humbling all who dared challenge them at darts. It saddened Cade to imagine his boon companion going off to war—and he felt more than a twinge of shame that he lacked the courage to enlist with him, even though he knew in his heart that it would be the right thing to do. Masking his self-reproach with bravado, he said, "Tell me you're not just doing this to prove some bloody point about Oxford men being patriots."

Miles didn't hide his disappointment. "I'd really hoped you'd come around."

"I could say the same of you."

The sergeant marched between them on his way to his desk. "If you two are quite finished?"

Before Cade could respond, his father's driver, Sutton, leaned through the doorway to interrupt. "Pardon, young master, but time and tide . . . ?"

"Coming." Saddened at parting from the man he'd loved like a brother for the past two years, all Cade could do was shake his head. "Take care. And try not to get killed."

Miles grinned. "Worried about me already?"

"Sod off. You owe me ten pounds."

Miles turned out his empty pockets. "Sorry, mate, I'm a bit short." A humble shrug masked the moment's sorrow. "Settle up next time?"

Cade embraced his friend. "Count on it." They gave each other's backs hearty slaps, then parted with a valedictory handshake. Miles returned to his chair in front of the sergeant's desk to finish his enlistment paperwork, while Sutton led Cade out of the recruiting office.

Outside, whips of rain lashed the street, and lightning flashed across the sky. Idling in the street was the Austin Ten, its headlight beams spearing the storm's curtain.

As Sutton scurried ahead to open the rear door of the Austin Ten for Cade, Cade heard steam whistles—the mournful cries of trains hurtling past Oxford Station, half a mile away.

Even from Exeter's secluded Fellows' Garden, Cade had heard trains rumbling across the countryside. By order of His Majesty's government, over the past two days tens of thousands of children and teens from every stratum of society had been evacuated from the urban and industrial targets of southern and central England, to the illusory safety of the rural north.

Cade's grim reflections were cut short by a hand on his arm. An older man with an ashen bramble of a beard and a Scottish accent halted him midstep. "Cade Martin?"

He eyed the stranger with suspicion. "Do I know you?"

"I'm here to recruit you for—"

"No thanks." Cade continued toward the sidewalk.

He made it only one step before the mad-eyed stranger seized Cade's collar. "I'm not done yet, Mr. Martin. The war effort *needs* you."

"Don't touch me!" Cade broke the Scot's hold. "I don't know who you are, but I'm not buying what you're selling. *This isn't my war.* Get it?"

Again Cade walked away. He made it as far as the sidewalk before the stranger caught up to him. "If you run, you'll endanger everyone near you." That stopped Cade, who turned back as the man added, "Including your parents."

Before Cade could demand an explanation, his father Blake bolted from the Austin Ten and put himself between Cade and the stranger. "Get in the car, son."

"Dad, what's—?"

"Get in the car!"

Cade backed away from the confrontation between his father and the older man. He retreated toward the Austin Ten, lingering just long enough to hear his father warn the stranger, "Don't *ever* talk to my son again."

The Scot sounded desperate. "It's too late, Blake. He can't hide forever."

"Maybe. But he's not going with you." Cade's father shoved the older man, who fell in a heap on the sidewalk. Cade stood mesmerized by his plight until his father, on the move, took Cade's arm and led him toward the car.

In spite of the downpour, a reek of sulfur haunted Cade as he and his father hurried to the Austin Ten. Cade winced at the odor as he glanced across the street to see another stranger staring at him: a pale, brown-haired man in his thirties, sporting a close-cropped Vandyke, a dark suit, and a fedora. The man tracked Cade's every step but made no attempt to approach; he just stood with his hands in his pockets, exuding malice.

Cade's father hustled him into the car's backseat, sandwiched him in the middle between himself and Cade's mother, then snapped at Sutton, "Go!"

Compelled either by instinct or by anxiety, Cade stole a look out the car's rear window. The older man was still sprawled on the sidewalk, but the stranger in the fedora had vanished.

The Austin Ten lurched into motion and sped away. Its chassis rumbled and clattered over the stone-paved streets of Oxford as rain slashed across its windshield.

Trapped between his parents, Cade found himself troubled by the altercation on the steps. "Dad . . . who was that?"

"No one who concerns you."

"What did he mean when he said I couldn't hide forever?"

"Just forget about him, Cade."

Cryptic looks passed between Cade's parents. His mother tried to mask her concern with a nervous smile. "Try to sleep, sweetheart. We'll wake you in Liverpool."

Tempest-drenched scenery blurred past. Oxford's suburbs gave way to rural countryside after less than thirty minutes of driving. Outside the rear window, Cade saw only billowing clouds of exhaust, as if his past had been erased.

He felt hypnotized by the road's ambient drone. The patter of raindrops on the roof, the white noise of tires on wet asphalt, and the purr of the engine lulled Cade to sleep. His mind protested at the thought of sleep, but his eyes fluttered closed.

A moment, then. Just a few minutes' rest. . . .

———— ∽∽ ————

Cade awoke with a start and squinted into hazy morning light.

The car was stopped, and he was alone in the backseat. His eyes adjusted as he looked around. The Austin Ten was parked beside a crowded dock where a massive steamship was anchored. The trunk was open. Burly porters pulled the Martins' luggage from the car and carried it toward the ship's gangplank. His parents stood in front of the car, talking with Sutton.

Cade got out of the car. Muggy heat pungent with the stink of low tide made him miss the car's air of clean leather and sweet pipe tobacco.

His father shook Sutton's hand. "I'm sorry I can't offer more than a week's severance, after all the years of service you've given us."

Sutton waved away the sentiment. "It's nothing, Mr. Martin."

"I disagree." Cade's father handed the driver a folded slip of paper. "The car's title. I've signed it over to you. Call it a parting gift."

"Most generous, sir," Sutton said, with strong emotion in his voice. "I'll keep it in good order until you return." He tipped his cap at Cade. "Safe travels, young master."

Cade waved good-bye to Sutton, then was guided away by his parents, across the dock and up the gangplank of the steamship *Athenia*.

A steward with callused hands and an Edinburgh accent met them on the main deck. "This way, folks!" With the sway of a man whose sea legs didn't know what to do on land, he led them belowdecks to their cabin. Three porters laden with their luggage plodded behind them.

Their cabin was a tidy space made claustrophobic by their luggage, which the porters stacked in haphazard fashion. Noting the family's dismay, the steward smiled and tipped his cap. "It's wee, but it's private. There's even a porthole somewhere in there!"

Cade's mother did her best to be polite. "How luxurious. Thank you."

An awkward silence made it clear the steward expected a tip. Cade's father pressed a few shillings into the man's palm, then shut the door. "I need a drink. Valerie, where's my flask?"

"In your trunk, where you put it."

The ship's horn blared, shivering the deck with its voice. Cade put his back to a bulkhead as his parents wrestled their luggage and each other to retrieve his father's flask. On another day, Cade might have found their foibles amusing, but the cabin was too tight for his comfort. He opened the door. "I'm going topside to watch the castoff."

His announcement drew an anxious look from his father, but his mother answered first. "All right, dear. If we go out, we'll leave a light on for you."

"Thanks, Mom."

Cade made his way up to the main deck. From there he gazed out at Liverpool's haze-obscured rooftops. Hundreds of passengers crowded the ship's railings. Most of them waved and blew kisses to the teeming masses on the dock below. Others stared into the distance as if they feared they might never again see England—at least, not the England they knew.

The crew cast off the ship's arm-thick rope moorings. Clanking chains and humming motors announced the weighing of the anchor, and the *Athenia*'s horn split the air loudly enough to make Cade wince. Deep rumblings resounded through the hull, and the ship crept out to sea.

A breeze offered fleeting relief from the humidity. Cade considered moving to the bow for a view of the open ocean—until he saw someone on the dock staring at him.

The silent stranger from outside the recruiting office.

As if immune to the swelter, the pale man was still garbed in his suit and fedora. Even from several dozen yards away, Cade felt the weight of his gaze. Whoever the man was, whatever he wanted, it was no coincidence he was here.

Maybe I should point him out to Dad. Cade turned to hurry to the cabin, but then he wondered if he had fallen prey to his own imagination. He looked back; the stranger was gone. Whether he had vanished into the crowd or into thin air, Cade couldn't say.

I guess it doesn't matter. As long as he's gone.

Cade walked aft. Lonely hours passed while he gazed from *Athenia*'s stern. He pushed from his mind all thoughts of Miles marching into peril, and of the peculiar stranger on the dock, while he watched England recede by degrees beyond the horizon.

Farewell, Britannia, he brooded. *I guess I'll see you when the war's over.*

A flick of the wrist cast a match into the empty fuel drum. Flames shot upward with a roar, and heat stung Siegmar Tuomainen's face.

He stepped back to keep the fire from crisping his Vandyke but took care not to scuff the double circle he had chalked around the barrel, which he had found behind the docks' motor pool, safe from prying eyes. Between the concentric rings he had scribed glyphs to prevent his enemies from detecting this minor magick. Outside the larger circle he had written the astrological signs in their zodiacal order, with Gemini to the north.

From his pocket he took a knot of cheese cloth packed with rock salt and exorcised Mercurial incense of powdered black dianthus. He cast it into the fire. Golden sparks fountained from the blaze, and the day's heat was dispelled by an unearthly chill.

Siegmar extended his hand into the jet of fire and phosphors, and uttered the incantation for distant communication: "*Exaudi. Exaudi. Exaudi.*"

Tongues of flame twisted then merged to reveal the face of Kein, his master in the Art. Siegmar bowed his head. "*Ave,* Master."

Kein spoke in syllables of ash and shadow. "Ave. *What news?*"

"I was unable to reach him in time. He was warded against attack."

A solemn nod. "*As we feared. Where is he now?*"

"On a ship with his parents. The *Athenia*. It left Liverpool at three minutes past one o'clock, bound for North America."

"*You have done well. Return to Wewelsburg. We have much to do.*"

"What of the boy?"

Through the flames, a wan smile. "*He is at sea. He has nowhere left to run.*"

3

Thirty-six hours of nausea and a restless night had reminded Cade how much he hated sea travel. Members of the *Athenia*'s crew had assured him the ocean was calm and the weather fair, but his stomach insisted they were lying. Seasickness had robbed him of his appetite within hours of the ship's departure—an ailment that had come to seem a blessing when he spied the meals being served in the dining room.

I love the English, but I hate their cooking.

He stood on the promenade deck, white-knuckling the port railing as he fought the urge to retch. The sea air helped clear his head. To the south the sky was a dusky pink, and the sun descended into the horizon ahead of the westbound *Athenia*.

Footsteps crossed the deck behind Cade, drawing closer. In no mood to make things easy for his father, Cade pretended not to notice his approach.

His father stepped to the railing on Cade's right. "You left dinner in a hurry. Feeling all right?" He saw Cade shake his head. "Hm. You do look a bit green in the gills. Maybe the ship's doctor can give you some bicarb. Settle your stomach."

"You want to settle my stomach? Toss the chef overboard."

They passed a moment admiring the sunset. His father packed the bowl of his briar pipe with a sweet Cavendish tobacco, then looked at the horizon. "There's something we should talk about, son." His joviality turned to shame. "A truth I've kept from you for far too long."

Cade had never heard his father speak that way before. "Truth about what?"

He struck a match on the railing and lit his pipe, filling the air with aromas of cherry and bourbon. "Decisions I made before you were born. Burdens I cursed you to carry."

"Dad, I know I complained about boarding school, but it really wasn't that bad."

"You love to pretend everything's a joke, but this is serious, Cade. All these years . . . I should've been training you."

"You teach history and Mom's a chemist. What're you gonna train me in? Alchemy?"

"Dammit, Cade! Just *listen* for once in your life! I have to prepare you for what's coming, before it's too late. I should've told you the truth years ago, but your mother and I were afraid." He stared at his shoes. "You're all we have. We don't want to lose you."

Startled into focus, Cade began to share his father's fear. "Dad . . . what're you talking about? What *exactly* do you think is coming? And what's it got to do with me?"

Just as his father mustered the courage to reply, there came a fluttering of wings above their heads. They recoiled from a large black bird. It landed on the railing and turned to face them. Cade marveled at the creature, whose eyes shone with hypnotic power. "Is that a crow?"

His father stared at it, horrified. "A raven." He swatted at the bird. "Shoo! Get lost!"

The raven flapped its wings, jabbed its beak at his hand, and let out a piercing caw. Then, in a scratch of a voice, it squawked, "Lifeboat!"

Shocked silence. Cade backed away from the raven. "Dad . . . the bird *talked*."

"Go below, son."

"Ravens don't talk. Parrots talk. Mynah birds talk. Even starlings. But not—"

"Lifeboat!" the raven cried.

Terror possessed his father. He pointed forward, toward the hatchway. "Get to the dining room! Find your mother, bring her—"

"Why does it keep saying 'lifeboat'?"

"Just find your—" His voice trailed off as his gaze shifted past the bird, toward the sea. Cade stepped to the railing and saw what had mesmerized his father: a straight line of white froth churning beneath the waves—and speeding directly toward the *Athenia*.

A torpedo.

His heart pounded as he grabbed his father's coat. "Dad, c'mon!"

There was no time to run. The explosion boomed louder than thunder. An icy spray of seawater doused them as the *Athenia* lurched starboard, away from the blast, slamming them against the superstructure. A fireball climbed skyward from the aft quarter of the ship, which recoiled hard to port, throwing them against the railing.

Cade lost his footing and started to tumble over the railing. His father dropped his pipe and caught Cade's arm. "Hang on, son!"

The ship settled onto its keel with a list to port. Alarms sounded, and the crew scrambled to general quarters. The raven was nowhere to be seen as Cade's father pulled him away from the railing and pointed him forward. "Get to a lifeboat!"

"What about Mom?"

"I'll find her! Go!"

He followed his father. "I'm staying with you!"

The captain's voice blared from speakers on the superstructure: *"All passengers, this is the captain: Abandon ship. Proceed to the main deck and board the lifeboats."*

Cade's father tensed to argue, then changed his mind. "Stay close."

They scrambled across the pitched deck, fighting for balance. At the hatchway they collided with a flood of bodies—the first wave of crew and passengers fleeing topside. Shrieks of panic filled the air as another blast rocked the ship from its bowels, knocking out the lights. Fear swirled inside Cade, churning up sickness worse than any the sea could inflict.

His father elbowed his way down the corridor. Cade followed, blading through the crowd to make sure he and his father didn't get separated. They charged down the forward staircase, only to be halted by a rolling wall of black smoke that stank of motor oil and diesel fuel.

A junior officer blocked them with his palms against their chests. "Go back!"

Cade stunned the man with a punch in the face, then followed his father past him.

Smoke stung Cade's eyes and burned his throat. He coughed and spat out the fuel residue in his mouth as he struggled to keep up with his father. Retreating passengers streamed past them on either side. Then someone ran right into them.

Instead of pushing away, Cade's father embraced the shape in the darkness. Cade blinked and recognized his mother's profile. "Mom!"

She let go of Blake to hug Cade, kissed his cheek, then pushed them into motion. "I'm fine! Go!" They followed the evacuation up to the promenade and joined the queue for lifeboats, which snaked up two sets of steps to a boarding platform above the main deck.

At the head of the line, the ship's crew did its best to keep things under control, but Cade could barely hear the officers' instructions over the shouting passengers vying to be the first to abandon the sinking Cunard liner. "Be patient, ladies and gentlemen!" said a lieutenant. "We have lifeboats for everyone, and time to launch them! Stay calm!" His words calmed the throng until a dip to stern sent the North Atlantic's waves coursing over the aft deck.

The line pushed forward, only to recoil as the ranking officer drew his sidearm. "Order!" The lieutenant swung his pistol. "You'll board when we bloody tell you!" He glanced at his crew, who fumbled with the first boat's tangled ropes and a rusty crane arm. "Faster!" A sweep of his revolver at the encroaching masses. "You'll board based on cabin assignment! First-class passengers to the front!"

Booing and protests filled the air.

An old lady shrilled, "Women and children first!"

The tumult hushed at the crack of a gunshot. The lieutenant stood with his pistol aimed at the sky, smoke climbing from its muzzle. "First-class passengers! Board now!"

Cade's father pulled him and his mother forward. "That's us."

Tourist- and steerage-class denizens glared at Cade, his parents, and the other first-class passengers as they shouldered their way to the front of the line, hectored by curses. A young woman clutching an infant to her breast regarded Cade with terrified eyes as he and his parents ascended the steps to the lifeboats.

Ahead of them, the first lifeboat finished loading, a mass of nervous passengers between two young crewmen of the *Athenia,* one each at the boat's bow and stern. As Cade and his parents watched its launch, Cade realized being among the first to abandon ship might be more a curse than a blessing. Tangled ropes and bad timing of the crane arm's outward swing tilted the boat. Its posh complement yowled as they clung to seats and gunwales, desperate not to be pitched overboard. Their less wealthy fellow passengers still on the *Athenia* snickered at the toffs' predicament.

The laughter ceased as the ropes went slack and the lifeboat plunged out of control. It righted itself just before it struck the water, but it landed hard, and its splash showered the crowd on the deck.

Above them, officers barked orders full of jargon at the launch crews. Most of the terms made no sense to Cade, but the lieutenant's summation was easy to grasp: "No more cock-ups, you bastards! Drop another boat and I'll shoot every last one of you!" He turned his wrath toward the passengers on the steps. "Keep it moving!" The line scurried forward. He pointed at the Martins as they neared the top of the steps. "You three! In the bow!"

Cade was sandwiched between his parents as they were directed into the last spots, at the second lifeboat's bow. His mother boarded first. Cade wondered if his father might try to give up his place for someone else, but his illusions of paternal chivalry shattered as his father sat down to his left on the narrow bench seat. "Hang on, son," his father said.

The two crewmen assigned to the lifeboat prepared for launch. Cade's mother wrapped her arms around him, as if she could shield him from the crew's incompetence. The ropes went taut and the boat wobbled as it was hoisted off the top deck. The crew swung the crane arm over the port side to put it above the water. Cade's mother kissed his cheek. "Close your eyes, sweetheart." Looking into her tear-stained eyes, he realized she was seeking courage more than offering it.

Pulley wheels squeaked as the ship's crew labored to launch the boat. The lifeboat was halfway down when someone lost his grip and sent them into free fall. Cade's stomach lurched into his throat, and only the fact that it was empty kept him from spewing more than acid. The drop ended with a jolt, and freezing water exploded over the gunwales, soaking him and everyone else aboard. The ocean's roar muffled the sounds of panic from the *Athenia* until Cade and the rest of the lifeboat's lucky few surfaced and gasped for air.

"Someone start bailing," shouted the crewman in the rear of the lifeboat.

The crewman at the bow said, "Set the oars! Start rowing before the next launch!"

The lifeboat's passengers fell over one another fixing the oars into the locks so they could move clear of the launch area. A pair of men in the middle of the boat rowed, while the aft-end crewman steered the boat toward the *Athenia*'s half-sunken stern.

Cade stared in horror at the wound the torpedo had torn in the ship's hull.

The gash in the ship's aft quarter gulped seawater and belched smoke. The flooding lower decks glowed with spreading fires.

Behind them, another lifeboat launched. It fell nose-first and pierced the surface like an arrow. Screams of terror split the air, only to be smothered by the sea.

Athenia rolled farther to port, hurling a dozen souls over the railings into the frothing waves. Its stern sank deeper with a groan that sent a shudder down Cade's spine.

Clear of the foundering ship, the oarsmen rowed harder. They pushed the lifeboat around the stern, then north into open water in pursuit of the first boat, which was several dozen yards ahead of them. Cade's father asked the man at the bow, "Shouldn't we stay near the ship?"

"Got to avoid getting pulled down with her when she sinks," the crewman said over the thud-and-creak of the oars. "Trust me, we know what we're—" The boat juddered.

Cade's mother's jaw trembled and fell open, but no words came out. She pointed past the the bow, at the open sea, and his father tensed. Cade strained to see what had alarmed them.

A whirlpool yawned ahead of the boat.

It was no ordinary vortex; Cade sensed there was something unnatural about the speed at which its maw expanded and its swirling throat sank into the deep. Within seconds the first lifeboat tipped over its precipice and vanished. Spectral light weltered in the gyre, and a cold miasma gusted from its bowels. Cade's father recoiled from the stench. Then a tentacle lashed out of the whirlpool, plucked the crewman from the bow, and dragged him screaming into the depths.

"LEVIATHAN!" Cade's father said, as if the name were a curse—and then he ceased to be the bookish Cambridge professor Cade had always known. Now he had a killer's eyes. He stood, propped one foot against the prow, reached under his jacket, and pulled out a twisted wand of carved white wood. "Valerie! Stay down!"

Cade stared in disbelief at the wand. *What the hell is he doing?*

Seven massive tentacles erupted from the vortex and flailed at the lifeboat. All that kept them at bay were daggers of fire that spat from the wand as Cade's father bellowed in hoarse, garbled Latin: "*Vindicta! Morietur, et draconi!*"

The oarsmen rowed in frantic strokes, desperate to put as much distance as possible between themselves and the thrashing tentacles. Bolts of lightning leaped from Cade's father's wand, cowing the black limbs of the deep one at a time, as Blake shouted, *"Transferam vos!"*

Magic? Monsters? Cade's rational worldview imploded: *This can't be real—*

One giant arm slammed down beside the lifeboat, sending up a wave that launched the wide-bottomed craft like a toy through the air. The lifeboat landed at an angle, and the aft crewman was thrown overboard. Water surged over the passengers and knocked Cade's mother into his arms. She shook her head and spluttered out a mouthful of brine.

"Mom! Are you okay?" He waited until his mother nodded. He turned aft. The rest of the passengers were falling over one another to reach the rear of the lifeboat. He grabbed one of the oars and wrested it free of its mount. Hefting it like a quarterstaff, he pivoted forward and moved to stand beside his father.

His mother sprang to her feet and seized his coat. "What're you doing?"

"Helping Dad!" He swung his oar wildly at tentacles undulating overhead. She tried to pull him down. "No, Cade! Don't!"

"Mom, he needs me!" He swatted at a tentacle that snapped toward his father, only to shatter the blade of his oar against it.

She clutched fistfuls of Cade's coat. "You don't know what you're—"

Another tentacle burst from the water, coiled around her torso, and stole her away before Cade could retaliate. "Mom!"

His cry turned his father's head. The elder Martin swung around and hurled barbs of fire at the arm that held his wife. *"Occidere monstrum!"*

Crushing force snapped shut around Cade's waist and chest. He lost hold of the broken oar and hollered. His mind went blank from fear as a tentacle hoisted him into the air, high above the lifeboat, beyond his father's reach. The massive limb coiled tighter as it whipped him back and forth. Another cry escaped his lips as his smallest ribs fractured.

Unable to breathe, he panicked. He kicked, flailed, pushed against the leathery hide and iron sinew that held him. He saw his mother in the other tentacle, suspended nearly a dozen yards above the water, trying to scream but unable to make a sound, suffocating like he was.

They swung toward each other. He reached out, tried to take her hand. Their fingers brushed but didn't connect. The tentacles holding them swayed apart, but his mother's eyes never left him. His tears mixed with seawater running from his hair.

Below, a third tentacle bashed his father overboard. He disappeared into a cresting wave, then surfaced a moment later, his wand aimed in Cade's direction. *"Iustitia et libertas!"* Arrows of ghostly light from the wand skewered the tentacle, which went slack and let Cade fall. He plunged toward the waves as he struggled to make his chest expand and draw breath.

Seconds before he met the sea, Cade pinched his nose. He plunged feet-first into the water. Under the surface he was engulfed in funereal wails, as if all the dead men ever claimed by the sea were serenading the ocean with their regrets. Instead of fathomless darkness, the depths were aglow with infernal flames that filled Cade with terror.

Fighting the knifing pain in his ribs, Cade kicked to propel himself away from the fire. He broke the surface a few yards from the boat, coughing out salt water. His father had made it into the lifeboat; he leaned over the side and reached toward Cade. "Take my hand!"

Agony and cold had sapped Cade's strength. A primitive survival urge drove him toward the boat, even as it drifted closer to the whirlpool. As soon as he was close enough, his father pulled him up onto the gunwale. Doubled over the lifeboat's edge, Cade looked for his mother, hoping she, too, had been blasted free of the creature's grip.

She wasn't in the water. He looked up. She was still trapped in the tentacle that had stolen her from the boat. He called out, his throat burning, his voice a rasp: "Mom!"

A sickening crack of breaking bones filled the air. Her body went limp.

"No!" Blind with fury and grief, Cade let go a hoarse, inchoate cry of sorrow. It was too late to help her, but he raged at his father, "Do something!"

His father cocked his arm to hurl another blow at the creature. One of its tentacles shot from the water, curled around the lifeboat, and crushed it. Wood splintered and water flooded in. Two more limbs snaked from the sea on either side of the wreckage. A third seized his father's legs and began to drag him off the fractured remains of the prow, into the vortex.

"Dad!" The beast had already slain his mother; Cade wasn't going to let it take his father. He caught his father's hand, then clutched his own hunk of wreckage. "Hang on, Dad!"

The fear left his father's eyes, leaving only love tinged with sorrow.

"Leave a light on for me, son." He aimed his wand at Cade: *"Fuge!"*

A pulse of light struck Cade and sent him soaring far away from the vortex.

Tumbling, rolling out of control, he splashed down half stunned. He surfaced and looked for any sign of his parents—only to see the tentacles pull them down into its swirling chaos. His mother's body drooped backward with a grotesque kink in her spine, but his father resisted his fate with a storm of vulgarity and a wand throwing fire.

Sprays of color streaked over Cade's head and struck the beast. He twisted around as he treaded water, then marveled at the sight of three strangers joining the battle. A gray-bearded man hovered in midair, his long coat fluttering as he hurled orbs of fire at the sea creature. A young man in a suit sprinted over the waves while conjuring shimmering arrows. A third man, too far away for Cade to see clearly, stood on the pitched deck of the *Athenia;* with balletic gestures he levitated unconscious survivors from the water and planted them in a bobbing lifeboat whose passengers were all unconscious.

A fearsome sizzling and a shriek turned Cade's head toward the whirlpool. Lightning arced from his father's wand and stabbed into the gyre that swallowed him, the monster, and Cade's mother.

The vortex shrank from sight and the North Sea rushed in to take its place.

"No!" Cade paddled with weary arms toward the last vestige of the whirlpool, driven by the irrational hope he might still rescue his parents.

A thunderclap marked its closing, releasing a pulse of icy blackness that slammed into Cade, leaving him dazed. His arms closed around a hunk of flotsam that seemed unequal to the task of keeping him afloat. Wounded and exhausted, he felt his strength ebb. His limbs grew slow and stiff, until he was unable to move at all.

I failed them. They're gone. Mom and Dad are gone.

He shivered. The ocean called, beckoned him to follow his parents into its embrace. His grief was unbearable, a ballast he couldn't bring himself to abandon. He was ready to accept the sea's invitation, to let go and vanish into the depths.

So cold . . . so tired . . .

He let go of the flotsam and surrendered to the ocean. It pulled him downward—until a slender hand seized his wrist and dragged him to the surface.

All he saw of his savior was the silhouette of a long-haired young woman.

"Hold on," she said in a Slavic accent.

The raven landed on the driftwood beside Cade's face.

Its angry caw was the last thing he heard as he lost himself to the darkness.

———⁂———

Sounds carried in the stone halls of Wewelsburg Castle. Footsteps could echo for hours, and even whispers took on lives of their own in the Renaissance-era fortress. So it came as no surprise to Briet Segfrunsdóttir when, from two floors away, she heard the grandfather clock in the east tower's study strike midnight and fill the castle with its melody.

Her steps passed in silence as she climbed the stairs. She delighted in her magickal stealth. This was how she preferred to move through the world: with the grace of a ghost.

The study's door was ajar. She tapped twice on its jamb. "Master Kein?"

He was slow to answer. "Enter."

She opened the door and stepped inside. Kein sat in a high-backed armchair upholstered in burgundy leather. His feet were propped on the chair's matching ottoman and extended toward the black marble fireplace. The room, like the rest of the castle, had recently been remodeled and furnished at great expense. Marring the image of luxury was a profusion of Nazi icons: swastikas carved into the mantel, Himmler's "Black Sun" mandala adorning a tapestry on the wall behind the desk, and the banner of the Third Reich above the hearth.

Kein, by contrast, embodied simplicity. Tall and spare of build, he had a handsome, clean-shaven face. His golden hair was cropped short and slicked flat. He wore a dark suit of tailored silk and a bone-white shirt that flattered his whipcord physique. The tack in his four-in-hand burgundy necktie and the links in his French cuffs were steel with onyx pentacles. His bespoke black leather shoes were as immaculate as the rest of him, down to their soles.

He shut the book he was reading. "What news, Briet?"

"A telegram from Oberleutnant Lemp on U-30, via the Kriegsmarine. As you requested, he torpedoed and sank the *Athenia* roughly two and half hours ago."

A knowing smirk. "Yes, I've already heard the news from Below." He shifted his book to an end table and stood. "The Martin family is *not* among the survivors."

She stepped forward and passed him the telegram she had carried up from the castle's radio room. "Lemp swears he expunged the incident from his log."

"Good. Now Admiral Dönitz can call it an accident."

"If he does, the British and Americans will cry murder."

He shrugged off the consequences. "A small price to pay."

Briet had been trained not to pry, but she had to ask. "Does this mean we've succeeded?"

"Now that Cade Martin is dead, the last obstacle to our labor is removed." He crumpled the telegram and threw it into the fireplace. "Tell the Führer he is free to proceed as we have discussed." Firelight danced in his eyes. "'Long is the way and hard, that out of Hell leads up to light.' . . . When Siegmar returns home, our great work begins."

1940

DECEMBER

Silence within yielded to silence without. Oblivion was supplanted by the weight of mere being, and the comfort of darkness slipped away. Formless thoughts reclaimed their shapes. Atoms of identity returned, single spies at first, then battalions. Respiration's familiar tides asserted themselves. Consciousness dawned, languid and foggy.

Then came a flood of fear and inconsolable grief.

Cade awoke gasping. His mind was still at sea, caught in the frigid water, his soul gutted and raw from watching his parents sink into the depths. He masked his eyes with his palms and poured out his sorrow in throaty sobs until his body felt as empty as his heart. *I can't remember the last time I told them I loved them; now I never will again. They're gone. Gone forever.*

His tears were still warm upon his face when a stillness overcame him.

Am I dead? Cade slowed his breathing and gave his eyes time to adjust. He was in a dark room, one he had never seen before. He wasn't dead, but he was alone in a strange place, without company or explanation. That boded ill.

Where am I?

Dim violet light spilled through a window behind him on his left. A jumble of logs smoldered in the hearth to his right. He lay on a narrow bed in a room with a wood floor and plain walls. The oak door opposite the window was shut. To the right of the fireplace, in the corner farthest from the door, a small archway led to another room with at least one window.

This is no hospital. Am I a prisoner?

He pushed off the bedcovers and sat up. His feet were bare, and the flannel nightclothes he wore were baggy and ill-fitting. A quick look around yielded no sign of his own clothes. He cinched the waist tie on the pajama bottoms as tightly as he could tolerate. *That should do.*

He got up. It felt odd to stand. The floor was cold, and his legs trembled under his weight. His stomach growled, and he wondered how long it had been since he'd eaten.

Halting steps brought him to the window. On the other side was a crenellated battlement mantled in snow and ice. Beyond it sprawled a panorama of lakes and hills slumbering under wintery shrouds. It was a landscape Cade had seen before only in photographs: the Scottish Highlands. *How the hell did I get here? And why here?*

A caw from outside the window startled him. He turned to see a raven perched on a crenellation. The bird stared at him as if it were looking for a fight. It cocked its head, then thrust it forward and let out a croak, as if to scold him. Cade backed away from the window.

That can't be the same bird I saw on the Athenia, *can it? What's going on?*

Curiosity drew him into the alcove. Atop the low dresser he found a wireless—or, as he used to call it before moving to England at the age of fourteen, a radio. He turned it on with the twist of a dial, then fiddled with the tuner knob. Static spilled from the box until he found a live channel, and a distant voice with a dry English accent broke through the noise.

"—as firefighters struggle to contain what many now call 'the Second Great Fire of London.' Reports from the Ministry of Information indicate the overnight raid was the deadliest since the start of the Blitz, killing more than one hundred sixty persons in metropolitan London, and bringing the estimated total of civilian casualties since September to approximately forty-one thousand. Home Secretary Herbert Morrison hastened to confirm, however, that St. Paul's Cathedral has survived this latest night of the Blitz. On behalf of Prime Minister Churchill, he vowed, 'It will not fall while free Britons still draw breath.'" A somber pause. *"Only a few hours remain in nineteen-forty, dear listeners, and the coming of a New Year brings with it—"*

Cade switched off the radio. He felt hollow and numb.

New Year's Eve 1940? I've been asleep for sixteen months? He met his reflection in the mirror over the dresser. His hair was mussed, and he'd grown a beard—yet he recalled no dreams, and his muscles hadn't atrophied. *If I've been out for a year and a half, I shouldn't be able to stand, never mind walk. And there's no medical gear here, so I couldn't have been in a coma.* The longer he pondered his situation, the less sense it made. *What the hell's going on?*

Another thought occurred to him: Someone must have given him the oversized pajamas he was wearing. Maybe they had left other clothes he could take.

Borrow, he corrected himself.

He opened the dresser's drawers and found what he needed—underwear, brown trousers with dark gray suspenders, a wrinkled linen shirt. They were old but felt comfortable to the touch. *Good enough.*

As he traded his pajamas for regular clothes, he saw in the mirror a reflection of his back on the window behind him. There was something between his shoulders.

He turned away from the mirror, then craned his head to peer over his shoulder at the symbol drawn in sepia ink between his scapulae:

What the . . . ? He had no clue what it was or who had put it there. *This gets weirder by the minute.* He finished getting dressed, then spotted a pair of broken-in black leather boots in front of the window perch. *There we go.* He picked them up and held one against the bottom of his left foot. They were his size. He sat on the window bench and put the boots on. As he finished lacing the second one, he saw a pile of old newspapers in the corner beside the dresser. Their folds were sloppy, the stack uneven; they had been read by someone.

He plucked the top newspaper from the stack.

It was a London *Daily Mail* from many weeks earlier. Plastered across its front page was an image of smoldering ruins beneath a headline touting how many Luftwaffe bombers the RAF had shot down before that night's bombing. A detail in the photo snared Cade's attention. He recognized the architecture of a gutted tower: it was all that remained of the chapel at his old boarding school. Studying the footprints of buildings described by rubble, he realized the Yarrow School had been obliterated. A small headline in the right-hand column confirmed his fears: NORTHWEST LONDON SCOURED BY INCENDIARY BOMBS IN OVERNIGHT RAID.

He flipped through other, older newspapers. Germany had been pummeling Britain with an air war since May of 1940 and showed no sign of relenting any time soon. Earlier papers recounted grimmer tales: the Nazis' swift conquests of France, Luxembourg, Belgium, and the Netherlands. With Italy's help, they had seized western Europe and much of northern Africa. Except for the Soviet Union, no one had shown any willingness or ability to resist the Nazis' advance. *This must've been what my father wanted to warn me about.*

Cade returned to the room in which he had awakened. The raven stood on the ledge outside the window, its beak half open as it squawked.

Christ. The whole world's gone to shit. I have to get out of here. He crept to the door and tried its knob, moving it just enough to see it wasn't locked. But was it guarded?

Cade took the poker from the hearth and held it like a broadsword as he returned to the door. With his free hand, he opened the door. He peeked down the narrow hall. There were no guards. It was a start.

Dark blue-gray plaid carpet. Pairs of electric lights shaped like candles overhead. Along the opposite wall, two long, red-cushioned benches of dark wood flanked a closed door. To Cade's left stood a stately grandfather clock. The hands of its modern-looking face stood at 8:41.

Makeshift weapon in hand, Cade ventured out of his room and skulked to his right, toward a windowed door that led outside onto the castle's battlements. It was locked. Wind rattled the door in its frame.

Cade stole down the corridor, past the benches and the clock. He passed a few more closed doors; then, at the corner, he paused and clutched the poker with both hands, tensed to strike. He pivoted left around the turn—and found no one there.

At the end of the L-shaped hallway's shorter leg, past an open door to a lavatory and a bath, was the top landing of a spiral staircase. Cade edged over to the stairs. Tantalizing aromas of roasted meat and baking bread wafted up and roused the hunger in his belly.

His fists tightened on the poker. *Could be a trap. But what choice do I have?*

Careful steps muted the scrape of his soles on the stone stairs. He kept his right shoulder to the outer wall during his counterclockwise descent, hoping to glimpse anyone who might be coming up before they saw him.

He paused at the next floor. It resembled the top floor, though its halls described a T. Opposite the staircase landing, at the other end of the top of the T, another windowed door led outside to the keep's lower battlements. Cade was tempted to see if it, too, was locked, but promises of bacon and cinnamon lured him farther down the stairs.

I should be looking for an exit, not a free lunch. So why can't I stop?

Golden light and hushed voices spilled over Cade as he neared the bottom of the stairs. He passed a closed door on his left as he huddled in an archway that opened into a banquet room. Suspended by a thick chain from a ceiling of oak timbers was a wrought-iron chandelier with electric lights. The room's mortared stone walls were decorated with tapestries, trophies, and painted portraits of Scotsmen in kilts or uniforms of centuries past. Wool rugs whose crimson had faded to hues of dusky rose lay parallel to one another on the hardwood floor.

From his vantage in the archway, Cade saw two peaked arches on the far side of the banquet room. Between them stood a white marble piscina similar to ones he had seen used for ritual ablutions in church. In the middle of the room, a dining table with matching Windsor chairs extended beyond his view. The voices he heard came from its far end.

Arrayed on the long table was a feast: roasted duck, glazed ham, bowls of sautéed beans with bacon, a platter of baked potatoes. Wicker baskets were piled with baked rolls, and a pie with a golden lattice crust sat on a trivet at the end of the table nearest him, venting vapor and teasing him with scents of apple and caramelized sugar. Crystal decanters of red and white wine stood half empty next to a bottle of scotch.

A gruff Scottish voice called out. "Come in, already!"

Cade froze and held his breath. He hadn't made a sound, he was sure of it, and he'd been careful not to lean out far enough to be seen. Surely that summons hadn't been for him?

"Aye, Mr. Martin, I'm talking to *you*. Do come in."

Dueling impulses froze him in place. Fear told him to charge around the corner, swinging the poker at anyone between him and the nearest way out. But a morbid curiosity compelled him to find out how a man who couldn't see him had known he was there.

Still holding the poker, Cade rounded the corner.

Seated at the table, a motley quartet looked at him: the strangers he'd seen at the battle in the sea. At the table's head was the well-weathered gent who had accosted Cade in Oxford. The man was stoutly built and dressed in rumpled clothes in need of a washing. His unkempt gray beard partly hid his yellowed teeth as he stood and smiled. His Scottish brogue was thick. "Hello, Cade. I'm Adair." A queer look at the poker. "I don't think you'll need that, do you?"

"Not sure yet."

"Healthy suspicion. Can't say as I blame you." He gestured to the trim, flaxen-haired man seated on his left. "This is Stefan Van Ausdall."

Stefan set down his napkin and rose to greet Cade with a bow of his head and a shy smile. He appeared to be in his twenties, but he dressed like a gentleman twice his age. His voice had a strong Dutch accent. "Pleased to make your acquaintance."

Adair nodded at the man next to Stefan. He was younger, with light brown skin, a wavy crown of black hair, and dark eyes. He dressed like a man born to a rural life and hard work, but there was a spark of genius in his countenance. "This," Adair said, "is Nikostratos Le Beau."

A blinding smile. "Call me Niko."

Cade tried to place his accent. "Algeria?"

His observation amused the rustic-looking youth. "*Oui!*" He tugged his earlobe and waggled a finger at Cade. "You've a good ear!"

The master turned toward the last of his cadre, a young woman who Cade guessed was close to his own age, or maybe younger. "And this is Anja Kernova."

Her pale, oval face was framed by unruly curls of sable hair. She possessed a cold beauty, but when she turned her head to look at Cade, he felt her gray eyes pierce his mask of normalcy, as if she could look into his deepest core of weakness and shameful secrets. Unnerved, he wanted to look away, but he was captivated by her scar. An old wound dominated the left side of Anja's face: an asymmetrical Y-shaped gouge that branched from the corner of her mouth to the bottom of her eye and the lobe of her ear. Her gaze was cold and aloof, and it made Cade want to shrink into the shadows. He was grateful when she turned away without saying anything.

Adair cleared his throat, freeing Cade from Anja's fearsome affect. "I'd introduce you, of course, but my apprentices already know who you are."

"All too well," Niko muttered.

"Manners," Stefan said, his correction firm but kindly, like that of an elder brother.

Cade noted the crests on the front of the mantel, as well as the two flags on either side of the fireplace: Britain's Union Jack to the left, and Scotland's red Lion Rampant on a field of gold to the right. "I know we're in Scotland, but where, exactly?"

"Eilean Donan Castle," Adair said, "just outside Dornie."

"This is *your* keep?"

A humble shrug. "I'm not its laird, but I'm kin. Clan Macrae, to be precise."

"How did I get here?"

"I plucked you from the sea and brought you. For your own good, of course."

Hearing of the sea dredged up Cade's grief. Despite the months he had lain insensate, for him the tragedy was still raw. Memories overwhelmed him: Fleeting visions of the *Athenia* ablaze and sinking. Tentacles crushing his mother and dragging his father into the abyss. The blast of cold darkness that had plunged him into temporary oblivion. His sorrow was too fresh and the hole in his life too deep to pretend they were in the past. Tears stung his eyes, so he faced the stag's head displayed high above the fireplace while he fought to recover his composure.

Adair struck a somber note. "You were all but dead by the time we got you here."

"Petrified," Stefan said. "Like a victim of Medusa."

Niko balanced a steak knife on his fingertip. "I took you for a statue." He set the blade spinning. "Thought you might look nice downstairs in the billeting room."

The master glowered at Niko. "No cantrips at the table."

The youth palmed the knife and set it by his plate. Adair softened his aspect as he looked at Cade. "LEVIATHAN's parting shot left you stuck between life and death. We spent the last sixteen months working to pry you from the reaper's embrace." He tilted his goblet toward his taciturn female colleague. "But to be honest, Anja did most of the work. Healing magick is mostly her bailiwick."

It was hard for Cade to believe he had heard correctly. "Magick?" His query drew odd reactions from the foursome. "So everything I saw the night my parents died . . . that was real?"

Adair's mien darkened. "Very much so. And quite deadly."

His grief found a new companion: fury. "What killed my parents?"

The apprentices and their master exchanged troubled glances. Adair stalled by taking a long sip of his wine and clearing his throat. "Would you say you're a pious man?"

Cade struggled to reconcile all that he'd once believed with all that he'd now seen. "I was, as a boy. After I got to Oxford, I started reading a lot of scripture as metaphor. But now . . ."

"Now you're not so sure." Adair nodded. "The attack was set in motion by the Nazis' top magician, but the agent of your parents' demise was a demon called LEVIATHAN."

"But why? Why them?"

Niko blurted, "It was not there for *them*. It was sent for *you*."

"For . . . me?" He remembered the warning Adair had given him in Oxford. *The warning I ignored.* "You told me this would happen. That if I tried to run . . . I'd put my parents in danger." Panic clouded Cade's mind. "They died because I didn't listen." A desperate look at Adair. "The other passengers who died? I did this to them, too?" Adair said nothing, but Cade's heart filled with guilt to match his grief. Tears ran down his cheeks, and he fought to keep himself from going to pieces. He dropped the poker. It clanged on the floor as he backed away from the table.

Adair shuffled toward him, one hand extended, palm up. "Hold fast, lad, it's not that simple. It wasn't your—"

Shattered, Cade interrupted with a raised hand, "Which way leads outside?" Adair pointed at the archway to Cade's left. Cade verified the passage was empty. "I'm sorry I didn't listen to you in Oxford. But, please"—he took the scotch from the table—"just let me go." Whisky in hand, he left the banquet hall, desperate to find comfort in solitude, oblivion, or both.

<hr>

A freezing wind blew in off Loch Duich, but Cade's face felt as if it were on fire. Lacking a coat, he had blundered out of the keep into the winter night. Ice had made a hazard of the stone steps that curved down to the castle's multilevel courtyard. Now, hunched in an archway looking out on moonlit water, he winced as his pulse pounded in his temples. Breathing came only with effort, as if his lungs had forgotten how to work. Anguish collided with denial; then both were consumed by his anger before his guilt devoured and disgorged them all to repeat the cycle.

He downed a long swig of peaty Ardbeg and savored its bite in his throat. Questions and accusations flew through his troubled mind. *My fault. But I didn't know. How could I have known? Why didn't Dad tell me? And why'd that thing want me?*

Behind his back, he heard the bump of the door at the top of the steps. He looked at Adair, who'd had the wisdom to don a heavy coat before braving the weather. The master navigated the stairs with caution, then crossed the grounds to Cade's side beneath the seawall. "We should have a word."

Cade downed another mouthful of scotch. "It's your house. Talk all you want."

Even through his overcoat, Adair stank of wine, whisky, tobacco, and sweat. Looking more closely at the man's careworn features, Cade noted irregular gaps in his graying beard and scabbed-over scratches inside his ears. The haggard Scot sighed. "First, I want to be clear. Your parents did not die *because* of you, Cade. They died *for* you."

Cade was too tired and morose for semantics. "What's the difference?"

"It wasn't your fault. You didn't cause the attack."

"Yes, I did. You said it yourself: I put them in harm's way by staying with them."

Adair sighed. "You can't blame yourself for that."

"Watch me." Cade looked west into a darkness with no horizon. "How long to get to Glasgow from here?"

"Why?"

All of Cade's words came out in anger. "I need to get home. I have to tell my grandparents what happened. This isn't the kind of story you put in a telegram."

Adair's frown deepened. "I regret to bear more bad news, but you've nowhere to go."

"What are you talking about? My grandparents—"

Adair shook his head slowly. "Gone. All of them."

Cade felt the foundations of his life crumble beneath him. "What? How?"

"On the record, their deaths were accidents. But I have it on good authority they were killed by a demon like the one that took your parents. One sent by the same enemy."

"The Nazis?"

"Their chief karcist. A dark mage who goes by the *nom de guerre* Kein Engel."

"Never heard of him. What does he have against me?"

"You're his competition, and he wanted you out of the way. I knew he'd come for you, but I had no idea he'd be so . . . thorough. Even if you'd heeded my warning in Oxford, your family would still be dead and gone."

Through the gloom, Cade thought he glimpsed a silver lining. "If the rest of my family is gone, that means I inherit *everything,* right? Am I rich, at least?"

More regret. "You were declared dead when the *Athenia* sank. That and the magickal ward I put on your back were the only way to hide you from Kein.

Alas, your father was an only son, just like you, so when you were all declared lost at sea, and your grandparents were found dead, the Martin estate was claimed by the American government."

Cade simmered with resentment. "So I'm not just an orphan. I'm broke and I'm legally dead? Twenty-one years old, and I'm a ghost without a country?"

"Chin up. Could be worse."

"Really? How?"

"If not for me and my adepts, you'd actually *be* dead."

He recoiled from the older man's smug insinuation. "Am I supposed to thank you?"

"A wee bit o' gratitude might be in order."

Cade stalked into the middle of the dark courtyard, then turned to shout at Adair. "If you wanted gratitude, why didn't you save my parents?"

The master's anger surged like a river breaking through a dam. "You don't think I wanted to? That I didn't try? I told your father to bring you here! You *and* your mother. I promised him you'd be safe here, that I could protect you. But he didn't listen. He scarpered off, as if there's anywhere on the face of the earth that Hell couldn't fucking find him!" He paced in the archway while he reined in his temper. "By the time my familiar Kutcha found you on the ship, I barely had time to warn you about the torpedo. And I'd no idea Kein had called up LEVIATHAN until I saw it rise out of the water. By then, there was fuck all I could do."

Reproached, Cade moderated his tone. "You knew my parents?"

"Aye. I knew your father well. We were mates a long time."

"Did you—?" Cade paused; he couldn't believe he was asking such a bizarre question without jest. "Did you learn magick together?"

A sad smile hinted at fond memories. "Not exactly. I was his teacher."

"Teacher? But you're not *that* much older than him."

Adair chortled. "I'm older than I look, laddie." He folded his arms. "Guess my age."

"I don't know. Fifty-five?"

"Close. Three hundred fifty-seven." Adair grinned as Cade stared, jaw agape. "One of the benefits of a life in the Art." He lifted his arm, and Kutcha the raven fluttered down to perch on his wrist. "Your father was a good pupil, but his interest in the Art was more academic than practical." He gently stroked the bird's feathers. "All the same, he meant the world to me. Which is why

I spent the last sixteen months searching for some way to free you from LEVIATHAN's spell."

"You spent sixteen months just trying to save me?"

His question made Adair frown. "Not *just* that, no. I also spent the last year training new magicians. . . . And sending them to their deaths." He fed a crumb to Kutcha, then dismissed his familiar with a twitch of his arm. He pulled a flat silver case from his coat, opened it with one hand, and with the other plucked out a cigarette. "All the mages I sent to Europe were murdered by Kein and his adepts—a woman named Briet and a man named Siegmar." Adair stuck the cigarette in his mouth, put away the case, and flipped open a stainless-steel lighter. He lit his smoke and took a drag. "I've lost more than ninety apprentices in the last year. I'm fresh out of qualified recruits, so I've had to focus on making my last few adepts the best they can be. Quality over quantity, as the saying goes."

A pungent cloud from Adair's cigarette enveloped Cade. "What now?"

"First, I'll tell Churchill about your recovery, news I'm sure he'll be glad to hear."

"Wait—you answer to the prime minister? Who *are* you people?"

A weary drag; then Adair replied through a mouthful of smoke. "A top-secret magickal warfare program. One I convened within the Special Operations Executive, at His Majesty's request. Our mission: stop Kein and destroy the Thule Society, his army of black-magick dabblers. We've been ordered by the Ministry of Defence to deprive Hitler's war machine of its magickal support at all costs. Until Kein and his followers are dead, the Nazis' hold on Europe will be unbreakable. Unless we succeed, the Allies have no chance of liberating Europe."

Another drag. Like a dragon, Adair exhaled gray vapor from his nostrils. "As of now, the Soviets are the Eastern Front; England is the Western Front. And the five of us left alive in this castle . . . are the Midnight Front." Another slow puff, followed by a series of smoke rings. "Forgive my manners—care for a fag?"

"I don't smoke."

"If the war doesn't push you to it, the Art will."

"Excuse me?"

"Wielding magick is one of the most grueling things mortal flesh can do. It won't be long before you need to take your mind off the misery that demons bring."

Cade realized he was being invited to embark upon a bold and dangerous path.

Can this really be happening? Magick? Demons? He couldn't deny what he'd seen. *I watched a nightmare murder my parents. I felt it try to kill me.* It seemed impossible, but the horrors he'd faced at the sinking of the *Athenia* told him that the orderly, logical world he'd always believed in was a lie. Now he wanted to know the truth, about everything.

Even more than that, he wanted *justice*.

Self-conscious about being so easily read—or perhaps manipulated—by the master magician, Cade adopted an aloof pretense. "Who says I'll be studying magick?"

The tip of Adair's cigarette flared as he took another pull. Smoke spilled from his nose and mouth as he spoke. "I don't have time to sugarcoat this. Like it or not, the Midnight Front is all you have left. And not to put too fine a point on it, we need you. There's lots to be done, and little time to do it. So . . . are you ready?"

It rankled Cade to be bullied into a decision, but he had more pressing matters to address. "Will learning magick help me avenge my parents?"

"It's the *only* thing that will."

Cade steeled his gaze and straightened his spine. "How do I start?"

A wide smile brightened Adair's craggy face as he slapped a callused hand on Cade's shoulder. "You just did."

1941

JANUARY

The new year dawned gray and cold. Cade awoke from nightmares to stare at the ceiling. He had feared the night before that he might have trouble sleeping after lying insensate for sixteen months, but in fact he had found himself exhausted, physically and emotionally.

He considered rolling over and returning to sleep. Rising to face the day would mean confronting his grief, but surrendering to dreams would plunge him back into the past, a prison of nostalgia. Awake and in motion he might distract himself. Work seemed his only hope for restoring his equilibrium. He tossed the sheets aside.

Half an hour later—shaved, showered, and dressed in clean clothes—Cade entered the banquet room to find himself without company. He circled the table and looked for any sign of Adair or his apprentices.

"Hello?" His voice echoed in the keep, but no reply came.

One place was set at the table, so he sat there. Two servants, a man and a woman, both tall, dour, and of indeterminate age, entered from the same passage he'd followed outside the night before. Their hands were laden with items of silver: She carried a four-piece coffee-and-tea service on a tray; he held in one hand a circular platter covered by a dome.

Cade nodded at them and smiled. "Morning." Neither servant acknowledged his greeting. Both regarded him with unblinking stares he found unnerving. He wondered if he had violated some point of etiquette. "Was I supposed to wait before I sat down?" His question was met with more silence. "I'm sorry, but do either of you speak English?"

They had all the verve of mannequins.

"*Parlez-vous français? . . . ¿Habla usted español? . . . Sprechen Sie Deutsch?*" He sighed in frustration. "Look, I've never had servants, so I don't know what

I'm supposed to do here." He lifted his empty cup from its saucer. "Can I just get a cup of coffee while I—"

The woman reacted with speed and precision. She circled the table, balanced the heavy tray in one hand, and filled Cade's cup with the other. After she put the pot on the tray, she stood beside him as if she were a statue.

He nodded at the tray. "You can put that down if—" She set it on the table, backed up, then returned to stand beside her colleague.

Spooning some sugar into his coffee, Cade told the manservant, "If that's my breakfast, you can serve it whenever you're—"

The mute steward walked around the table, set the platter in front of Cade, and removed its lid to reveal a plate piled with scrambled eggs, sausages, beans, and a buttered scone.

Cade cracked an awkward smile at the retreating man. "That's great, thanks."

Hunger took over. He picked up his fork and knife and dug into his breakfast. Between bites he smiled again at the servants. "Nice to meet you, by the way. My name's Cade. What're yours?" Innocent inquiry collided with mute indifference.

He'd had at most one bite of each item on his plate and two sips of coffee when his repast was interrupted by Adair's foghorn bellow from the staircase.

"On your feet, lad! Time to go."

Cade mumbled through a mouthful of egg and scone, "I just started."

"Too bad." Adair grabbed Cade's collar and hefted him out of his chair. "No time for pity." To the servants he added, "Clean this up."

The servants cleared the breakfast dishes. Cade rescued his half-full cup of coffee and did his best not to slosh it on his hands as he pursued Adair. They walked down the courtyard passage, detoured left into a short transverse, then turned right at a T-shaped intersection.

The old Scot's voice resounded off the stone walls. "Long day ahead."

Cade trailed the master through a narrow corridor and down some dark stairs. Halfway across a long passage he had almost caught up when he tripped, and a splash of hot coffee seared the back of his hand. "Son of a bitch."

His grumbling drew a look from the master. "Not much for pain, are you?"

"Not if I can help it."

"Learn to deal with it." He led Cade down a switchback stair.

"Where are we going?"

"Workshop." He pointed at the cup in Cade's hand. "Finish up. I need your hands free."

Cade gulped the last of his coffee on his way downstairs. At the bottom another servant—a pale, humorless woman—relieved him of the cup. She carried it upstairs while Adair led Cade down the corridor. Cade glanced over his shoulder for another look at the servant, but she was gone. "Tell me you didn't hire your staff for their charm."

"Hired? They were summoned." He unlocked the workshop door, then faced Cade, whose confusion must have been evident. "They're lamiae. Demonic servants." He opened the door and welcomed Cade into the tidy confines of the workshop.

Looking around at the rock walls, the workbench, and the array of tools, Cade remained fixated on the lamiae. "You let demons walk around free in your castle?"

"Far from it. They're minor spirits, so low they don't even have true names. Their kind get pressed into service for years, sometimes decades. They don't talk, but they can follow simple orders: 'Serve the food.' 'Wash the dishes.' 'Do the laundry, make the beds.' You're lucky to get one that can cook." With a wave of his hand he shut the workshop's door. "But make no mistake: Lamiae *are* demons, and they hate us more than you can ever know. If they weren't properly summoned and bound, they'd kill us all."

"Then why use them?"

"Because they're cheap. And since they don't sleep, they'll serve at any hour without complaint." He pressed a mallet and chisel into Cade's hands. "Unlike apprentices."

Cade was befuddled by the implements. "Woodworking tools?"

"Aye."

"I thought you were gonna teach me magick."

"If you want to learn the Art, first you need to learn to make your own tools. Thirteen blades, your own grimoire, a wand—"

Disbelief raised Cade's eyebrows. "Can't I just buy some of that?"

"There are no shortcuts in magick, except to the grave. An operator needs to make all his own implements, according to—"

"Wait. What's an 'operator'?"

A long-suffering sigh. "I'm getting ahead of myself." He picked up a list from the workbench and gave it to Cade. "These are the items you need to make before you can start learning the Art. Do you have any skill for glassblowing? Woodcarving? Metalwork?"

"Some." A humble shrug. "My mom was a chemist. She taught me glass-blowing. Don't know much about wood or metal, though."

"I'll have Anja teach you metal, and Niko can show you how to carve. Stefan'll help you get the rest of your kit together, and get you started on the books."

"Books?"

"Aye. Magick is a skill, one that most persons can learn, given time. But it's also an Art, which means some are born with more of a knack for it than others. And I have it on good authority that you possess just such a knack." Adair clasped his shoulder. "It takes most new adepts a year to learn how to make the tools of the Art. . . . You'll have four weeks."

He was sure he'd heard the master wrong. "Four weeks?"

Adair dismissed Cade's objection with a raised hand. "It usually takes three years to master the basics of the Art. I need you ready to go into battle at my side in three months."

"Are you crazy? You just said there aren't any shortcuts in magick."

"There aren't."

"Then why rush my training?"

The master skewered Cade with a black look.

"Haven't you heard? *There's a war on.*"

6

Four weeks had sounded to Cade like too short a time in which to master several complex skills. Only after the work had begun did he realize how long a day could be, never mind a week or a month. January was only half gone and already he was exhausted.

Most days Anja rousted him from bed before dawn. The young Russian permitted him less than a quarter hour each morning to bathe, dress, eat, and ready himself for the day's teachings. She was by far the strictest of the three apprentices. Once her lessons started, she always demanded Cade's complete attention. The first thing he'd learned was how much she hated being made to repeat herself. The second thing he'd learned was that she hated his guts.

After suffering a few hours of Anja's tutelage every day, Cade had found working with Stefan and Niko to be a relief. Each, in his own way, treated Cade like a brother.

Hours sped by as Niko told Cade of his youth in Algiers, and of how he and his younger sister Camille—children of a Greek mother and a French Algerian father—had escaped lives of poverty by smuggling themselves to France as teenagers. Somehow, while regaling Cade with his life story, Niko also taught him the basics of woodcarving and engraving.

Stefan was less talkative. His manner was quiet, kind, and unfailingly polite. Despite his reticence, it was clear to Cade that the Dutchman possessed a keen intellect. But what Cade liked best about him was that he comported himself as a gentle soul.

The first week of Cade's training had been a success, as far as he could tell. His experience with blowing glass had proved useful, inasmuch as it had spared Anja the need to teach him the basics. While she had taught him about metal ores, Niko had instructed him in identifying different types of wood, and Stefan had helped Cade assemble a reading list.

Week two had been far more trying. Forging metal was new to Cade. Melting down raw ore, separating liquefied metals by temperature, and then casting them into shapes was draining both physically and mentally. He and Anja did their smelting outside in the courtyard. The blaze had no bellows, but Anja used magick to make it burn white-hot. Its heat felt as if it could cook the front of Cade's body while his back went numb from the winter cold.

His hands had ached when he woke this morning, the fifth day of his second week of training. Every time he struck the hammer to metal on the anvil, he winced as needling shocks radiated up his arms, into his shoulders. He grimaced at the crescent-shaped lump he was beating into shape. "What'd you say this is called?"

Anja answered in a monotone. "A boline. You might call it a sickle."

"Actually, I'm calling it a pain in the ass."

"Stop whining. Focus."

He brought the hammer down again. Sparks danced from the point of contact. He sighed. "Why can't I start with a straight blade and make the fancy curvy thing later?"

"Because the boline is the only tool without runes. You must use it to inscribe all the other blades you will make." She gestured at the hunks of steel waiting to be worked. "Those you will use to inscribe your other metal pieces, and to carve your grips and your blasting rod." She noted his confusion and clarified, "Your wand."

Another ringing strike of the hammer kicked up orange sparks. Cade sleeved sweat from his brow. "So the order in which I make the tools matters?"

"Yes."

"Good to know."

He cleared his mind of questions and tried to recall what she had shown him about folding and shaping the metal. In different circumstances, he might have resented her for the torrent of information she'd dumped on him, but as matters stood he was grateful. Every moment he spent on the minutiae of his training was one he didn't spend stewing in grief and anger.

***

"Let the knife do the work," Niko said. Cade let Niko correct his grip on his carving blade, then his hold on the narrow branch of hazelwood in his other hand. "Turn the wood but keep the blade steady to cut a spiral up the length of the wand."

Cade resumed his practice carving. "Like this?"

"*Oui, très bien.*" An encouraging smile. "You'll be ready to carve the real thing any day now. If I didn't know better, I'd think you were born a carpenter."

"Hardly." It was difficult for Cade to keep the angle of the spiral cut consistent with each turn of the branch. "I'll be lucky to finish this without losing my thumb."

Niko studied him. "What did you want to be? Before all this, I mean."

The question took Cade by surprise. He stopped carving. "No idea. I was on track to take a First in Classics at Oxford, with a bit of Arabic on the side, but I've no idea how I planned to make a living at it. Anyway, I've always wanted to tackle the big questions: 'Why are we here?' 'What does it all mean?' 'Why does my toast always land jam-side down?' That kind of thing."

"If arcane truth is what you seek, the Art will suit you well."

"What about you?"

A broad grin lit up Niko's face. "My sister and I always said we'd open a café in Paris. She would be the hostess, and I would be the chef." He dug his wallet from a pants pocket and from it pulled a cracked and faded portrait of a young woman who bore him a strong family resemblance. "This is Camille."

"She's lovely," Cade said.

"Too much for her own good." Niko tucked away the photo, then shoved his wallet into his pocket. "Be glad you never had a sister. They are nothing but trouble."

Cade dreaded the end of each day's work. He kept telling himself it had been over a year since the sinking of the *Athenia* and the deaths of his parents, but his grief remained too fresh to bury.

Lying in bed each night, with no one to crack jokes at, he struggled to find the peace to sleep. After hours of reading musty tomes of the Art, all he could do was lie awake and listen to the wind howl across the loch to shake his windows.

Being alone with his thoughts felt like teetering on a precipice, one step from a plunge into despair. He had been ready to sink into the darkness that night in the water; part of him still imagined that such a surrender could bring only relief.

Then he would think of vengeance, and his urge for self-destruction would abate.

And so he ended each day, nurtured by dreams of violence.

———≈≈≈———

Anja's words guided Cade's hands. "Feel the curve take shape. . . . Heed the metal. When it resists, take it to the fire. . . . Remember what I showed you. Fold the steel." She punctuated her instructions with bursts of Russian profanity Cade was happy not to have translated.

Her lessons had taken on a rote quality that let Cade empty his mind of everything but the task before him. He found solace in simplicity. His past was forgotten, his future out of view. All that mattered was the present—the fusion of heat and pressure in a strip of steel caught between a hammer's head and the back of an anvil.

He became one with his work, and in those brief moments he had peace.

———≈≈≈———

Columns of stacked books surrounded Cade like a literary Stonehenge. Dust caked the tomes' spines and dulled the shine of gilt pages. Motes lingered in dying rays of daylight slanting through the study's windows, lending the keep's most secluded room an aura of timelessness.

Open on the table in front of Cade was an ancient volume bound in oak and calfskin: *Clavicula Salomonis Regis,* which was also called the *Lemegeton* but was better known by its modern name, *The Lesser Key of Solomon.* It claimed to be an instruction manual for the conjuration, binding, and control of demons. The edition Cade was reading, which Adair had insisted was the "definitive version," had been obsessively annotated by hand. Much to Cade's dismay, its marginalia had been scribbled using the same archaic Latin as its main text.

At least I get to read by electric light, Cade consoled himself. The codices in Adair's library of magick were too valuable to risk being exposed to flames, which meant Cade had no need to fear he would go blind straining to read by faltering candlelight. *I just hope I don't go mad trying to parse ancient Greek and Aramaic.*

He knew that at any moment he might fall asleep sitting upright, and then he would end up facedown in the gutter of an open book. He marked his place with a white feather, closed the book, and sat back to rub his tired eyes.

In the corner of the study, Stefan looked up from the book he was reading. He had been so silent while hunkered down in his favorite armchair that Cade had forgotten the senior apprentice was still there. "Have you already finished with the *Lesser Key*?"

"Just halfway." He quailed from the mountain of words before him. "How the hell am I supposed to memorize all this in three months?"

Stefan adjusted his wire-frame glasses. "You have less time than that, I think. Most of this you need to know before you conjure your first spirit."

"Tell me you're not serious. I have to read all this just to summon one demon?"

The Dutchman stood and walked to Cade's reading table to survey the books stacked upon it. "At the least, you must know the rituals of Waite's *Ceremonial Magic*. And we will all be safer if you have read *Pseudomonarchia Daemonum*."

"But the rest—"

"Are still vital. The *Heptameron*. Agrippa's *Occult Philosophy*. Weyer's *Officium Spirituum*. Any of them could save your life one day." He lifted a book from the top of the stack nearest him and read its title aloud. "*Necronomicon*." He set it down. "Maybe not that one."

Cade remained intimidated by the mass of knowledge he was being asked to cram into his brain in so brief a span. "Is it really possible for one person to learn all this? Did you?"

"I read every one of these books during my training."

"And how long did it take you?"

Stefan hesitated to answer. "Four years and three months."

"*Four years?* Then why does Adair think I can do it in four weeks?"

Cade had meant his question to be rhetorical, but it garnered a thoughtful reaction from Stefan. "The master does not tell me all his secrets, but if he pushes you this hard, it is for one reason only: He sees greatness in you." He set his hand on Cade's shoulder. "As do I."

～～～

Cade held up the crescent blade of his boline and admired it against the faded pink of dusk. "How's this?"

Anja tested its edge. "Good blade. One more firing and you can temper it."

"You said I'll use this to make my other tools?"

"Most of them. First your white-handled knife. Then your athamé—"

"The black-handled knife?"

Her expression soured. "Yes. Then your other blades."

"Thirteen in all."

His interruptions stoked her impatience. "Yes. Each cast from unused steel, fired three times, then quenched in a bath of magpie's blood herbed with *jus de foirole*."

"I thought blood quenching went out with Damascus steel."

"In the Art, the old way is still best."

Cade harbored doubts. "But modern quenching baths—"

"This is magick, not science. There is no substitute for blood."

He looked at the blade in his hand and thought about what Anja had said. "If it's not about chemistry, is it about symbolism?"

"In the Art, everything is. You temper your spirit as you temper your tools." She stepped away from the fire and nodded for Cade to follow. "Prep the rest of your blades tomorrow so we can finish them Wednesday, while the moon is still full."

"I know, in the first or the eighth of the daylight hours, or in the third or the tenth of the night hours, under a full moon." A question nagged at him. "Which times are better?"

"The grimoires disagree on which hours are best. Contradictions are common in the Art. What matters is obedience of the operator in all steps of preparation."

He recalled that by "operator" she meant him, in his upcoming role as the one performing a magick ritual. "Once I do all this, I'll be ready to start learning magick?"

She averted her eyes but failed to veil her contempt. "That is for the master to say."

He put down his unfinished boline. "Is it worth it? Magick, I mean."

A suspicious look over her shoulder. "It can be. If you do the work."

Cade wasn't sold yet. "What've you learned?"

"Besides battle magick? I have a way with animals. And I can heal and change shapes."

"What do you mean 'change shapes'?"

She hesitated to answer. "I can turn myself into animals and back again."

He was impressed. "If you have a knack for healing, why don't you—" The rest of his question caught in his throat; he'd realized too late it was one he had no right to ask.

Anja inferred his query and turned the marred half of her face away from him. "You wonder why I still have my scar." She met his stare. "No magick can erase this wound. But even if it could, I would keep it so that I never forget who I am—or who did this to me." Her haunted gray eyes narrowed; she wore her sorrows and grudges as badges of honor.

"I'm sorry if I—"

"Clean your tools, then get dinner and go to bed." She walked past him and climbed the steps to the keep. "We resume work at dawn."

***

Adair stood in the workshop, his adepts gathered behind him. He inspected Cade's newly crafted magickal tools and concealed his wonder. *I set impossible goals and he beat them all. But am I pushing him too hard?* It wasn't clear how much praise was due to his apprentices for Cade's training, and what measure of credit belonged to Cade alone, so Adair erred on the side of caution. "Fine work. And done sooner than I'd thought. You'll make a fine apprentice." He threw an approving look at his adepts. "No doubt because I gave you good teachers."

Cade looked relieved. "*Now* I start learning magick?"

The master let his smile fade, and a low gurgle resounded from the raging sea of whisky and bile in his stomach. "Walk before ye run, lad. You've still got a mountain of reading to do. Besides, it'll be at least a week before the stars align for an Infernal compact, and you haven't exorcised your tools yet." His other adepts cleared a path as he turned away from the workbench. "Follow me, all of you."

He led the four of them out of the workshop, upstairs, then through the service passage to the door near the banquet hall. Tucking his hands into his pockets, he took his adepts outside and across the courtyard. A marble sky threatened snow, and a meat-ax wind carved a furrow in Adair's brow. He guided his four disciples to the castle's southwest building, a blocky edifice of mortared stone with a narrow peaked roof.

Inside, a high-ceilinged corridor of closed doors stretched away to the right. "The Macrae family apartments," Adair said to Cade. "Presently unoccupied." Adair brought his pupils to a door that led downstairs. A brass knocker shaped like a dragon's face hung on it at eye level. Its forked tongue reacted to the group's presence with a slow flick, then retracted behind its fangs when Adair touched its snout. He noted Cade's surprise and nodded toward the knocker. "A guardian, to protect our lab and tools." He opened the door and led the adepts downstairs.

The lower floor and basement level had been gutted. Remnants of beams jutted from the stone walls, betraying the absence of floors that had been discarded. Three small windows on the south wall, and one in the middle of the west wall, admitted a diffuse glow that failed to pierce the shadows pooled in the deepest corners.

Cade drank it all in. "What happened down here?"

"When the king borrowed the castle for the Midnight Front, I had the lower levels—" It took Adair a moment to summon the right word. "—*converted* for my use." He walked his adepts across the smooth concrete floor, on which scuffed and faded chalk marks from previous labors remained visible. "I'm sure they'll fix it when the war's over. And none'll be the wiser."

Along the windowless north wall stood five Victorian-style wardrobes. "The closest is mine," Adair said to Cade. "The farthest is yours, for your tools and gear." Adair opened Cade's wardrobe, which he had equipped with essential supplies. "Virgin parchment. Candles made with the first wax from a new hive. Blessed chalk. Incense, basic oils, a thurible. Plus your vestments, and silk for wrapping your tools after they're purged." He gestured at an empty leather roll-up that hung by a hook from the center rod. "For your blades."

The youth sighed. "Can I also get a mule to help me tote all this crap?"

"Learn to lead experiments and you can make demons carry your bags."

"Experiments?"

Anja scowled at Cade. "Did you not memorize Waite's *Ceremonial Magic*?"

He answered her disdain with sarcasm. "I was too busy making swords."

Stefan bowed his head to Adair. "I failed to prepare him, Master. Forgive me."

"No worries. He'll have plenty of time to read 'twixt now and the full moon." Adair faced Cade. "Let me lay out the basics for you. Give you the jargon, as it were. You ready?"

"No, but that hasn't stopped any of you yet."

Adair let the youth's sarcasm pass unremarked. "All magick, from the simplest trick to the grandest miracle, is based on the conjuring and control of demons. No exceptions."

"We're demon-worshippers?"

"We don't *worship* demons. We *control* them. Conjuring a demon is called *an experiment*. The magician conducting an experiment is called *the operator*. Those assisting the magician are called *tanists*.

"A person who practices magick is *an adept*. The lowest order of adept is a novice. After that comes acolyte. Then the highest class, which we call *karcist*." Adair paused and gauged Cade's state of mind. The youth was alert and focused. "Any of this familiar?"

A tiny nod. "Tell me more."

"A karcist gets power from signing demonic pacts. When you make a deal with a major spirit from the Pit, you earn the right to strike pacts with all the other demons who answer to it. But you need to choose your patron wisely. There are six ministers of Hell, but a karcist can have only *one* of them as a patron. Choose a lesser minister, and it'll be easier to sway—but it won't have as much to offer. Choose one of the greater spirits, and you might find yourself enslaved."

Glimmers of fear began to show through Cade's mask of bravado. "How do I choose which one to seek as a patron?"

"Research. Read the old grimoires, then decide which one has what you need."

"How am I supposed to know that?"

"That's why you have me—" A wave at the others. "—and them."

The youth didn't look encouraged. "Anything else?"

"Just a few last basics. Making a demon do a task for you is called *a sending*. If you send a demon to harm or abduct a person, the target is known as *the patient*." He pointed at the chalk smears on the floor. "You'll need to learn how to draw magick circles, to protect yourself and your tanists during experiments. One mistake in a circle, and you'll get yourself and everyone else killed."

"Okay. So, I get a patron, sign a Faustian bargain—"

"If Faust had been a better magician, he wouldn't have died. But go on."

"And then I summon demons to do magick?"

The boy was getting ahead of himself. "To wield the kind of magick you saw us and your father use, you need to learn how to yoke demons."

Noting Cade's lack of comprehension, Stefan added, "You bind demons to your will. For as long as you can hold them, you can use their powers as if they were your own."

"Powers? Like hurling fire and lightning?"

"That's only the start of it, lad." Adair opened his arms. "Anything you can imagine, there's a spirit to make it happen. You could fly, change shape, turn to smoke, turn invisible . . . but there's a cost. Harnessing a demon is miserable work. Yoking even one can turn your guts to mud and leave your head feeling like it was used for horseshoes. Bind too many spirits, or hold them too long, and the strain can drive you mad."

Niko spoke up. "Demons poison your sleep with nightmares. Use your hands when your mind is idle. Make you pull out your own hair. Make your flesh crawl until you scratch it off."

Now it was clear Cade was spooked. "How many demons is too many?"

"Only you can know where your breaking point is," Adair said. "But first, learn to draw glyphs and wards, learn the rituals. Today's the twenty-first. You have three weeks until the next opportunity for striking a compact." He shot a look at Stefan. "Make sure he bones up on Waite, then walk him through the *Grimorium Verum*."

"Yes, Master."

Adair slapped Cade's shoulder. "Chin up, lad. We'll get you trained yet."

"If you'd told me magick involved more reading than most of my classes at Oxford, I might've thought twice."

"Too late now. But if you don't mind, just call it 'the Art,' with a capital 'A.' Babble on about 'magick' and you'll sound like those berks at the Thule Society."

"Sorry."

"Don't be sorry, be careful. The Art is many things, but one thing it's not is forgiving of mistakes." He shooed his adepts up the stairs. "Back to the keep! You've books to read, and I've Glenmorangie to quaff." Adair wore a brave face as he trailed his adepts upstairs, but in his heart he knew he had likely just set Cade Martin on the path to an early and gruesome demise.

Heaven forgive me . . . but I don't know any other way to win the war.

7

An argument filtered down from above Kein, tainted with the stink of demons. He climbed the spiral stair, while two flights above him, on the third floor of Wewelsburg Castle's north tower, his two disciples sniped at each other like marksmen.

What Siegmar's voice lacked in bass it made up for in volume. "We are wasting valuable time! There is no reason for us both to be consumed with this chore."

"The master's orders left no room for debate." As ever, Briet's words cut like knives. "I've seen to the security of occupied France. He wants you to secure Poland."

"There's nothing in Poland worth defending!"

Frustration sharpened Briet's anger. "It's about protecting *Germany,* you idiot—not Poland. You heard the warning from Below, just as I did. The Nazis and the Soviets will be at war by summer. When that happens, Poland will be the Russians' first target."

Kein reached the third floor and interrupted his apprentices. "She is correct, Siegmar. The Germans need Poland as a buffer for the war with Russia."

The bespectacled Finn looked surprised. "Then it's true? Hitler is *that* reckless?"

"If I take him at his word? Yes." Kein crossed the circular room, which served as their library and study, to stand in front of Briet and Siegmar. "Which makes me wonder what you think is more pressing than securing Poland."

Siegmar masked his embarrassment by glowering at Briet. "Adair and his adepts."

"This again?" Despite his attempt at stoicism, Kein sighed in disappointment. "We killed all the adepts he sent to Europe, hunted down all his prodigies. Adair is *contained,* Siegmar. We need to focus on more pressing matters." He threw a look toward the stairs. "And the two of you need to learn to keep your voices down when we have company."

His disciples' reactions made it clear they took his meaning: Reichsführer Heinrich Himmler and his entourage had just returned to the castle, whose restoration Himmler had financed and overseen, with just enough interces-sion by Kein to ensure their respective efforts did not conflict. When their Nazi benefactor was in residence it was best not to draw his attention, especially not when one was daring to criticize the Führer.

Siegmar lowered his voice but remained insistent. "We are wasting an impor-tant opportunity. Adair's power is at an ebb. Now is the time to neutralize him."

Despite Kein's earnest wish to view both of his students as fully trained kar-cists who deserved to be entrusted with responsibility, he was reminded that, of the two, Briet possessed the more serious mind while Siegmar was ruled by his emotions. Hoping to teach by example, Kein stripped all emotion from his tone. "First, my dear Siegmar, I feel compelled to point out that despite our successes to date, we have not killed *all* of Adair's apprentices. I am quite sure he continues to train new adepts, even now."

"All the more reason to hunt him down and finish this!"

It grew more difficult for Kein to maintain a sanguine demeanor. "Very well. And how do you propose to stop him? Master Adair is one of the most skilled karcists in the world, second only to myself in power and experience. What makes you think you can stand against him?"

"No defense is perfect, not even his."

Briet ran him through with a condescending look. "That is an aphorism, not a plan."

Her gibe strengthened Siegmar's resolve. "We could compel VASSAGO to reveal—"

"Adair is guarded by spirits far greater than VASSAGO," Kein said.

"But not greater than those who answer to you."

"Few things in Hell are costlier than the breaking of a ward. It has taken me *centuries* to earn political capital with the powers Below. I will not spend it rashly."

His disciple took the warning to heart and changed the topic. "I could hunt Adair and his adepts the old-fashioned way, on the ground. All I would need is cash and time."

"And more magickal protection than the three of us combined could pro-vide." Kein lifted a hand to forestall further objection by Siegmar. "Do you remember when the war started? When I sent you to Oxford to eliminate the last of Adair's prodigies?"

"Of course. I succeeded."

"To a degree. You were on English soil for less than two days, but protecting you from Adair and the British took all three of us *weeks* of preparation. Even still, you barely escaped with your life. Now imagine the lengths to which Briet and I would need to go in order to protect you during a siege on the enemy's strongest redoubt."

Siegmar stewed. "I could breach his defenses within days. A week at most."

"You'd never get within half a mile of him—or the last of his adepts. But why waste the effort? Adair and his pups are cornered. *Neutralized*." Kein pressed his palms together, as if in prayer. "No, my friend. Hunting them is a fool's errand, and I will not permit it. Not when I have far greater need of your talents in Poland."

"What could I possibly do there that would be of more use?"

Kein angled his fingertips toward Siegmar. "Hunt down the last of the Kabbalah masters and their students. I have reports from Below that half a dozen of the old rabbis are on the run outside Kraków—and that Adair has been trying to contact them for months. Bury those old fools so deep that Hell itself could not find their bones." He shifted his gaze toward Briet. "And I need you in Paris, to take direct control of its coven."

Siegmar grew angrier. "Are you serious? You send me to Kraków, but she gets to go to Paris?"

"She did not vex me by clinging to suicidal fantasies." Thinking it might take the sting out of the task he had given Siegmar, Kein added, "If it is any consolation, I will be up to my neck in dabblers while I supervise the founding of new Thule covens. Because you know how highly I regard the skills of amateur magicians."

His wrath defused, Siegmar bowed his head. "As you command, Master."

"Excellent." He steered them toward the stairs. "Now, let us repair to the dining room. Herr Himmler has brought home a case of wine from Burgundy"—he punctuated his thought with a smile—"and I, for one, do not plan on letting the Nazis drink it all without us."

* * *

Cade was almost done getting dressed when the door to his bedroom swung open. Adair and Anja stood in the corridor, both garbed in ceremonial vestments—white albs, fur girdles, pale paper crowns inscribed with the word "EL," bleached leather shoes—and carrying swords for the grand "experiment" Cade was to conduct.

The master eyed Cade's nearly identical garments. "You look ready." A hint of suspicion. "You said the prayer of vesting?"

"I did." Feeling doubted, he added, "Should I strip and do it again?"

Adair swallowed his annoyance. "It's late. We should go."

Cade tucked his silk-wrapped wand under his lion-skin belt. "Ready."

Adair led Cade and Anja down the keep's spiral stairs. "You cleaned your blades? The room's prepared?"

"I followed the grimoires to the letter."

Anja added, "I made sure the candles and incense are pure."

The master remained anxious. "What about the charcoal?"

"Newly consecrated," Cade assured him. "And in a new brazier. We're all set."

They didn't speak again until they were inside the southwest building. Stefan and Niko, both in their own robes, met the trio at the door to the basement.

The master faced Cade. "Remember: You're the operator tonight, and the rest of us are just your tanists. Once the experiment starts, you're on your own. We can't speak or step out of our circles. We can't give you advice or help you tame the spirit."

"I know. It's 'against the rules.'" Cade opened the door. Odors of lavender and camphor drifted up from the laboratory, which was lit by open flames. "Let's do this."

They proceeded downstairs.

There had been so many details to learn, so many points of minutiae, that Cade had no idea if he'd mastered them all. He had checked his work, but doubts plagued him. The task had been a welcome diversion from his grief. Few things could distract him from his sorrow like memorizing reams of Enochian, Hebrew, and Latin phrases, or the seemingly endless names of JEHOVAH, or the details of what herb had to be mixed with what oil in the skull of what dead beast at what hour of the day while wearing what color robe.

Had he never witnessed magick's deadly effects, he would have found his labors absurd. Instead, he was now confronted by a dilemma he would have dismissed as fantasy before that night on the *Athenia*. This ritual required him to accept the reality of the supernatural and, by extension, the existence of his soul. But if his soul was a genuine commodity, then bartering it to a de-mon threatened to bring the damnation he'd been taught to fear as a boy.

If Faust had been a better magician, he wouldn't have died, Adair had said. Did that mean there was a way to cheat the Devil? A secret to shortchanging Hell?

Making the pact would give Cade a path to power that would let him avenge his parents, and a doorway to knowledge otherwise beyond the reach of man. If that wasn't worth the risk of his eternal soul . . . what was?

Cade stopped when he realized that while he, Stefan, and Niko were pro-ceeding to their places, Adair and Anja had halted at the bottom of the stairs. "What's wrong?"

Horror had opened the master's eyes wide. He pointed at the grand circle of protection Cade had inscribed. "That's not the seal of PAIMON."

There was no point denying the truth. "No, it isn't."

Adair prowled around the magickal ward, whose border had been described in strips of skin cut from a sacrificial kid with the hair still upon it, and fas-tened to the floor at the cardinal points of the compass using four nails from the coffin of a child.

The master pointed out details of Cade's preparation as if he were a pros-ecutor presenting charges. "A male bat drowned in blood . . . The skull of a parricide." He continued to pace the circle. "The horns of a goat." A grim frown. "And my own familiar, Kutcha."

His raven squawked at him.

Anja stepped forward beside Adair. "The triangle and glyphs have been drawn in hematite." She and Adair turned to look east.

Another large circle abutted the rear wall. Inside it, atop a crude altar, lay the nude body of one of the keep's lamiae servants. Her paper-white body had been decorated head to toe with symbols—some astrological, others Enochian—drawn in red and yellow greasepaint, a detail whose garishness accentuated her nudity. Coiled above her navel was a twist of violet fabric, tied in a knot around a broken communion wafer.

Adair was aghast. "How did you make a sacrifice of *my* lamia?"

"It's bound to obey."

"To obey *me,* not you."

Niko shrugged. "Stefan and I might have provided some assistance."

Grumpier by the minute, Adair continued his perambulation. Scowled at chi and rho superimposed beneath the base of the triangle. Tapped the six-foot candles of virgin wax ringed by crowns of vervain. Shook his head at three circles joined by a cross within the triangle—the northernmost of which was adorned by horns. He faced Cade. "Are you taking the piss, boy? Why are you trying to raise *this* beast? Why face the fury of Hell's prime fucking minister?"

"Because he can give me the most power."

"But at what price? It's too dangerous!"

Cade kept his voice steady, his expression neutral. "You want me to go to war with a Nazi karcist who you say has insane power. I can't fight him unless I can match his strength, and I'm just as damned no matter what spirit I deal with, so I might as well go for the top dog." He walked to his position inside the protective triangle, then closed its perimeter with a pull of his sword's tip over its edge.

The master was incensed. "One scuff of my foot, and this circle's ruined."

"Then what? We spend another month arguing? You said it yourself: That's time we don't have. You want me to help you fight Kein? Get in your circles."

A toxic silence prevailed for several seconds, until Adair motioned for the others to take their places. Before he moved to his own circle, he sidled up to Cade and spoke in a confidential hush. "No matter what you see or hear, don't leave your circle, or we *all* die." With that final warning, he withdrew to the eastern circle and waited for the experiment to begin.

There was no need for Cade to instruct the others. They rested their swords across the tops of their feet. Each took up the bottle by the brazier beside his or her station—brandy for Anja, camphor for Adair, holy oil for Stefan, and ram's blood mixed with Abramelin oil for Niko—and stood ready to ignite the charcoal inside their brass containers.

Cade reached to the lectern beside his circle, opened the grimoire of blank pages he had prepared under Stefan's guidance, and picked up his pen of the Art, which he had crafted with equal care under Niko's tutelage. He was about to forge the contract of a lifetime. A touch confirmed that a hunk of bloodstone—a talisman of protection he had secured, as the Covenant instructed—was still under his robe. Nothing could be left to chance.

"Light the candles."

Adair snapped his fingers, and flames danced to life on the wicks.

Cade spread his arms, striking a pose that felt sacrilegious given the circumstances. "Pass me the brandy, then the camphor."

Anja handed Cade the brandy; he dribbled some onto the charcoal, then returned the bottle to her. Next he took the camphor from Adair and sprinkled some onto the unlit coals before handing the vessel back to his master. "We're ready. Everyone, light your vessels."

His tanists ignited their braziers of incense.

The room was prepared.

Cade cleared his mind. Remembered why he had fasted and prayed for three days. His mind and body were unsullied. His tributes were in order and the sacrifices were in place. He squatted—with great care, so as not to dislodge the sword he had perched atop his own feet—to light his brazier of consecrated charcoal. When he straightened to his full height, he incanted in a clear and commanding tenor:

"I present thee, O great ADONAY, this incense as the purest I can obtain; in like manner I present thee this charcoal, prepared from the most ethereal of woods. I offer them, O grand and omnipotent ADONAY, ELOIM, ARIEL, and JEHOVAM, with my whole soul and heart. Vouchsafe, O grand ADONAY, to receive them as an acceptable holocaust. Amen."

His brazier shot up a geyser of indigo sparks that rebounded off the high ceiling. Doleful howls and cries filled the conjuring room, and a macabre mist encompassed the grand circle. A window to the nether realms had been opened. It was time to begin the conjuration.

"Hear me, SATAN MEKRATRIG! Heed my summons, PUT SATANACHIA, also known as BAPHOMET: Behold my gifts and send me thy agent and minister, free of evil noise or odor, as the Law commands!"

He procured a pinch of incense from his robe and cast it into the brazier, turning its flames a sickly green. The vapors outside the circle flared red and reeked of sulfur, burnt hair, and rotting flesh. The stench threatened to gag him. He fought the urge to dry-heave and forced himself to speak again:

"I conjure and command thee, LUCIFUGE ROFOCALE, by all the names wherewith thou mayst be constrained and bound: SATAN, RANTAN, PALLANTRE, LUTIAS, *traditore, tentatore, adulatore, divoratore, conciatore, seminatore, e seduttore,* where art thou? I conjure thee, by Him who created thee, to fulfill my work! I invoke thee, by the names ADONAI, EL, ELOHIM, ZABAOTH, ELION, ERETHAOL, RAMAEL, TETRAGRAMMATON, SHADDAI, and by the names ALPHA AND OMEGA, by which Daniel destroyed BEL and slew the Dragon; and by the whole hierarchy of superior intelligences, who shall constrain thee against thy will—I adjure thee, LUCIFUGE ROFOCALE, appear before me in a pleasing form and voice, or feel the pain of my rod!"

He thrust his twisted wand of hazel into the brazier of charcoal.

Roars of suffering and hatred beyond measure struck terror into Cade. His hands shook, and he feared he might lose control of his bladder. Vertigo swept over him, and for a few seconds he was sure his balance had betrayed him and he was falling.

At once he felt steady, recovered his wits, and pulled his wand from the coals. "LUCIFUGE ROFOCALE! Show thyself in a pleasing form, or feel my wrath again!"

A roll of thunder passed through Cade, followed by a chill that gave him his first taste of the oblivion that awaited all mortal flesh. Then came a voice unlike any he'd ever heard; it was the rush of a bonfire and the crashing of waves.

I AM HERE. WHAT DOST THOU SEEK OF ME?

A figure wreathed in steam and bathed in light without evident origin appeared outside the grand circle of protection. Over nine feet tall, it loomed above Cade and regarded him with mad yellow eyes. From its bald head protruded three twisted horns. Its jaw gaped open, revealing a mouth of fangs above its pointed chin. A tattered ruff ringed the collar of its copper-hued jerkin, which was adorned by a fringed skirt. Below that extended a pair of caprine legs ending in black hooves, and a tufted tail that twitched with nervous energy.

Cade fought to overcome his terror and recall his next part in their scripted pas de deux. "Hadst thou appeared when I invoked thee, I had by no means smitten thee. Remember, if the request I make of thee be refused, I am determined to torment thee for all eternity."

SAY WHAT THOU DOST REQUIRE.

"I require that thou shalt communicate with me, or with those to whom I entrust my present book, which thou shalt approve and sign, whenever I or they shall invoke thee by the names of power; that thou shalt grant me dominion over all those spirits of the Pit that call thee 'master'; and that thou shalt grant me the gift of seven hundred years of life, youth, vitality, and freedom from poison, pestilence, and disease. Such is my demand."

The monster regarded Cade with loathing and fear. YOU ARE NOT SOME MERE EVE-SPAWN. YOU BURN WITH A BRIGHTER FLAME.

He had been warned not to succumb to the demon's flattery. "Speak plainly! Will thou grant my request, as stated, and without additional condition?"

VERILY, I PLEDGE TO GRANT YOUR REQUEST, AND TO APPROVE THY BOOK, TO WHICH I SHALL AFFIX MY SEAL AND TRUE SIGNATURE, AND TO APPEAR

AT THY REQUEST, PROVIDED THOU OFFER ONCE EACH YEAR THE SACRIFICE AND TRIBUTE, AS PRESCRIBED BY THE LAW.

Cade reached under his alb, pulled out a live mouse, unwrapped its leg bindings, and released it outside his circle. The rodent let out a squeak as it raced toward the demon; then it circled the monster thrice before darting from the room. As soon as it was departed, Cade drew from the same pocket a gold coin engraved with the demon's seal, and lobbed it to him.

The beast's mouth opened wide like a serpent's and snapped the coin from the air. ABIDETH BY THE TERMS OF THE COVENANT, AND MY PATRONAGE SHALL BE THINE. BUT IF THOU FAILEST, THOU SHALT BE MINE EVERLASTINGLY. It picked up Cade's pen of the Art from the lectern and inscribed its demonic marks into Cade's grimoire. As it set down the pen, it bared a smile that stank of urine and blood. OUR BUSINESS IS CONCLUDED.

"I thank thee, LUCIFUGE ROFOCALE, and discharge thee by the terms of the Covenant. Depart in peace, and return when, and only when, I call for thee. Begone, spirit, in the name of ADONAY, ELOHIM, ARIEL, and JEHOVAM!"

A stroke of thunder trembled the flames on the candles.

The demon was gone.

Cade finished the ritual with a single word: "Amen."

The master left his circle. "You had me worried there. But that was well done." He clasped Cade's shoulder. "Tomorrow we'll call up a minor spirit and teach you how to yoke it." With an arch of his brow he added, "Then the *real* fun begins." He headed for the stairs.

Niko and Stefan approached Cade. "That was quite something," Niko said. "I hope I never see its like again."

Stefan laughed, and then Niko and Cade laughed, too. When their mirth faded, the senior apprentice said, "So your journey begins. But you have many miles to go, and tomorrow will be a long day indeed." Still in their robes, Stefan and Niko followed Adair upstairs.

Cade removed his vestments and stored them in his wardrobe rather than bring them to the keep, since he would have to wash and exorcise them and his tools in the lab. He closed the wardrobe's door to find Anja standing in front of him, her normal air of disdain replaced by one of rage. "You nearly killed us all."

He recoiled from her accusation. "What? What are—"

"When you heard the cries of the damned—you started to step backward. Had I not used the hand of PALARA to keep you in your circle, you would have broken the ward, and LUCIFUGE would have devoured us all." She poked his chest. "Had the rest of us not been at risk, I would have done nothing. But know this: If you *ever* make another mistake like that, I will *let you die*."

Enraged past the point of decorum, Anja threw open the door to Master Adair's bedchamber. He was half out of his alb, and startled as his door rebounded off the wall. He cast aside his robe and fixed Anja with a look. "Explain yourself."

She was so angry, she couldn't stop shaking. "Tell me you saw it."

"Saw what?"

"What he did! During the experiment!"

The master's dudgeon dissipated. "You mean his half step backward."

She felt vindicated and dismissed in the same breath. "You *did* see it."

"Of course. And I saw you keep him in place—just as I asked."

"He could have killed us all."

Adair sat down to remove his ceremonial shoes. "A risk I foresaw. Sparing him that mistake was our job as his tanists."

"You taught me the operator protects the tanists. Not the other way around."

"Special circumstances." He tucked his shoes inside a bag of velvet, then cinched it shut with a pull on its silk drawstrings.

Anja had no words, just a growl of frustration. She paced and pushed her fingers through her hair. "All he cares about is taking his revenge."

"So?"

"He is selfish. He cares nothing for our cause."

"Aye. But if that's what it takes to get him trained in time, so be it."

"His training." She seethed. "It makes no sense. Not the pace, not the forgiveness. You told him to raise PAIMON, he called up LUCIFUGE ROFOCALE—and *you let him*. Why?"

"You heard why. We don't have time to—"

"No! Do not lie to me. We have been together too long, lived through too much." She pointed an accusatory finger. "You would never have let me, or Niko, or Stefan do that."

Adair pushed his shoes under his bed, then set to folding his alb. "Is that what this is about? You're cheesed because someone other than you is getting special treatment?"

Stung, she tensed. "How *dare* you—"

"Don't play coy, lass." He stood tall. "It's never been a secret that I love you like you're my own. You've *always* been my favorite. If anyone other than you *ever* spoke to me like this, they'd spend the night as a toad in the castle cistern—*and you fucking well know it*." He stepped away to his dresser. With his back to Anja, he pulled the stopper from a decanter of Irish whiskey and filled a glass. Then he turned, downed half the drink in one tilt, and let out a gasp of satisfaction. "So what's *really* got your dander up?"

She found the truth embarrassing. There were many emotions she was willing to own, but envy wasn't one of them. "Cade. He made all his tools in three weeks."

"Aye, with help."

She shook her head. "Not as much as you think. When you helped me, it still took me more than a year to make my first tools."

Adair took another sip of his drink. "Cade had more previous training than you did."

Anja sensed her master's rhetorical evasions—not in what he said, but in what he was careful not to say. "And how did he memorize so much of Waite, and the *Clavicula Salomonis Regis*, and the *Grimorium Verum*, in just two months?"

"I don't mean to be rude, my dear, but when I found you, you were a peasant girl from a Russian logging town. Cade was a student at Oxford, one of the most prestigious universities in the world. What you think he lacks in experience, he makes up for in first-class education."

Everything the master was telling her was true, but she sensed there still was something he was hiding. "You have had apprentices who were good students before they came here. None ever learned as fast as he has." Her temper got the best of her. "He has done more in two months than I did in three years! If I was your favorite, why did you not speed *my* training like this?"

"Because if I had, you'd be dead."

She recoiled, offended by his undertone of pity. "Damn you."

He looked almost remorseful but said nothing as she hurried out the door into the hallway—where she collided with Cade.

He backed up, hands raised. "Hey! Sorry, I—"

"Must be nice to be *special*," Anja said, cutting him off and leaving him speechless. She pushed past him and sprinted up the spiral stairs, wanting nothing more than to leave him and Adair and everyone else behind. She stormed into her bedroom and slammed the door.

Every passing day made her oath to Adair more painful to honor. Over a year had passed since the war began, and with each day her urge to join the battle grew more acute. After all the master had done for her, the notion of leaving him felt unthinkable, but every day she spent helping train this self-ish young American was another day her duty to the Soviet went postponed.

Someday soon, she knew, a more solemn vow would call her away. And when it did, she would have no choice but to answer.

Until then, she would continue to do her master's bidding.

But only until then.

———

Yoking a demon, Cade learned the next night, was not substantially different from striking a pact with one. In some respects, it was easier. The circles of protection were simpler to draw and required fewer elements. In one regard, however, it was more tedious, and that was the wording of the agreement. Cade was daunted by the verbiage Adair had asked him to memorize.

"Do I really need to say all this?"

"Every word," Adair said. "Demons come in all shapes and sizes, but one thing the fiery gits have in common is they honor their pacts *to the letter.* Some'll let you use their powers for a specific *duration,* some'll let you use their powers only a *limited number of times.* Each demon's terms are unique, so it's vital that every word in a demonic pact be *perfect,* and leave nothing to chance. Get sloppy and you'll wind up empty-handed in the middle of a fight."

"It's all just so arbitrary," Cade said. "All the grimoires told me to ask Lucifuge for seven hundred years of life. But if he can give me seven hundred, why can't I ask for a thousand? Or just simple immortality?"

"Because the beast would have refused and offered you seven hundred, in accordance with the Law."

That sounded to Cade like a cop-out. "And I'd have been obliged to accept it? Why? Because that's just the way it's always been done?"

"I didn't write the rules of magick, lad. I just teach them."

With a grudging shake of his head, Cade continued to review the language of his pending pact with the spirit known as XAPHAN, a demon whose body was composed of the Flame Everlasting. The pact gave Cade the right to yoke the demon for up to ninety consecutive days and during that time wield all of its powers as his own, without restriction, before having to discharge it and summon it again. The catch—because there always was one with demons—

was that for every day of power XAPHAN gave to Cade, it demanded payment in the form of Cade's submission to a century of torment in the afterlife.

Before the sea battle, Cade would never have worried about selling a soul he hadn't believed existed. But now he had seen demons with his own eyes. Knowing that they and Hell were real made it hard for him to be blasé about pledging himself to eons of Infernal torment.

He held up the contract to Adair. "This thing wants to grill me a hundred years for each day I use its powers. Are all the deals like this?"

"Eternity's a long haul. They need something to pass the time."

Cade shook his head. "Do your contracts have these terms?"

"Aye. It's just boilerplate. Nothin' to get on about."

A rueful chuckle. "Yeah, sure. Just eternal damnation. No big deal."

"Trust me, it's a hard debt to collect. Do as I say, and it'll never happen."

The ritual went off without a hitch. It was packed with dreadful howls, stomach-turning odors, and acts of petulance by the spirit, all of which Cade had expected. A few thrusts of his wand forced XAPHAN to stop presenting itself in false forms—first as a beautiful maiden, in a transparent effort to seduce him; then as a mass of gelatinous flesh, eyestalks, and tentacles meant to intimidate him—and appear in its true shape: a tall slender man with a body of fire. Its voice was the hiss of steam dancing across hot iron.

Once the spirit was subdued, Cade calmed his mind before reciting the details that would govern his pact with the demon. XAPHAN simmered through the dictation of terms, which took Cade nearly twenty minutes to enumerate.

When he finished, the demon asked with droll boredom, Is THAT ALL?

"Do you feel underexploited? Should I demand more?" He raised his wand. Adair had warned him not to let demons seize the upper hand, whether by threats, flattery, or sarcasm.

I ACCEPT YOUR TERMS. I WILL AFFIX MY SEAL AND TRUE SIGNATURE IN YOUR BOOK.

Cade rotated the lectern to face his grimoire toward the spirit. XAPHAN took up the pen of the Art and added his imprimatur to the book of pacts, just as its Infernal master LUCIFUGE ROFOCALE had done the night before.

It set down the pen and shrank while awaiting its servitude. I AM PREPARED.

With one hand, Cade raised his wand; with the other he cast a fistful of gold dust into the brazier of smoldering coals at his feet. "*Adiuro animae meae anima tua potestate mea sit potestate, in condicionibus foederis.*"

The spirit faded until it was almost invisible, and then it leapt forward and shrank as it merged with Cade, vanishing inside him as it did. Silence reigned over the grand circle, and the odor of burnt metal that had announced the demon's arrival dissipated.

Adair, who had observed the ritual from the protection of a secondary circle outside the main seal, asked, "How do you feel, lad?"

The sensation pulsing through Cade's body was almost narcotic. "Amazing."

"Enjoy it while it lasts. The hangover's going to be a bear. Tomorrow I'll show you how to scribe circles for calling up several spirits at once."

"When do I start learning how to *use* this?"

"Patience. Right now you've got a belly full of fire. Tomorrow we'll get you a shield and a way to see magick coming. Once you've got those, we can teach you how to fight."

Cade forced his emotions into check. "So, by tomorrow I'll have three demons yoked at once?" His master nodded. "What's the most you've ever yoked?"

"Eleven."

"What's the most anyone's ever yoked?"

The Scot shook his head. "The most I've ever heard of was thirteen."

"Who did that?" He inferred the answer from Adair's dour expression. "Kein."

"Aye." He stepped out of his circle and snapped his fingers to extinguish the ceremonial candles, leaving the room dark but for skewers of moonlight through the windows. "But you've a long road to walk before you brave a stunt like that." He pointed Cade toward the stairs. "Tomorrow's another long day, so sleep tonight—if you can."

"Meaning what?"

"Meaning, I'd put a bottle of whisky on your nightstand if I were you."

FEBRUARY

"Magick is a science," Adair said to Cade as he juggled three orbs of fire. "Master its rules and you can learn to bend them." He made the fiery globes orbit above his head. "And even break them." The tiny fireballs turned to ice, shot off in separate directions, and shattered against the castle's walls of stone. "You try."

Cade concentrated on the names and powers of the four demons he had yoked. XAPHAN, the first, let him conjure and control fire. He held out his right palm and envisioned a ball of flames. Short-lived tongues of reddish fire danced above his hand. A deep breath slowed his racing heart and helped him imagine the fireball with greater clarity.

It popped into being, an orb of cold flames swirling above his hand.

"I did it!" He looked to Adair. "What's next?"

"Make another in your left, but with blue flames. And hot as hell this time."

Again he focused his thoughts on the demon and its native talent. More reluctant licks of fire danced in his left hand before the teal-colored fireball appeared. Its heat shriveled the hairs on the back of his hand. "Okay," Cade said. "One hot fireball, one cold. Now what?"

"Toss 'em in the loch," Adair said. "No way you're bringing those in the keep."

Cade hurled the fireballs into Loch Duich. The red orb spawned a patch of ice on the lake's surface, and the blue orb blasted it to bits that turned to steam in midair. "That was wild," he said, stunned to have seen such raw power in his own hands.

"That was nothing," Adair said. "Before I can teach you to fight, you'll need to be able to attack and defend at the same time, and switch from one power to another on the move."

"Are you serious? I can barely call up one power at a time."

The master took Cade's complaint in stride. "Wielding yoked powers is always hard at first. It's like learning to play music."

"Music?"

"Aye. When you start, it takes all your focus to make one perfect note. You worry about the note itself, about where your fingers go . . . and then you worry about the next note. But the more you practice, the easier it gets to follow one note with another. And each demon is like a new instrument, with its own quirks and techniques. Then, one day, you'll find that you never even think about the notes anymore. Then you're free to just play."

It was a beautiful metaphor, one Cade could finally understand. "Okay. So now . . . ?"

"Learn to tell your sharps from your flats. When you can do that, we'll start on chords. Until then . . . let's see if you can throw some lightning."

"Magick is fun, *mon ami*." Niko passed the wine to Cade. "And never let anyone tell you different!" They had nearly finished off their third bottle of Côtes du Rhône for the afternoon, in between what Niko said were sessions of instruction but which were really little more than him showing off his knack for the magicks of mind control.

A swig of red wine vanished down Cade's gullet. He sleeved some from his chin. "What the hell is fun about having demons in your skull? I've had a headache for three days, and I'm starting to think I might never shit right again."

"Your stomach will adjust. As for your head"—Niko took the bottle—"drink more."

Cade laughed while Niko drank. "Was it this hard for you at first?"

"Harder. Took me eighteen months to make my tools. Another eighteen before Adair said I could make my first pact. Three years I was a novice—you will be a karcist in three months. Count yourself lucky." He passed the bottle to Cade. "Want to see a party trick?"

"Who wouldn't?"

Niko snapped his fingers, and the near-empty bottle was instantly full again. "Better than Jesus! But drink it fast—an hour from now it'll turn to piss."

"I'm pretty sure that'll happen after I drink it, with or without a demon." He downed a mouthful of the summoned wine. "Not bad. Is there a whole field of hooch magick?"

"It is called a cantrip. Minor magick. Still uses demons, but for trivial things."

"Adair told me never to use magick for anything that can be done some other way."

Niko let slip a cynical chortle. "Adair says lots of things."

Now Cade was curious. "Something I ought to know?"

"Just that there is more than one way to work magick. And some—" He took the wine. "—are more fun than others. Case in point: truth magick. I will ask you a question; when you answer, try to tell me a lie." He leaned forward and looked into Cade's eyes while marshaling the power to compel the truth from someone: "What do you really think of Anja?"

"She scares the shit out of me," Cade said. His eyes went wide. "Jesus. I wanted to say, 'She seems nice but a bit tense.' Hell of a trick you've got there."

"Now imagine what you could do with power like that in a poker game." An impish grin. "As I said: Magick is *fun*."

<hr />

"Magick is beauty." Stefan delivered his proclamation without, as far as Cade could tell, the least hint of irony or self-consciousness. They were alone in the conjuring room; Stefan had said they would review the finer points of demonic control, but as usual he had spun himself off on a tangent. "Hidden within the mysteries of the Art are the secrets of the universe." He paced around Cade, fading in and out of sight with every other step, and each time he reappeared, some detail of his attire or person had changed in color or style. "Science has only begun to grasp what magick has long known: that we live in a realm of mysterious connections. Our cosmos exists on scales both greater and more minuscule than we can possibly comprehend."

More than with any of the others, Cade loved to listen to Stefan talk. "Is that why you chose to study magick?"

He stopped circling Cade and faced him. "No. My . . . friend . . . was a student of Kabbalah." He took off his glasses, pulled a cloth from his pocket, and polished the lenses. "I was going to join him and his rabbis. Then I met Adair. When he showed me what the Goetic art could do . . ." He lost himself in a memory. "I knew then what path I had to follow." He put away the cloth and fixed his glasses on his slender nose. "The question, my friend, is what path will you take?"

"Path? You mean like the Left-hand Path or the Right-hand Path?"

"Forget the dogma. Magick is poetry, and vulgarity. Its power comes from darkness but can be used to shed light. It is yin and yang. But *we* must choose. Our will defines it. So what path will *you* choose? Light? Or darkness?"

"Does it have to be black or white? Can't there be a middle path?"

Stefan paired a slow nod with a troubled frown. "The path of shadow. A difficult road. One never knows where it might lead. Take that path with great caution."

"I think you could say that about any aspect of the Art," Cade said. "From where I'm standing, it looks like there isn't a single part of it that can't get you killed."

His observation made Stefan chuckle. "Very true. A dangerous way we follow."

"So what's the secret? The real secret, I mean. How do I do this and not die?"

It seemed to Cade that if anyone would give him a straight answer to that question, it would be Stefan. The master's senior apprentice considered the matter in earnest.

"Some would call my advice foolish or naïve," Stefan said, "but it is all I know to be true. Ground your actions in love and compassion, in empathy and generosity. Never act out of hatred, or for selfish gain. The Art elevates those who humble themselves before the Divine, and it humbles those who seek to clothe themselves in glory. Only when you let go of the ugliness of this world will magick reveal to you its true and endless beauty."

Forked lightning stung the wand from Cade's hand. An unseen blade of ice pierced his gut and dropped him to his knees; then an invisible hand slammed him against the keep's western wall hard enough to rip open his forehead and paint his face with his own blood. He staggered backward and collapsed in the snow, stunned and gasping for air.

Anja regarded him without pity. "Magick is pain. Forget that, and you will die."

Fire crackled in the billeting room's hearth. Cade lay in front of it, stretched out on a champagne-colored antique rug, letting the warmth soothe his aches. "I really think she's trying to kill me."

"If she was, you would be dead," Niko said. "She just wants you to suffer." He and Stefan sat at the small round Chippendale gaming table in the center of the windowless room, nursing glasses of the master's best scotch. The bottle of thirty-year-old Macallan was already half empty, though it had been open less than an hour.

Stefan nodded between sips. "Niko is right. She toys with you."

"Lucky me." Cade watched firelight dance with shadows on the low, barrel-vaulted ceiling. "I just want to know what I did to make her hate me."

Niko drained his glass with a tilt. "'Hate' is a strong word."

"Then why did she tell me she hopes I die in training?"

The senior apprentices laughed. Stefan refilled Niko's glass as he said to Cade, "She resents the attention you receive from the master."

Cade sat up and felt the blood rush from his head. "Resentment I can handle. But she acts like she's got it in for me. How can I trust someone who hates me to train me?"

"She respects the master too much to let you come to harm." Stefan tipped some scotch into a third glass and passed it to Cade. "Be patient. Your training has been hard for her."

"Why? I've done everything she's told me."

Niko said, "You are a good student. Better than expected. And that is the problem."

Stefan added, "You mastered the basics faster than anyone else we have ever trained."

"Why is that a problem?"

"Because," Stefan said, "though Anja is skilled, it took her many years to master the Art. It did not come naturally to her."

"She got this far only because Adair treats her like his own." Niko lowered his voice. "Had I been as slow as her, he'd have thrown me in the moat and told me to swim home."

Knowing more about the dynamic between Anja and Adair only made Cade worry more. "I've heard Adair say you two are leaving soon."

"*Oui*," Niko said. "Special missions. Behind the lines."

"Great. Who'll save me from Anja after you've gone?"

Stefan topped off Cade's glass. "You will just have to win her over."

"And if I can't?"

Niko grinned. "Be patient. Her feelings are hurt, but she will get over it." He took a long swig of scotch, then added, "Or she will stab you in your sleep. Either way, it will work out."

Cade sipped his drink. "Thanks for reminding me why everyone hates the French."

9

Another bolt of lightning flared against Cade's shield of REJECH. The bolt raised the hairs on his arm. He circled left to keep Adair in front of him, and relied on SATHARIEL's disorienting 360-degree vision to watch for minor spirits under the master's control that might appear behind him.

Adair taunted, "Don't hold back, you gutless prat!"

"I'm not." He threw a jet of fire at his master, who dodged it with ease. Then he launched a fireball, only to see it be absorbed into Adair's demonic shield.

The master cracked a knowing grin. "How's your head?"

Cade grimaced. "Same as yesterday." In truth, it was worse. The pounding in his noggin was half hangover, half demonic malice. He was sure that one morning soon his skull would split open, his pulverized brain would spill out, and he'd be grateful for the release.

Electricity leapt from Adair's hand, struck Cade's shield with enough force to knock him back a step, then ricocheted off the keep's stone walls.

"Concentrate! Shields don't just deflect. They can also scatter, absorb, and bounce back."

"I can send your attacks back at you?"

"Or scatter them into a group of enemies. Trust me, that can be handy." Sparks danced on Adair's fingertips. "*En garde.*" He threw a fistful of lightning at Cade.

Racing to keep pace with the mock duel, Cade let his imagination run free. He pictured his shield reflecting the incoming burst, then summoned a wall of flames between himself and Adair. The lightning ball rebounded off Cade's shield and shot back, through the fire, straight at Adair. Using the Sight, Cade saw the reflected attack knock the master off his feet. With a thought, Cade banished the flame wall.

He smiled at his supine mentor. "Like that?"

"Exactly." Adair looked pleased as he rose and slapped mud and snow from his coat and britches. "You learn fast. Pairing a bounced attack with a wall of fire as a distraction—very smart. Tonight you'll yoke a few more spirits. Tomorrow, I'll show you how to combine their powers. Putting XAPHAN's fire on VAELBOR's weapons, for instance." Perhaps noting a change in Cade's expression, he frowned in concern. "What's the matter, lad?"

"Nothing. I'm fine." Cade had never had much use for self-pity—not in prep school, not at Oxford, not now. He pretended that his head didn't ache as if it were trapped in a vise, and that his guts weren't churning from heartburn and diarrhea, all of it demonically induced. "How many spirits am I yoking tonight?"

Despite Cade's feigned confidence, Adair clearly sensed something was amiss. "Been a long time since I was an apprentice, but it's not something one forgets." He struck a sympathetic note. "How've you been sleeping?"

"Like shit."

"Nightmares?"

"Not every night. Just when I sleep."

"Whisky's not helping?"

"I ran out a few—" He raised his shield to absorb Adair's surprise lightning attack and funneled its energy into himself to mitigate his fatigue.

The master gave an approving nod. "You've learned not to drop your guard."

Cade touched his chest. "I still have the scars from your first two lessons."

"The words you seek are 'thank you.'" He tilted his head toward the steps to the keep. "'Senough for today. Let's head in, get supper, find you another bottle of Oban." He started up, but Cade lingered in the courtyard. After a few steps, Adair turned. "I know that look. Something else is on your mind. Out with it."

It was hard for Cade to overcome his self-consciousness. "It's Anja."

"Had another one of her turns, did she?"

"She talks like she wants me dead."

"Bothers you, does it?"

"It does if you expect me to go into combat with her. How can I trust her to have my back when it's obvious she hates my guts?"

A weary frown. "It'll pass." Under his breath he added, "I hope."

"Niko and Stefan said that, too. But what if it doesn't? That's a lot to take on faith."

"Listen to me: You can trust her. Anja's nothing if not loyal. You will never have an ally as trustworthy or as brave as her. On that, I give you my word."

His assurance satisfied Cade. "All right." Wind off the loch sent a shiver down his spine. "As for yoking more demons—you got anything stronger than scotch?"

Adair cocked a ragged eyebrow. "You mean like opium?"

"Do you have any?"

"A wee bit. But I don't plan on giving it to you."

The bait and switch irritated Cade. "Why not?"

"I'm saving it." He plodded up the steps to the keep, with Cade close behind. "Yoke six spirits and you can crack on with absinthe. If you want laudanum in your cocktail"—he shot a smile over his shoulder—"show me you can yoke nine."

<hr />

Morning arrived too early for Cade, as it always had. He was roused by voices from the keep's second floor. Groggy, he considered returning to sleep until he remembered the date: Stefan and Niko were leaving that morning. He got up, dressed in a hurry, and scrambled down the spiral stairs, hoping to catch them before they left.

All the doors on the second floor were closed save the one at the end of the corridor, the room beneath Cade's. He moved closer and recognized Stefan's courtesy and Niko's chiding.

"*Mon Dieu!* How long does it take to pack a bag?"

"Longer with criticism than without, I should think."

Cade stood outside the half-open door. The room looked much like his; it had the same floor plan, but the window was farther to the left, near the wardrobe alcove, and had a deeper sitting area with a pair of padded benches that faced each other. Niko was splayed across an armchair in the corner, one leg draped over an arm. His overcoat and scarf were piled in his lap. "Perhaps you hope to postpone our departure? Until summer, for instance?"

"I will soon be done." Stefan stood at the foot of his bed, his back to Niko as he folded a pair of suit pants and then rolled them up.

From behind the door came Anja's voice, surprising Cade. "Not everyone packs a bag the way a butcher stuffs a sausage, Niko."

"Maybe they should. It is faster than this, *n'est-ce pas*?"

"Faster it may be." Stefan pushed the rolled-up trousers into his shoulder bag, then started folding a dress shirt. "But I would rather be slow than live as a walking wrinkle."

Anja laughed, and Niko stuck his tongue out at her. Then he noticed Cade and beckoned him with a long sweep of his arm. "*Entrez-vous!*"

Stefan and Anja turned toward the doorway as Cade stepped into the room. The young Dutchman greeted Cade with a dip of his chin, but Anja regarded him with suspicion. Unsure what to do or say, Cade lifted his hand in a half-hearted wave. "Morning."

"*Goedemorgen,*" Stefan said.

Cade looked at Niko's duffel, then Stefan's bag. "Leaving without breakfast?"

"We ate before dawn," Niko said.

A sympathetic nod from Stefan. "Master Adair has us on strict schedules." He packed his last shirt and then laid his folded neckties atop his impeccably folded clothes. Cade noticed the ties were ordered by color, from brightest to darkest.

Anja drifted into the wardrobe nook and stared out a window.

Cade watched Stefan close his bag. "Where's he sending you?"

Stefan sighed. "The master loaned a grimoire to a circle of Kabbalah masters in Poland. He has charged me with securing its safe return."

"And I," Niko said, "am to find shelter in Paris, then set to work destroying all Thule covens in the *zone libre.*" He checked his watch, glanced at Stefan's bag, and cleared his throat. "If I can get to France before the war ends, that is."

"Enough. I am ready." Stefan picked up his overcoat and hat from the bed. The gray fedora he settled onto his head; his coat he draped over his arm. Niko groaned as he got out of the chair and shuffled into his winter coat and scarf.

Their imminent departure coaxed Anja out of the wardrobe. She moved to Stefan's side and clutched his arms, prelude to an embrace. "Be safe. And come back to me." She hugged him and pressed her head to his chest. He hugged her with equal affection.

Stefan let her go and stepped back. "I will miss you, Anja. Be well until we meet again."

She pushed a stray lock of his hair into place, then straightened his tie. "You, too." She aimed a faux scowl at Niko. "And you: Stay out of trouble!"

"But that is where all the fun is!" Anja lifted her hand to smack him. He retreated, and she chased him, both of them laughing like children. She got in one last good slap before he grabbed his duffel and hurried out of range. "*Arrêter!* I already *have* a sister!"

Niko followed Stefan to the door. They paused at the threshold and turned to face Cade. Despite the Dutchman's relative youth, there was a calm wisdom in his eyes. "You have much to look forward to, my friend. Adair is a fine master, and you will find no better guide to the Art than Anja. Soon you will find the world is made of wonders."

Niko added, "Just take care those wonders do not kill you."

The older apprentice waved away Niko's pessimism, then shook Cade's hand. "Feel no fear. The universe shall bend to your will." A conspiratorial gleam. "And it will be beautiful."

He let go of Cade's hand and led Niko out of the room and down the hall to the stairs. Cade stood in the doorway, watching them leave. As they rounded the corner at the end of the T, he felt the weight of Anja's stare. He looked at her. The sisterly affection she had shown to Niko and Stefan was gone, replaced by an unforgiving aspect. "You could not even let me have *this* to myself." She shouldered past him and disappeared down the hall.

He noted her departure with dread.

She's gonna kick my ass worse than ever.

<hr/>

The passage out of Eilean Donan Castle was short and steeped in shadow. Daylight bled in from the courtyard on one side and from the outside world on the other. Stefan walked ahead of Niko, his bag tucked close behind his shoulder. This was the first time in five years that either of them had left Eilean Donan for anything other than a short jaunt out. Ahead of them, the castle's three-arch stone bridge stretched east toward the mainland.

Adair's voice echoed through the passage behind them. "Wait!"

They turned to see their master hurry out of the castle. He wore a patchwork flatcap, a dingy overcoat, and a long scarf decorated with his clan's red-and-black tartan pattern. His shoes crunched on the gravel as he caught up to them. "I can't believe I almost let you go without these." He reached into his coat's pockets and pulled out two small metal hand mirrors. He handed one to each of them. "Both made in Hell. They'll never break unless you want them to."

Niko admired his mirror. "Very nice. What are its control words?"

"Hold it and say '*fenestra,*' then the name of the person you want to talk to. Stefan, if you want to talk to Niko, say his name. If you want to speak to him *and* me, say both our names. To close it, say '*velarium.*'"

Stefan turned his mirror over and saw the glyph etched on its back: the sigil of HAEL, a spirit that served as an Infernal messenger. "Magickal radio."

"Better. Just like my large mirror, we can pass small objects between them. Anything that can fit between its edges—a key, a note, a bullet. They work over any distance, and they're immune to eavesdropping." He rested his hands on the men's shoulders. "Do *not* let the enemy capture them, and *never* tell anyone the control words. Unlocked and plumbed with the right charm, one of these could let Kein spy my every move. If you think there's even the slightest risk he or his people might get their hands on your mirror, hold it in your left hand and say '*discutio.*' Think you lads can remember that?"

Niko tucked his mirror inside his coat. "*Fenestra, velarium, discutio.* Simple enough."

"Thank you, Master." Stefan opened his bag just enough to slip the unbreakable magick mirror inside, then zipped it shut. "I'll contact you in a fortnight, as agreed."

"Watch your steps, both of you. Europe might seem familiar, but under Nazi control it is terra incognita, I guarantee it." Adair spread his hands in a gesture of blessing. "Let the wind be at your backs, and may the hand of God stand between you and harm."

Stefan and Niko overlapped each other as they answered, "Thank you, Master."

Adair waved to the two men as they turned away and walked over the bridge. They were halfway across when Stefan heard the gears of the castle's portcullis, followed by the ringing of iron against stone as the barred gate dropped into place over the main entrance.

He glanced over his shoulder to make sure they were alone, then said quietly to Niko, "Thank you for not telling Adair my secret."

"The truth would have done more harm than good."

As a specialist in divination and truth magick, Niko had long ago discerned Stefan's hidden agenda, the personal mission he intended to pursue while he worked to recover the Iron Codex for Adair: Stefan's lover, Evert Siever, was one of the Kabbalah students who had gone missing and silent after the Nazis' invasion of Poland in September 1939.

The master would not have sent me to find the Codex had he known how urgently I need to find Evert. How many times had Adair railed against the folly of risking many lives to save one? It was a lecture all his adepts endured sooner or later: the cold arithmetic of wartime moral calculus was a lesson of which Adair seemed never to tire.

At the end of the bridge, Niko offered Stefan his hand. "Here we part ways."

Stefan pulled Niko into a tight embrace and fought the urge to shed tears. "You have been my good friend, Niko Le Beau. I shall never forget you."

"We will meet again, when this is over." He slapped Stefan's back, a hearty affirmation of their camaraderie. They faced each other. "And you *will* find him."

"I hope so."

"Love, eh? It will not be denied! Trust me. Love is stronger than hate. It is the wellspring of hope. And hope will carry us." He kissed Stefan's cheeks in that rough but affectionate way only the French can commit with panache. "God be with you, brother."

There was nothing left to say. Stefan watched Niko walk west toward Broadford, from whence he would seek passage to France. Meanwhile, a boat had been summoned to meet Stefan in Inverness, and from there it would carry him to Europe by way of Malmö, in neutral Sweden.

Stefan walked east. He feared that Adair's warning would prove prescient. There was no telling what the Nazis and their cult of overzealous amateur magicians—the Thule-Gesellschaft, or Thule Society—had wrought in Europe. Stefan's inner pessimist feared he might not recognize places he once had called home. The Nazis had made no secret of their anti-Semitic rhetoric in the years leading up to their invasion of Poland. He feared it could only have grown worse in the years since he had left the Netherlands to study with Adair, and the loss of contact with the Kabbalah masters seemed to confirm his most dire suspicions.

As for what would come of the master's new adept—who could say? Cade had seemed unremarkable when first they had brought him to the castle. Just a youth frozen in the stone grip of death, more a likeness of a person than a flesh-and-blood human being. Yet the master had been willing to defy heads of state and postpone many of his own grand designs for the war in order to bring that one young man back from the edge of oblivion.

Mine is not to question, Stefan reminded himself. *I am a soldier, and I have my orders.*

His feet carried him eastward, toward an appointment long overdue and a quest too long delayed. He knew his duty was to find Adair's missing grimoire, but in his heart, he knew his courage served only one objective: to find Evert and spirit him to safety, at any cost.

Niko's words echoed in his memory.

Love, eh? It will not be denied.

10

Knee-deep in snow on the lowest portion of the island, beneath the crenellated seawall, Anja focused on shattering large stones with a demonic whip, then melting the fragments in midair with blasts of hellfire. A single stone caromed off the wall of the keep's guardhouse and ricocheted over the lower seawall toward the loch. She split the fist-sized piece of falling rock with one arrow from the bow of LERAIKAH.

A voice at her back halted her practice: "Nice shooting."

The master shed his invisibility and faded into view, hovering a few feet above the ground. Anja sulked at the intrusion. "I could have killed you."

"Fat chance. But I'm glad you care." He drifted to the ground. His feet sank into the churned-up snow. "Up with the sun, are you?"

"I never went to bed."

The master nodded in understanding. "Can't sleep?"

"Not for a few nights." She massaged her right temple, then looked his way. "And yes, I tried absinthe. And no, I don't want the opium."

"You've got eight spirits yoked. A touch o' the poppy could take the edge off."

Anja shook her head. "It does bad things to me. And it took me weeks to quit last time." She studied Adair. "This is not what you came to discuss."

"No." He seemed uncomfortable. "You're supposed to help me train Cade."

She searched the grounds for a new target against which to unleash her fury. "He does not need my help."

With an invisible hand, the master spun her to face him. "I need to know I can trust you in battle."

The implications of his demand stung her. "How can you ask me that? After all I have done? All I have lost? You would question *my* loyalty?"

"I don't fear for myself, lass. I'm worried you won't protect *him*."

Her denial soured into contempt. "Let him save his own skin."

"Not good enough, my dear."

"Why not?"

"Because I—" He stopped himself, regrouped. "Because *we* need him. And he needs us." He trudged through the snow to hold Anja by her shoulders. "This is bigger than you, or me. Cade's our best hope of winning this war—but not if we fail him."

"I think he will fail us. Good in the circle is not the same as good in battle—and he is not that good in the circle."

Adair's patience waned. "He made one mistake, and you stopped it. He's done well since then. He's already mastered the basics."

"The basics? We need to fight a war, against an enemy with much greater numbers, and you want me to risk my life with an amateur at my side?"

The master regarded her with incredulity. "And what are you? A seasoned veteran?"

"Not in war. But I know more magick. And at least I have shed blood."

He cupped his right hand over the scar on her left cheek, his affect suddenly mild. "Aye. I know." His touch calmed her. Then he looked her in the eye. "But I need to know you won't turn your back on him out there. Or lead him into danger."

She suppressed her envy. "I did not betray your other 'special' students."

"No, but you were never so hostile to them, either. Why Cade?"

"You tell me. Why did you risk us all to save him that night at sea? Why make me spend so much time working to free him from LEVIATHAN's curse?"

"I have my reasons, lass. Let that satisfy you."

It didn't, but his tone made it clear he was no longer willing to suffer questions. Wary of his wrath, she changed the subject. "Is he ready for combat?"

"Some blades need to be proved in action. They either break, or draw blood." A sigh. "What I do know is we can't wait any longer. Thule Society covens are spreading like a cancer. If we don't start carving them out now, the war's as good as over." He floated upward, parallel to the keep's wall, and called down to Anja as he levitated away. "Pack a ruck, lass, and travel light. We leave tonight at sundown."

Realizing that the day for which she had so long prepared was upon her, she was filled with foreboding. "Where are we going?"

His countenance was grim. "To war."

A shriek filled the train car as the brakes engaged. Momentum hunched the passengers forward in their seats as the locomotive slowed to a halt, and Westphalia's bleak winterscape emerged from the blur of motion outside its windows. The late-afternoon sky had faded to the color of a blanched peach; long shadows and streaks of reflected light filled the streets of Hamburg.

Stefan lowered his copy of *Mein Kampf*—a pandering choice of reactionary tripe he had only pretended to read during the ride south from Fehmarn.

During his brief stay in Sweden, his contact had advised him to eschew his usual three-piece suits in favor of a workman's clothes, so as not to draw attention. Her counsel had proved useful for his predawn sea crossing by skiff into Denmark, and also afterward, when he had been forced on short notice to slaughter an entire Thule Society coven in Copenhagen.

After leaving Denmark by ferry and arriving in Fehmarn with forged papers identifying him as a citizen of the Großdeutsches Reich, Stefan had reverted to habit and attired himself in a suit of dark gray wool with a silk vest and tie. Some might have accused him of vanity, but he thought of it as playing his part. He had, after all, booked first-class accommodations all the way to Warsaw, from whence he planned to arrange alternative transportation to Kraków, the last known whereabouts of the Kabbalah masters who had vanished with Adair's precious grimoire.

The plan was not without risk. It entailed traveling in public through two of Germany's largest cities: Hamburg, its principal seaport, and Berlin, its capital. Even so, Stefan had felt certain his disguise and persona were sufficiently nondescript as to let him pass without detection, a ghost by virtue of anonymity.

Then four Gestapo entered the carriage behind his. The plainclothes officers headed his way. Stefan felt his confidence take flight. Alone and only moments away from a confrontation with the Nazis' secret police, he was no longer certain of anything.

Do I run? Or trust in my papers?

Though he'd made every effort to be inconspicuous, he was paralyzed by the fear he had missed something, some detail that would betray him—if not as a Jew, then as a homosexual or an Allied spy. He feared the Nazis might search his bag and find the photos of him and Evert that he kept tucked away, between the pages of a copy of Yeats's collected poems, and discover the truth that seemed so evident in those images of happier times.

In the next car, the Gestapo moved from one row of passengers to the next, demanding papers and asking questions. They moved in pairs, with each duo working one side of the aisle. Their black trench coats and fedoras were just as menacing as any SS trooper's uniform.

Were it just one man, I could make his death seem an accident. But four of them? He stole another look over his shoulder and considered turning himself invisible. *No, they have a passenger list. If I vanish, I might as well run. But the moment I do, they'll start looking for me.* He took a breath, but his heart refused to slow its mad tempo.

A clatter announced the opening of the carriage's rear door. The four Gestapo marched to the closest row of occupied seats and began asking for passengers' papers.

Acid crept up Stefan's throat; sweat beaded on his forehead. In small motions, he mopped his brow with his handkerchief, then tucked it away.

What if they arrest me?

He had more than enough demonic power at his command to kill all four Gestapo, but how would he attenuate the consequences? *If only I had yoked* FORNEUS, *I could erase the memories of the Nazis and the other passengers.* It was an error of omission he vowed to correct and never make again—but first he had to avoid being arrested or killed.

"Papers, please."

Stefan forced a polite smile. "Of course." He fished inside his suit coat, pulled out his papers, and handed them to the officer looming over him.

The other two Gestapo moved down the aisle; the pair studying Stefan's papers lingered. Cupping their hands in front of each other's ears, they traded whispers. One of them hurried away with the forged papers while the other remained at Stefan's side. The young karcist affected his most humble demeanor. "Is there a problem?"

"Be quiet," said his new watchdog.

Chancing a glance to his left, Stefan saw his Nazi minder drape his hand over the grip of the Luger semiautomatic on his hip. At the front of the carriage, the other two Gestapo continued forward, leaving Stefan's captor alone. Through the windows on the other side of the carriage, he saw the officer who had taken his papers confer with a knot of black-uniformed German SS.

It took only a thought to set Stefan's escape in motion.

In your heart, I strike at thee. Stefan pictured the invisible dagger of Orias piercing the Gestapo man's chest, and thus it was done. Without sound or fury, without blood or obvious wound, but a killing blow all the same.

The officer crumpled to the floor of the train, clutching at his chest, his gesture a pantomime for the shredding of his cardiac muscle beneath his sternum.

Stefan sprang to his feet. "This man needs a doctor!"

In the moment between his declaration and the crush of charitable reactions from the other passengers, Stefan grabbed his leather roll of tools off the luggage rack, then his shoulder bag. He slung one over each shoulder and hurried aft to the closest exit.

By the time the two Gestapo in the next car had doubled back, and the one with Stefan's papers realized something was amiss, Stefan had disembarked from the train and made his way into central Hamburg, concealed and abetted by its throngs of pedestrian traffic.

As an escape, it had been well timed, even artful. But it had left Stefan without papers in the heart of enemy territory, a great distance from his destination. To his chagrin, his only reliable means of reaching Poland now was to do so on foot, and under cover of darkness.

So much for traveling in style. He adjusted the roll-up, which contained his tools of the Art, and his satchel, which held his clothes and personal effects, and he was grateful Adair had encouraged him to travel light. His path had grown longer and more perilous than it had been just an hour earlier—yet his thoughts now were dominated by one pragmatic regret.

Had I known I would be walking to Poland, I'd have worn more comfortable shoes.

———

Winter had reduced Paris to a sketch of itself. Avenues, boulevards, buildings, and monuments all were nothing but outlines on a pale canvas of knee-high snow. Only the weaving paths of tire tracks and the broad cuts of panzers' treads marred the shroud that blanketed the City of Light.

Trudging down a *rue* in the Ninth Arrondissement, Niko pulled his scarf over his nose as much for warmth as for anonymity. In the weeks since he had waded ashore at Carantec after crossing the English Channel in a skiff piloted by a besotted old Welshman, he had hiked from one town or village to the next, always under the cover of darkness.

Along the way he had seen enough of the Germans' atrocities to know he needed to avoid being noticed in Occupied France. Just as Adair had warned, his adopted home had come to feel strange and hostile. In a country village, he had seen SS troops execute two boys for stealing a loaf of bread. On a road outside of Sainte-Suzanne, he'd borne silent witness from the woods as a squad of Wehrmacht opened fire on a dairy truck that had refused to stop at their command; when the soldiers searched its wreckage, all they had found was a young woman in an apron, a pool of milk and cream from a dozen shattered bottles, and fifty pounds of bullet-ridden cheese.

Niko pulled his arms to his sides and quickened his step.

An hour earlier, after he'd crossed the Pont de la Concorde, he'd noticed a crowd of anglers stooped over the railings along the Right Bank, their lines cast into the Seine. Niko couldn't remember ever having seen so many people try to fish the river at once, so he'd paused long enough to ask an elderly gent, "Any luck?"

The old fisherman looked at him with sunken eyes. He wore a dense stubble of white whiskers on his gaunt cheeks. "As much as one would expect."

Attuned then to the crowd's air of desperation, Niko had nodded and moved on.

At the midpoint of his climb up the tiered steps of the Rue Foyatier, he passed a squad of German soldiers. The half dozen Nazis shouted anti-Semitic slurs as they beat a frail elderly man and woman under one of the steps' lampposts. The Germans paid Niko no mind as he drifted past, his chin down and his eyes averted in fearful shame from the spectacle unfolding in plain sight on the steps of Montmartre's famous Sacré-Coeur Basilica.

I am a pilgrim in an unholy land.

He shook with rage and suppressed an urge to vomit. The conflict between his impulse to wreak vengeance on the Nazis and his duty to carry out his mission, which required him to remain undetected in enemy territory, stung his eyes with tears.

How many must I sacrifice for the greater good? And how do I forgive myself for the lives I do not save? Pushing onward, he found no answers and no solace, only distance from the pain.

Once he reached the Rue Saint-Éleutherè, he found the streets deserted. The glow of lamplight was dulled by the blizzard, and his steps were muffled by deep snow. He didn't see another soul the rest of his way through Montmartre, and when he reached the Café Étoiles on Rue des Cloys, it was—as he had expected—closed, locked, and dark.

He tried the adjacent door, which led to the apartments above the restaurant. It was unlocked, so he opened it and stepped inside. He passed through the foyer, then climbed the switchback staircase to the third floor. He stopped in front of the door to its only flat and knocked twice with the side of his fist.

Thumps and rumblings from the other side. Muted voices, anxious whispers. Then the thunk of a deadbolt being retracted. The door cracked open. Through the sliver, Niko spied a tall man, who asked with naked suspicion, "What do you want?"

It wasn't the greeting Niko had expected. "I'm looking for Camille."

From behind the door he heard a revolver being cocked. The bruiser's one visible eye narrowed. "And who are you?"

"Niko. Her brother."

A flurry of commotion pushed the lunk aside, and the door was pulled wide. Looking at Niko, beaming with joy, was his kid sister—who now was more grown-up than he had ever thought possible. "Niko!" Camille threw her arms around him and laughed as she peppered his cheeks with kisses. Pressing her palms to his face, she leaned back. "It's been so long! When the Germans came, I was afraid I'd never see you again."

"Don't be silly, Cami. Even the hordes of Hell couldn't keep us apart."

Their moment was spoiled by the bruiser. "We should search him."

Camille glared at the big man. "You're not searching my brother."

"We can't trust anyone. Not after what happened to Luc and Adele."

Niko wanted to enjoy his reunion with Camille, but it was clear he had to cut to business. He stepped inside the apartment. "You mean the Lamarck Maquis?"

The big man pressed his revolver's muzzle to Niko's forehead.

Camille tried to leap between them. "Ferrand! Don't!"

Ferrand pushed her aside and kept his stare on Niko. "How do you know that?"

"British SOE sent me."

A bead of sweat trickled down Ferrand's right temple. "Prove it."

"The Allies will need help when they come to free Europe from the Nazis. They'll need a strong resistance here in Occupied France. A fifth column to pave the way."

Ferrand pressed the revolver's muzzle harder against Niko's head. "We know that."

"Then you know the Nazis have guerrilla units in France, pretending to be occult groups. They call themselves the Thule Society. The SOE sent me to wipe them out in the *zone libre*."

"The SOE sent *one man* to fight the Thule cult? I'm not sure I believe you."

"Why should I give a damn what you believe?"

"Ferrand, stop." Camille nudged the pistol away from Niko and put a hand to Niko's chest, signaling him to back down. "Niko . . . Ferrand Clipet is my husband."

Niko chortled, then set down his duffel and tool roll. He rubbed his eyes and sighed before facing his sister and his brother-in-law. "A thug, just like Papa. I should have known."

Still itching for a fight, Ferrand took two steps toward Niko. "Oh, *pardon me*. Was I supposed to get your blessing first? Maybe I would have if you hadn't run off to England!"

Niko had no patience for an argument with an aggressive cretin. He gestured toward the door. "Monsieur Clipet, would you mind giving us a few minutes alone, please?"

"Yes, I do mind. This is my home. You can't just strut in here like a peacock and—"

"*Give us a few minutes,*" Niko said, projecting the coercive force of DANTALION. "Put down your pistol and take a walk outside."

Ferrand froze, struggling between his free will and the magickal compulsion thrust upon him. Then he set his revolver on the table, walked out the door, and continued down the stairs, leaving Niko alone at last with his younger sister.

She radiated disapproval. "That was rude."

"Rude? He put a *gun* to my head. An offense I would forgive had he not also put a ring on your finger." He lifted her hand to look at her wedding band. "What were you thinking?"

She pulled her hand back, offended. "That you were dead, like Mama and Papa."

"Why would you think that? I wrote you every week."

"Until the Germans took Paris."

"That's my fault? I'm to blame because the Nazis won't deliver my letters from Britain?"

She shut the apartment door, then turned and lowered her voice. "You don't know what it's been like here since the Germans came. They take most of the food and fuel, then make us beg for scraps." A nod toward the kitchen. "It's been months since we've had cooking oil. Thin as our ration cards are, most days the markets don't have enough food to fill them."

"That explains the fishermen on the Seine."

"The Nazis banned fishing on the coast to stop men from sailing south to join the Free French." She pulled a chair from the table and sank onto it. "The Vichy-loyal police and the Nazis arrest hundreds every week. Jews, Communists, anyone who looks different or says anything they don't like. Whenever someone so much as bruises a Nazi, they kill *dozens* of innocents." She palmed tears from her cheek. "We're in Hell, Niko."

It pained him to see her so frightened, so bereft of hope. A decade earlier, when they had come to Paris as teenaged refugees after the deaths of their parents, he had promised to keep her safe. Watching her weep, he knew it was time to honor his vow.

He leaned forward and clasped her hands. "You are *not* in Hell, Camille. And I'll prove it to you—and to your prick of a husband, if he'll let me."

She studied him with tearstained eyes. "How?"

"I'll help you and Ferrand unite with other resistance groups. Once you all start to work together, you'll find you're stronger than you know."

Camille stood. "Count me in." She patted his shoulder on her way into the kitchen nook. "Now, ration stamps be damned: My brother is back from the dead! I must have a wedge of Gruyère and a bottle of cabernet stashed in here *somewhere.* . . ."

❧

Cade hurried down the stairs to the conjuring room. Each plank groaned beneath his weight. Over one shoulder he toted a ruck of well-weathered canvas. He wore his heavy leather roll of blades diagonally across his back. Bounding off the last step, he adjusted his tool roll's strap, which was snug against the front of his overcoat.

Adair stood at the far end of the laboratory, his tools and ruck nowhere in sight. Noting Cade's arrival, he produced a pocket watch from under his trench coat. "Early for a change." He tucked the watch away. "Only by a minute, but I'll take all the miracles I can get."

Eager to get on with whatever Adair had planned, Cade crossed the room to stand with the master. "I thought you were going with us."

"What makes you think I'm not?"

A confused look around, coupled with a shrug. "Where's your gear?"

"I have a demon tote that shite." A wink and a crooked half smile: "Pays to keep your hands free." His brow creased as he studied Cade. "Growing a bit o' scruff, eh?"

"Yeah." The mention of his new facial hair reminded Cade of the itching that had come with it. He scratched at either side of his chin. "Figured I might as well. They weren't banned at Oxford, but they weren't in fashion, either. Besides, I kind of like it."

"Hrmph." The master didn't seem to approve. Before Cade could ask why, Adair turned to face the wall. "I guess we should get started."

"Shouldn't we wait for Anja?"

"I am here," she said, from behind his shoulder.

Cade jolted at the nearness of her voice. "Where the hell did *you* come from?"

"Shadow is my friend. So is silence." She moved to stand with Adair. "I am prepared."

"Right, then. Close behind me, both of you." A wave of his arm cast off a shroud that had hidden a huge mirror on the room's western wall. Adair drew his wand and pointed it at the mirror. "*Haec reflexio fit per fenestram, hoc autem speculo fit porta.*"

The trio's reflections vanished, supplanted by clouds of smoke that churned from black to imperial violet. Adair closed his eyes and concentrated while keeping his wand aimed at the mirror. A scene took shape from the mists. It was like spying on a house whose interior was steeped in fog. Adair frowned, shook his head, and dispelled the image with a wave of his wand.

Cade asked, "What was that place?"

"A house outside Brisbane, Australia," Adair said. "Not a useful portal."

"Portal?" The mirror filled once again with turbulent vapors. Cade wondered what would be revealed next. "We travel by stepping through mirrors?"

"Aye, if I can find a portal glass Kein hasn't smashed."

"So you need to have a special mirror on both sides?"

Adair's brow creased. "If you want to use it as a portal, yes." He paused to catch his breath, and the mirror reverted to normal when he opened his eyes. "I can also use it to scry people and places that aren't warded, but that doesn't do us much good right now." He steeled himself for another go. "I need to find a working portal glass somewhere in northern Europe, one big enough for us to walk through."

Cade wondered if he was missing something obvious. "Why not just make a new one and have a demon take it to wherever you want to go?"

The master turned a stink-eye stare at Cade. "Because I don't make the bloody things. Hell does, by request. A mirror big enough for a man to walk through takes seven years to make, and costs a fortune. The handheld buggers I gave to Niko and Stefan only take a year, but they're not cheap, either." The master's grouchiness worsened. "I spent the better part of two centuries putting mirrors like this all over the world. Kein broke nearly every last one in just under a year."

It was a dismaying state of affairs, but Cade clung to hope. "Isn't there any other way of making a portal big enough for us to use?"

"A permanent one? Not that I know of. In a pinch we could try a saint's portal—" The master shifted gears at the first sign that Cade didn't know what he was talking about. "It's a one-time portal made with dust from consecrated stained-glass windows and a lot of holy oil."

"Okay," Cade said. "Why not use that all the time?"

"Because," Anja said, "stealing a blessed window is harder than you think. And most churches refuse to share holy oil with karcists."

"Not to mention," Adair added, "it depends on having a major demon yoked, and the few that can work that charm are a fright to have kicking around inside your head." He raised his wand, closed his eyes, and concentrated on the mirror. "Let's have another go, shall we?" The clouds reappeared, erasing the trio's reflections. The image rippled, only to settle upon more fog. "Fuck! Kein's been a busy bastard."

Cade had an idea. "What about southern Europe? Do you have mirrors there?"

"One, in Tuscany—but it won't help us."

"Why not?"

"Because it's Axis territory, and there aren't any Thule covens in Italy. Part of a deal Kein made with the Vatican, to make sure the Synod's white mages stayed out of the fight." He added under his breath, "Bloody wankers."

Another wave of Adair's wand, and the mirror's liquefied surface trembled. When it calmed, it revealed what looked to Cade like a warehouse strewn with cobwebs. "There we go," the master said. "Bruges. An old dress shop." He frowned at the scene visible through the mirror. "Looks like they went under. No matter. That's our way into Europe. We go on three. Set?" Nods from Anja and Cade. "Right. One. Two. Three!"

The trio moved single-file through the mirror and emerged inside the shop.

It felt to Cade like stepping through a gap in a wall. Then he noticed a shift in the quality of the light, and in his bones he felt the weight of having traversed a hole in reality. He looked back, expecting to see the laboratory in the mirror behind him. All he saw were reflections of his own surprise, Adair's amusement, and Anja's boredom. He swallowed and pretended not to notice he was the butt of the joke. "All right. We're here. Now what?"

Adair swatted through cobwebs and navigated a maze of dusty sewing machines to an exit. "First, we find a way out. Then we nick a ride and head north, to Amsterdam."

"What's in Amsterdam?"

"The nearest Thule coven." The master paused at the door, pressed his ear to it, then tapped its knob before turning it. He peeked through the crack between the door and jamb, then opened it and led Cade and Anja down a staircase to another door. "They've about thirty major covens in western Europe. Maybe ten in Germany, the rest in occupied territories."

He pushed open the door at the bottom of the stairs. It let out onto a cobblestone street flanked by buildings that looked to Cade as if they'd been lifted from fairy tales. Adair paused on the sidewalk to savor the night air; then he smiled. "Good to be back on the Continent." He fished a pack of cigarettes from his coat, lit one with a snap of his fingers, and offered the pack to Anja, who plucked a smoke from the box and lit it off the end of Adair's.

The master thrust the pack at Cade, who waved it off. "No, thanks."

"As you like." He put away the cigarettes and crossed the street. "This way."

It took Adair less than a minute to find a car he deemed suitable. The vehicle was locked, but the same charm Adair had used on the door in the dress shop opened the car's doors and turned over its ignition. Anja climbed in the front to drive. Cade moved to get in the rear, only to be shooed to the front seat by the master. "I like room to stretch out."

Cade got in the car and did his best to avoid eye contact with Anja. She seemed to have no trouble ignoring him as she put the car into gear and sped down the forgotten roads of Bruges. Rather than stare ahead, half paralyzed with fear of a collision, Cade looked at Adair, who had settled in for a nap across the backseat. "What do we do after we get to Amsterdam?"

"Find the dabblers' lair, wait for them to meet, then kill them."

"Sounds easy." Cade scratched an itch under his beard. "What's the catch?"

Anja said, "We will be outnumbered."

"By how many?"

Adair said, "Don't know. Some covens are small, maybe half a dozen strong.

Others might be as big as twenty, or bigger." He opened one eye. "But there's more to battle than numbers. Most of the enemy's ranks are amateurs."

"Then why does it take three of us to attack one coven?"

Anja replied, "Even amateurs get lucky."

The car rattled as Anja steered it down another narrow street. Outside the windows, quaint buildings and arched bridges blurred past.

Questions continued to nag at Cade, who was too keyed up to keep his worries to himself. "If the Thule covens are amateurs, why waste time fighting them?"

"What they lack in skill they make up for in numbers. They constitute an invisible line of defense the Allies can't break, though they won't know why. We need to get the dabblers out of the way *before* the Allies come to free Europe." He sat up, apparently abandoning his hopes for a nap. "We can't wage the Allies' war for them, but we *can* give them a shot at a fair fight."

"But why not just go after Kein now? Why waste time on small fry?"

Adair shook his head. "Kein's too strong for us to attack right now. Part of his power comes from having an army of followers who feed his strength. It's like chess: One thins the board before attacking the king. Trust me, lad, this is the way." He leaned forward against the front seat. "Lass, turn left up here."

"I know the way."

"Aye, but I know the shortcuts. Make the next left. We'll drive through the night, then find some petrol before we bed down for the day." He pressed his hand onto Cade's shoulder. "And if I were you, I'd think about shaving off those whiskers."

"You don't like my beard?"

"I like it fine. But I don't think you realize what you're doing to it."

Confused, Cade pressed his palm to his face and felt strange gaps in his facial hair. Adair passed him a hand mirror. Facing his reflection up close, Cade saw that irregular bald patches marred his beard on either side of his chin, and extended to the corners of his mouth and below the curve of his jawbone. "What the—"

Then, as he watched himself in the mirror, he saw his hand stroke at a damaged area of his beard, catch a hair under the thumbnail, and pluck it out with a sharp jerk. He was aware of what he was doing as it happened; he didn't want to do it, but his hand did it anyway.

And he understood: "Demons."

"Can't say I didn't warn you." Adair pointed at the ragged tufts of his own eyebrows. "There's no stopping them. Yoke the buggers long enough and the bad habits become part of you. Then you end up doing it even when there's no one in your head but you."

"So what do I do?"

"Lose the beard. Trim your brows. And if you can bear it, shave your head."

It might have been a trick of the moonlight, but Cade thought he saw Anja smirk.

He passed the mirror to Adair. "I'll take that smoke now."

Eight days and counting. It wasn't the waiting that bothered Cade; it was the lack of momentum right after having been in such a goddamned hurry to get there.

The drive from Bruges to Amsterdam had taken just over eight hours, thanks to Adair's insistence that Anja use only secondary roads, to avoid Nazi patrols. Even so, they had found a route into the city in the wee hours and taken shelter while the sky was still dark, in an abandoned dye works not far from the Jewish quarter, near the Nieuwmarkt.

And there they had stayed for the past week. Waiting.

Most days, Cade and Anja had occupied themselves with clearing the central part of the factory floor so it could be used for magickal rituals. It was menial labor, but Cade was thankful for it. When there was nothing else to do, his thoughts turned to dark memories. That was when his yoked demons did their worst, spurring his hands into acts of self-destruction. A few times he had snapped out of a sulk to find he'd chewed his fingernails to the quick.

Tonight, rain pounded the factory's roof, and thunder shook its foundation. Cade had no experience with hideouts, but he was sure this one left much to be desired. Its walls were patched with mold, and dank odors infused its every square inch. Broken machines cluttered the space and collected dust. Most of the windows were thick with grime that Adair had insisted not be disturbed, since it protected their privacy. Never one to do as he was told, Cade had cleared the corner of one window with his thumb, just to enjoy a view of the outside world.

From what little Cade had seen of Amsterdam during the midnight drive into the Dutch capital, the Nazis had spared it the wanton destruction they had inflicted on Rotterdam. Even so, the Germans had wasted no time making their mark on Amsterdam. Swastika banners hung on every prominent structure from Haarlem to Amstelveen. And there had been no ignoring the barbed wire with which the Germans had demarcated the city's Jewish neighborhoods.

Cade paced beside the front door, wondering when Adair would return. The master made nightly forays into the city. Often he returned with sacks of pilfered canned goods, hunks of cheese, stale bread, or wine. A few times he had scavenged—or stolen—wrinkled cigarette packs with two or three smokes left in them. For all of Cade's initial resistance to smoking, he had come to appreciate nicotine's ability to clear his mind of demonic whispers.

Anja lay on her cot, staring at the leaking roof. Noting Cade's back-and-forth, she eyed him with disdain. "Sit. I am tired of your footsteps."

In no mood to argue, he sat on his cot and pushed his hand over his scalp—a habit he had developed since trimming his hair to a crew cut. He liked the texture of shorn hair under his palm and the scratch of his stubbled chin, but he resented the compulsions that had necessitated them.

The deadbolt on the warehouse's rear door slid free of its whistle, guided by an unseen hand. Anja and Cade sprang to their feet and drew their wands, ready to attack if their visitor was anyone other than Adair.

Rain gusted in as the door swung open. The master hurried inside and shut the door, but didn't lock it. "Suit up."

Cade and Anja pulled on their coats. For the first time he could remember, she looked excited. She asked Adair, "You found the coven?"

"I'll explain on the way." He opened the door and conducted them into the storm.

The master led Cade and Anja in silence, guiding them past German patrols into a residential quarter of the city. "I was misled," he said at last. "Thule has no coven here. Not yet." They turned onto a side street. "It's being created tonight at midnight."

Adair darted down a narrow alley between two old brick buildings. "Kein sent one of his better pupils to be its leader. If we're quick, we can kill him before he swears in a new band of dabblers." He stopped and faced Anja and Cade. "Hans Boerman is a coven master, a karcist of some ability. He won't be a soft target, so you'd best take him by surprise and finish him fast." He handed black-bladed knives to Cade and Anja. "You get close enough, use these."

Cade studied the play of light across the blades. "What're they made of?"

"Onyx. Just in case Hans warded himself against metal." Adair dug into his coat's other pocket, pulled out a compact semiautomatic pistol, and handed it to Anja. "In case he hasn't." At the end of the alley, he pointed them toward the rear of a town house. "Go in through the back. I'll take the front." Then Adair melted into the shadows, leaving Cade and Anja to forge ahead with only each other for company.

A wave of fear hit Cade. The reality of his training came into focus: He had spent the past three months training to kill. Now it was time to put his skills to the test. The prospect of facing a real person in a fight to the death stirred up sickness in his gut and rooted his feet to the ground.

Anja shoved him. "Go."

"I can't." The knife almost fell from his shaking hand.

She pushed him harder, with enough force to propel him into the open. Once he was moving, his feet took over. He felt as if he were floating toward the rear door of the town house, a spectator in a nightmare. Rain pelted his face. A low thudding inside his head left him dizzy and gasping for breath as he reached the back door.

Anja grabbed his collar and leaned in so close that all he saw of her were her gray eyes. "Calm down. Look at me. Breathe in. Hold it." She twisted his collar to drive her point home. "Now let it go." He exhaled while she maintained eye contact. "Again."

His pulse abated; his breathing slowed. His stomach was still a pit of bile, and he had to piss, but when Anja asked "Good?" he nodded. She pointed at the door. "Spring the lock."

He stared at the knob. *Time for all the pain to be worth it.*

Calling forth the talents of ARIOSTO, Cade dispelled the charms of protection on the lock, then worked its tumblers and retracted its deadbolt, which he sensed had been thrown. Success felt like scratching an itch inside his mind. He turned the doorknob, then eased the door open. He looked at Anja. She signaled him to lead the way.

They entered a dark hallway thick with the scents of snuffed candles and lavender incense. Dim glows emanated from rooms on either side of its far end. To Cade's right were stairs to the upper floor.

Footsteps clomped above them, accompanied by creaking floorboards. Cade looked at Anja and glanced upward. She pressed her index finger to her lips, then pointed him to the stairs. He shifted his dagger to his left hand so that its pommel was toward his chest and its blade pointed outward—a grip he had learned from his fencing instructor at Oxford. Then he led Anja up the stairs while trying to remember to breathe.

At the top of the stairs, Anja stopped him with a hand on his shoulder. She motioned for him to fall in behind her and watch their backs; then she skulked down the long hallway toward the room from which they had heard the footsteps.

All of Cade's focus was on the space in front of him and Anja. The town house's décor went by in a blur: old furniture, framed photos on the walls, bric-a-brac on the shelves, dim electric light in the wall sconces. The one detail Cade noted with clarity was the carpeted floor, which muffled his and Anja's steps as they neared the end of the hall.

When they reached the last door, it was ajar. From the other side came a tinny voice from a wireless spitting out a news report in Dutch.

Anja steadied the pistol in her right hand, then arched her left above her head, a prelude to unleashing demonic violence. She glanced at Cade to make sure he was ready.

He steadied his knife and conjured a fistful of fire in his right hand. With a nod, he signaled her to attack.

She kicked open the door. It rebounded off the wall while she searched the room. He charged in behind her, then flinched at a spark from his right—

A man with a banker's fashion sense hurled lightning at him.

Cade raised his shield of AZAEL and deflected the forked bolts, only to see them ricochet toward Anja. She used her own shield to send the lightning caroming into the ceiling, where it cut a jagged wound that bled smoke.

She swatted Cade aside. "Down!"

Her left arm snapped forward, and a spectral whip blazing with green flames lashed at Hans, who parried it with a spirit sword that appeared in his left hand. The whip tangled around the blade. Anja jerked her arm but failed to disarm Hans or free her whip.

Cade hurled a fireball at Hans. It erupted against his shield, then vanished inside it. Hans threw a jet of arctic cold at Cade, who ducked low while trying to block the attack. The numbing bite of magickal frost stole the feeling from Cade's arm.

Earsplitting cracks made Cade wince. Anja was firing the pistol at Hans. Her left hand steadied her right, and she aimed her shots with a marksman's precision. Her first few shots—head, chest, gut—would have been killing blows if not for being deflected by Hans's shield.

She changed her target and put a bullet through Hans's left foot. The leather of his shoe ruptured, spewing blood and bone.

Hans staggered forward as fog choked the room.

Anja cried *"Tempestas!"* Wind blew from her outstretched palm. It tore framed photos from the walls, toppled small tables in the hallway, and blew open doors as it scattered Hans's camouflage—but by then Hans had vanished.

Anja closed her fist, ending the gale. *"Koshka!"*

At the risk of angering Anja further, Cade shushed her. He invoked the sight of SATHARIEL and spotted Hans, cloaked in demonic invisibility, creeping down the stairs . . . and leaving bloody footprints. Cade conjured another fireball—

Anja cried, "Cade! Get down!"

Hans pivoted and struck with a tentacle just like the one that had killed Cade's parents. A whiff of briny putrescence confirmed this appendage belonged to LEVIATHAN.

It swatted Cade against the wall, and nearly through it.

As Cade collapsed to the floor, Anja stepped between him and the demon. Her wand unleashed demonic arrows that sent the monster into retreat, along with Hans.

Dazed and aching, Cade was barely conscious as Anja pulled him upright. She held his sleeve until he stopped swaying like a willow in a storm. "Can you walk?"

"Yeah. Let's get him."

They moved toward the stairs. A cacophony from below stopped them before they took the first step down. It was the whistling of steel slicing through the air then cutting through flesh. Screams gave way to gurgling sounds, followed by a grisly patter of fluid and shredded meat that filled Cade with disgust. When he dared to look downstairs, he saw the walls of the lower floor festooned with viscera and wild sprays of blood.

Acid pushed up his throat, but he forced it down. It took all his focus not to be overcome by the carnage. When he looked at Anja, he was somewhat relieved to see that she, too, looked revolted by the abattoir at the bottom of the stairs.

Down below, Adair stepped into view, taking care not to tread in the deepest puddles of mangled sinew. "'Sall right. I finished him. You can come down."

Cade trudged down the steps to join the master and met him with his head bowed. "Sorry. I froze." He looked up the stairs and tried to ignore Anja's accusatory look. "When that tentacle hit me, I thought I was finished."

"We're alive and this tosspot's dead. You've nothing to be sorry for." He spit on the shredded remains of Hans's body. "One down, three hundred to go."

Adair tossed a handful of fire up the stairs, turning the second floor into an inferno, and then he walked out the front door, into the storm.

Cade moved to follow him, only to be halted by Anja's iron grip.

Her words dripped with contempt. "Learn to think *before* you act." She pushed past him, out the door into the rain. "And before you get us all killed."

MAY

The screaming stopped when gusts of fire blasted out the chateau's windows, peppering the road outside with molten glass. The stately manor had become a crematorium. Niko stood in the midst of the inferno, as intangible as a dream, and watched it all burn.

It would have been a lie, he knew, to think there had been any art or style in his attack on the Thule coven. The truth was simple and ugly. His assault had been a brazen display of power. Twenty dabblers under the wing of a halfway proficient Nazi karcist might have posed a danger to him had he given them a chance to fight back. He hadn't.

Now they were a mound of charred corpses piled in the house's root cellar, thanks to Niko crushing the floor beneath their feet before dropping a burning ceiling on their heads.

He was thankful he hadn't hesitated when the time came to shed blood, and grateful his yoked demons had proved stronger than the coven's patron. There were a thousand ways the battle could have gone wrong, but for tonight, he had prevailed alone against many.

Cracks and groans announced the collapse of the roof. Sparks shot from the gutted house as its upper floor plunged into its basement.

The conflagration would draw the neighbors, and Vichy-loyal police from the nearby town of Limoges would soon investigate. Niko needed to be gone before they arrived.

Time to move on.

He willed his ghost form to drift out of the house. When he was a safe distance from the fire, he let his flesh return to its normal state, and then he walked south from the chateau, knowing his Maquis allies would be waiting for him down the road.

This might be a good time to check in on Stefan.

He pulled his enchanted mirror from inside his coat and clutched it in his right hand. *"Fenestra, Stefan."* His reflection in the looking glass darkened to a shadow.

Stefan's visage appeared. *"Niko? You look unsettled."*

Angling himself and the mirror to show Stefan the burning chateau behind him, Niko replied, "I just killed a house full of dabblers."

Stefan reacted with grim recognition. *"Much as I did last night here in Warsaw."*

"Have you had any leads to the Kabbalists? Or the grimoire?"

"No. All I find, everywhere I go, is this." Stefan shifted his own mirror to reveal the squalor behind him: a tiny space with no furniture, in which ten Jewish refugees lay piled on top of one another, huddled on the floor. Another turn of the mirror brought Stefan into view. *"Every place I go is the same."*

"Stacked like cordwood. *Mon Dieu.*"

In recent weeks, each conversation with Stefan had brought news of some new atrocity the Nazis were inflicting on the Jewish people of Poland. First it was being rounded up into ghettos; then Stefan had shown Niko dozens of Jewish temples that had been vandalized, burned, or gutted to serve as stables or supply dumps for the Nazis. Inside the gravestone walls of the ghetto, the Jews' furniture and valuables were stolen to be redistributed to Germans and Polish Christians. Then came the beatings in the streets, followed by the removals of anyone deemed unfit for manual labor or potentially subversive.

So grim were the latest reports that Niko began to think even his worst tale of misery could only offend Stefan, who dwelled amid horrors too numerous to count.

"I wish I could help. If there is anything I—"

"Cigarettes?"

Niko reached into his pants, pulled out a crumpled box of Gauloises, and passed them through the mirror. "Half a pack. It's all I have right now."

Stefan snatched the pack from his side of the mirror. *"It's enough."* He plucked a brown cigarette from the box and lit it. He savored a long draw, then blew smoke through the mirror to perfume the air around Niko with the aroma of Turkish and Syrian tobaccos. *"Thank you, brother."* Another drag, and he seemed almost his old self again. *"Your fight goes well? The Maquis make good allies?"*

"Good enough. So far they've helped me find three Thule covens in Vichy France." He smirked at the snap and pop of burning timbers he had left behind.

"Eight or ten more, then I just need to cut off the head in Paris. How about you?"

"I cleared Prague and Poznan before Warsaw. Tomorrow I leave for Kraków."

Niko saw headlights closing in. "My ride is almost here. Travel safe."

"We will speak again soon. Velarium!" With the link between their mirrors severed, Niko tucked his inside his jacket as a Maquis-driven lorry pulled up alongside him. He opened the cab's passenger door and climbed inside. "Nice night for a drive, eh, Etienne?"

Etienne Charbonneau, who had been a professional bureaucrat before becoming an amateur gunman and getaway driver, looked ready to shit himself as he laid eyes on the burning chateau. "My God! What've you done, Niko?"

"I sent the enemy a message. And I plan to send many more." He took out a map that had been marked by his informants and pointed to their next destination. "Head south. There are Nazi spies in Toulouse I need to kill."

JUNE

Everything depended upon timing, Adair had said, and Anja had taken the master's warning to heart. Wearing the form of a rock dove, she circled above the center of the Belgian city of Ghent, her eyes trained upon an ivy-clad house along the River Leie.

Below her, Cade sprinted across the narrow river using his newest demonic talent. Despite using magickally enhanced sight, she was unable to spot Adair, but she knew he was preparing to assault the manor's front entrance as a diversion.

The witching hour, three o'clock in the morning, drew near. When it arrived, the Thule Society's Coven of Ghent would summon a great minister of the Descending Hierarchy to work a charm that would entrench them in the city's body politic, like ticks burrowing into flesh.

That was an outcome Adair, Anja, and Cade would not permit.

At the river's edge, Cade reached the house. His body became a wisp of smoke that slipped inside the building through gaps around its storm-beaten windows. That was Anja's signal to begin. She plummeted toward the house's roof. Just before reaching it she leveled out and fluttered her wings, alighting behind the guard.

The young man turned, noted what must have looked to him like a common pigeon, then resumed his lonely vigil, staring out across a sea of rooftops.

In silence, Anja shed her avian form.

The sentry was faced away from her. She had a choice of means for disposing of him. Her savage impulses wanted to drive a knife into his back, to feel the resistance of bone and sinew as she twisted the blade to grind his lung into pulp—but Adair's teachings compelled her to dispatch him with speed and as little commotion as possible.

She conjured a bone javelin and hurled it at the guard, piercing his spine and heart. The weapon vanished as soon as the dead man collapsed onto the rooftop.

Anja stepped over his body and approached the door to the house's main stairwell. A glimpse through the eyes of Vos Satria confirmed there were no charms of protection on the portal, no magickal guardians set to warn of intruders. Confident the path was clear, she opened the door, slipped inside, and hurried downstairs, eager not to miss the battle to come.

Unlike the house she and Cade had invaded in Amsterdam, this one seemed modest. There were no decorations, no carpeting, no accent furnishings. Just blank surfaces and narrow, empty hallways lined with closed doors.

Every step she took toward the house's basement heightened her dread. As much as she had tried to forgive Cade's clumsy mistakes in Amsterdam, she feared that he would put her or the master in danger again, not out of malice but out of incompetence. That was something she couldn't allow—not with so much at stake.

Shy of the first floor, she stopped. She heard the breathing of a Thule sentry standing beside the bottom of the stairs. Before she could devise a plan of attack, she heard a rising wind outside the house; then the front door slammed inward, pushed by a hurricane-force gale. The sentry drew a wand in one hand and a pistol in the other as he pivoted to face the open door.

Anja sprang from the stairs, locked one arm around the dabbler's throat, and thrust her athamé into his spine. It gave her satisfaction to feel his vertebrae snap under her blade.

Adair strode through the open front doorway as Anja broke the Thule guard's neck with a twist. She dropped his body. It sagged to the floor and landed with a slap. The master paid the corpse no mind as he walked past it and led Anja through the house's ground floor. "It's almost time. Let's get downstairs."

She followed him down the hall and through the kitchen, to the basement door. As he opened it, she asked, "What about Cade?"

"If he did as I said, he's already there."

He opened the door.

Howls and rumblings emanated from the darkness below. A musky fragrance of sandalwood saturated the basement; it was almost strong enough to mask the odors of mold and mildew lurking beneath it. Adair whispered over his shoulder to Anja, "They're trying to raise Belial." He closed his eyes, then vanished from sight. His disembodied voice added in a cautious hush, "Tread with care, lass."

Muffling her steps with the tufted paws of PSYTHRIOS, Anja descended the steps with slow caution, just to make sure she didn't collide with her now-invisible master.

Halfway to the basement, the steps reached a platform that led to a switch-back. Pausing there, Anja saw the experiment taking shape mere yards away. A Thule coven master stood at the operator's position inside a grand circle of protection, backed by a pair of tanists. Outside the grand circle were six more dabbler adepts, each secure inside his or her own pentagram.

Unable to turn without upsetting the sword balanced across the tops of his white shoes, the coven master spoke over his shoulder to his adepts. "It is vital that none of you talk during the ceremony. Even the smallest sound will risk breaking my control over the demon. And I am sure I don't need to re-mind you what will happen if you leave your circles, so don't move." He raised his wand in one hand and opened his grimoire with the other.

That was the cue to attack. Cade was nowhere in sight, but Anja didn't dare wait: once the dabblers raised a demon, anyone outside the circles was as good as dead.

She struck the two adepts on the left. She broke the man's neck with the fist of BAEL and throttled the woman with the whip of VALEFOR.

Adair, still invisible, slew the pair in the middle with simultaneous stabs between their shoulder blades. Both men twitched and gurgled up blood while impaled on his knives of the Art.

Cade appeared from a patch of shadow behind the men on the right. With a twist of his open left hand he magickally spun one man's head to face back-ward with a crunch of splintered bones. The other man he skewered on a ghostly spear. It took the shocked dabbler a few seconds to die and go limp on the weapon's barbed shaft.

All six dead adepts dropped to the ground at once.

Inside the grand circle, the coven master and his two tanists spun about. The master was older, balding with pinched features and beady eyes. His tanists looked to be in their forties; the man sported blond hair, a pencil-thin mus-tache, and wire-rimmed glasses, while the woman had a long nose and a squar-ish chin, giving her an equine quality.

The coven master seethed at the sight of his dead adepts. "So brave against the defenseless." Forked lightning leaped from his hand, with one tongue each directed at Anja, Cade, and Adair. All three invoked magickal shields as they spread out to flank the dabblers.

The two tanists moved apart. The man lobbed fire at Anja as the woman sprayed icy needles at Cade, leaving their master to train his lightning upon Adair, whose charm of invisibility faltered, leaving him visible.

Anja used her shield to absorb the male adept's assault, and she fed it into a focused blow from the hand of BAEL. She hoped it would shatter the man's leg, but the attack was blocked by another demon's protection.

On the other side of the room, Cade reflected the female tanist's needle attack. She, too, deflected it with a demonic shield—only to find her feet entangled by writhing serpents.

The male tanist filled his right hand with electricity and cocked his arm to throw it. Anja occupied his shield with LERAIKAH's envenomed arrows— and in the same thought racked him with the agonies of XENOCH. His screams were drowned out by the premature detonation of his lightning strike. The blast threw him against the wall. His blazing corpse dropped to the floor.

The coven master and Adair traded furious barrages of electricity and ghostly missiles, with neither gaining a clear advantage. Then, as the female tanist collapsed, overwhelmed by a riot of serpentine, Cade hurled a sphere of light at the coven master. It exploded against the man's shield in a blinding pulse. Aided by that distraction, Adair disintegrated the concrete beneath his opponent's feet. The coven master plunged through the hole and splashed into waist-deep water—which came alive in a vortex, spinning him like a leaf in a gale until Adair ended the man's abuse by bifurcating him at the waist with one cut of a spectral scythe.

Everything went quiet.

Anja watched Adair survey her handiwork and Cade's. "Not bad. You hit your marks and you stayed out of each other's way. It's a good start." He clapped his hand on Cade's shoulder. "Distracting him with a light charm: brilliant! And the waterspout was a fine touch." He gestured at Cade and Anja. "As soon as you two learn to match your attacks, we'll be ready to take down the coven in Calais. But for tonight—" He gathered the gunk from his throat and spit on the dead coven master. "We've earned our wine."

The master returned to the stairs and left the basement. Cade looked around the room, then at Anja. "I liked watching you work tonight." A wan smile. "It was . . . educational." He followed Adair upstairs, leaving Anja alone amid the carnage they had wrought.

Conflicting emotions left her rooted in place. She envied the raw power Cade had learned to wield in so short a time—far more than she'd ever been able to harness at once—and she resented him for it, though not as much as she had a few months earlier. In weeks past, she would have used his meek compliment as an excuse to insult him. But tonight, when the naïve young American had smiled at her, she had almost smiled back.

Almost.

Perhaps I will not kill him in his sleep. At least, not tonight.

⌁

If asked to catalog the world's most underappreciated gifts, Kein Engel would have rated the Kehlsteinhaus very near the top of his list. The chalet boasted walls of hand-cut stone, floors polished to perfection, and breathtaking views of the Bavarian Alps. Designed by Martin Bormann as a gift for the Führer on his fiftieth birthday, it sat empty the majority of the time. To the best of Kein's knowledge, Hitler had visited the chalet fewer than six times in the past three years, and then for usually no longer than half an hour.

What a waste.

Summer had turned the valley below lush with shades of green, and a zephyr caressed Kein's face. He gave the last of the '34 Duhart-Milon-Rothschild in his glass a swirl before he downed the claret in one tilt. Though he was resigned to the necessity of chemical relief whenever he yoked multiple demons for extended durations, he saw no reason to debase his palate with inferior vintages. Fine wines were his drug of choice; opiates and rotgut he left to the weak, the dabblers, and the philistines.

He set his empty glass on one of the outdoor patio's tables. It disappointed him that there was no need to kindle a blaze in the chalet's central hearth. The red marble of the main dining room's fireplace was a thing of beauty—a gift, he had heard, from Benito Mussolini.

Kein settled instead for conjuring twin plumes of hellfire in his upturned palms. Flames twisted harmlessly above his flesh while he trained his mind upon their diabolical dance and projected his will through them. "*Exaudi. Exaudi. Exaudi.*"

He concentrated upon his adepts' names and faces. *Siegmar. Briet.*

Familiar visages flickered inside the flames. In Kein's left hand, Siegmar; in his right, Briet. He greeted them with a nod. *"Ave,* friends."

Briet bowed her head a few degrees. "Ave, *Master."*

Siegmar mimicked Kein's own subtle dip of his chin. *"Master."*

"I bring bad tidings. Our enemy has come to Europe, and is on the attack."

Briet asked, *"How much do we know of their actions?"*

"Enough to concern me. Their first victim was Hans Boerman, the karcist I trained to lead our new coven in Amsterdam. Since then we've lost several more."

Siegmar's composure crumbled. *"What? When did this happen?"*

"Boerman died the same night he was to consecrate the Amsterdam coven. The Ghent coven was killed a week later. Over the last month, we've lost contact with covens in eastern Europe and France's *zone libre.* All of which suggests our foes are picking up their pace."

Briet echoed Siegmar's concern. *"Why are we hearing of this only now?"*

"Before tonight I wasn't certain what had happened. Herr Boerman seemed to have perished in a house fire: unusual and tragic, but not unheard of. As for Ghent, its members lacked experience. Their deaths could have been caused by a mistake during an experiment; they would not have been the first amateurs to die as a consequence of ineptitude." He exhaled frustration. "But the swift eradication of multiple chapters? That is no coincidence. My old friend Adair is at large on the Continent, and he has brought the last of his adepts with him."

Slow nods from his disciples.

Briet swept a lock of hair from her face. *"I have a spy within the Maquis. I can use him to help me set a trap for whoever is attacking our covens in Free France."*

Kein arched an eyebrow. "Defending the Paris coven is your chief concern."

"We can strike without showing our throat."

"Very well. Proceed, but be careful. Adair would not send his last remaining adepts into battle unless he was sure they were fully trained."

Siegmar cleared his throat. *"We might have a related issue on the Eastern Front. I've heard reports of a 'miracle worker' in the Jewish ghettos. An outlander who asks questions about Adair's missing Kabbalists."*

"This could present an opportunity. Identify this 'miracle man' and make certain he finds his way into our control. I trust you know how to make that happen."

"*I do, but I'll need some time. I'm still in Kovno.*"

"That's not done yet?"

"*The Einsatzgruppen finished the executions but aren't done plundering the bodies.*"

"How long will that take?"

An arrogant shrug. "*I don't know. I've never seen a hundred cretins try to rob three thousand corpses before. I'll be on a train as soon as I'm able.*"

"See that you are." Kein felt the future taking shape at last. "Our enemy has come calling at last. Let us give them a welcome they will never forget."

Everything had gone according to plan, right until the moment it all went to hell.

The front of the coven house outside Toulouse had been too exposed, too naked of cover for Niko's liking, so he had come at it through the woods behind. Nothing about the house had suggested it was any better defended than the ones he had toppled farther north in the *zone libre*.

Then his fireball had rebounded off the house's rear door, engulfed his shield, and knocked him on his ass. Now he was on his back, stunned and confused, as machine guns filled the air with a deafening chatter and ripped divots across the lawn.

Niko rolled over, pushed himself off the ground, and sprang toward the trees, harried by gunfire every step of the way. *Merde!*

Inside the house, German voices cried "Alarm!" as bullets ripped the bark from trees on either side of Niko. He zigzagged through the woods as searchlights snapped on behind him. Their beams slashed from side to side, throwing shadows in all directions.

Footsteps and orders barked in German hounded Niko as he stumbled in retreat. Pops of semiautomatic rifle fire filled the woods, and a wild shot lanced through Niko's left triceps. He clutched at the wound to stanch the bleeding as he ran.

More shots zinged past his head. He was half a minute's run from the clearing where his ride was waiting for him, assuming the Maquis hadn't fled at the first sound of gunfire. Recalling how much open ground lay between the truck and the tree line, Niko feared he wouldn't make it into the vehicle alive, not with the Germans so close behind him.

He looked for the Nazi troops. It was too dark for him to target them directly. *Have to settle for slowing them down.*

He swept his hand in a broad arc and invoked HARATHOR's gift of "tanglefoot," animating tree roots and undergrowth into troublesome snares for anyone passing over them. He was instantly rewarded by a break in the gunfire, followed by strings of German profanity from the shadows. *That should do.* He went on running.

As he neared the clearing, he was intercepted by Ferrand and another Maquis, named Michel. They had entererd the woods with pistols drawn. "What happened?"

"A trap," Niko said, still on the move. "Get back to the truck!"

Michel and Ferrand fell in behind Niko. As the trio emerged from the woods, harsh snaps from behind announced the Germans' escape from the cursed roots. Then a light flooded in from dead ahead, blinding the three of them.

Camille shouted, "Move! They're right on you!"

Niko squinted to see that Camille had moved their truck forward to the edge of the tree line, to effect a faster retreat. Now she stood on the running board and balanced their one working submachine gun atop the frame of the open door. "Get in the back!" she cried, just before she fired three quick shots over their heads into the woods. "Hurry!"

Ferrand pulled her off the running board and yanked the weapon from her hands. "Get in the back." He pivoted and tossed the SMG to Michel. "Two more bursts, then you drive." To Niko and Camille he barked, "In the back! Now!"

Niko, his sister, and her husband scrambled to the rear of the truck and clambered inside its cargo area. Outside, two more stutters from the SMG were answered by crisp reports from the Germans' rifles; then the truck's engine rumbled to life. It groaned in protest as Michel shifted it into gear and accelerated. Its chassis and panels banged and rattled as they sped down a rocky dirt road that was the only passage to or from the clearing.

After his sister tied a handkerchief around the wound in his arm, Niko lit a cigarette to calm his jangled nerves. He took a drag, then passed it to Camille. "Good thing you moved the truck. We wouldn't have made it if we'd had to cross the clearing."

He saw his sister's smile in the cigarette's cherry glow as she inhaled. "No big deal."

"The hell it isn't," Ferrand said, his tone sharp. "I told you to hang back."

"I heard gunshots."

"All the more reason you should've stayed put. I told you to retreat if we came out under fire—not charge in to save the day. Do that again, and I'll beat the lesson into you next time."

Niko bristled. The last person he'd ever heard threaten Camille that way was their father, Marlon Le Beau—the first man Niko had ever wanted to kill. "Shut up, Ferrand. She saved our lives back there. You ought to be thanking her, you fucking ingrate."

Ferrand grabbed Niko's jacket collar with one hand and stuck a knife to his throat with the other. "Don't forget who's in charge here." He put just enough pressure behind the edge to drive his point home. "And don't you ever tell me how to talk to *my* wife."

Just like Papa would have done. Marlon Le Beau was dead and buried, but Ferrand made Niko feel as if that sorry excuse for a man had been resurrected in all his hateful, booze-drenched squalor. Niko seethed but said nothing. He knew at least two ways to kill his brother-in-law with magick that would be silent, traceless, and not leave a mark or spill a drop of blood. And if he wanted to slip from Ferrand's grasp and vanish, he could do so on a whim.

Instead, he satisfied himself with staring the man down until Camille talked Ferrand into putting away his knife and letting the matter drop.

That was for the best, for the moment at least. There was nothing to be gained from answering the threats of the small and petty, not when far more pressing dilemmas obtained.

For starters, how did the Germans ambush me tonight? Who told them I was coming?

Niko considered Ferrand, then Michel. Neither of them nor any of their compatriots had anything to gain by walking into a trap. But who else might they have told? And how could he get those names from them without arousing their suspicions?

One problem at a time, he told himself.

He reached up and tested the wound from Ferrand's blade with his fingertips. As much as he wanted to keep his mind on his mission, all he could think about was whether Ferrand had ever put a knife to Camille's throat. The thought of it filled his mind with visions of revenge. *He doesn't know pain. Not the way a demon could teach it to him. . . .*

He closed his eyes and calmed his thoughts. *Those are the demons pushing forward,* he realized. It was getting harder to separate their goading from his own inner voice, especially when he was forced to go more than a day without a stiff drink.

Camille passed him the half-burned cigarette. Niko took a gratifying pull, then exhaled through his nostrils while he reminded himself what Master Adair had always said when his apprentices got on one another's nerves: *Save your hexes for the Nazis.*

It was good advice, and Niko planned to heed it.

Just as long as Ferrand never raised his hand to Camille again.

Reading a map written in Polish was hard; trying to read it in the dark was enough to set Stefan to cursing. Around him sprawled the outskirts of Kraków, the city's residential Dębniki district. He knew he was close to his destination, but the hours he'd spent wandering pitch-dark streets left him fearful he had missed a turn or was going in the wrong direction.

Stefan paused to orient himself. He heard the rumble of vehicles and machinery in the distance; the core of the town lay ahead to the northeast. A bank of clouds parted to reveal the waxing moon, a thumbnail's edge of light in a heaven full of darkness.

This is the way. I just need to keep going.

Soon he found himself in front of a two-story house set back from the road. The half acre of property around it was well tended and populated with oak and linden trees. There were no lights on inside—at least, none that he could see. The Nazi-occupied city had for months forced residents to paper over their windows, to hide the city from Russian bombing raids.

Piercing the night with the eyes of SŌZAY, Stefan saw the house glowing with magickal wards. It was without a doubt a Thule coven lair. He took off his ruck and tool roll and entrusted them to his demonic beast of burden. For what would come next, he knew he would want to move quickly and have his hands empty.

Blue flames wreathed his fists as he strode to the front door.

The talents of TERAGOR unraveled the wards of binding on the door and swung it open to grant Stefan entrance. He whispered two words of ancient Enochian to banish the demon that had been set as a sentinel on the other side. Then he stood in the entryway, unchallenged.

By the azure light of the fire in his hands, he saw that furnishings were sparse in the foyer, but sumptuous appointments packed the front room to his left and the dining room to his right. Ahead of him, beside a steep staircase, a hallway barely wide enough to let two skinny people slip past each other led to a handful of rear rooms.

There were discreet ways for Stefan to search the house and obtain the information he needed. But after weeks in lonely transit, he was in no mood for subtlety.

His magickal senses felt the presence of three people in the house, plus a handful of minor spirits attached to one of those persons. *That would be the coven master,* he deduced.

He shattered the silence with a bellowed command: "Wake up, scum!"

Sounds of confusion filled the brief hang-fire between Stefan's challenge and the dabblers' response. The coven master and two of his adepts raced out of three upstairs bedrooms, each in pajamas. They nearly collided at the top of the stairs, and one of the adepts fumbled his wand and watched it fall to the ground floor, hopelessly out of reach.

The coven master aimed his wand at Stefan—who flung the man against the ceiling hard enough to break half his bones. On the stairs, the adept who still had his wand prepared to take his best shot. Stefan threw a jet of blue fire and set him ablaze. It took a few seconds for the adept to stop screaming and tumble dead down the stairs to land at Stefan's feet. By then the last adept, alone on the landing at the top of the stairs, had pissed himself.

Stefan let the coven master—far too lofty a title for such an amateur, he thought—drop from the ceiling. The man tumbled down the stairs and landed, gasping, atop his dead apprentice. Stefan drew a knife and released the man from his suffering with a slash of his throat.

That left the urine-soaked youth at the top of the stairs.

"Come here," Stefan commanded him.

The youth descended the stairs in trembling steps.

He stood in front of Stefan, quaking.

Stefan set a demon's hand around the young man's throat to make sure he understood the consequences of lying. "I seek a group of Kabbalah masters. They would have come from Warsaw. Have you seen them?"

Frantic nods. "They were here."

"Did their leader have a large book bound with iron?"

Terror put a tremor in the dabbler's voice. "I don't know. I never saw one."

"Where are they now?"

"Gone, months ago."

Stefan hid his frustration at having missed the Kabbalists. "To where?"

"No idea." Fresh urine soaked the youth's leg. "Maybe the Jews in the ghetto know."

"Perhaps. Where is Kraków's ghetto?"

"In the Podgórze district. Trust me—you will know it when you see it."

"I trust you. I also have no further use for you."

A turn of Stefan's wrist cued SATOR to snap the dabbler's neck. The vertebrae splintered with a series of cracks. Released, the body slumped to the floor.

With a mental command, Stefan dispatched SAPAX, a spirit known to be good at finding things. *Search the house. Bring me a list of this coven's members and their addresses, and any supplies of the Art that don't need to be made by the operator.*

As YOU COMMAND, the demon replied, commencing its task.

Stefan visited the house's cellar. As he'd suspected, it had served as the coven's conjuring laboratory. One of its walls bore the house's sigil of protection. He used his white-handled knife to mar the sigil, neutralizing its power to protect the house.

He walked upstairs, then out of the house and down to the road. Less than a minute later, SAPAX returned with the list and a haul of oils, unguents, and other supplies that would help Stefan keep his roster of yoked spirits intact for weeks to come. His hellbeast of burden GAIDAROS gathered up the plunder, which vanished into its custody.

In his imagination, Stefan pictured the coven house being reduced to a pile of rubble. Then he sent SATOR to turn his vision into reality while he continued his journey.

Behind him a demon razed the house, but Stefan knew that a far greater horror lay ahead of him—in the form of yet another Nazi-created Jewish ghetto.

13

JULY

The bodies of the slain littered the conjuring room. Under pools of blood and ash lay remnants of magick circles. Candles, wands, swords, and daggers rested in heaps. Grimoires smoldered down to their spines, filling the windowless space with smoke.

It felt wrong to take pride in such carnage, yet Cade reveled in the victory. Hellfire danced on the ends of his fingers. Lightning crackled around his wand. His mind and body coursed with Hell's most destructive energies. Only a sense of decency and a modicum of shame reminded him this was no time for celebration.

Adair drifted from one body to the next, checking for pulses. He paused over two of the fallen to slash their throats with his athamé. On the far side of the room, Anja used a dead man's pant leg to clean the blood from her dagger.

Queasy from the mingled odors of incense and slaughter, Cade looked for an excuse to step out of the basement killing jar. "Master? Should I search the house?"

"Aye. Grab the basics. And if they have anything exotic, take that, too. Never know when something rare might come in handy."

After the battles in Calais and Le Havre, Cade had internalized the routine: Slay the members of a Thule coven, then raid their stronghold for its best and most unique magickal supplies. This lair gave up a wealth of useful ingredients: fresh beeswax, virgin parchment, various herbs and unguents. It was a better haul than they had taken from other covens.

Minutes later, the master and Anja met Cade in a room upstairs. Adair inspected the provisions. Those he deemed suitable vanished into the hands of AKROTH, his invisible hellbeast of burden; the rest he threw into the fire under the hearth. Then he wrapped his wand in red silk. "Well, then. You two finally know how to protect each other in battle." He smiled at Anja. "And the way you threw water under those wankers' feet—" He grinned at Cade. "—and then you hit it with lightning! That's teamwork. Well done, both of you."

Their synergy had been accidental, but Cade shrugged and said, "It was her idea."

"I thought as much." Adair gave Anja's chin a paternal nudge. "You're the keenest blade I've ever honed." He pointed at Cade. "Keep doing as she says. You might live through this."

"Yes, Master." Out of the corner of his eye, Cade noticed a peculiar look from Anja. When he shifted his gaze to acknowledge it, she turned away.

Adair walked to the door. "Let's move. We need to lay low and gear up for a *real* battle."

"A *real* battle?" Cade looked at the mangled, scorched bodies. "What was this? A sissy slap-fight?"

"I've let you cut your teeth on small covens." He led them out of the coven's lair, a large house on the outskirts of Cherbourg. "Now we go after the plonkers." He added with a fretful look, "I won't lie: After this, it gets ugly."

The master mumbled to himself as he quickened his stride.

Several yards behind, Cade kept a slower pace, happy to steal a moment alone. After months of sneaking and hiding with Adair and Anja in the most dilapidated corners of northwestern Europe, Cade had come to find that the one thing he missed most about his old life was privacy. He wondered if he would ever know such a privilege again.

Anja invaded his solitude, falling into step by his side. She didn't look at him as she asked, "Why did you praise me for what we both know was an accident?"

"You saw how much it pleased him. He wants to believe we can fight as a team."

"Your lie will bring him no comfort if we fail in our next battle."

Cade waited until she met his stare. "Then maybe you should actually *talk to me,* so we can plan our attacks and defenses." She turned away in denial, but he wasn't done. "Stop treating me like the enemy. We *need* to be allies. I *want* us to be friends."

"What you *want* means *nothing.*" She strode ahead of him. "This is *war.*"

Surviving an ambush had taught Niko a valuable lesson: Trust no one. Getaway vehicles and support from the Maquis had provided a safety net for his first few assaults on Thule covens, but a spy within the Resistance meant that the luxury of backup had become a danger. Of course, it was just as perilous for him to act alone, but at least now he was able to take the enemy by surprise. It had worked in Nice, Marseille, and Lyon, all of which he had rid of Thule covens in a matter of weeks. Now, excepting Paris, only one target remained in Niko's assigned territory.

A late-night thunderstorm scoured the coven house outside Toulouse. Lightning stuttered across the sky, creating stark snapshots of flooded streets. The tempest had driven the locals to take refuge behind closed shutters, leaving no one to bear witness to Niko's return.

He stopped in front of the house. It was warded by sigils and defended by spirits: he felt their energies from several meters away. Neither would stop him tonight.

All day he had watched the house from a safe distance. Starting in the late afternoon, the coven members had begun to arrive, just as Niko had suspected they would. Dabblers tended to be more beholden to the prescribed dates and hours for magickal operations than were expert karcists. A glance at an ephemeris a week earlier had enabled Niko to predict when the Toulouse coven would meet again. And here they were.

The midnight hour drew near. That was when the dabblers would start preparing their circles for the night's experiment. Niko wasn't going to let them get that far.

He pulled off his hood and let the storm wash over him. The rain brought relief from the region's muggy heat. Reaching out with demonic talent, he extended his senses into the thunderhead. Gathering its power, he raised his fist and focused his thoughts as Master Adair had taught him. "*Ut fulgur gladium meum!*"

Niko swung his arm toward the house—and called down the demon MOLOCH in a stroke of lightning. An earsplitting boom and a white-hot flash split the coven house in half. Its sigil of protection was broken, its guardian spirit banished, its shattered frame ablaze. Burning victims tumbled out of the inferno. Some screamed and staggered; others crumpled to the ground. In the time it took the storm to douse the flames on their backs, most of the dabblers were dead.

This had been a crude, noisy means to an end, one that had defied all of

Adair's warnings against drawing attention by using magick in too public a manner—but Niko resented being ambushed, and he intended to make an example of this coven as a message to the enemy.

Smoldering timbers flew into the air from the middle of the collapsed house. More debris followed, hunks of smoking wood and furniture ejected from the wreckage as if hurled by a giant. Niko stood his ground in the downpour and prepared himself to face the coven's handful of competent magicians, who were fighting their way out of the house's now-buried cellar.

Three figures holding wands emerged from the flames and smoke—a white-haired older man, a young man with a shaved pate, and a flaxen-haired woman in her thirties. They parted to flank Niko as they stalked away from the burning house. The white-haired man, who had led the others out of the cellar, spoke with a German accent. "You should not have come back."

"You should not have stayed."

The dabblers charged, wands blazing through the storm.

The youth on the left hurled orbs of green fire; the woman turned raindrops into ice needles that sped toward Niko with deadly accuracy. Their master lobbed lightning with one hand and invisible blows of bone-crushing force with the other. It was an expert attack, too much for Niko to stop all at once. Frozen shards sliced into his thighs as he deflected the fireballs and absorbed the lightning—only to be knocked backward, launched through the air by whatever unseen fist the coven master controlled.

Niko landed on his back and slid down a street of mud. He mustered his shield just in time to dissipate another volley of jade fire from the bald apprentice.

Then with a wave of his left hand he snapped the bald man's neck with the barbed whip of BANOG, and a thrust of Niko's right hand flayed the flesh from the woman's head with the winged blades of ZOGOGEN. The two adepts collapsed in the mud, and their master froze as he realized they were dead.

Then he fired a bolt of red lightning from his wand, a blast mighty enough to wipe a normal man off the face of the earth. It crackled and sparked against Niko's shield—and then Niko reflected the pulse at the coven master. The white-haired amateur's shield fizzled and popped like a balloon, knocking the man on his ass in the mud.

A crowd of villagers spilled into the road, drawn from their homes by the magicians' duel. In no mood to contend with the superstitions of farm folk, Niko waved the entire group to sleep with the power of NEBIROS. Then he turned his attention to the coven master, who lay in the road, still steaming from his self-inflicted wound.

Niko kneeled on the wounded man's chest and seized him by his shirt's collar. "You were here the last time I attacked this house, yes?" He accepted the German's pained but silent nod as confirmation. "Who told you I was coming?"

"The Red Woman—the leader of the Paris coven."

"And who told her?"

"A spy, she said. Inside the Resistance."

Niko pressed the tip of his athamé under the man's jaw. "A name, damn you! Give me a name."

In spite of the blade at his throat, the German was defiant. "She never said. You want a name? Ask her."

"I plan to." Niko drove his knife into the man's jugular, then into his brain. "I hope she's as helpful as you've been."

14

AUGUST

Five minutes past midnight, the streets of Caen were quiet. Cade huddled with Adair and Anja in a doorway on Rue Guillaume le Conquérant. His shirt collar was starched and snug around his throat. Seeing himself in the garb of the enemy made his skin crawl. He turned an imploring look at the master. "You're sure there's no other way?"

"Positive." The gruff Scot tugged the jacket sleeves of the black Waffen-SS uniform, then straightened the red armband on Cade's left arm, to make sure its white circle and black swastika were centered. "Right. Where's the hat?"

Holding the black peaked cap by its brim, Anja handed it to Adair. As soon as he took it from her, she made a show of wiping her hand across the front of her shirt.

The hat felt heavy on Cade's brow as Adair patted it into place. He imagined that its weight came from the metal in its eagle pin and death's-head insignia, as well as its braided chin strap, which marked it as the cover of an officer. "Shouldn't I be armed?"

Adair shook his head. "No weapons inside." A downward glance. "Boots fit?"

"They pinch like a vise. I can't feel my toes." In truth, he appreciated the sensory distraction. His ten yoked demons had filled his nightmares with itching sensations so that, in his sleep, he had scratched his lower legs raw with his own toenails. Now the scabs prickled and burned, inviting him to claw at them again and exacerbate the damage.

With a few final tugs, Adair cinched the uniform's belt and corrected the angle on the leather strap that crossed Cade's torso from his right shoulder to his left hip. "Remember: Say nothing unless someone speaks to you first. And if anyone asks, you are . . . ?"

"Untersturmführer Dietrich Hoffmann, Fourteenth Company, SS Division Totenkopf."

"Good. Which spirit did you yoke to fix your German?"

"CAELBOR. He lets me speak, hear, read, and write."

A nod. "Good choice. And your target is . . . ?"

Cade's patience waned. This was the third time Adair had quizzed him on the mission's details. "I climb the rear stairwell—"

"Which is accessible only from . . . ?"

"The northeast end of the second-floor hallway. On the top floor, I find the binding circle that controls the spirits inside the building, then I change the glyph inside the circle from that of the coven's patron to mine. The demons do the rest. . . . And what'll you two be doing?"

"Making sure no one but you walks out that door and lives." The master slapped Cade's back hard enough to start him walking. "Off you go. Chop-chop."

Cade had no choice but to keep going. Turning around would only draw attention to himself as well as Anja and Adair. He put on his best air of confidence and walked toward the row of three-story buildings on the far side of Rue Saint-Manvieu.

As he approached his destination, the door opened. Green light spilled out, silhouetting a pair of drunk German soldiers who stumbled into the street, hanging on to each other as if that made their blundering any less awkward. They tripped over the curb and caught each other just shy of pitching chins-first onto the pavement. When they recovered their stride, they looked up, saw Cade, and almost knocked each other over trying to stand straight while lifting their right arms in the Nazi salute and slurring in near unison, "*Heil Hitler!*"

He returned the salute as if it were an irritating obligation, which it was. "*Heil Hitler.*"

Out of anxiety he avoided eye contact with the two men. As they scurried away from him, disengagement seemed in retrospect to have been the right tactic. Over the past few months, he had observed a fair number of Nazi officers interacting with their enlisted men, and most seemed to regard the lower ranks as either objects of scorn or as walking, talking furniture. Channeling their example in a display of contempt had felt true to form.

To Cade's advantage, it fit his mood perfectly.

He slipped inside the building. Just past the door, curtains obstructed the view of the corridor beyond. Cade pushed past them and was greeted by what appeared to be a tall, beautiful woman with ebony skin, brown eyes, and a wild mane of black curls. She wore a negligee and exaggerated makeup. Her perfume was musky, her gaze intense, her smirk seductive. She caressed the lapel of Cade's jacket. "Welcome, Untersturmführer," she said in flawless German. "Is this your first time here?"

Calling upon his demonic agent of tongues, Cade replied, "It is. I'm told you have delights to suit every taste, no matter how exotic."

"True. For a price, of course."

"Of course." He reached inside his jacket and pulled out a fistful of reichsmarks that Anja had liberated from the Thule coven's lockbox in Le Havre. "What will this get me?"

"Let's see." The dark lady plucked the paper currency from his hand. As she counted his tribute, he looked more closely and saw, concealed in her curls, two small but telltale horns on her upper forehead—marks of a succubus. She finished tallying the cash. "For this? Anything you can imagine." She turned, walked down the hall, and beckoned him with a crooked finger. "Follow me."

The nameless demon in female guise led him to a staircase in the center of the corridor, then up a flight to the second floor. Splashes of blue-green light painted the walls above the gel-wrapped sconces, and a haze of opiate smoke lingered from chest height to the ceiling. In either direction, the hall was lined by doorways, some open, some shut. Peculiar sounds emanated from the hidden spaces—snapping whips, whimpers of pain, moans of suffering and delight, a symphony of perverse appetites being sated.

They stopped before an open doorway. She sent Cade ahead with a balletic sweep of one dark arm. "After you." He nodded and stepped inside. The room was lavishly appointed, with a large bed and brocaded curtains drawn in front of towering windows. Between the bed and the windows stood an antique end table, atop which rested a china basin. The succubus snapped her fingers, and at once the bowl was half filled with steaming water. She faced Cade. "In three minutes, you will hear a knock at the door. Bid your visitor 'enter' three times, then open it. You will see no one there, but when you close it again, she—" The demon studied him with a curious leer. "—or *he*—will be with you."

"I understand. Thank you."

She shut the door on her way out.

Cade moved to the door and put his ear to it. All was quiet. With the sight of SATHARIEL he gazed through the door and confirmed the way was clear. Having no desire to meet whatever monster the madam had in mind for him, he opened the door and slipped into the hallway.

Treading toward the stairs at the far end of the corridor, he succumbed to morbid curiosity and used the Sight to spy on the assignations transpiring

around him. Most were banal couplings, young Nazi officers and senior enlisted men being pleasured by demons in a variety of feminine shapes. Some
of the officers were being serviced by two succubi at a time, while others preferred to watch two succubi pretend to pleasure each other.

Cade knew the demons' moans to be empty; the Fallen were not capable of
taking pleasure from such encounters. All the men seemed oblivious of the
fact that, come dawn, the succubi would be dispatched as incubi, to plant the
Nazis' demonically corrupted seed into other clients around the world, so that
women and girls could birth monsters.

By contrast, the two German officers pleasuring each other while a succubus stood in the corner, present apparently only to conceal their forbidden
tryst, seemed almost innocent.

Such pedestrian sights Cade could forget. It was the horrors interspersed
among them that burned themselves into his memory as he continued toward
the stairs.

In one room, a Nazi in full regalia savagely beat a succubus that wore the
form of a young woman crowned with a saint's halo. The louder she cried,
the harder he laughed.

Cade halted when he saw through a closed door what looked like a Wehrmacht officer raping an angel—its white-feathered wings spattered with blood,
his fist closed on and pulling its flowing golden hair, while he thrust himself
into the Seraph from behind. Then Cade perceived the even uglier truth beneath the illusion—the withered shape of the succubus, like a child's charred
corpse, hidden inside the phantasm of the angel.

Behind the last door before the stairs, a fiftyish man handed a photo to a
malevolent, sable-haired beauty. "My daughter," he told the succubus. "Can
you look and sound like her?"

In the blink of an eye the demon changed into a blond woman, then handed
the photo to the *Oberleutnant* and said with affected subservience, "Will this
do, Papa?"

A predatory grin. "Perfect, sweetheart."

Cade swallowed his revulsion and continued up the northeast stairs, more
eager than ever to reach the third floor and leave the brothel's repugnant spectacle behind. He stole upward with bated breath, unsure what defenses awaited
him. At the midflight switchback, he paused. There was sound from above,
scuffling steps on the tiled floor, huffing pants.

Heavy breathing inside a brothel. That never bodes well.

He drew an obsidian blade and continued up the steps.

Once his eyes reached the level of the floor at the top of the stairs, he searched for the source of the footfalls. At the end of the corridor, a hellhound padded away from him, its muscled bulk rippling as it moved. It would have been invisible to Cade had he lacked the Sight. The monster was near the end of the hall, where it would have to stop and turn around. At most, Cade had a few seconds to act. Neither fire nor lightning was viable; he didn't want to set the building ablaze while he was still inside it. That left him few options, but he was out of time.

What the hell. I bought the ticket—time to see the show.

He advanced to the third floor and conjured a shield.

The hellhound turned, growled at Cade, then charged, barking all the way. It snorted green flames as it ran. Just yards from Cade it sprang toward him, its fanged maw gaping wide—

Cade pushed his shield forward, knocking the beast on its ass. As it scrambled to get up, he struck it with weapons from the arsenal of VAELBOR—a glaive, a spear, and a morning star—and savored the creature's howls and whimpers. Wounded and cowering, it retreated. He finished it with a thrust of the spear. It dissolved into green mist, banished to the Pit, where it belonged.

Down the length of the third-floor hallway, doors opened. Three men hurried out to investigate the ruckus. First they traded confused looks, then they trained their stares on Cade. The oldest of them, a fortyish-looking man with prematurely white hair, reached under his smoking jacket for a wand. The others drew pistols.

The Nazis had their weapons only half raised when they staggered in the grip of ORNIAS. Cade knew not to fight fair when outnumbered. He let the demon crush the dabblers' windpipes and snap their necks like cheap pencils. As they collapsed to the floor, he stepped over and around them while he peered through closed doors in search of his objective.

When he found it, the door to that room was locked, as he had expected. Imbuing his hand with the gift of ARIOSTO, he turned the knob and felt the lock surrender to his will.

The glyph of binding filled the room's floor. An equilateral triangle formed its outer boundary. Within it was a double circle; its outer border was twelve feet in diameter, the inner circle ten. Between them were names from many languages and a variety of arcane Enochian symbols. In its center there dwelled only one sigil: the seal of ASMODEUS, one of the six ministers of the Descending Hierarchy, and this coven's patron:

Cade used his jacket's sleeve to erase the chalk sigil. Through the floor he heard plangent wailing from the floor below, as the succubi—no longer under direct control—howled in protest.

He took a piece of consecrated hematite from inside his jacket, and from memory drew upon the floor the Infernal seal of his patron, the Prime Minister of Hell, LUCIFUGE ROFOCALE:

It took nearly two minutes for him to scribe the seal, but when it was done he felt the power of the grand circle course through him. All the spirits bound to this den of iniquity were now under his control, and awaiting his command.

"Hear me, unclean spirits. I charge thee with two tasks: First, kill those with whom you now lie. Second, when all those are slain, kill those who before me called this lair their own. When those two directives are fulfilled, I shall discharge and dismiss thee without further requirement. *Audite vocem meam, et dolore esse parcendum.*"

He employed Ariosto to secure the room's door against intrusions, then folded his arms and bowed his head to listen. Beneath and around him, the coven's song of cruel desires became a nightmarish chorale of well-earned retribution.

A fading ember of his youthful naïveté almost made him pity the men being savaged by demons . . . until he thought of that night at sea, when he'd watched the *Athenia* sink, and saw his parents murdered by a monster raised from Hell. Men such as these gave the order to torpedo an unarmed ship, fired the shot, and summoned the terrors of the abyss to kill him and his family.

Cade refused to take pleasure from the Nazis' screams of pain and terror . . . but he refused to feel guilty for serving as the instrument of their deaths.

They brought their war to me. I'm just returning the favor.

Walking in a world without color was peculiar, but Stefan had grown accustomed to it during his months of sneaking from town to town under the cover of night. Monochromatic vision was the consequence of invoking invisibility through Foras. When he considered the advantages of being unseen in enemy territory, perceiving the world in shades of gray was a minor sacrifice.

Tonight he had taken the extra precaution of silencing his movements with the power of Andromalius. Concealed from the Nazis' eyes and ears, he had strolled unnoticed inside their Kraków headquarters. He was relieved to find no glyphs or wards on the exterior of the building, nor any warning signs of demonic presence within its walls.

This place must not be important to Kein and his adepts.

The Wehrmacht's command administration building had been commandeered from the city's government. What once had been busy municipal offices now were storage rooms packed with boxes piled atop filing cabinets that occupied every inch of floor space.

Only a small number of larger offices on the uppermost floors were being used by the Nazis, but they had done their best to spread out and take up as much room as they possibly could, whether they needed to or not. One large and windowless storage room on the top floor had been set aside for the Nazis' records, which were kept locked away.

A futile effort, Stefan thought. Extending Teragor's knack for locks through his own hands, he pulled off the padlock that secured the door's latch, opened the door, then shut it behind himself. He illuminated the room with a cone of BERAGOR's light projected from his palm, even as he hid it from passersby with a pool of the same demon's shadow over the door.

Now to find what I came for.

The Nazi army was as meticulous as ever in its record keeping. Deployment orders, supply requisitions, personnel transfers, duty logs—all had been filed with regularity. Stefan searched one batch of files after another, skipping those that didn't answer his only question:

Where were the Kabbalists and Adair's missing grimoire?

Police activity logs, arrest records—then he found it: lists of Jews. He was getting closer. There was a separate collection of records for arrests made in the Jewish ghetto. He narrowed his search to documents filed during the month when witnesses told him they had seen the Kabbalists hauled away by the Nazis. Most of the files divided the people of the ghetto into two categories: those fit for manual labor, and those not. Those who were, the Nazis attempted to match with work assignments. Those who were not were transferred to sites whose names Stefan didn't recognize: Sachsenhausen, Płaszów, Dachau, Auschwitz.

He pulled another page of transfer orders from the box, and his eyes landed on a cluster of names in the center column: those of the Kabbalah masters and their students. Among them, near the end of the list, was his beloved's name, Evert Siever. They all were marked as having been transferred to the ghetto in Kiev.

Stefan puzzled over the detail. No other Jews in Kraków had been transferred to Kiev, nearly nine hundred kilometers away. Why would the Nazis move so small a group of prisoners so far? Had they discovered the Iron Codex? And if so, why send the rabbis to Kiev?

He put the files back as he had found them; then, as he turned to leave, he pondered all the evils the Nazis would wreak with those lists of names and addresses.

Stefan lobbed an orb of flame over his shoulder on his way out of the filing room. As the room and the rest of the floor around it was swept up in an unstoppable blaze, he retraced his steps out of the headquarters. Only after he was many blocks away did he shed his gifts of silence and invisibility and turn to watch the building burn in vivid hues of crimson.

It soon would be dawn. He had to be indoors, hidden once more, before then.

During the morning, Stefan would sleep. Come afternoon, he would impose upon a few trusted friends in the ghetto to procure for him some items he needed to summon ASARADEL, a spirit that could grant him the gift of flight, and GAIDAROS, his preferred hellbeast of burden.

Flying would be a perilous gamble: passing over a ringing church bell would banish ASARADEL and leave Stefan in free fall, so he needed to plan his route to Kiev with precision.

More dangerous, he had to decide which two of his presently yoked spirits he would release to accommodate GAIDAROS and ASARADEL. Giving up one exotic power for flight was a fair trade; it vexed him to sacrifice one of his gifts for something as mundane as a demonic butler, but it was necessary. Eleven spirits was the most Stefan had ever held at once, and after months, the strain of traveling with fallen angels bound to his soul was breaking him. His days had become running battles against nosebleeds, night terrors, headaches, chewed fingernails, and his soured stomach. Riven by war and picked clean by the Nazis, Poland didn't have enough vodka or opiates to quell Stefan's pains. The idea of adding to his demons' legion of torment was too daunting for him to consider. No, he would have to let two go.

It will be worth it, he promised himself. *Once I find Evert.*

Ferreting out a spy from the ranks of the Resistance was proving to be messier work than Niko had anticipated. Forced to conduct his investigation from a borrowed bedroom in Camille and Ferrand's apartment, Niko stared at a mess of notes, photos, and timetables, all of which he had stuck to the wall with wads of gum and glue.

Linked by lengths of yarn in a rainbow of colors, Niko's evidence had evolved from a collage into a web. At its center was a grainy picture of an unknown red-haired woman. A Maquis informer had seen her scribe symbols on walls inside a Nazi officer's temporary dwellings—symbols that were later hidden with wallpaper. As if that had not been enough to draw Niko's interest, in the photo he had chosen for his web's centerpiece, a wand was barely visible tucked under the woman's belt in the shadow of her trench coat. She was a karcist.

But is she Kein's adept Briet? That is the question.

Radiating from her photo were chains of acquaintance that connected her by degrees to Nazi officers, Vichy-loyal officials, and members of the Resistance supposedly embedded within its ranks. Whoever she was, she wielded significant influence with the Nazis.

None of the usual divinations had enabled Niko to discern her whereabouts—not scrying, Tarot, or runestones. Not even a Lull Engine had granted any insight. *Magick will not find her,* he concluded, *so I must rely upon more prosaic methods.* He sighed. *Her ability to hide herself suggests she is Kein's disciple. If only I had—*

Frantic knocks on the bedroom door startled him. His heart slammed inside his chest as he pulled it open and snapped at Camille, "What?"

She grabbed his nightshirt. "We have to go! Now!"

"What?" He pried her hand free. "Why?"

A fearful whisper. "They're here! The Nazis! They have lists. They're dragging people from their homes!" She grabbed his sleeve. "We need to go!"

He eluded her grasp. "Go *where,* Cami?"

"I don't know! The roof? We can reach the next building, get to the street—"

"They'll be in the alleys, looking for anybody who runs."

Down the hall, Ferrand emerged from the master bedroom with a suitcase in each hand. He looked even more frightened than Camille. "Is he ready? We have to go!"

"Not yet." Camille turned toward Niko and pleaded with her eyes. She stepped out of the way as he left his room and hurried to the front door.

Niko put his ear to the door and pretended to listen for clues from the hallway, when in fact he was deploying ALAKATH's ability to hear distant conversations and events. From the street below, he heard two men speak in German:

"Is this the place?"

A ruffling of papers. "Yes. Ferrand Clipet. And a wife, Camille."

"Ready the dogs in case they go out the back." Cold clacks of magazines being slapped into pistols and rounds being chambered. "Let's go."

Convinced he had heard enough, Niko stepped away from the door to face Camille and Ferrand. "It's too late, they're coming up the stairs. Hide in the bedroom. I'll handle this."

Ferrand's face wrinkled in disbelief. "How?"

"I can be very persuasive. Now go!"

Camille and her husband hesitated until they heard the clomps of booted feet outside their door. Panicked, they retreated into the bedroom and shut the door as softly as they could.

Niko had only moments to prepare. From the kitchen he took a bottle of bathtub gin Ferrand kept under the sink. He swished a mouthful, spit it into his cupped hands, let some dribble down his shirt, then massaged the rest into his greasy, uncombed hair and unshaven face.

Three knocks at the door. One of the men he'd heard from downstairs demanded in German-accented French, "Ferrand Clipet! Open the door!"

With a bit of effort, Niko summoned a belch from his diaphragm as he plodded to the door. He pretended to fumble with the latches and locks before pulling it open to confront the two armed SS noncommissioned officers outside. "What do you want?"

"Ferrand Clipet, you are—"

"Who?"

The German stiffened at the interruption. "Monsieur Clipet, you are—"

"Never heard of him." Niko feigned a hiccup and sleeved gin-scented spittle from the corner of his mouth.

"This is his address." The *Scharführer* pushed a warrant toward Niko's face.

Niko squinted at the warrant, then made a show of leaning closer to read it. "Must be a mistake. No one by that name here. Only me."

The almost boyish *Unterscharführer* studied Niko, as if looking for a sign of deception. "And who are you, *monsieur*?"

"Jacques Boulanger," Niko said, resorting to his *nom de voyage*.

The *Scharführer* held out one hand. "Papers, please."

"Of course." He shambled away from the door and scratched his balls on the way to his bedroom. He dug up the false traveling papers he had brought with him from Scotland months earlier and returned to the main room.

The two Nazis were inside the apartment. The *Scharführer* poked through the kitchen and looked inside the cabinets. The *Unterscharführer* perused the contents of the bookshelves in the main room. He was closer to Niko, so he took the papers for inspection.

After a look at the forged identity documents, the *Unterscharführer* handed them to his superior, whose brow creased deeper the longer he looked at them. "Where are you from?"

"Marseille."

Cryptic looks passed between the Germans; then the *Scharführer* nodded. "There are many . . . *immigrants* . . . in that part of the country, are there not?"

"No more than usual, I think."

The boss Nazi's eyes seemed to drill through Niko's pretenses. He eyed a glass that had Camille's lipstick stain on its rim, then rested his hand on the grip of his holstered Luger. "Are you alone in this apartment?"

"I live alone, if that's what you're asking."

Also gripping his semiautomatic pistol, the *Unterscharführer* moved toward the hallway. "You won't mind if we check the bedrooms. Will you, *monsieur*?"

Niko had tried being polite; he had tried simple diversions. Now it was clear the Nazis were about to turn this situation bloody. He couldn't permit them to find his wall full of evidence, or Ferrand and Camille cowering under a bed.

Channeling the mind-bending power of DANTALION, he said in a steady voice, "Why would you? You've already searched them. They're empty."

The *Unterscharführer* halted in midstep. His body and mind seemed locked in a struggle, with one half of his will urging him forward, the other resisting. On the far side of the apartment, his superior snapped, "Mueller? What's—"

"He is obeying your orders." Niko met the *Scharführer*'s eyes and captivated him with his now hypnotic stare. "You confirmed those rooms were empty with your own eyes. You are wasting your time here. The man you seek is long gone. You and Mueller need to go."

Both the Germans stood frozen for a few seconds. Then the *Scharführer* blinked, and he spoke as if he had just been roused from a long sleep. "Mueller, we checked those rooms. They're empty." His subordinate blinked then faced him, and he continued. "We're wasting time here. Clipet's long gone. Let's get back to command and file the report."

"*Jawohl*," said the second German.

They left without apology or valediction. Niko locked the door behind them, then audited their departure with ALAKATH's far-reaching ears. When he was confident they weren't coming back, he knocked on the door of the master bedroom. "Cami? Ferrand? They're gone."

Behind the door he heard scuffling. Then it opened, and Camille emerged, her eyes red, her face streaked with tears. Ferrand was behind her, looking pale and shaken. He said nothing as Camille wrapped her arms around Niko and sobbed into his shoulder. "My God, Niko! I thought they had us!"

"It's all right." He held her close and stroked her hair. "I got rid of them. They won't come back." He glanced at his brother-in-law, who looked undone. "And you, Ferrand? Are you all right?" All the man could do was nod. Despite his size and brawn, he looked powerless and terrified. "What would they have done had they found you?"

"Killed me for certain." His eyes were wet with tears. "Camille, too."

As Ferrand spoke, Niko listened with the discerning ear of CALIEL, which could detect lies with even greater ease than it compelled truth. There was no falsity in Ferrand's voice, no echo of lie by omission, no vibrato of exaggeration. He spoke the truth: He was deathly afraid of being captured by the Nazis. There was no way this man was in league with the Germans or with Kein. Whoever was to blame for the Maquis's misfortunes, it was not Ferrand.

Camille broke from Niko's embrace. "What do we do now?"

"Learn which of our friends were not as lucky as we were," Niko said. "Then see where the Nazis have taken them—and find a way to set them free."

15

SEPTEMBER

Sirens keened in the dark and misty streets of Strasbourg.

No matter how hard Anja pressed against the wound in her gut, it wouldn't stop bleeding. Syrupy warmth pushed between her fingers and pulsed under her palm. Parched and dizzy, all she wanted was to stop moving and quench her thirst, but Adair and Cade dragged her down one dark street after another. "Water," Anja mumbled. Cade shushed her.

Adair halted them at a corner. They pressed their backs to a wall. From the street ahead came running steps. The master raised a shadow to hide them from the squad of Nazi soldiers who charged past. As weak as she was, Anja held her breath and made herself believe, if only for a few seconds, that she was one with the wall: cold, impervious, oblivious.

The soldiers' footfalls melted away. Then Adair and Cade were in motion, pulling Anja with them, to a destination unknown. Her memory, like the streets, was thick with fog.

Harsh floodlights snapped on far away down a tree-lined avenue. Cade and Adair whisked Anja across a deserted street toward a great pillared edifice of granite. "Hurry," Adair whispered, his voice taut from the effort of carrying Anja.

Overwhelmed by the size of the building ahead, Anja was surprised to find herself in front of an unassuming door at one of its side entrances. Cade opened the door with magick; then he and Adair sidestepped through it, supporting Anja between them.

The master told Cade, "Lock it behind us."

"Done."

"This way." Adair led them through pitch-black corridors, down steps Anja couldn't see, into the bowels of a building so voluminous that even its silences echoed.

A fever surged through Anja's body. Delirium followed. Next she was flat on her back, atop something cold and hard. She blinked to sharpen her blurred vision. Rising up on either side of her were endless rows of books on shelves.

Her voice sounded remote to her. "Where are we?"

"The Strasbourg University national library," Adair said. "Well, *beneath* it, to be precise." He snapped at Cade, "She's still bleeding!"

"It's a magick wound. I don't know how to make it stop."

"Find a way." Adair leaned over Anja, his affect once again paternal. "Hang in there, lass."

It hurt her throat to speak. "What happened?"

"Ambush. The dabblers saw us coming." The master shook his head. "It's my fault. 'Twas only a matter of time before Kein got wise to us. I should've been more careful."

Cade dug through Anja's shoulder bag for clean gauze, which he stuffed into the puddle of blood seeping from her abdomen. "Keep her awake," he said, dusting the wound with white powder that numbed all it touched.

The master took Anja's hand. She blinked again, and now she saw that Adair and Cade were bloody, bruised, and scorched from head to toe. "Are you hurt?"

"We're fine, thanks to you."

"What did I do?"

"You don't remember?" Anja shook her head; Adair smiled. "You took a shot meant for me." The master used his shirtsleeve to sop blood from Anja's face and forehead. "If not for you, it would've ripped out my heart." His eyes misted, and his voice broke. "That's the *second* time I owe you my life." Tears fell from his eyes as he glared at Cade. "Why's she still fucking bleeding?"

"Because I don't know what demon stabbed her!"

"Dammit! Reason it out! The coven's sworn to Sathanas! A barbed sword—?"

"Hadragor," Cade said, suddenly realizing. "Keep her talking."

Adair cupped his palm to Anja's cheek. "Still with me, lass?"

A faltering smile. "Still here, Master."

Stabbing pain overpowered the morphine powder caked into her gut. She looked down and saw Cade sew her ragged wound shut while he mumbled in broken Latin, making a hash of a healing charm. She wanted to slap him but couldn't move her arms.

Cade finished his closing stitch. His shoulders slumped. "I've stopped the bleeding. I can fix the rest later, but she needs to rest. And so do I."

The master dismissed Cade with a nod, then stood by Anja's side. "The worst is over. But now you need to leave us for a while."

"I understand."

Adair brushed his leathery fingers over Anja's eyelids, coaxing them shut and ushering her into a dreamless sleep.

———※———

It took hours for Cade to finish the healing charms Anja needed to recover from her wounds, and the effort left him feeling more drained than he had ever thought possible. Sitting on the floor, he cast his eyes about the subterranean library and noted arcane symbols engraved into the stone pillars that surrounded them. "This isn't a normal part of the library, is it?"

Adair drank in the nostalgia. "Sixty years ago, this was a secret Freemason temple. Its members are gone now. Most dead, the rest in hiding. But this place is still a sanctuary, hidden from the enemy." A rueful chortle. "If only it had a mirror."

The master paced between the stacks and let his fingertips brush the spines of books that were almost as old as he was. "Magick wasn't always like it is now. Great brotherhoods of White magicians once sought wisdom from the Celestial powers, and they used that knowledge to give rise to Science." A deep sigh. "Answering questions beyond human ken—that's why man took up ceremonial magick in the first place. Not for *this*. Not for murder. War. Genocide. Not to pave a road to the Apocalypse, but to light the way to objective truth."

The next question seemed obvious to Cade.

"What happened?"

"What always happens. Greed. Hubris. Lust for power." A melancholy settled over Adair. "Kein and I were taught by the same master, many moons ago. I thought we learned the same lessons, but time proved me wrong on that count. The first time Kein threatened to meddle in human affairs, he helped Napoleon run roughshod over Europe. I begged him to stay out of it, but he didn't listen—not until our master intervened. A few years after Waterloo, our old master vanished. Kein swore he had nothing to do with that . . . but I knew then that the next time Kein decided to take sides in a war, it would be up to me to stop him."

Listening to Adair talk left Cade awash in doubts and questions—a state of unrest the master clearly recognized. He ceased his wanderings and planted himself in front of Cade. "Something on your mind?"

After months of stifling his curiosity for the sake of mastering the Art, Cade realized this was the first time he was being invited to ask the master anything he wanted. "You make it sound like Kein is some kind of villain. But what are we? If we all use demons for magick, is there any difference between us and him? Or are we just monsters of a different stripe?"

The master nodded. "Church propaganda aside, demons are like any other tool. Using them doesn't make us evil—it's what we use them for that matters."

"So what's the difference between us and Kein?"

The question drove Adair to a soul-searching pause. "We have conflicting visions for the future of man. Kein resents science and technology. Calls them 'blights on our collective soul.' He doesn't just want them destroyed—he wants them *disgraced*. Shamed into oblivion so that he and his ilk can use magick to lord over the broken remains of 'a simpler society.'"

"And what do *you* want?"

A wistful smile. "My hope? One day, after science defines the *rules* of the physical universe, the Art'll be ready to ask the one question science can't answer: *Why?* And when that day comes, I pray magick will still be there, ready to dispel the old superstitions and bridge the last gap in humanity's understanding of itself—and the universe." He lit two cigarettes and handed one to Cade. Exhaling smoke, he turned toward Anja, who still lay sleeping on the table, and cupped her head in one hand. "Those are the *true* stakes in this fight, lad: a future of light—or an eternity of darkness."

───

It was a crude fence, but an effective one: thick posts sunk deep into the ground, sharp pickets bound closely together, all topped with barbed wire. The only breaks in the perimeter were gates manned day and night by Vichy gendarmes who seemed to revel in doing the Nazis' bidding.

Beyond the fence rose an oddity in the French landscape: a five-story modernist residential complex in the shape of a zigzag. Its designers had erected it in the center of Drancy, a northeastern suburb of Paris, as a model of peaceful urban dwelling; to wit, they had taken to calling it "the Silent City." Now that the complex had become an internment camp for Jews, members of the Resistance, and anyone else who ran afoul of Vichy or Berlin, its old nickname had taken on sinister overtones.

Niko strolled on the opposite side of Avenue Jean Juarès, his hands stuffed inside his pockets as he passed the main gate. It was dusk but still hours shy of the city's curfew, so the guards ignored him. At the next corner he turned and strolled to his borrowed car, which was parked on the narrow street where he'd left it.

He slumped into the driver's seat and twisted around to make sure he was alone. Then he pulled his enchanted mirror from inside his jacket. *"Fenestra, Stefan and Adair."*

Several seconds elapsed while he awaited a response. The master was the first to appear. *"Niko, lad. Still in one piece?"*

"So far."

Stefan rippled into view and split the frame with Adair. *"Niko! You are well, I hope."*

"As well as can be. Master, how is Anja?"

"Almost healed. Another week and we'll be back in the fight. Stefan, any word?"

"No. But I have found a clue I am following to Kiev."

Adair shifted his eyes to Niko. *"And you, lad? What word?"*

"My lost comrades were sent to the Drancy internment camp, along with seven thousand Jews rounded up from Paris and beyond."

His revelation darkened Stefan's dejected mood. *"This is happening all over Europe. The Nazis have made ghettos for the Jews in Warsaw, Kraków, Łodz . . . everywhere they go."*

"The good news," Niko added, "is I can think of at least three ways in and out of the Drancy camp. I can smuggle in food and medicine, then find ways to bring our people out."

The master shook his head. *"No. That's not the mission."*

"Pardonnez-moi?"

"No mercy missions. We can't risk it. Not with active Thule covens still at large."

That was an answer Niko couldn't accept. "People are *starving* in there."

"People are dying all over. You need to see the bigger picture."

"They have no heat. Some of them are without blankets or coats. What happens when winter comes? Should I just let them freeze?"

"Aye, if necessary." Adair massaged his bloodshot eyes. *"I respect your sense of charity, lad, but that's not why I sent you there."*

Niko rolled his eyes in disgust. "Every time I get close to finding the Paris coven, they slip away. Their spy sabotages me at every turn."

"Then set a trap and flush the bastard out."

"I'd no idea it was so simple. I will just ask the spy to raise his hand and expose himself, *mais oui*?" He met Adair's keen gaze. "If I find him, then can we help the Drancy prisoners?"

Stefan added his own plea: *"And the Jews in the ghettos?"*

The master frowned. *"There's fuck all we can do for them until we stop the Thule covens and get back the Iron Codex. Once that's done . . . maybe then."*

His answer stoked Stefan's desperation. *"Then might be too late!"*

Adair sighed. *"Lad, if Kein finds the Codex before we do, it'll be too late for all of us."*

<hr />

They came by the thousands, carrying all they owned and cherished. Bundled in layers of clothing, toting suitcases and duffels, the Jews of Kiev queued up for kilometers, with the head of the line somewhere in the city's Syrets district, out of sight around a bend in the road.

Plastered all over Kiev were printed notices—in Ukrainian, German, and Russian—posted only the day before by the city's German occupiers. Their directions were clear:

> **All Yids of the city of Kiev and its vicinity must appear on Monday, September 29, by 8 o'clock in the morning, at the corner of Melnykova and Dorogozhitskaya streets (near the cemetery). Bring documents, money and valuables, and also warm clothing, linen, etc. Any Yids who do not follow this order and are found elsewhere will be shot. Any civilians who enter the dwellings left by Yids and appropriate the things in them will be shot.**

A damp chill suffused the early-morning air. Stefan shivered inside his wool overcoat, unseen by the crowd because he had been rendered invisible by the talent of FORAS. He had traveled light that morning by entrusting his tools of the Art and other gear to his demonic porter. It meant he would need to fumigate and exorcise his tools before he could use them again for magick, but it was the price he had to pay to keep his hands free, just in case he found the Codex.

Beside him was an old Jewish man whose beard reached nearly to his belt. He mumbled as he walked, praying under his breath the way Stefan's father once had done. Ahead of Stefan, a mother carted two small children—an infant in one arm, a toddler in the other—while a third youngster plodded beside her, restless and crying like his siblings.

The great mass of humanity shuffled forward. As the gate to the Jewish cemetery came into view, Stefan felt sick with suspicion. Standing on either side of the gates were not just Ukrainian police but also Waffen-SS troops with machine guns, and hundreds of SS-Sonderkommandos. *How do these people not realize what they are walking into? Or do they know, but are too scared to resist or retreat?* He had seen this happen throughout Poland, but still it baffled him to watch thousands march to their doom.

As he passed through the cemetery's gate, he couldn't help but recall Hell's motto from *The Divine Comedy*: "Abandon hope, all ye who enter here."

Inside the gate, a fat German officer sat behind a table. He wore the uniform of the Einsatzgruppen and was flanked by armed Waffen-SS troopers. More Nazi soldiers and Ukrainian police stood nearby. Most of them brandished submachine guns, but a few held snarling, barking attack dogs on taut leashes. They took turns corralling the new arrivals.

Stefan slipped away from the line and took as wide a path as possible to get behind the Germans. Self-preservation was his chief prerogative. No matter how much he wanted to let loose with every magickal assault in his limited arsenal, he knew his strength and reserve of yoked talents would expire long before the Germans ran out of soldiers. Magick was a powerful tool, but not an omnipotent one. A single karcist couldn't last long against an army when all it would take was one lucky shot to break the magician's concentration.

And then there were the dogs. Bred for aggression, trained for alertness, they were the most troubling enemy of all. Like many animals, dogs possessed keener senses than humans. As such, they were not easily fooled by charms of invisibility. Escaping the Nazis was hard enough, but their damned dogs were a nightmare. Stealing along the edge of the woods, Stefan did his best to avoid dried leaves and twigs, or anything that might betray his presence.

Just as the Germans had done at other roundups he had witnessed in the ghettos, they separated arriving Jews from their possessions with bureaucratic coldness. Portable valuables were seized first, up front. Luggage and larger possessions would no doubt be confiscated farther down the line. And so it would go, until the Jews were left with nothing.

It is possible the Codex was taken with the valuables, he reasoned. He needed to search the stacks of stolen goods without moving anything, or else the Germans would become suspicious. Using the sight of SŌZAY he peered inside closed crates and sealed boxes, past one layer after another of jewelry, watches, cash, and precious knickknacks. After several minutes of scrying the Nazis' first cache, he was certain the Codex was not there.

He waited for the next large group of Jews to be moved down the line. He followed them, hoping the Germans' attention would be on the group and not on him passing behind them, skirting the tree line on his way to their next checkpoint.

Several meters ahead, he saw other Jews being relieved of their luggage. Bags large and small, from the most stylish suitcases to the cheapest canvas duffels, all were hurled into a heap behind the Nazis while their owners were forced onward empty-handed.

Once more he ducked behind the line and used SŌZAY's talent to look inside locked suitcases. In one case near the bottom of the pile he glimpsed a large book. Could that be the Codex? He peered closer only to find it had no sigil on its cover, no warding glyphs on its pages. It was an old book, an antique, but not the Iron Codex. *If it is here, it could take hours—*

A wild snarl preceded the white pain of fangs piercing Stefan's calf. Taken by surprise, he cried out in pain, his charm of invisibility broken.

A trio of Einsatzgruppen converged on him. He wanted to run for the trees, but the dog's jaws were locked on his lower leg, leaving him hopelessly anchored.

The muzzle of a rifle was thrust into Stefan's face. He raised his hands in surrender.

"What are you doing out of line?"

Stefan stammered, "I—I don't—" A rifle's stock slammed into the side of his head.

One of the Germans whistled, and the dog let go of Stefan's leg. The other two Nazis dragged Stefan away from the luggage pile and threw him on the trail with the Kiev Jews. An SS officer stepped in front of him. "Where are your papers?"

"I don't have any."

The officer pointed at Stefan and told his men, "Search him."

In seconds they relieved Stefan of his eyeglasses, billfold, and a tarnished old pocket watch—the first gift Evert had ever given him. "Please," Stefan begged, "that's all I have."

"Keep moving, Jew!" Stefan was hounded down a gauntlet of German soldiers, who shouted obscenities and slurs at him every step of the way. More barking dogs, their fangs glistening with saliva, threatened to slip their leashes.

At the next clearing, Stefan blanched. Prisoners were being forced to strip naked. Outer garments in one pile. A stack of shoes. Women's dresses in a heap. Men's trousers. Children's clothing, separated by gender. Shirts in a ragged mound. Undergarments of all kinds, tossed together without regard.

Cold morning air prickled Stefan's body with gooseflesh as he shed his clothes and handed them over to the Nazis. He kept looking for an opportunity to escape, to use his remaining reserve of yoked magick to flee this death march, but there were no breaks in the gauntlet of SS-Sonderkommandos, Einsatzgruppen, Waffen-SS, and Ukrainian collaborators.

Turns and twists in the trail made it hard to see far ahead, and the loss of his glasses made it that much more difficult for Stefan. But before he saw the fate that awaited him, he heard it, in spite of the forest's knack for smothering sound—

Short controlled bursts: the staccato rip of submachine guns.

Each step brought him that much closer to the source of the shots, and carried him that much farther from his desperate need to deny what was happening.

All around him, naked Jews—old and young, men and women, teens—whimpered and wept as they were corralled toward what they now all knew to be their impending doom. From ahead came sounds to turn Stefan's stomach. Howls of suffering, the shrieks of frightened children, pitiful keenings—all cut short by the chattering of guns, only to be supplanted by different voices crying out the same song of terror.

Then he saw it, yawning ahead of them, through the trees:

Babi Yar ravine—a wooded gully thirty meters across and fifteen meters deep whose edges dropped off in steep slopes. Curtains of gunsmoke lingered in the morning air and sharpened the wind with a sulfuric tang.

The Nazis lined up their Jewish prisoners ten across at the ravine's edge. Last into the line was a young mother clutching a nursing infant to her breast. She screamed as an SS officer tore the infant from her grasp and flung it like so much garbage into the ravine. She screamed and leaped from the edge in pursuit of her son. Gunshots tore into her back and shrouded her in scarlet mist as she dropped, lifeless, into this scar on the earth.

Terror left Stefan speechless as tears streamed down his face.

My God.

He was still in shock as the Germans prodded him to the ravine's edge. Behind him he heard the clack and clatter of weapons being reloaded and primed to fire.

None of his yoked magick would make him impervious to bullets. If he hoped to survive, he needed to pull off the most complex magick he had ever attempted—and he had only seconds in which to do so. *Remember the training,* he admonished himself. *Clear your mind.*

It was an illusion in four parts, all happening at once, in the span of two seconds.

Through ANARAZEL, he created an illusion of himself, around himself.

With the gift of FORAS, he turned himself invisible.

By the power of ANDROMALIUS, he wrapped himself in silence.

And as he leaped into the ravine and felt gravity take hold of him, he cast a glamour of ASOCLAS on the illusion of himself that still stood with the prisoners on the edge.

A barrage of gunfire ripped into the trembling victims. Stefan made his illusion erupt in bloody wounds and pitch into the ravine, his anguished howl provided by the glamour.

He landed hard, his long fall cushioned by the multiple layers of bodies that already filled the bottom of the ravine. The prisoners' bullet-riddled corpses slammed down around him, twisted into deformed poses, most with their eyes still open but no longer seeing.

Already the dead here were too numerous for Stefan to count. There were hundreds, maybe thousands. Men, women, children, all ravaged and broken, painted in blood and dirt. A charnel reek assaulted Stefan's nose, a stench of dead flesh and evacuated bowels and bladders. It was a worse stink than any he had ever known; not even the vapors of Hell compared.

Above him, the mass executions continued, a slaughter unabated. When one group of gunmen ran out of ammunition, a fresh squad relieved them, and the murders resumed. Once or twice each hour, Nazi gunmen descended into the pit and prowled among the carnage, looking for survivors. Those they found, they finished off with point-blank shots to the back of the neck.

There was nowhere Stefan could hide from the rain of the dead. An old woman's corpse landed on top of him, her impact mitigated only by the fact that she had been starving for so long that she had withered to a sack of bones. Her blood ran over his face, and he felt the contents of her bowels spill over his legs. He wanted to push her aside and free himself, but he didn't dare, for fear of drawing the attention of the gunmen who kept their sadistic vigil for survivors.

More bodies landed on top of Stefan. Their weight pressed down, suffocating him even as they shielded him. Trapped under mounting layers of the dead, Stefan lost sight of the sky.

The chattering of the Nazis' guns was endless. It was a factory for genocide, murder in an industrial fashion, with all the efficiency for which the Nazis were now infamous.

Unable to move or breathe, Stefan felt consciousness slip away. Surrendering himself to the darkness, all he could do was hope this was yet another of his countless demonic nightmares.

<p style="text-align:center">~~~</p>

A tease of fresh air woke Stefan. Hearing no sound from above, he risked shifting the old woman's body to see if there was any room for him to climb. The weight of the dead was oppressive, but fleeting tastes of air energized him.

It was slow work to excavate himself without upsetting the delicate balance of cadavers stacked on top of him. He snaked around one cold, naked body after another, following his nose, clinging to hope, and ignoring the odor of rotting flesh and human waste.

Loose dirt spilled into his face as he slithered around another corpse. Pushing upward, he found himself clawing a hole in a layer of loosely packed earth. His hand broke free of the grave. He cleared enough of a hole to raise his head and survey his surroundings.

High above, on the ridge from which he'd jumped, there were unsteady flames from campfires. Muted voices with German-sounding accents drifted down. Even at night, the Nazis were keeping watch over their killing field. Stefan had to be cautious.

Several dozen meters away, Stefan saw a teenaged boy and a young girl, both naked and filthy, helping each other climb the ravine's steep slope, on the side opposite the Germans' camp. They tried so hard to be stealthy, but as soon as they were out of the ravine they were spotted. One of the Nazis shouted a warning, and shots rang out as the young couple fled into the trees. After that, Stefan lost sight of them.

Weak and cold, he shaped his thoughts into a command.

GAIDAROS. Give me a set of clothes, my work shoes, and my spare glasses.

The requested items appeared in his hands. He dressed quickly but in small motions, taking care not to draw the Germans' fire.

In less than a minute he was clothed and on the move, skulking and sometimes crawling down the ravine, away from the soldiers. Babi Yar was about 150 meters long. He soon reached its northern end, where it gave way to level ground and a long expanse of forest. There was no sign of anyone pursuing him. All the same, he shrouded himself in silence so that he could run without giving himself away.

At first he sprinted, but his strength soon flagged. He slowed for only as long as he needed to revive his stamina, and then he ran again. All he wanted was to put as much distance as possible between himself and Babi Yar.

After what had felt like hours, he slumped against a tree to gasp for air. Out of habit he reached for the pocket where he kept his watch, only to remember the Nazis now had it.

At least I am still alive.

He looked up, hoping to gauge the hour by the stars, only to be thwarted by an overcast sky. The dawn could be hours away, or only minutes.

A ball of fire lit up the night.

Stefan's mental reflexes raised a shield and scattered the flames, which stank of demonic origin. He ducked for cover behind a wide tree while searching for the fireball's source.

From the darkness, an unfamiliar male voice taunted him in halting German.

"You're quick, Miracle Man. I'll give you that."

It was hard for Stefan to see in the dark so soon after the fiery detonation. He blinked, hoping to dispel some of the spots clouding his vision. He readied the dagger of ORIAS—the only combat-oriented talent he had yoked at that moment—and considered making a run for it. He replied just to buy time. "You must be Kein's puppet Siegmar, yes?"

"I prefer to think of myself as a peer."

A spectral sword stabbed through the tree's trunk and grazed Stefan's chin. Once he saw the rippled edge of the blade, he recognized it as the flamberge of QLIPHOR. Then it pulled back and vanished, no doubt a prelude to its next strike.

Stefan fought to control his fear, but he needed more time. He called out to Siegmar, "The Kiev massacre! That was you?"

"I didn't *plan* it, but I knew it was coming. Just as I knew *you* were coming."

Siegmar's declaration sent a shiver through Stefan. *How did he know I—?* Then the answer came to him. "The transfer orders I found. Forgeries?"

"As I said, Miracle Man! You're quick!" A cruel chortle. "You didn't think your precious Kabbalists were still alive, did you?"

Vowing to avenge the victims of Kiev, Stefan marshaled the last of his strength and put his yoked demons to work. It was time to give Siegmar something to shoot at.

⁂

Flushing out the renegade karcist hadn't been difficult, but it had required more patience than Siegmar preferred to expend. Now that he had the man cornered, he meant to finish him off—if only the cowardly Jew would show himself.

Another gust from AFAEL's furnace was taking shape in Siegmar's hand when he got his wish. The downtrodden enemy magician charged right at him, a ball of electricity in one hand and a revolver in the other. Lightning leaped from the young mage's palm.

Siegmar attuned his shield to absorb their power so he could hurl it back at his foe and sear the flesh from his bones. The blinding forks of energy passed through his shield and through him—as did a salvo of all six shots from the man's revolver.

Illusions, he realized. As the phantasms collided with his shield, Siegmar used it to scatter them into vapors. Then he searched for his foe's real attack, which could come from any direction—but when he looked up, he saw too late that he had misread his enemy's intentions. The diversion hadn't covered an assault, but an escape.

Almost as quickly as Siegmar spotted the blur of motion in the gray predawn sky, it was gone. Without a yoked spirit capable of flight, he had no means of pursuit.

We'll meet again, Miracle Man. And when we do . . . I will see you dead.

16

OCTOBER

The need for privacy had made it necessary for Niko to move his investigation materials into the basement of a derelict building behind the one where his sister and her husband lived, but he was starting to regret the change of venue. He found it hard to concentrate on timelines and reports of enemy activity when his nose was under constant assault by the stench of ruptured sewer lines, the fumes of motor oil and diesel fuel, and the odor of mildew.

His collection of notes and photos had grown, though now it was better curated. It wrapped around one corner onto an adjacent wall. He was closing in on the Thule spy and tightening his figurative snare around Briet.

In his pocket, the enchanted mirror vibrated, alerting him that someone was trying to reach him. Happy for an excuse to tear his attention from the wall, he pulled out the mirror. His elation subsided when he saw Adair in its frame.

"How goes the hunt, lad?"

"I might ask the same of you."

"We've broken the Thule covens in the occupied territories north of Paris. Now we're heading into Germany. But stop changing the subject. Have you found the spy?"

"Not as such. But I have given it a great deal of thought."

Adair struggled with his temper. *"And how do you plan to turn thought into deeds?"*

Niko aimed his mirror at his wall of words and pictures. "I have narrowed my suspects to three: Antoine Le Blanc; Michel Deniaud; and Françoise Perrault. All had access to the messages between multiple cells of the Resistance and the Maquis. Each also has ties to the Vichy government, and all have repeatedly evaded capture by the Nazis."

"So how do you mean to flush out the spy?"

He turned the mirror so that it faced him. "By remembering which lies I choose to tell."

Adair appeared intrigued. *"Explain."*

"Three shipments, coming to Paris from different sources. Each with a unique time, place, and means of delivery. Each set in motion by a different party, none of whom knows of the others, and none of whom are known to my suspects." Niko pointed at the yarn-linked data on his walls. "I've told each target I've arranged a shipment of supplies from the British. Antoine thinks it's coming tomorrow by truck from Le Havre. I told Françoise it's coming Thursday, by an airdrop north of the city, in the hills west of Clermont. And I told Michel the shipment comes on the Saturday train from Geneva."

"Then you watch the shipments, and see which one gets seized by the Nazis."

"Exactly."

"Not a perfect plan, though, is it? What if the Nazis learn of your shipments by other means? What if they all get seized?"

"To be safe? I find them all guilty, and I kill all three."

The master nodded. *"Aye. That's the safest way. Of course, you could do that now."*

"I would rather kill just the one who deserves it."

"As you like. But tell me this: How do you mean to find the Paris coven?"

A bone-weary sigh. "I don't know. Every time I think I am close, I find another dead end. Now I think I might follow the spy, to see if he leads me to Briet."

"Worth a try. But if you find her, mind your step. She's more dangerous than you know."

Niko grinned. *"Tu plaisantes?* You want me to devise another ruse? You know this is not my—how you say?—strong suit."

"I'm just saying, know what you're doing before *you do it."*

He had to chuckle at the advice. "Master, you know me. I am not like Stefan. I don't like plans. I prefer to just . . . *do things."*

The master was in no mood for levity. *"Well, whatever you do, be quick about it. This spy helped the Nazis send half a dozen cells to the Drancy camp last month alone. He's costing the Resistance men, money, and time—and the longer it goes on, the more it hurts recruitment. Mark my words: If you don't plug this leak soon, the Resistance is as good as dead."*

⌇⌇

Wind shrieked over the rooftops of Paris. Crouched in ankle-deep snow on the roof of the Gare de Lyon, Niko noted the approach of the train from Geneva. He pulled his hands from his coat pockets to check his watch. Its face was fogged, but he still could see its hands: 2:17 A.M.

My plan is either about to prove its genius or go down in flames.

Porters and cargo handlers ventured onto the platform, moving into position ahead of the train's arrival. As it rolled in, its brakes engaged with a screech.

Niko tucked away his watch, then cupped his hands and huffed warmth on them. The first two lures he had dangled for the spy had gone unbitten. Neither the truck delivery nor the airdrop had been intercepted or, to all appearances, even noticed by the Germans. The weapons, ammunition, and medicine had been welcome surprises for the Resistance.

All that remained to be seen now was what happened to the crates on the train.

The locomotive's brakes went quiet as it shuddered to a halt. Doors opened on several of the passenger cars. A few people disembarked. They all hunched their shoulders against the cold and moved with the haste of people seeking warmth on a night when gusts off the Seine were like knives that pierced even the thickest coats.

At the rear of the train, a shadowy quartet scampered across the tracks, on their way to the cargo railcar. Whoever the Resistance had hired for this job, they were professionals. It took them less than a minute to break into the train car, and thirty seconds later they were on their way out. Working in pairs, they carted two wooden crates onto the tracks.

Searchlights snapped on and froze them in a white glare.

A swarm of Vichy police, a handful of Waffen-SS officers, and a platoon of Nazi soldiers converged on the thieves, barking orders in French and German. The thieves again proved their professionalism by setting down the crates, dropping to their knees, and placing their hands on top of their heads. None of them were stupid enough to try to run.

There was no longer any doubt that Michel was the spy Niko had been hunting. He regretted the sacrifice of the men on the tracks, but such was the price of victory. *C'est la guerre.*

He was about to slip away when copper tresses caught his eye: Briet marched toward the arrested men—and Michel scurried along beside her.

Niko had planned to follow Michel and let the traitor lead him to her.

Instead, she had come to him. He resumed his place at the roof's edge and watched to see what happened next.

The Nazis opened the stolen crates to inspect their contents. Niko could almost hear their curses as they dug through layers of straw to find nothing but scrap wood. He had been prepared to lose a real shipment at one of the first two deliveries; it would have been the cost of business. But after those had passed unmolested, leaving only the third shipment's fate in doubt, he had made a last-second change. Why lose valuable supplies for no reason?

The redhead confronted Michel and berated him while poking his chest with one finger. Niko tried to eavesdrop on them with the clairaudience of ALAKATH, but he heard only muffled gibberish. Within seconds, he recognized it as magickal obfuscation.

She must be using a privacy charm.

He dug in his coat's pockets for his binoculars so that he might try to read their lips. No sooner had he focused it than Briet struck, searchlights gleaming off the blade of her black-handled knife as she slashed Michel's throat. The spy pitched face-first to the gravel between the tracks and painted them with his blood. She wiped her athamé clean on his back, then sheathed it under her trench coat. When she stood, she snapped orders at the Nazis, who fell over one another in their haste to comply. Then she turned away from the man she'd just killed and walked toward the train station.

Niko retreated from the roof's edge, then ran to the access door.

His steps thundered in the stairwell as he charged downstairs.

He reached street level two minutes later and nudged open the stairwell door. There was no sign of Briet. She wasn't on the platforms or on the tracks; she was nowhere on the main concourse. She wasn't on the plaza outside the main entrance.

Niko cursed himself for having let his yoke on ARUSPEX lapse. Without the spirit, Niko had no access to the Sight. If Briet was nearby but invisible, he would have no way of knowing. And with Michel dead he had no more leads to follow.

The master will have my head for this.

He prepared himself for a harsh reprimand as he darted into the shadows, his arms tucked close at his sides for the long trudge home to Montmartre.

〜〜〜

The brown-skinned man passed so close to Briet that she caught the musk of his cologne. He moved in a hurry. His every step and glance spoke of desperation. He stared right at her—and then she saw him strain to peer into the distance. He looked through her, thanks to the invisibility bestowed on her by SITHIROS. *He must not have a spirit yoked to grant him the Sight.*

Michel's news had seemed too convenient to be trusted. Briet had expected retribution ever since the misfire of her trap in Toulouse. As a precaution, when she'd arrived at the Gare de Lyon, she had reached out with the senses of PHENE-GREX. In seconds she had known there was another karcist nearby, one with several yoked spirits in thrall, so not a dabbler.

She wondered if her secret admirer had felt cheated of his vengeance by her murder of Michel. Once the crates were exposed as decoys, she'd known the young spy was burned. She'd had nothing to gain and much to lose by letting him return to the Resistance. He'd had to die.

Her observer fascinated her. She watched him search in vain for her. *Where is he from, I wonder? Morocco? Algeria?* The latter seemed more likely to her.

After a few minutes, he gave up his search. Briet didn't blame him. It was cold and late. Hunched against an icy scalpel of wind, he plodded off. If he was lucky, he might have a beautiful young woman waiting to keep him warm that night, as Briet did.

You're not getting away from me that easily.

She reached inside her trench coat, to a fur-lined pocket in which she toted her familiar. A palm-sized black rat with bloodred eyes, Trixim seemed impervious to heat or cold, and he was always ready to obey her commands. She pointed at the brown-skinned man.

"Follow him. Don't be seen. Don't get caught. Go."

The rat leaped from her hand and skittered across the pavement, then vanished over the curb into the gutter, all in swift pursuit of the departing enemy karcist.

She knew who the man must serve; it was the only reason she hadn't killed him. Kein wanted the location of the enemy's stronghold and leads to its future targets. Keeping watch on this man might provide both in short order. So for the time being, he would live. When he ceased to be useful or amusing, Kein would decide his fate.

Until then, Briet wanted to see how many of the brown-skinned man's friends and loved ones she could trick him into handing over to the Nazis.

NOVEMBER

Most of the Thule covens Cade had helped destroy in France had been hidden in plain sight. The one he was surveilling in Stuttgart was no different. In fact, this chapter of dabblers was downright brazen; they had ensconced themselves in a building near the Rathaus, or city hall. Their lair's peaked roof and ornate half-timbered fachwerk reminded Cade of the gingerbread houses he had seen in upscale London bakeries as a teenager.

He lurked on the far side of the plaza, watching from the shadows between two freestanding houses. His task was to watch the coven's front entrance and plaza-facing windows, note all persons who arrived or departed, and track which rooms had activity at which hours.

It was tedious work, but after the ambush in Strasbourg Adair had insisted on better precautions and more diligent preparations for future encounters. Now it could take weeks to reconnoiter a target to the master's satisfaction. So far, it had paid off. Armed with floor plans and timetables of its members' schedules, they had laid waste to four groups of dabblers in two months. Now they were in Germany, bringing the fight to the enemy's doorstep.

Across the street, two men approached the coven's entrance. At the door, one of them knocked thrice, paused, knocked once, paused again, then knocked a final time. It was always the same sequence. A keyhole panel was opened from the other side; then the door was opened to admit the men. As the door closed, Cade checked his watch. It was just after 1:30 A.M. He opened his journal and jotted down the event.

Another tiny step toward victory. He put away the pencil and pulled out a pack of Lucky Strikes. One shake of his wrist coaxed a cigarette's end from the soft package. He lifted the pack to his mouth, plucked out the loose smoke with his lips, and put the rest away.

A snap of his fingers, and a tongue of Xaphan's fire lit the Lucky.

If the coven's members remained true to form, Cade didn't expect to see anyone else come or go for at least another three hours. He wondered if the rear entrances were any livelier at this time of night. For Adair's and Anja's sakes, he hoped so.

Behind a curtained window on the building's upper floor, a light switched on. Cade reached for his journal to record which window and the time. As he touched pencil to paper, a voice from the alleyway behind him turned his head: "*Guten abend.*"

A tall and dapper man strolled toward him. The gentleman was lean of build, and as he passed through a spill of light, Cade noted his chiseled features and slicked hair. His suit looked as if it had been tailored just for him, and his shoes snapped on the pavement. He smiled at Cade, but there was no light in his eyes, just a gleam off of his perfect incisors. "What are you doing out on such a brisk evening?"

Cade hoped hostility would abbreviate the encounter.

"Minding my own business," he said in German.

The stranger held a lit cigarette between his thumb and forefinger, an effete posture Cade found peculiar. At a slow pace the man drew nearer. "And what are you scribbling? Poems, perchance?" The blond German made no effort to conceal his mockery. "Might I suggest a verse? 'So on this windy sea of land, the Fiend walked up and down alone bent on his prey.'"

Tucking his journal into his pocket, Cade decided he'd suffered enough abuse from the Kraut. "If you're looking for a bit of buggery, you're in the wrong place." He added the suggestive power of Esias to his valediction: "Now fuck off."

The stranger paused. Then he breathed in. "Ah. The sweet smell of demonic suggestion." He sounded nostalgic. "I haven't succumbed to *that* perfume in ages."

Cade realized the stranger must be Kein. *I'm not prepared to fight dabblers, never mind a master karcist.* It felt as if the ground had dropped away beneath his feet, and he was trapped in the moment before free fall. He raised his shield—but not soon enough.

Icy jolts ripped through his gut, and a demonic force threw him against the alley wall hard enough to crack his lower ribs.

His mind rebelled against surrender. He lashed out with a surge of fire, only to see it fizzle against Kein's shield. The Nazi karcist stretched open his jaw like a serpent preparing to swallow fat-bodied prey. A jet of cold spewed forth, stinging Cade's extremities and caking his face with hoarfrost. Another blow and Cade was airborne, tumbling out of control. He struck the ground head-first and felt pain slice across his scalp.

Disoriented, Cade forced himself onto one knee, determined to retaliate—

He barely raised his shield in time to block a stroke of violet lightning surging from Kein's outstretched hand. The attack pushed Cade backward several feet before knocking him over. He rolled through it, then hurled VAELBOR's spear.

Kein swatted the spectral weapon into mist. "You're the marauder who laid waste my French covens?" A flick of the Nazi magician's hand snapped Cade's right femur as if it were dry kindling. "I suppose, to amateurs, you might seem like a real karcist. But if you think I'm going to let you just waltz into the Fatherland . . . you are gravely mistaken."

Agony and exhaustion left Cade frozen on the ground, trembling, waiting for the killing blow to fall as Kein's open hand filled with fire.

Then the Nazi spun about to block a barrage of lightning and ghostly arrows.

Adair and Anja strode into the alley, both with hands full of deadly magick awaiting release. The master's voice was as dark as Cade had ever heard:

"Leave him be, Kein."

"My old friend. It's been too long." Kein glanced at Anja. "Your pet—how she's grown. Can't say the same for her brother, though, can we?"

There was no misinterpreting Anja's stare: she wanted blood.

"Leave my adepts out of this," Adair said.

Kein seemed almost remorseful. "You brought them into it, Adair. That makes them fair game. Not that war respects the laws of magick—or anything else, for that matter." To Anja he added, "Need I remind you which of us drew first blood?"

She started forward, but Adair restrained her with one hand; then he hurled more magick at Kein than Cade had thought possible. Infernal energies raged in both directions—fire and lightning, snaking clouds of blinding light and chilling shadow, whirlwinds of glass and sand. The longer they traded and repelled attacks, the larger the maelstrom grew, until Cade had to cover his face and flatten himself to the ground to avoid its scouring touch.

A thunderclap shattered every window in the alley and brought the tempest to a halt.

Cade looked up to see Adair and Kein on their backs, both scorched and bloody. Of the two, Kein was the worse for wear.

Adair sat up, pointed his smoking right hand at Cade, and told Anja, "Help him."

She ran to Cade. "Can you walk?"

"No."

"Then this will hurt."

She grabbed him under his shoulders and dragged him. And she was right— every inch of his body flared with agony. As she neared Adair, the master produced a leather pouch and a crystal flask as if from thin air. He emptied the pouch onto the pavement, creating a perfectly round patch of multicolored dust. Then he broke the flask in the center of the circle, and a puddle of oil spread to its edge and shimmered. Before Cade could ask what Adair was doing, the master intoned, "*Pulverem et oleum fenestram.*" Their reflections rippled in the oily puddle and then were replaced by a smoky curtain, roiling and churning.

In the alley, Kein shook off his torpor.

Anja grabbed Cade, then let herself plunge through the impromptu portal with him in tow. They seemed to float, weightless—

Then they fell out of the large mirror in the conjuring room at Eilean Donan Castle and slammed onto the stone floor, redoubling all of Cade's pain.

Adair tumbled out of the mirror behind them. He rolled across the floor, then pointed at the mirror and commanded in a hoarse voice, "*Absconde ostium!*"

The churning vapors in the mirror rippled, then vanished to leave only the trio's haggard reflections. "Home sweet home," Adair muttered—just before he fell unconscious to the floor.

DECEMBER

Two weeks Cade had been lying in bed. Every part of his body still hurt. He wanted to enjoy being in Eilean Donan—a thought that struck him as ironic when he considered how much he had resented awakening here nearly a year earlier—but the aches and stabbing pains that permeated his limbs, torso, and head made it difficult.

Outside his windows, the highlands of Skye were dusted with snow. The sky was perpetually overcast. Even at dawn the sun barely made a cameo appearance before it went into hiding above Scotland's omnipresent ceiling of clouds.

Two knocks on his door—Adair's trademark. Cade put down the ancient leather-bound book he'd been studying. "Come in."

The master pushed the door open with his foot and walked in carrying a tray. Kutcha was perched on his shoulder. "I brought breakfast," Adair said. A newspaper was tucked under his arm. To speed their recoveries, they all had shed their yoked spirits after returning to the castle, and Adair had banished its lamiae domestic staff rather than spend time or effort keeping them bound. Only Kutcha had been suffered to remain.

Adair set the tray on the table by Cade's bed. Breakfast that day was soupy porridge, burned toast, a boiled egg, and what looked to Cade like the weakest cup of Earl Grey ever brewed. He noted the meal with a polite smile. "Gee, Master. You shouldn't have."

"Not quite a feast, is it? Pantry's been a bit neglected in our absence."

Cade picked up a blackened slice of bread and bit off a corner. It tasted like charcoal. He put down the toast. "Well, at least you didn't make me limp downstairs to get it."

Adair laughed and slapped Cade's leg. "Truer words, lad!" He recoiled, embarrassed, when he saw Cade's wince of pain. "Sorry. Still hurt?"

"Only when I'm conscious." A pained groan. "I wish Anja could fix it."

The master shook his head. "Only so much she can do when the wounds come from magick. Some demons do harm that never heals." He held up the newspaper. "Ready for some good news?" He unfolded a copy of *The New York Times* to reveal its front-page headline:

JAPAN WARS ON U.S. AND BRITAIN;
MAKES SUDDEN ATTACK ON HAWAII;
HEAVY FIGHTING AT SEA REPORTED

Cade met Adair's expectant gaze. "This is good news?"

"Having your countrymen off the sidelines and into the scrum? I'd fucking well think so. 'Bout time the Yanks got down in the muck with the rest of us." With less of an edge he added, "Present company excluded, naturally."

"Naturally." He leaned closer to the newspaper. "When did it happen?"

"A few days ago. Your congress declared war on Japan yesterday, and the Nazis returned the favor today. So no more malingering for us. How long before you can go another round?"

"Another round of what? Getting my ass kicked in?"

Adair's hopeful cast became a mask of regret. "That was partly my fault. I knew you'd have to face Kein eventually. I just didn't think it would be so soon."

"What do you mean I'll have to 'face him eventually'?"

The master sat on the far corner of Cade's bed. "There's a reason Kein went after you. A reason he had the Nazis sink the *Athenia,* and why he sent demons for you and your kin." He wore a guilty look. "The same reason your father died to save you—and why I fought to bring you back." A deep breath, and a sigh of regret. "It's not just that you're bound to face Kein—it's that you might be the only soul on earth who can do it and hope to win."

"Why? What's so special about me?"

"Topic for another time." Adair got up. "You need to get right, then get to working magick like your life depends on it—because it bloody well does." He gestured at the book in Cade's lap. "Speaking of which—what've you got there?"

"*The Sworn Book of Honorius.*"

"A touch of light reading?"

"You could say that." He fixed the master with a sly look. "Does this work as well as the *Grimorium Verum*? Or the *Lesser Key*?"

Adair walked to the door and paused. "Drag your ass out of that bed one of these days, and maybe we'll find out."

"Challenge accepted."

The master took his leave, and Cade was alone once more with one of the most complex tomes he had ever opened, one of the worst breakfasts he had ever tasted, and the longest-lived headache he had ever endured. Yet all he could think about was what Adair had avoided telling him about Kein, and why Cade was the only one who could hope to stop him.

One thing's for sure: I won't find any answers lounging up here. He devoured his meager repast, gulped his tepid Earl Grey, and set the book aside.

He sat up. Shifted his legs over the bed's edge. Eased his feet onto the floor. *Enough moping. I'm getting out of this goddamned bed.*

The moment he put the least amount of weight on his legs, the spot where his femur had snapped blazed with white agony. He fell backward into his pillows.

Tomorrow. I'm getting out of this bed tomorrow. . . . I hope.

1942

JANUARY

Flying by magick was a dangerous proposition under the best of circumstances. Hovering above Chełmno nad Nerem, held aloft by the power of ASARADEL, Stefan felt vulnerable despite being invisible thanks to FORAS. Months in hiding had left him fearful of open spaces. After escaping the horrors of Babi Yar, all he wanted now was to stay out of sight.

At first he had told himself he was being pragmatic. He had needed time to rest; then it was weeks before he found a secluded space suitable for magickal experiments—one where the din and reek of demons would draw no attention. But even after he had fortified himself with all the yoked spirits he could bear, all he wanted was to retreat into the shadows. Now he knew the truth: He was terrified. The evils of men had put those of demons to shame.

Below, a convoy of trucks rolled toward the gate of an estate ringed by a wooden fence. Most of the property was flat and clear; it was dominated by a large manor. The trucks—which Stefan had followed the night before from the Łodz ghetto to an abandoned mill, where their hundreds of prisoners had been held until that morning—were waved through the gates by German troops.

One by one, the vehicles disgorged their passengers, whom the Germans herded single-file inside the manor. Most looked to be Jews deported from the ghetto, but among them were a few men in Russian army uniforms—prisoners of war from the Eastern Front. Everyone carried a ruck or a duffel packed with whatever possessions they had left in this world.

While the line shuffled indoors, Stefan surveyed the manor's grounds. There were no barracks, nothing that resembled temporary housing. Snow blanketed the ground and frosted the trees of the forest to the north, on either side of the road to Koło. Turning east, Stefan shielded his eyes against shafts of morning light breaking through the clouds.

Nothing he saw happening made sense to him. Why bring the prisoners here? There was no work for them in Chełmno nad Nerem, no place to house them. He looked toward the nearby River Ner, to see if there might be boats waiting, or perhaps an extension of the camp, but all he found was winter countryside. Then he let himself float on a breeze, which carried him behind the manor. There he saw three large trucks, each much larger than the transports that had delivered the detainees. These were a different kind of vehicle, with fully enclosed, hard-shelled rear passenger areas. Instead of canvas flaps in the back, they had heavy, windowless doors. Stefan had never seen anything like them.

He tried to descend for a closer look, but when he was still more than thirty meters above the ground, ASARADEL resisted his commands to descend—or so he thought at first. Opening his mind to the yoked spirit's protests, he understood at once: An invisible magickal barrier prevented the demon from moving closer to the manor or its grounds.

A powerful glyph or ward it must be to hold ASARADEL at bay.

No dabbler could have set such a defense, he realized. It had to be the work of Kein or one of his chief adepts—perhaps the one who had almost killed him at Babi Yar. Whatever was happening here, the enemy's karcists had ensured no one would interfere with it.

Most of an hour passed before Stefan again saw movement on the ground. A rear door of the manor opened, and the prisoners were marched outside— only now the men and children were naked, the women clothed in only their slips or underwear. None of them had the bags they had taken inside. Nazi soldiers shouted them up ramps into the hard-backed trucks—almost seventy people in the smaller ones, twice as many in the largest—then locked the doors. The Germans fired up the engines, idled a few minutes, then drove off the grounds.

Stefan followed them northwest, up the road to Koło. Two lanes wide, it cut through a dense forest that partly canopied the road with its boughs. Roughly four kilometers from the manor, the vehicles turned off the paved road onto one of packed dirt.

Looking up to track where the path led, Stefan saw another fenced compound inside a large forest clearing. Moving closer, he searched for barracks but found only a ramshackle shelter ringed with barbed wire. A platoon of Nazi troops guarded a group of thirty-odd emaciated prisoners, none of whom had adequate winter clothing.

The convoy halted at the gates. German soldiers standing guard opened the gates, waved the trucks inside the compound, then secured the entrance behind them.

Once more Stefan tried to float downward to investigate and perhaps intervene, and again he found himself obstructed by an unseen glyph of warding. He had no idea what form it took—a buried charm, an invisible sigil, a demon tasked to defend the area until Judgment Day—only that he lacked the skill and power to overcome it.

Two dozen meters beneath his feet, the trucks turned, stopped, then reversed toward a vast, recently excavated pit. After the trucks halted, the men in their cabs climbed out, and Stefan saw for the first time that they all were wearing gas masks.

The masked Nazis opened the rear doors of the vehicles.

Shifting his vantage point, Stefan saw his worst fears made manifest. All the passengers in the backs of the trucks were dead, piled in heaps, their lifeless eyes wide with horror and agony. He didn't know how the Germans had done it in transit, but they had.

After a few minutes, the half-starved prisoner-laborers were forced to drag the corpses out of the trucks and heave them into the mass grave. Once all the bodies were in the pit, most of the laborers were tasked with shoveling dirt over the them, while a few others were made to wash the urine and feces out of the interiors of the trucks, then wipe them dry before they returned to the manor to pick up the next group of the condemned.

Stefan watched the trucks roll away, heading south on the road to the manor. Even as he soared above the Polish countryside, his soul sank in despair.

All those lives in Kiev I could not save; all these souls here I have failed. I will remember them all—and I will avenge them.

Every step down the spiral stairs shot pain up Cade's spine and left leg. Despite all that Anja and Adair had done for him, his body remained wounded, and he knew it likely would remain so. He was learning to live with the ache inside his skull, the needles of heat that stabbed his heart when he drew deep breaths, and the twitches that haunted his muscles like a traveling freak show. It was time for him to accept his new status quo and get to work.

The problem was that Adair didn't agree. *He's worried I don't have the strength or the focus to control demons. He thinks if I go back in the circle, I might get us all killed.*

They were rational fears. But Cade was done being afraid.

He limped off the stairs and paused before entering the banquet room. It was quiet and dim, lit by a single lamp at the far end of the room. Cade closed his eyes and drank in the sounds reverberating inside the castle. He latched on to Adair and Anja's voices. They were muted, but if he could hear them they had to be somewhere in the keep. Then he noted the bite of woodsmoke in the air and deduced they were in the billeting room, directly beneath him.

Another awkward limping step, another shooting pain in his leg. He grimaced and pushed ahead to the next sets of stairs.

Have to control the pain. Can't let them see me like this.

If he could just get back in the circle and yoke another team of demons, Adair would let him resume his diet of whisky and opiates. Then he could suppress his pain for real.

He knew what they would say if they saw him struggling. They'd accuse him of being too proud for his own good, of having more courage than common sense. And maybe they'd be right. But he knew what compelled him to defy his body's complaints.

Guilt.

No matter how many times he asked them to carry on the fight without him, they refused. They wouldn't leave him behind, though it was obvious—to Cade, at least—that they were losing precious time. *Every day they wait for me is one the enemy has to roll back all our victories. Every day that I linger, Kein gets stronger. I'm done giving up ground.*

A deep breath, then he started up the stairs. This part of the keep felt like a Zen koan: one had to go up in order to go down. To get from the banquet room on the first floor to the billeting room below, one had to climb to a landing, from which one could reverse direction to descend a parallel flight of steps to the ground level.

It's fine, he assured himself. *I need the practice.*

His first challenge was to overcome his limp. He forced himself to walk at a normal pace, favoring neither leg, with his back straight and his head up. Then he concentrated to erase the pain from his face. Anja was perceptive when it came to discomfort, and the master had a keen eye for deceptions. Fooling them would be difficult but necessary.

By the time he reached the ground level, his charade was complete. Wearing a mask of joviality, he strode into the billeting room.

Anja and Adair sat across from each other at the gaming table in the center of the room, speaking in low voices while they pored over maps. A fire in the hearth threw warm light on the low curved ceiling. Cade cleared his throat. "Hope I'm not interrupting."

Adair smiled and stood. "Look who's up!" He met Cade a few steps inside the room and slapped his shoulders. "How do you feel, lad?"

Cade smiled when all he wanted to do was groan. "Ready to get back in the fight."

The master's elation turned to concern. "Let's not be hasty."

"Relax." He approached the table. "What're we looking at?"

Anja rotated a map of Germany toward him. "Targets."

"Outstanding." He eyed the map.

The master sidled over. "You sure you feel up to this? Yesterday you couldn't walk three feet without—"

"That was *yesterday*," Cade snapped. "I'm fine. Let's focus."

Perhaps sensing the futility of argument, Adair let it go. "We're not wanting for choices. The strongest Thule covens are in the border cities." He tapped at places on the map as he named them. "Bremen, Hamburg, Münster, Berlin, Dusseldorf, Köln, Stuttgart, Munich. Moving inland, we find smaller covens in Hanover, Frankfurt, and Leipzig. It might seem daft, but starting in the middle might be our best shot at getting a foothold in Germany."

"The question," Anja said, "is where to strike. Leipzig is the most remote of the inland targets, which we could use to—"

"Stuttgart," Cade cut in.

Alarmed looks passed between Anja and Adair. He said to Cade, "Lad, did you hear a word we said? Stuttgart coven's huge, and its leader is Johann Merganthaler."

"Just a dabbler," Cade said.

"Aye, but a gifted one." He collected himself. "Putting that aside—the fact that we ran into Kein outside that coven suggests he had a hand in raising its defenses. Even if he's not there now, that's got to be the hardest target in Germany outside of Berlin itself."

Cade nodded. "I know. That's why we need to burn it down." He looked up from the map to meet Adair's troubled gaze. "You want to knock Kein off balance? Don't go for his weak spots. He expects that. Hit him where he thinks he's strongest. Break his coven in Stuttgart. That'll put the fear of God into the others—and into *him*."

Anja looked pleased by that answer. "This is bold. I like it."

"Lots to do, little time." Adair cracked his knuckles and grabbed a pen. "Let's get to it."

20

FEBRUARY

The demon manifested inside a swirl of smoke that did nothing to hide its cloven hooves, three-horned bald head, or its radiant yellow eyes. Its voice emanated from all directions and shook the floor under Kein's feet: Why hast thou disturbed my repose?

Nothing was ever gained by losing one's temper while speaking to the Prime Minister of Hell, but Kein Engel was tempted. "I think you know why."

His accusation resounded inside the Chamber of the Eternal Flame—the most important room in Wewelsburg Castle. Situated in the basement of the north tower, it was a masterpiece of sandstone and blond marble, and as round as human hands could make it. In its center was a shallow pit from which rose a gas-fed pillar of fire surrounded by glyphs ancient and arcane, all bounded by a circle inscribed with the names of El written in Enochian script.

Standing inside that flame was Lucifuge Rofocale.

The object of Kein's wrath was unimpressed.

I would read thy mind, but you deny me that privilege. So speak.

"The Scottish dog and his pups vex me."

This old complaint. The demon shrank from its imposing height to that of a man, and its voice took on a human dimension. "What have they done now?"

"Laid waste my coven in Stuttgart."

"*Tsk.* What a shame." The demon made no secret of its mockery. "I know you can't have called me from the Abyss to commiserate."

Kein resisted the urge to rebuke the demon. "Of course not, mighty prince. I seek Hell's counsel on matters of strategy."

The beast laughed. "A pity, then, you didn't call for me sooner. All I can do now is tell you that you brought this upon yourself."

"Meaning what? Speak plainly! Or else thou shalt—"

"—*feel thy rod and its torments.* Yes, yes. You had the chance to win this war in Stuttgart, and you failed. You let yourself be distracted."

Its accusation baffled Kein. "Distracted? By what?"

A grin of fangs. "The grudge with your old rival. You let your hatred of him stop you from finishing off your real enemy."

Kein recalled the fight in the alley, yet he failed to grasp the demon's point. "The girl? She's no threat to my—"

NOT HER! The walls shook from the beast's roar. It swelled to its former height. DID YOU NOT RECOGNIZE THE ADEPT WHOSE SPARK YOU FAILED TO SNUFF?

The news left Kein's jaw agape. "He's alive? How? No one could survive what I—" His disbelief surrendered to a chilling revelation. "He's not just another karcist, is he?"

HE IS ONE OF THE *NIKRAIM.*

"Impossible. I killed them all. The last one died at sea just days after the war began."

DID HE? ARE YOU SO CERTAIN?

Hearing the question made Kein realize he was no longer certain of anything. "If the adept I met in Stuttgart was the one called Cade Martin, he must be eliminated."

IF THAT IS YOUR WILL.

"Where is he? Tell me, and I'll send MAMMON to reap his soul."

A growl of displeasure from the demon. HE IS PROTECTED BY GREAT WARDS AND PACTS. IF YOU WANT HIM DEAD NOW, IT MUST HAPPEN BY YOUR HAND ALONE.

Kein knew not to take a fallen angel at its word. "Hell has no wards you cannot break."

UNTRUE. I CANNOT BREAK MY OWN SEALS OF PROTECTION—OR PERHAPS I CHOOSE NOT TO. EITHER WAY, THE OUTCOME IS THE SAME.

It took Kein a second to parse the demon's revelation. When he understood, he was seized with rage. "You're his *patron*?"

HE PERFORMED THE RITUAL AND ABIDED BY THE COVENANT. The beast shrugged its arms and rolled its head into a mockery of Christ on the cross. I WILL NOT AID ONE SON AGAINST ANOTHER.

"Damn you! I banish and discharge thee, and command that thou return without delay or detour to the Flame Everlasting! Begone, I abjure thee! By the names ADONAI, ARIEL, ELOHIM, JEHOVAM, and TETRAGRAMMATON!"

Fire consumed the demon from its hooves upward, until its twisted horns vanished in puffs of cobalt smoke.

Kein tossed a handful of camphor into the brazier and let its perfume cleanse the chamber of the demon's lingering stink before he muttered a valedictory "Amen."

He remained inside the operator's circle, consumed by his own brooding. *Why did I not realize the* nikraim *was still alive? How could I not have recognized him when he stood in front of me?* Having to ask such questions galled him. They made him doubt himself, an affliction he'd thought was centuries behind him, a relic of his past long forgotten.

He reined in his resurgent insecurity. *Recriminations accomplish nothing. I have no time to waste on blame or regret. All that matters now is action.*

He extended his hands into the pillar of fire at the center of the pit and pulled out two handfuls of flame. Licks of golden fire swirled in his hands, then soured to a sickly green as he invoked the power of PARAGO: *"Exaudi. Exaudi. Exaudi."*

Reflecting upon his adepts' names made their faces appear above his blazing hands. "Siegmar. Briet. *Ave,* my friends."

They bowed their heads; then Briet cut to business, as usual. *"What news, Master?"*

"None I have not already shared. I hail you this evening to give you both an order, one that supersedes all of my previous commands. Do you both understand?"

Behind the veils of fire, nods of acknowledgment.

"Good. As of now, turn your every thought, word, and action to this goal: Find and kill Adair Macrae, and bring me his youngest male apprentice—the one named Cade Martin."

MARCH

Like their late peers in Stuttgart, the dabblers of Dusseldorf knew how to put up a fight. Not one of them asked for mercy.

That was just as well; Anja was in no mood to grant any.

A pair of Germans leaped through a doorway, only to be cut down by Anja's barrage of poisonous needles. At the end of the corridor, another one hidden by a weak invisibility charm shimmered into view for half a second as he spit fire at her. She drank his attack with her shield, then sent it back to him on a flight of ghostly arrows.

As he fell dead, she faced her next wave of attackers.

It felt good to release the power she carried pent up inside her. It was her just reward for dragging ten yoked demons all over Europe, week in and week out.

The upper floors of the nineteenth-century manor shook from a deafening crack of the whip, with which Anja tore off one dabbler's arm and another's leg in a single strike. As she coiled the whip behind her for another blow, she heard it rip chairs and tables into kindling.

One of the dabblers' Nazi guards stormed into the corridor ahead of her and swung his submachine gun in her direction. She ignited her whip with flames as it snapped forward. Before the soldier could pull the trigger, his weapon turned to half-molten scrap. He dropped it and went for his sidearm. Anja crushed his chest with one punch of a demon's fist.

As he collapsed, Anja found herself alone. From the floors above came the cracks of lightning striking magickal defenses, followed by the rumbles of explosions. Thuds of collision carried through the walls. Smoke choked the stairway; a dead dabbler fell out of it and struck the ground floor as a heap of bloody flesh and broken bones.

Then . . . silence.

No more sounds of battle from above, none from the cellar below.

Is it over? She felt a pang of disappointment. At most she had killed nine or ten dabblers. After all her preparations, she had hoped to slay twice that number.

Anja knew if she voiced such a complaint to Adair, he'd say that was the demons talking. But she knew better. She had lived so long with demons that the black fires of their nature had tempered hers; killing was no longer something she viewed with regret. It was a grim necessity.

Motion caught her eye—but it was only Cade. He returned from the dabblers' conjuring room in the basement with his clothes torn and singed. A wound on the left side of his head had left a smoldering slice through his crew cut. Anja watched him step over a dead dabbler.

He froze as he looked her way.

His hand shot up, palm out, ringed with electricity.

What the hell is he doing?

Lightning streaked from Cade's hand, straight at her. She conjured a shield and braced herself to reflect the attack back at him—then watched the stroke split in two. Each half of it arced around her. In the fraction of a second it took her to turn, the arcs converged and skewered a Thule dabbler holding a pair of spectral scimitars.

She was speechless as she watched the man slump dead to the floor, his demonic blades fading along with the light in his eyes.

Cade was at her side. "Are you all right?"

It took her a second to respond. "The split lightning—?"

"A trick I picked up from Honorius. He has a bunch of 'em." He touched her shoulder and looked into her eyes with genuine concern. "You sure you're okay?"

She nodded. "Yes." Her next words came only with effort. "Thank you."

"Anytime," he said with a smile, then turned toward the stairs as Adair clomped down the last flight. "All set upstairs?"

"They're all dead, if that's what you mean." He nodded for Cade to head up. "Go light the fires. I want to see this place up in flames when we walk out the door."

An obedient nod. "It's as good as cooked." The young man charged upstairs, taking the steps two at a time. Anja watched him leave, and for the first time realized she had developed a genuine respect for him—and maybe also a measure of fear.

Adair studied her. "What's that look on your face mean?"

"Cade. He's still gaining power."

The master stroked his ragged gray beard. "I noticed."

"He's more powerful than any of the other 'special ones' you trained."

"Aye . . . but only because he's survived longer than they did."

～～

Trains arrived day and night. Each disgorged prisoners by the hundreds—some of them Jews, some Poles, plus a few prisoners of war. All were processed with efficiency by the Nazis who manned the concentration camp outside Oświęcim—or, as the Germans had renamed it since annexing Poland into their ever-expanding reich, Auschwitz.

The camp was vast, larger than any other Stefan had seen in his travels. It comprised hundreds of barracks arranged in ranks and columns, all surrounded by walls punctuated at regular intervals by guard towers. It was subdivided into ten areas separated by electrified fences crowned with barbed wire and patrolled by SS troops with dogs. Its population numbered over a hundred thousand, by Stefan's estimate, and more prisoners arrived each day. The weak were culled; the strong were consigned to forced labor.

Huddled in the forest that surrounded the camp, Stefan could only bear witness and grieve. As at Chełmno, Auschwitz was defended not just by troops but by hidden glyphs designed to prevent spirits—and living beings, such as himself, who held them in yoke—from trespassing. It was a cruel irony. If he divested himself of his powers and defenses, he might be able to enter the camp, but doing so would be tantamount to suicide.

Stefan wanted more than anything to charge out of the darkness, to storm the gates of Auschwitz, to lay siege to a target he knew he couldn't defeat.

For months he had savaged Kein's network of Thule covens in eastern Europe. Kein's disciple Siegmar had established new covens to replace the ones Stefan had slain, but none had lasted more than a few weeks before Stefan reduced them and their adepts to ash. He had adopted the enemy's tactics since Babi Yar, and he refused to apologize for it.

Here he knew that without demons he wouldn't make it over the wall, or even within a dozen meters of it, before the Nazis mowed him down with their machine guns. Still he fantasized about halting the incoming trains. He'd free the prisoners and lead them like a modern-day Moses to some land of freedom, far from here, far from any place he or they had ever known. He didn't know where that place could be in a world that permitted atrocities such as he'd seen, but he had to believe one could be found. He had to believe.

But all he could do was watch from a distance.

After hearing Siegmar's taunt at Babi Yar, Stefan had given up any hope of finding the Kabbalists alive. After dismissing the lies that had lured him to Kiev, and poring over reams of Nazi records, he had concluded that, in all likelihood, the Kabbalists had all died here.

Which meant that if Kein hadn't yet found the Iron Codex, it was also here.

Dusk melted into darkness as a new trainload of prisoners rolled through the main gate. Stefan cloaked himself with invisibility and let ASARADEL's wings bear him aloft, high above the camp. Below, a familiar scene transpired. The Germans shouted the prisoners out of the railcars and lined them up for evaluation. The few deemed suitable for labor were assigned to barracks. Hundreds of others were marched away, toward the northwest corner of the camp.

Over the past few days, Stefan had observed those sent to the barracks. Tonight he summoned the courage to follow the condemned.

Most of those culled from the ranks were elderly or infirm, or children too young to care for themselves. Flanked by armed troops, they trudged north on the camp's westernmost path. They were marched inside a large building, from which they emerged minutes later naked and weeping. Shivering in the winter cold, they were led out of the camp.

Just beyond the camp's northwest corner, the prisoners were corraled inside a large red-brick farmhouse. Once the prisoners were inside, the Germans bolted the doors from the outside. A Nazi officer shouted to men stationed on the farmhouse's roof; they emptied canisters down its chimneys before capping them with metal plates. Then the Germans on the roof climbed down and departed with their brothers-in-arms, the prisoners inside the little red house forgotten.

Mystified and filled with dread, Stefan bade ASARADEL to set him down beside the brick house. Frosted grass crunched under his feet as he padded around the rear of the house. All of its windows were boarded over or bricked in. A smell like that of mothballs filled the air.

His foot struck something.

An empty metal canister. He picked it up and perused its label.

It was marked as Zyklon, a highly toxic pesticide.

The lawn around the house was littered with emptied canisters just like the one he held. He turned toward the house. Looked up at its capped chimneys.

Overcome by the horror of his discovery, he doubled over and emptied his stomach. When his body had nothing left to give, it racked itself with dry heaves until he coughed and dropped to his knees, where he wept until his well of grief ran dry.

When he had no more tears, he found himself alone with his fury.

He adjusted his glasses. Stood tall. *I do not care what glyphs guard this camp. No barrier is impenetrable. Nothing will keep me out. Nothing.*

ASARADEL carried Stefan high above the camp. He noted the Germans' movements. They pushed carts loaded to overflowing with clothing and personal property stolen from murdered prisoners, from the big building where they had stripped the condemned, and from the rail yard near the main entrance at the south end of the camp. The pilfered wealth was funneled inside one massive warehouse in the camp's northwest sector, near the processing center.

It was time, Stefan decided, to see for himself all that the Nazis had stolen.

Ever since being thwarted at Chełmno, he had prepared for this moment. Breaching the defenses here would draw the attention and potential reprisal of Kein, but if the Iron Codex was here as Stefan suspected, the reward would more than justify the danger.

Stefan commanded ASARADEL to dive toward the warehouse's entrance and invoked the power of VARAXAS to overpower the glyphs of warding that shielded the camp from scrying or intrusion by karcists with yoked spirits.

Penetrating the sphere of protection stung Stefan like a thousand hornets, but the pain passed quickly and then he was on the ground—still invisible, alive, and unharmed.

He followed the Nazis inside the warehouse. It was worse than anything he had imagined. There were piles taller than he was, composed of naught but confiscated eyeglasses. Mountains of clothing. Purses, jewelry, knickknacks of every kind. At one table, a husky German weighed rough-edged ingots of gold that Stefan belatedly recognized as tooth fillings. When he imagined how they had been acquired, his stomach almost betrayed him with another urge to vomit.

No time, he reminded himself. *Kein and his ilk know I am here. I must be swift.* He spared a moment to calm his racing heart, then set to work. *SAPAX, search the warehouse. If the Iron Codex is here, lead me to it by the swiftest route and without delay or deception.*

AS YOU WILL.

The demon could not touch the Iron Codex because of the book's wards, but if the grimoire was here, SAPAX could guide Stefan to it.

A cold, fetid breeze moved through the warehouse. The Nazis paid it no mind. *Toiling in a place such as this,* Stefan reasoned, *they must take the reek of the damned for granted.*

Every passing moment felt like an invitation to disaster. Stefan knew the spirit could search the warehouse faster than any mortal ever could, but how long would—

IT IS HERE, the demon said in Stefan's thoughts. *LET ME GUIDE YOU.*

It was like moving in a dream. Stefan allowed the demon to steer him through the horrific canyons of plunder. In the heart of the warehouse, they stopped.

There, in a stack of old books, was the unmistakable binding of the Iron Codex. A quick check with the Sight confirmed that its sigils and wards were intact; no one had tried to open it without permission. Stefan plucked it from the pile and hugged it to his chest.

It was time to go, but there was one more question to which he needed an answer. *SAPAX, if anything that belonged to my love Evert Siever lies in this house of rapine, bring it to me.*

The spirit went forth, its progress swifter than thought, its presence little more than a cold whisper on the neck of the unassuming. It returned in seconds and appeared before him, a silhouette watery like a mirage. Its ram-horned head was bowed, and its clawed hands were outstretched and bearing a leather billfold into which Evert's initials had been seared. Stefan took it from the spirit and inspected its contents. It held no money, no identity documents, but Stefan knew where to look for what mattered. He pulled loose its interior lining and found a small photograph hidden underneath. A faded gray snapshot of him and Evert, their cheeks pressed together as they beamed with delight on a bridge in Amsterdam many years earlier.

The wallet fell to the floor as Stefan kissed the faded photo. Tears rolled from his eyes; his beloved had met an unjust end in this accursed place, at the hands of monsters.

Stefan's heart flooded with darkness. He wanted to repay agony with agony, sorrow with sorrow. But this was not the time, not the place. He wasn't ready. But soon he would be. Then those who took Evert from him would suffer, they would rue the day they had robbed him of love, and they would know what it meant to feel true fear before they died.

Colors of alarm from SAPAX warned Stefan his enemy was near. It was time to withdraw and regroup. It made him sick to leave behind so many innocent souls as he retreated to safety, but he consoled himself with a promise: When the time was right, he would return to this place.

And when he did, he would bring the host of Hell with him.

22

APRIL

It had seemed a simple task to Cade: Now that Stefan had recovered the Iron Codex, all he had to do was get it into Adair's hands before the enemy realized that stealing the grimoire was why Stefan had been sent to Europe in the first place. But, as with most things that seemed rudimentary, the return of the Codex had proved damnably hard.

A number of factors complicated the matter, Adair had explained.

The first was that the Codex was protected by a variety of sigils and wards. Most were designed to prevent persons from opening or using the book unless they knew its shibboleths. A few were intended to protect the book from damage of all kinds, including fire, water, and cutting or tearing. But one glyph was proving to be the real wrench in the gears: the one that prevented demons from making contact with the book.

That defensive measure meant that Stefan was unable to entrust the tome to his demonic porter, because the spirit couldn't touch it to take on the burden. It also precluded the possibility of having a spirit carry the book to Adair. Had there been a working mirror portal large enough, Stefan could have come home carrying the book himself, but an exhaustive search of eastern Europe confirmed what Adair had already known: Kein had tracked down and destroyed all the man-sized enchanted mirrors in that region of Europe.

That had left only the hand mirrors, but they were far too small for the massive grimoire to fit through. At best they could accommodate something the size of a pack of cigarettes, or maybe the magazine of an automatic pistol, but nothing larger.

And so the Midnight Front had found itself at an impasse.

It was too dangerous for Stefan to linger in enemy territory with the Codex, but it was even more dangerous for him to try to travel with it. As a consequence he had spent weeks in hiding, surrounded by ever-growing circles of magickal defense and wards against scrying and divination. Meanwhile, Adair had sequestered himself inside Eilean Donan's library, where he had plumbed all his dustiest books of magick in the hope of finding a solution.

Six days later Adair had emerged with a plan scribbled on sheets of foolscap that he passed through a hand mirror to Stefan, who had perused them and pronounced the plan "mad." In the absence of a better idea, however, he had consented to give it his best effort.

Now Stefan stood alone on his side of the mirror, with the Iron Codex in his hands. Cade and Anja stood on either side of Adair in the castle's conjuring room, watching Stefan through the master's hand mirror, waiting to see what would happen next.

"If this works," Stefan said, *"I should be able to pass the book to you. If this fails, I suspect you will bear witness to my most horrible and painful demise."*

"I knew I should've brought the camera," Cade said.

"Enough jabber," the master said. "Get on with it."

The Dutchman pressed his hands on either side of the Codex—and it shrank, as if he were compressing it like soft dough. When he had squashed it down to the size of a deck of playing cards, he pushed it through the mirror. *"Hold it with both hands, Master."*

Adair pulled it through with just his thumb and forefinger, then studied it with a queer look. "But it's light as a feather."

"That will change." Stefan snapped his fingers, and instantly the book was its full size again. It fell from the master's hand and landed with a loud thump on his foot. Adair fumbled the hand mirror, but Cade caught it as the master hollered curses and hopped on his good foot.

Stefan shrugged. *"I told him to use both hands."*

Cade suppressed the urge to laugh, since he knew it would only draw the master's ire. Instead he told Stefan, "Nice work. What spirit did you yoke for it?"

"TAQLATH," Stefan said. *"From the Arabic text."*

"Good choice." Cade picked up a flask of whisky he had brought along for Stefan. It barely fit through the mirror to him. "To take the edge off."

"Too kind." A distant sound turned Stefan's head. His next words were whispered. *"I must go. Good luck with the Codex.* Velarium!"

His image vanished from the mirror. Cade saw that Adair had himself under control, so he handed the master the mirror. "One mission accomplished. Was it worth it?"

"I should bloody well say so. If Kein had got this—"

"I know: fire and brimstone, French and English living together, total chaos. Let me ask you: If the Codex is so important, why'd you risk loaning it out in the first place?"

The query drew a withering glare from the master. "Because I'm not a fortune-teller, am I? When I let the mystics take the book, I didn't know they'd get caught up in the bloody war."

His answer perplexed Anja. "How long ago did you loan them the Codex?"

"Fifteen years, give or take."

Cade thought he'd misheard. "Fifteen years?"

"Magickal research takes time. Done wrong, it can cost lives. So you do it slow." Adair picked up the Codex from the floor—and grunted from the effort. "Though if I'd known what was coming, I might've asked the scholars to come do their work here."

Cade led Adair and Anja upstairs. "So now that we have it back, what do we do with it?"

"Pray to God we never need to use it."

For months Briet had watched from the shadows, noting the brown-skinned man's every action. Twice he had come close to uncovering the location of her coven in Paris. To protect her adepts and preserve the coven's secrecy, Briet had been forced to move their lair twice in the past six months. Now that their final, permanent lair was nearly finished, she was determined never to move it again. *If he finds us now, I'll just have to kill him—whether Kein approves or not.*

YOU ARE SWORN TO OBEY YOUR MASTER.

KUSHIEL's brazen mental intrusion rankled her. *Be silent or know my wrath.*

Tracking her foe this evening had taken Briet all over the city. It amused her that the City of Light sported so many dark corners, and that the enemy karcist—who was called Niko by his associates and accomplices—seemed to be familiar with all of them.

This evening his wanderings had taken him from Montmartre to the tony boulevards of the Élysée, the storied lanes of the Marais, and a row of brownstones on Rue Cassini in Montparnasse. All his stops had been at places he had visited before. Most were rear entrances to buildings that looked abandoned, doors that led to basements and underground lairs the Resistance had established in the Catacombs, Paris's labyrinth of ossuary tunnels.

When Niko ventured into such places, Briet preferred to keep her distance and monitor him through the eyes of Trixim, her black rat familiar. It took extra effort to filter her perceptions through the gifts of DESMOS, but it was worth it to be spared the stink of rivers of human excrement when Niko detoured through the city's sewers.

Tracking him was tedious work. It ate up night after night of Briet's time, filling her with resentment. *I would much rather spend my evenings entwined with Victor and Sandrine than—*

Niko emerged from his latest meeting—most of which had been devoted to the mundane details of smuggling and sabotage by the Resistance—and breezed out of the alley, then down a side street, apparently unaware that Trixim dogged his every step.

Rendered invisible by SITHIROS, Briet masked her steps with silence and got ahead of Niko, then darted into an alley. After he passed by she emerged, scooped up Trixim, tucked the rat inside her trench coat, and followed Niko at a discreet distance.

It was dangerous to get too close to him. She had learned to sniff out the presence of demons not yoked to her control, so it was possible Niko had, as well. Kein had stressed to her how important it was that she not lead Niko to the Paris coven's lair, or reveal to him that he was being tracked, because he was their only lead to Adair and his other adepts.

Each week it seemed another Thule coven was slaughtered, yet Kein counseled patience. Briet was sick of waiting. She wanted to strike.

THE MASTER HAS A PLAN FOR THAT ONE.

Kein keeps his plans to himself—as you should do with your thoughts.

Being clearheaded enough to not give herself away while tailing a trained spy and karcist like Niko meant staying sober more often than she liked. Life was easier when she could blunt her demons' edges with wine or liquor. On nights such as this, she had to wage two battles at once: one in the material world, against a foe whose attention she couldn't afford, and the other inside her own mind, versus enemies whose attention she couldn't escape.

Niko did all he could to force Briet to reveal her presence: doubling back, detouring into dead ends, and resorting to invisibility charms that required her to employ the Sight to track him as he passed over the Pont Royal into Saint-Germain on his way north.

She followed him to Montmartre, expecting him to disappear inside his warded apartment building, whose walls and foundation Trixim had been unable to breach. Instead, he stopped at the Café Étoiles, knocked in a stuttered pattern on its window, and slipped inside as someone shut the papered-over front door behind him.

Briet approached the restaurant. She worried its occupants might have posted a lookout to keep watch over Rue des Cloys, but when she reached its façade she saw no one at the window. She edged closer. Voices carried from inside.

Through the brick walls and dusty glass, she felt the resistance of Niko's warding glyphs. When she tried to peer inside using the clairvoyance of VE-RAKOS, all she heard was the roar of the Inferno and the clanging of bells. The café, like the rest of the building, was warded against scrying and intrusion. That meant she couldn't send Trixim inside as her proxy, and she couldn't cross its threshold while she held yoked spirits.

More primitive methods are in order, then.

She drew her Luger semiautomatic, fired four shots through the café's window, and reveled in the music of shattering glass and panicked cries from beyond its drawn curtains. Then she strolled around the nearest corner and waited, secure in the protection of her invisibility.

The café's front door swung open. Three men raced out: Niko and two Frenchmen—one a pudgy gent of middling years, the other a hulking specimen of Gallic peasant stock. The big man toted a shotgun, while Niko and the older fellow brandished revolvers. They searched for their harasser only to find the street deserted and silent. They lowered their weapons, apparently satisfied the threat had passed.

Briet was disappointed. Exposing a handful of Maquis did not interest her. Then she noted the woman who emerged from the café and went straight to Niko: a young, pretty thing who shared his Mediterranean ancestry—tawny brown skin, sable hair, dark eyes. Who was she to Niko? A lover? A wife? The look in the woman's eyes suggested the two shared a bond of affection. But of what nature?

The huge Frenchman pulled the woman away from Niko, and Briet had her answer. Such casual thuggery, and the woman's acquiescence, was a scenario she recognized from her own youth in Reykjavík: only a husband would dare to treat a woman that way, like property, as if she were no better than a piece of cattle. Just as familiar to Briet was the rage in Niko's eyes as he stood by, powerless to intervene.

She's his sister.

Armed with new information, Briet hurried south out of Montmartre. After she put a few blocks between herself and the Café Étoiles, she filled her open palm with the fire of PYRGOS and invoked her master's attention. *"Exaudi. Exaudi. Exaudi."*

Kein's eyes shone through the flames. *"Ave, my dear. What news?"*

"Niko has a sister, here in Paris."

"Interesting. Is she dear to him?"

"Quite."

"Good." Behind the fire, a diabolical smirk. *"You've done well, Briet. Now it's time to force our enemies into the open—and finish them, once and for all."*

MAY

All had been quiet in Montmartre when Niko left his sister's building to make his nightly rounds of check-ins, strategy meetings, and surveillance. There had been no sign of anyone following him, no indication that anything was amiss. It was as if the Nazis had gone on holiday.

Nine minutes after four o'clock in the morning, he turned left onto Rue des Cloys and stopped in midstride, petrified by the scene unfolding less than two blocks ahead of him. A company of Wehrmacht and a platoon of Waffen-SS crowded the street outside the Café Étoiles. A troop transport modified to hold prisoners idled in front of Camille's building. Exhaust fumes lingered and mixed with cigarette smoke exhaled by the Germans watching over the street.

How did they find us? Did someone talk? Is there—

A pair of SS men dragged Camille from the building. She was barefoot, clad only in her nightgown, her hair a mess. She cursed and spat at the Germans, who laughed at her. Next came Ferrand, his hands bound behind him, one soldier on each side dragging him forward while a third kept a pistol jammed between Ferrand's shoulder blades.

A German sentry looked in Niko's direction. Niko turned himself to vapor and rode the wind, unseen and unheard. A gust carried him closer to the commotion outside the café.

An SS officer caressed Camille's face. He met her scowl with perverse curiosity. "*Jude? Afrikanischer?*" He lifted her negligee and thrust his hand between her legs. "*Mischlingshure!*"

Ferrand broke free of his handlers. His hands were tied behind his back, but he slammed his forehead into the SS officer's face, crushing the man's nose. The *Obersturmführer* crumpled to the ground. Roaring with anger, Ferrand lifted his foot to stomp the German's head.

A gunshot echoed as Ferrand's head shattered, painting the street and the fallen SS man with blood and brains. Camille fell atop her husband's corpse and screamed in anguish, while the *Obersturmführer* shouted at his men for soiling his uniform. For a minute it seemed everyone in the street was yelling at someone, until a woman's voice cut through it all, barking orders with clarity and fury: it was Briet.

She who'd cut Michel's throat at the Gare de Lyon, she who Niko had come to suspect was protecting the Paris chapter of the Thule Society. She was here, and the SS officer's reaction to her upbraiding made it clear she was in charge. On her orders, the Nazis threw Camille in the rear of the truck with the other prisoners. The Germans piled into their vehicles and drove off, leaving Ferrand's half-headed body lying in the street.

Sick with guilt, Niko cast off his charm and solidified next to his slain brother-in-law. He fell to his knees beside the man, overwrought. He'd disliked Ferrand; they had not been friends. But Ferrand had been Niko's ally, his host, and his kin. Now the man was dead, gunned down like an animal and left to rot. And Niko was certain it was because Briet had come looking for him. *She must have tracked me here. Now she has Camille, and I need to get her back.*

He had no way of following the convoy that had taken his sister, but that was of no consequence. He already knew where they would take her.

She was on her way to the Drancy prison camp.

※

"Mon Dieu! *You must be joking! We cannot just leave her in Drancy!*"

Adair crossed his arms and, through the conjuring room's enchanted mirror, fixed his hotheaded adept with a glum scowl. "What would you have us do, Niko? Storm the gates with wands blazing? Drancy's locked up tighter than a nervous virgin. Those walls might as well be guarded by SATAN itself."

His admonition fell upon unreceptive ears. *"We don't need magick to get her out. A bribe could do it. Demons used to fetch lost treasures. Why can't we do that? Pay off the guards?"*

"First," Adair said, vexed at having to explain what Niko should damned well already have known, "any treasure worth finding was dredged up long before I was born. Most of the world's wealth is locked away in vaults under the Vatican, the banks of Switzerland, or Fort fucking Knox. And you'd best believe they're all guarded by magick more than strong enough to rip the bones from your back if you so much as look at 'em.

"Second, even if you dig up some lost fortune and put it in the hands of the guards at Drancy, how do you know they'd keep their word? I bet you they're all scared shiteless of Kein and his ginger witch. Even the ones who don't know what she is probably know she's not one to be fucked with. And if she went to all that trouble to ward Drancy, don't you think she'd be smart enough to put charms of protection on its fucking guards? I know I would."

Niko seemed possessed by a spirit of denial. "Merde! *I cannot just give up! She is all that remains of my family! I will not stand by and let the Nazis dispose of her like garbage!*"

Cade chimed in from the stairs behind Adair, "He's right."

Adair glowered at Cade and at Anja, who stood by Cade's side. The master knew they had been eavesdropping from upstairs, but their interruption came as a surprise. "*Et tu,* lad?"

A look of disbelief. "You want Niko to sacrifice his only kin, but you expect me to feel like the bad guy? Try again." He and Anja left the stairs to stand with Adair in front of the mirror. "With our help, he could be in and out before the Nazis know what hit them. Bring in Stefan and we'll mop the floor with these chumps."

"Oh, it's that easy, is it?" It was hard for Adair not to get upset, and easy for him to forget that in spite of their talents for magick, they were all young and foolish. "Has it occurred to you that maybe—*just fucking maybe*—that's *exactly* what the enemy wants? That maybe the reason Niko's sister got grabbed was to goad us into doing something stupid?"

Niko's face creased with anger. "*Possible?* Mais oui. *But just as possible— she was taken because she was a Maquis. Because she was a leader in the Resistance. Or because she was in the wrong place at the wrong time. Or had skin the wrong color!*"

It was like debating a bull whose mind was already set upon the charge. Still, it was Adair's role to teach and counsel, then hope his adepts listened. "Lad, I've made up my mind. I can't risk you, the Resistance, and the entire fucking war effort, all to save one woman, no matter who she might be to you. The answer's no."

Seething, Niko resorted to grumbling. "Va te faire enculer!" Then he snapped, "Velarium!" Instantly, his image vanished from the mirror, leaving Adair looking at the reflection of his careworn features and of Cade's and Anja's frowns of disapproval.

"Don't you two start. I'm in no fucking mood."

A strange silent accord manifested between Cade and Anja. Then, without a word she turned away and climbed the stairs, leaving Adair alone with Cade. For the first time since Adair had met him, the young man regarded him with disappointment. "You talk a good game. I'll give you that much. When you want us to charge into the belly of the beast, you talk about duty, and honor, and loyalty. But when one of us needs something—"

"Are you under the delusion that I owe you something? *Any* of you? Without me, you'd all be *nothing*. Just bits of bone in the meal, getting ground up by the gears of war. But I sought you out, took you in, taught you secrets only a handful of human beings have ever seen. I filled your hands with power, and *this* is how you thank me?"

His attempt to change the subject didn't fool Cade. "You didn't give me anything I couldn't have taken for myself. All you did was show me that it was there to be seized." He stepped closer, unafraid of confronting his master nose-to-nose. "What's the point of having power if we're too fucking scared to use it?"

"The *point* is to use it *wisely*."

"Saving innocent lives isn't a wise use of power?"

"What I'm trying to tell you is that power like ours shouldn't be used carelessly, not with so much at stake. It's not that I don't feel pity for the souls this war chews up. And trust me, there are millions of them. It's that I don't have the luxury of feeling sorry for them. And if I might speak frankly? *Neither do you*."

Cade was adamant. "But this is his *sister* we're talking about! This has to be the exception to the rule."

"No, it doesn't. Because I absolutely guarantee you that *this*—" He pointed at the mirror. "Is a fucking *trap*."

24

JUNE

Through the window of Kein's study came a breath of summer, but from the flames in his black marble fireplace surged Briet's torrent of invective. *"It's been over a month and they haven't even tried to contact the girl, never mind rescue her!"*

"As I feared. Adair is no fool. And his apprentices are young, but they are also loyal."

His reproach stoked Briet's determination. *"You didn't see Niko and his sister. He loves her. I don't care how much loyalty Adair commands—he can't trump family."*

"We don't know that." Kein carried his glass of wine to the nearest window to escape the heat of his fireplace, and admired the rolling landscape of Wewelsburg. "All we know is that Adair seems unlikely to let his people risk themselves to rescue this woman."

Briet considered that. *"Maybe we set the bar too high. If the defenses on the complex hadn't been so robust—"*

"I doubt it would have made a difference." He took a sip of his 1865 Beaune Grèves Vigne de l'Enfant Jésus, one of the most transcendent Pinot Noirs ever bottled. Though most of mankind's so-called progress disappointed Kein, wine continued to impress him. "If strong defenses were enough to deter these people, they would never have sacked our Stuttgart coven. No, I think the problem is that we have not set a high enough price on their failure to act."

As ever, Briet was quick to take his meaning. *"They can tolerate her being imprisoned. But if she were facing imminent execution. . . ."*

"Precisely, my dear. But what will make this trap work is not her death, but ensuring that this Niko fellow knows of it *in advance*. If he is as devoted to her as you say, he will either persuade Adair to lead a rescue mission, or defy his master to stage one himself."

A nod of understanding. *"How much lead time should we give them?"*

"Today is what? The fifteenth?" He envisioned a few possible scenarios. "A prisoner train is scheduled to leave Drancy in a few days. Have one of the guards sell the news to a member of the Resistance. It should reach Niko quickly enough."

"What then?"

He enjoyed another swallow of Pinot Noir. "Then? Put his sister on the train—and make certain you are on board when he comes to her rescue."

———

It was after dark, there wasn't a soul for a kilometer in any direction, and Stefan was well hidden inside an abandoned farmhouse nestled in the trees south of the River Wisła—but still he feared someone would hear Niko's shouts through the enchanted mirror: *"I do not have time to be calm! We must act, before it is too late!"*

Stefan employed his most soothing timbre. "Yet you must be calm." He pushed past the aching of his empty stomach. "Tell me what has happened."

Niko pulled a hand over his stubbled face while he struggled for composure; he regarded Stefan with bloodshot eyes. *"One of my spies in the Drancy complex sent me a message. The Nazis are transferring a thousand prisoners out of Drancy, on tonight's train. Camille, my sister—she is on that list!"*

"Have you told Adair?"

"Of course I did! But he says the same as when the Germans took her: she is not worth saving." Grief wrinkled his features. *"He knows what she means to me. She is all I have. But still he orders me to give her up!"* He thrust his finger at Stefan, who half expected the digit to poke out of his own mirror. *"Mark my words: I will not abandon her. Not now. Not ever."*

"Yes. You must save her. But the enemy is prepared. This will be most dangerous." Stefan racked his imagination for some way he and his friend could overcome the odds against them. "What of Anja? Or Cade? They would be of great help."

"There is no way to reach them without going through Adair." Niko lifted his mirror over his shoulder, giving Stefan a view of the emaciated prisoners being forced onto a train. Just as Niko had described, the Nazis were herding droves—men, women, and children—into the railcars at gunpoint. The sight made Stefan sick as he recalled all the trains like it he had seen at Poland's concentration camps.

Niko angled his mirror toward himself. *"Over a thousand souls, mon frère. All going to some place called Auschwitz. You have heard of it?"*

The very name made Stefan want to retch. He felt his face blanch. "I have." His eyes burned with tears as he remembered the red farmhouse. A deep breath steeled his nerves and cleared his vision. He met Niko's anxious gaze with one of grim resolve. "Tell me your plan."

"A group of Maquis will help me stop the train. I—" He took a moment to choose the precise word. *"—coerced the train's route from a German officer, who then suffered an accident. My friends will sabotage the tracks a few miles outside Fleury, then keep the Germans busy while I open the railcars and free the prisoners."*

The last detail surprised Stefan. "All of them?"

"Oui. What kind of a man would I be if I save my sister but let a thousand others die?" A humble shrug. *"It also will create chaos to cover our escape."*

Stefan appreciated Niko's ethics as well as his tactics. "Most clever."

"Once she is off the train and in our truck, we will take her to a man who knows how to smuggle people into Spain."

"Sensible. What do you need of me?"

Niko's trademark optimism faded. *"You . . . are to be my insurance. If my plan fails, for whatever reason, and the train gets past us . . . I need you to get Camille out of Auschwitz."*

Stefan's courage faltered. "The camp is warded, Niko. I breached its barriers once, to get the Codex. The enemy has taken steps to ensure I cannot do so again. And you should know: Most prisoners are killed on arrival. If your sister enters Auschwitz, her chances will be slim." Reading the dejection on Niko's face, he was quick to add, "But I know their train routes. If need be, I will set my own ambush and halt the train before it reaches the camp."

"Can you get to Auschwitz ahead of the train?"

He wondered how Niko would react to the truth. "I never left."

"You've been there this entire time?"

"Since returning the Codex, yes. Watching. Trying to find a way to save those inside." Stefan hesitated to play Devil's advocate, but now he felt compelled to try. "Niko . . . the master has been correct before. And I think he is right about the train: this feels like a trap."

"It is only a trap if you do not see it coming. This is an invitation to a fight. And I plan to come ready to give them one. My only question is . . . are you with me?"

Stefan couldn't let Niko face this alone. He smiled. "Who doesn't love a good fight?"

"Merci beaucoup, mon frère." From somewhere beyond the mirror's frame, other voices whispered to Niko. He tucked his mirror out of view as he answered in a secretive hush, then returned to the conversation. *"The train departs in four hours; I need to leave so I can get ahead of it."* He leaned in closer. *"If we save her, I will contact you. But if you do not hear from me by morning, then our plan has failed, and my sister's life will be in your hands."*

"I understand. Depend on me."

A smile and a salute. *"Until we meet again."*

"See you in Spain, my brother." He closed the astral window between their mirrors with a muttered *"Velarium,"* then tucked it inside his satchel.

If Niko failed to stop the train from Drancy, it would reach Auschwitz in just under four days, assuming the Germans adhered to their notoriously rigid schedules. Stefan considered which spirits he had time to summon and yoke before that hour arrived. Most of those he could call up would be of little use, but he knew of at least three whose powers might prove decisive—assuming he could keep them under control long enough to wield them.

It was a gamble worth taking, he decided.

He unrolled his tools of the Art and set to work preparing the room for magick.

A pinpoint of light in the darkness announced the train's approach from five kilometers out. The engine's headlamp seemed to flicker as the locomotive raced through a cluster of trees in the distance. In moments it would reach the straightaway where the Maquis had set their ambush.

Niko regarded his trio of accomplices. "Gaston, trigger the charges on my order. Jules, André, get on either side of the tracks and cover me while I free the prisoners. If any Nazis show their faces after we stop the train, kill them."

All three men acknowledged his instructions, then fanned out into the night to await the train, whose approaching mass shook the ground beneath them.

It was an ideal spot for an attack—secluded, without any nearby German garrisons or Vichy sympathizers, and numerous farms where the escaped prisoners could find food and, if they were lucky, shelter.

The most difficult part of the plan would be gauging the right moment to set off the dynamite on the tracks. If Niko gave the order too soon, the train would stop shy of the cross-fire point and give any German troops on board time to retaliate; if he triggered the charges too late, he ran the risk of derailing it and killing not only the Nazis but also their prisoners, including Camille. To time the detonation, Niko had set two bullets on the tracks, spaced a hundred meters apart, with the one nearest him two kilometers away. He would measure the delay between the bullets' sparks as the train rolled over each in turn, and use that to time the detonation.

He confirmed that his revolver was still in its holster, and that his athamé was in its scabbard. Then he crouched beside the tracks and watched for the sparks to start his countdown.

Sweat teased the nape of his neck as the locomotive drew near. The first spark went off, and Niko started his silent count. Five seconds later, the second bullet sparked. After a fast round of math in his head, he estimated the train would need about one kilometer to stop to avoid derailing, which meant giving it one minute's warning.

He checked his watch. "Gaston, blow the tracks in three . . . two . . . one . . . now!"

Gaston sank the plunger on the detonator.

Nothing happened.

Niko's temper flared. "Did you check the wires?"

"Of course I did!"

"Then what—?" An icy shudder up Niko's spine and the bite of sulfur in the air told him who had cut the wires: *demons.*

He engaged the Sight, and his suspicions were confirmed. Two spirits raced in front of the train, clearing the tracks of obstacles. That meant there was at least one karcist on the transport, and a wily one at that. *As I expected—we both have come ready for a fight.*

The demons flew past Niko and his comrades, apparently deeming them insignificant. That meant the train was only seconds away from passing them, as well. *Time to improvise.*

Niko sprang to his feet and ran along the tracks as the train raced up from behind him. He shouted over its clamor, "Gaston! Get the truck! Follow me!"

His bearded ally was befuddled. "Wait! What—?"

It was too late for words. Niko had to act while he still could.

A wedge of air traveled in front of the train and pushed Niko away from the tracks as the locomotive roared past like a speeding wall of noise. Niko stumbled in the dark over uneven ground, then righted himself and sprinted onward.

If it is a fight they want, I will give it to them.

Channeling the strength of MADRIAX, which a century earlier had been the favored spirit of a British prankster known by the nickname Spring-heeled Jack, Niko leaped into the air above the train—high enough that he feared what would happen when he landed. The demon excelled at going up, but coming down was a challenge it left to others.

It was hard to see the train. Only the engine and a few forward cars had interior lighting, and those were far ahead of Niko as he fell earthward. Moonlight glinted off the metal frames of the middle railcars as they blurred past beneath him.

He struck the top of one car and tumbled backward, as if he'd had a rug pulled out from under his feet. Landing on his back knocked the breath from his lungs, and he rolled to one side until his fingers found purchase between the wooden slats of the railcar's roof.

Wind stung his eyes and whipped at his hair and clothes. Struggling for balance, he recovered his footing. Steady for a moment, he commanded AMON, a spirit of divination, *Find my sister Camille!*

Like an iron shaving drawn toward a magnet, Niko felt AMON's guidance lead him forward atop the train, onto the next car closer to the engine.

Gravity and momentum conspired against Niko. The train cars rocked through every curve and threatened to toss him over the side as the locomotive picked up speed.

He hopped over the gap between cars and scurried forward. All he cared about was finding Camille as quickly as possible. With each step he bellowed her name over the roaring wind and the clattering of steel wheels.

"Camille! Do you hear me? Camille! It's Niko! Camille!"

He heard her voice issue from the railcar beneath him: "Here! Niko!"

He kneeled and peered through a gap between roof slats. He saw her huddled in the shadowy throng of prisoners. "Camille! Hang on, I'm going to get—"

She shouted something, but the train's steam whistle drowned her out. When it ceased, she hollered again, "Niko! It's a trap!"

At the front of the train, movement. Niko stood to confront a foe whose face he had come to know all too well: Briet.

She stood with her feet wide apart. Ribbons of dark vapor shrouded her right hand; licks of violet flame swirled in her left. "So predictable."

"Yes, you are." Niko charged, hurling ghostly daggers and green lightning.

She ran at him, unleashing fire and poisonous smoke, her strides as sure as if she were on solid ground instead of atop a swaying railcar.

Fireballs slammed into Niko's shield. He deflected them, then dodged her cloud of poison, which scattered in the wind. He tuned his shield to leach power from her next fiery assault to feed his counterstrike—a crack of BANOG's barbed whip.

She parried the spectral whip; then an invisible force swept Niko's legs and slammed him onto his back. He bent his shield around himself to buy time to regain his feet, and as he did he used BARATO's talents to unlock the doors of the railcars.

Briet leaped onto the same railcar as Niko and hurled lightning at him. He reflected it toward her. The bolts slammed into her shield and knocked her backward, onto the railcar behind her. Niko used the many hands of ALASTOR to open all the railcars' doors.

Camille is almost free! I just have to stop the train.

Briet charged again. Niko drew his revolver.

A snap of her burning whip broke his hand and knocked away his pistol.

He lashed out with the fist of ALASTOR, hoping to swat her off the train, but she blocked it. He tried to sense a weakness in her mind, one he could attack with mind control—

A phantasmal spear ripped into Niko's thigh, and a flurry of needles left his face burning, as if wasps had swarmed him. Briet's fiery whip lashed his chest, and a barrage of lightning broke through his shield and left his limbs quaking and his tongue tasting of tin.

Briet was on him. She seized his throat with her right hand and forced him to his knees. "Niko! You've no idea how much I've looked forward to this."

"That makes one of us," he choked out.

With a wave of her left hand, she closed all the railcars' doors; a turn of her wrist locked them. She reached down, plucked the enchanted mirror from Niko's coat pocket, and held it up like a prize. "Lead me to your master and his adept Cade, and I will set you and Camille free."

Niko felt his strength ebb. He couldn't muster any more magick. His yoked spirits felt his weakness and broke away, retreating to the abyss and leaving him to his fate.

Briet waved the mirror at him. "Tell me!"

Niko thrust his left hand upward to pinch the mirror's edge. "*Discutio!*"

The looking glass shattered, peppering the right half of Briet's face with burning-hot motes. She let go of Niko, then swatted him away with a titan's strength.

Half blind and racked with pain, Niko twisted through the night, soaring, then sinking into free fall. Then came the impact, hard and unforgiving.

Stone and wood rent flesh and broke bones, snapped teeth and crushed gums. The world around Niko was black, his world was reduced to bloodred bursts of pain.

An end to the rolling, to the confusion. He came to a halt surrounded by a scattering of split logs and large stones, and he realized he had crashed through a rock wall and a stack of firewood. It was agony to lift his head, but he needed to see the train with his own bloodied eyes. It chugged away without him, continuing its journey to Auschwitz with his sister locked inside and his nemesis on top of it, sorely wounded but still alive.

His soul wanted to continue the chase, but his flesh was beaten. Jagged ends of broken bones protruded from one arm and leg; each breath he took reminded him of his cracked ribs.

He would have wept, but his voice was lost, along with the battle.

Camille . . . I have failed you. Forgive me. . . .

The train disappeared into the night. From somewhere behind it came the buzzing of motorcycles and the hoarse growl of a truck's engine. By the time Gaston and the others found Niko, he was too weak to move or talk—not that it mattered anymore. Without the mirror, he had no way to warn Stefan the train was too well defended for him to face alone.

I should have listened to you, my friend. I should have listened. . . .

His allies carted him away. Gaston pleaded in hoarse shouts for someone to summon a doctor. Niko wished he could ask his friends to leave him where he lay. What was the point of saving his life now? They were too late.

His sister was gone.

25

Four days without word from Niko. Attempts to reach him using the mirror had failed. Stefan had considered hailing Adair to seek his counsel, but he knew what the master would say: that Niko should never have attempted a rescue, that Stefan should have told Adair sooner, and that he should abandon this foolish crusade and learn to see "the big picture."

I have seen enough of "the big picture." Memories of Chełmno and Dachau, of Bergen-Belsen and of Auschwitz, haunted Stefan whenever he closed his eyes. If this was the wider world of which Adair spoke, no further reminders did Stefan need. It was time to fight back.

Yet common sense nagged at him. There had been no word from Niko. That suggested his bid to halt the train had failed. Stefan knew from experience that Niko was a strong and clever karcist. If he had been neutralized trying to save the prisoners from Drancy, it was likely the arrest and deportation of his sister had been part of a trap, as they'd suspected. If so, the most rational course of action for Stefan was to retreat, to preserve his cover and await new orders.

The very notion churned bile into Stefan's throat. *No. I have run for too long. Witnessed horrors and done nothing. I will not stand by and watch the Nazis deliver another thousand lives to that abattoir. Live or die, it is time to stand and be counted.*

Behind his courage, he hoped he was wrong. He prayed Niko had already stopped the train, freed its prisoners, and simply had been unable to contact him. If the train did not round the bend in the track within the next hour, Stefan promised himself, he would consider its passengers liberated, and he would slip into—

A light pierced the darkness. The Drancy train was coming.

Stefan was in no mood for subterfuge. In his mind the train was more than a machine, more than a simple conveyance. It was an engine of evil, a force unto itself, a cursed vessel bearing innocent souls toward a Hell made by human hands.

He had come ready to meet its power in equal measure.

It was half a mile away. Stefan stepped between the tracks and walked toward it, his mien proud, fearless, and vengeful. He raised his right hand, and it was ringed by a white halo as he reached out with the unyielding might of SATOR and forced the train to stop.

The engine's pistons screamed in protest, and the steel wheels whined as they scraped across the rails. The iron behemoth ground to a stop mere feet in front of Stefan. Clouds of vapor jetted from vents on either side of the train.

Stefan stood bathed in the light of the train's headlamp.

On either side of the engine, Waffen-SS troops disembarked and charged toward Stefan, their submachine guns ready for action. He could have put them all to sleep with the breath of RAGORAS, but he felt no inclination to show mercy. The men on his left he cut down with a saw-toothed blade of VESCAEL; the squad on his right he slew with forked lightning before any of them had time to shout a threat or pull a trigger.

All was quiet. Then three figures climbed down from the train's first passenger car and walked toward Stefan. Their manner was calm, their pace unrushed. In the center was a man Stefan had heard described many times by Adair—the Nazis' master Black magician, Kein Engel. He wore a suit that filled Stefan with envy.

On Kein's right walked Briet in a dark trench coat; Stefan recognized her from Niko's wall of photos, though the pitted scar that marred the right side of her face was a new detail. On the dark magician's left was Siegmar, the cruel-faced man Stefan had faced at Babi Yar.

Kein moved ahead of his adepts and stopped several meters from Stefan. "Hello, my young friend. You—"

"I am not your friend," Stefan cut in.

"As you prefer. I take it you are one of Adair's pupils. I trust you know who I am."

"The Devil's agent on earth."

The man seemed almost modest. "You give me far too much credit." He made small gestures toward his adepts as he continued. "These are my adepts. Briet Segfrunsdóttir. And I believe you've already made the acquaintance of Siegmar Tuomainen."

Stefan watched their eyes and hands as he prepared his own magickal arsenal.

Kein assessed the standoff with sad resignation. "Must it always come to this? Transparent deceptions and a futile struggle?"

Stefan threw down the proverbial gauntlet: "It will not be futile as long as I take one of you with me to the grave."

Smoke and lightning filled the air; the world became a blur of blood and fire. Ghostly weapons clashed and cut flesh. Stefan deflected one of Kein's own fireballs into Siegmar, snared Briet in a spiral of steel track that he bent like soldering wire, and nearly fooled himself into believing he might achieve a Pyrrhic victory—

Then an icy stab of pain scattered Stefan's thoughts, and his yoked spirits started to desert him, vermin fleeing his fast-sinking mortal vessel.

He fell to his knees and looked down. A semitransparent spear jutted from his abdomen. It dissolved into mist as a burning whip snapped around his throat. Invisible forces seized his wrists and pinned his hands behind him.

Briet and Kein were bloodied but unbowed. Siegmar remained on his knees while he slap-extinguished patches of fire on his scorched clothes.

Briet searched Stefan's pockets. Blood ran down her forehead; smoke rose off her back. Empty-handed, she faced her master. "He doesn't have a mirror like Niko's."

"Oh, I am sure he does. I think he has learned to hide it better, is all." A shrug. "No matter. He will surrender it soon enough—along with the location of Adair and his adepts."

Stefan spat at Kein. "I will tell you nothing."

"Not all at once—and not without a fight, I am sure." With a small motion of his hand, he levitated Stefan from the ground. "Even mountains succumb to the elements. It is merely a question of pressure, and time." He moved Stefan clear of the tracks; then with balletic gestures he straightened the piece of track Stefan had bent and fused it back into place, as good as new.

Kein motioned for the train's conductor to roll on toward Auschwitz. Then he towed Stefan toward a conjured column of fire, with his wounded minions limping close behind. "Let us repair to someplace more private, shall we? We have much to discuss."

~~~

Waves of pain, cold fear, stutters of color and sound—Stefan reeled from the sensory overload of Kein's torture by magick. More precise than blunt force or the cruel cuts of steel, more insidious than drugs, it plumbed the darkest recesses of Stefan's thoughts and stirred all his long-buried terrors into the light.

Sunlight blinded him. He was alone on a barren plain, a child crying for his mother.

Thunder crashed; the sky turned black. On hands and knees, Stefan was old and broken, pawing at the freshly turned earth of an open grave that he knew in his soul was his own.

Cymbals crashed, and a thought-piercing shriek of noise ripped through his brain. Then came a cool kiss of air against his spleen, his liver, his intestines. He was flayed and restrained, his body an open book on a steel table. To his dismay, his gutted state was no demonic illusion, no lie—it was his reality.

Kein looked and sounded profoundly sad. "Herr Van Ausdall, have you not had enough of this? In spite of what your master told you, I take no joy in hurting you. My methods are cruel, but only because you force them to be so." He pressed a cool, damp cloth to Stefan's cheek. Wiped the blood and spittle from Stefan's chin. Refolded the cloth, then used it to mop the perspiration from Stefan's feverish brow. "The mirror my adept found in your possessions— how do we activate it? And please do not try to trick me into saying '*discutio.*' Your comrade Niko has already shown us what that word does."

Desperation made Stefan want to confess. His body was weak, full of pain, sick to its core. The prospect of another bout of demonic torment clouded his mind with panic. Then he remembered his master's parting words about the mirrors: *Do not let the enemy capture them. And never tell anyone the control words. Unlocked and plumbed with the right charm, one of these could let Kein spy my every move.*

It took all Stefan had left to mutter, "Kill me."

Kein looked at Briet and Siegmar. Each of them stood inside a circle of protection. She poured a tipple of brandy into the smoking brazier at her feet; he dribbled camphor into the smoldering brass pot in front of his. Clouds of vapor climbed toward the ceiling and merged into a swirling mass that assumed the shape of something monstrous.

Stefan looked down. Traced the lines inside the grand circle that encompassed them all. He saw that Kein was inside the operator's circle, his sword balanced atop his white-shod feet. The convergence of other lines in the room confirmed Stefan's worst fear: he was in the open, exposed to the conjured spirits under Kein's control.

Kein asked, "Shall we continue?"

"Please. . . ."

"You wish to stop?"

To beg for mercy was to condemn his master and friends to death. But Stefan knew the horrors demons could inflict, the tortures they could impose. Not just violations of the flesh but torments of the mind. Undefended as he was, he would be chum for a demonic feeding frenzy. A swift death would be out of the question: a plaything for spirits, he would be reduced to a broken vessel, a conduit for transient terrors until his body rotted around the husk of his intellect.

If only I still had a spirit yoked. Any of them would do. I could make one kill me, snap my neck and set me free. But I'm alone—and Kein will never let me go so easily. He will prolong this for as long as it takes to break me. Tears of shame and defeat rolled from his eyes. *I can't fight him forever. How much longer can I resist?*

Kein leaned close to Stefan. The dark master's whisper caressed Stefan's cheek. "You know what the Fallen are capable of, Herr Van Ausdall. They can boil your eyes in their sockets. Break all your bones, knit them back together, then shatter them again. Tie your guts into knots that would turn a sailor green with envy. Must we go down that road?"

All Stefan wanted was vengeance, but it was beyond his reach. Tears of rage and despair spilled down his cheeks; a hacking sob racked his chest. He shook his head. "No."

"Tell me how to use the mirror."

"I can describe his defenses. Eilean Donan is vulnerable."

"I need to see its wards for myself. You understand, yes?"

A frantic nod. "Yes."

"The mirror. How do I unlock it?"

"To open it, *fenestra*. To close it, *velarium*."

"How do I focus it?"

"Attune it to another of its kind . . . by saying the owner's name."

"Splendid." From beneath his robes, Kein produced Stefan's mirror. He held it at his eye level, concentrated a moment, then pronounced in a clear voice, "*Fenestra Adair, occulta speculis.*" He smiled at whatever he saw. "Good. Very good."

Stefan was spent, shattered, beyond resistance. "Kill me."

Kein waggled an index finger. "Not yet." The dark master banished his demons and opened the circle.

Briet and Siegmar carried Stefan to a cot in the corner of the conjuring room. Up close, Stefan noticed that the wounds he had seen on Briet's face had almost entirely healed.

No doubt at my expense, he realized.

The two adepts tended Stefan's wounds, bound his wrists, then left him to rest. It seemed as if his tortures had come to an end, but he knew better. This fight was far from over.

Kein's revenge had only just begun.

It was alarming to watch how quickly Cade learned magick. Anja had never seen anything like it, in all the years she had lived with and studied under Adair. None of his other adepts had taken to magick like this; not the ones who had come before her—a select group that had included only Stefan, Niko, and a few others—or any of the hundred recruited after the Nazis invaded Poland.

She sat across from Cade at a long table in the library. He had piled the main table high with old grimoires and codices scribed in languages Anja had never seen before. Several lay open between them, and he pointed from one to the next as he gushed with excitement over his latest discoveries.

"And here, in the Sumerian Book of the Damned, there's a binding spell that lets you yoke not just a demon but all the others who answer to it. Picture it: We could yoke one of the lesser dukes and command its legion of spirits against other demons. Why take one power when you can wield an army?"

The markings on the calfskin pages were unintelligible to Anja. "How can you read that? LIOBOR said it would grant me any tongue I desired, but even it cannot translate this."

"These aren't human writings, this is proto-Enochian script—the alphabet the angels used *before* the Fall. Among the many things the host of Hell gave up when they rebelled, one was the ability to read this. For them, looking at this is like rubbing lye in their eyes."

"So how can *you* read it without their help?"

A boyish smile and a look of mischief. "Truth? No idea." He traced a line of angelic text with one fingertip. "Yoking all of a duke's legions would hurt worse than anything we've ever tried, but we're still outnumbered by the Thule Society, and the ones that are left are getting stronger by the day. We need a way to even the odds."

He was right, but his ambition troubled her. "When I was younger, Adair told me stories. He said Kein saw power in old magick, did things no one else dared. It made him strong, but it also drove him mad. Are you sure you can handle that many demons at once?"

He met her caution with a foolhardy smile. "I guess we'll find out." He snatched up a quill and scribbled notes on a scrap of paper. "I don't know where we'll find half this stuff, but I didn't ask why Adair had a jar labeled 'nails from a child's coffin,' either. If he—"

A thunderclap blasted in the windows.

Shattered glass and splintered wood tore into Cade and Anja as the blast threw them across the library with tables, chairs, and dozens of books.

Anja tucked her arms to her face, but shards of glass scoured the nape of her neck and shredded her clothes. Stony shrapnel ravaged her flank as she landed on the floor. When she looked up, Cade was lying next to her, his hand pressed to the right side of his head. Blood ran from under his palm and down his neck. His arms and hands were bleeding, too.

She clutched his shoulder. "Are you all right?"

He nodded, his breaths quick and ragged. "What hit us?"

Anja darted to the blown-apart window. Below in the courtyard stood a trio. Kein, the master's smartly attired nemesis, she recognized from Stuttgart. With him were a copper-haired woman in her twenties and a dark-haired man in his thirties: Briet and Siegmar.

On the ground at their feet twitched a bloody tangle of black feathers, fragile bones, and spattered blood that had been Kutcha, the master's familiar.

How did they know we were here? How did they get past Adair's defenses? Did the master hear them arrive? She faced Cade. "Kein is here. With his adepts."

Cade was on his feet. His hand fell from his bloodied ear. "Let's go."

Reason told her to urge caution, but he was already halfway out of the library, heading for the stairs, charging into the fray. Without protest, she ran after him.

Demons accosted them on the stairs. He dispelled two with a wave of his hand, banished another with a barked Latin curse. She fended off a pair that attacked from behind, then exorcised another as it reached up through the floor in a mad grab at Cade's feet.

A legion of spirits harassed them all the way down to the courtyard, and at every step she and Cade cast more of the nameless fiends back into the Pit with words that were ancient when the world was young. Deadly to laymen, the demons were but pests to prepared karcists, obstacles to wear down their strength and resolve. All they did for Anja was whet her appetite.

Cade blasted open the door to the courtyard. He and Anja ran outside to face the invaders.

On the far side of the courtyard, the keep's ground-level door flew open and Adair strode out, his countenance grave. He taunted Kein. "Come to fall on your sword?"

"Hardly." The German cocked one eyebrow. "I must say, old friend—you and yours are looking quite the worse for wear. One might think you found the practice of the Art taxing."

There was a cutting truth in his observation. Kein and his adepts were portraits of perfection. Every detail of their appearance—from their hair and complexions, to their shoes and sartorial elegance—expressed pride and power. By comparison, Adair, Anja, and Cade all looked as if they had been dragged through fields of blood and barbed wire. Scorched and scarred, with beards and eyebrows ripped ragged by compulsive hair-pulling, their complexions sallow from months of sleep deprivation and substance abuse, they were a sorry excuse for . . . well, *anything*.

Murderous silence filled the courtyard.

Then came bedlam.

Fire and lightning, blasts of light in every color Anja could imagine, roars of fire and monsters. Spectral missiles and ghostly blades. Invisible fists and storms of sharpness.

A demon threw Anja against a stone wall. She bounded off of it and hit the ground hard. She sprang to her feet and resumed her attack, cracking VALE-FOR's whip and filling the courtyard with hellfire, but none of it could touch Kein or his adepts. She hurled a sweep of demonic arrows at the dark master, but he swatted them away like flies. Siegmar squelched her flames with a jet of water from his wide-open mouth.

Kein and Adair volleyed barrages of raw energy that prickled Anja's skin into gooseflesh. An electric tingle filled the air as the masters traded salvos—

Then Briet—who had vanished while Anja was distracted—reappeared behind Cade. Before Anja could shout a warning, the ginger witch slapped her palms against the sides of Cade's head. He twitched and went limp in her grasp.

Siegmar barked a word, and in gouts of fire he vanished with Briet and Cade.

Anja had no time for regret—Kein harried her and Adair with a cascade of lightning and a lion-dragon chimera that belched a cloud of biting insects, an assault that forced them to their knees in defensive postures, huddled behind overwhelmed shields.

When the attack ceased, the dark magician was gone.

A stench of sulfur and burnt wool filled the air.

Every part of Anja hurt. Her joints ached, her muscles burned, her skin felt as if it had been gnawed by a billion fangs. Nausea swirled in her gut and left her desperate to retch and empty herself of poisons real or imagined. Her strength ebbed and she fell to her knees, her face burning as much from the enemy's assault as from the shame of defeat.

All she wanted was to collapse, fall apart, and hide.

A hand seized her biceps and pulled her into motion.

Adair's voice was gruff. "Up."

Staggering in his grasp as they raced inside the southwest building, Anja realized rest was the last thing on the master's mind. "Where are we going?"

"To strike back." He shouldered through the door that led to the conjuring room in the basement. They stumbled downstairs.

"How did they find us? How did they get in?"

"Don't know. Doesn't matter."

He pulled her away from the stairs to the middle of the room. "Stand here. Don't move." He walked a few paces more, then took from his pocket a large pearl and lifted it over his head. "*Eripe me Angeli Dómini a malo!*" He smashed the pearl on the stone floor.

It erupted in a flash that forced Anja to shut her eyes. When she opened them, an eldritch fog rolled around her and Adair. They both had been changed—they were attired in their ceremonial robes. Around their feet, circles of magickal protection had appeared. Beyond them had been described a thaumaturgic triangle inside a grand double circle, but the glyphs and symbols that populated its spaces were ones Anja had never seen before. A gleaming golden sword was balanced on Adair's feet, and the Iron Codex sat upon his lectern.

"Stay still," he cautioned. "Don't speak. I'm going to yoke spirits to you like you've never felt. It'll burn in ways that words don't do justice. But it has to be done."

For the first time in years, Anja was afraid. "Master? I do not recognize these symbols. What demon are you conjuring?"

He looked over his shoulder at her. "Demons won't cut it if we want to see

Cade alive again." He opened the Iron Codex. "You might want to close your eyes."

She did as he said. His voice filled the conjuring room with words unlike any she had ever heard. Then came a light so powerful that even with her eyes shut Anja knew it could not have been spawned in Hell. Somehow, Adair was doing what all the scriptures and grimoires ever written had sworn could never be done.

He was calling down the arsenal of Heaven.

He was yoking angels.

26

"Wake up, Herr Martin."

Cade navigated to consciousness by slow degrees. He winced at the pressure in his sinuses; patterns of pain felt etched into his thoughts. His eyes fluttered open to reveal that his perspective of the world had gone blurry and dim. After his vision adjusted, he saw he lay on the floor in a candlelit, circular room of stone. The tapers' flames cast feeble light on the walls and were unable to illuminate what he presumed was a high ceiling lost in shadows.

The tiled floor had been inscribed with an intricate magickal pattern. Circles enclosing pentagrams lay within triangles, all sporting symbols from the zodiac and the ancient grimoires, the seals of demons, and decorations macabre and profane. Coals smoldered in braziers, filling the room with scents of aloe, resin, cedar, and alum.

He tested his bonds; he was trapped in place by a short chain connecting a shackle on his left ankle to an inch-thick metal ring sunk into the floor. His heart raced as he grasped his predicament: *I'm inside a circle used for sacrifices.*

Across from him, Stefan lay sprawled outside the circles. His clothes were torn and filthy. Blood seeped from wounds on his face and head, and an X-shaped incision on his torso had been stitched crudely shut. The Dutchman cracked open one eye and looked at Cade, but gave no outward sign of recognizing him—unlike their three enemies, who stood watching them.

Kein was the closest, inside the operator's circle. His adepts were behind him on either side, occupying the tanists' positions. All wore white vestments.

The master noted Cade's return to awareness with a birdlike cock of his head. "We haven't been properly introduced. I am—"

"A dead man."

The interruption didn't seem to bother Kein. "Then permit me to introduce my adepts: Briet Segfrunsdóttir. Siegmar Tuomainen."

Cade's attention fixed on Siegmar. "Oxford. And the pier in Liverpool." He winced at cruel memories—torpedoes hitting the *Athenia*; bone-chilling water; the suffocating embrace of LEVIATHAN. Hatred welled up from his darkest places. "You told the Nazis to sink us."

Kein shook his head. "I gave that order, Herr Martin. Though it was Siegmar who provided me the name of your vessel, and its destination." He briefly held up one hand and closed his eyes, signaling a shift in his direction of thought. "I did not bring you here to rehash history. I compelled your presence so that we could discuss the future. *Our* future."

"You don't have a future. Not after I get free."

The threat didn't faze Kein. "Confidence, bordering on arrogance. I expected no less." He studied Cade, as if scrutinizing his every reaction. "We are much alike, you and I."

"I don't see it." Standing up made Cade's head swirl with vertigo, but he refused to falter.

"We both respect power. It is why we chose the same patron spirit. You see, yes? We are *meant* to unite! As allies, we could work miracles. We could change this world."

"I'd rather change the shape of your face—with my fists." Cade kept his eyes on Kein, but with his mind he sought his yoked demons, any indication he might be able to fight back. He was disheartened to find that his indentured spirits had been exorcised. He was disarmed, and his only remaining defense was bravado: "Tell your Nazi pals I'm not playing ball."

"I assure you, the Nazis are not part of this equation." Perhaps reading Cade's confusion, Kein reacted with interest. "That surprises you?"

"You are their Teutonic ideal."

"Yes, the Führer certainly likes to think so." The ancient but youthful-looking karcist turned pensive. "Forgive my curiosity: What has my old friend Adair told you about me? Does he still peddle his fantasy that I seek world domination?"

"Something like that."

Kein shook his head. "I regret to say, you have been misled. For centuries, he has been a slave to outmoded notions of good and evil. He fell in love with the Enlightenment and the Industrial Revolution, but never asked himself if humanity was ready for either of them."

"What does that have to do with helping the Nazis murder millions?"

"Join me, and I will explain everything."

A cough and a splutter turned Cade's head toward Stefan. His fallen friend croaked through cracked, bleeding lips, "Don't . . . trust . . . him."

The warning made Kein more emphatic. "Side with me, Herr Martin, and I will heal your friend and set him free."

"Even if I trusted you—"

"Together we can end this war in a matter of months and save millions of lives."

"By handing the world to the Nazis? Pardon my French, but fuck you. I seem to recall the Bible says the meek shall inherit the earth."

"True." Invisible fangs of ice bit into Cade's guts and forced him to his knees, screaming in agony. Kein smirked. "But it never said they would get to keep it." The pain abated when Kein snapped his fingers. "Humanity has been seduced by Science, led down a path to its own destruction. Think of how men used to make war. Now look upon the terrors they wield. Science has given men powers they cannot control. In time it will lay waste to countries, then the world itself. Nietzsche said it best: 'Oh, how much is today hidden by science! Oh, how much it is expected to hide!' Heed me, Herr Martin: Left unchecked, Science will herald the end of mankind, unless we bring it to heel. *We* must save the world."

"Why would you think *you* have the right to make that choice?"

"Who should make it, then? The masses? They are in no position to oppose the horrors of Science. They are oppressed by robber barons. Magnates. Men of industry who spent decades preparing to supply a war they created. How can ordinary people stand against such institutional villainy?" Kein paused to collect his wits and calm himself. "This is not some ruse, Herr Martin. Humanity does not realize it stands at a crossroads, a juncture at which it seems doomed to choose the wrong path. We must not let that happen."

Cade suppressed a deep tide of sickness in his gut so he could feign courage. "Science has done great things for the world. So why should I believe you?"

Kein folded his hands atop his grimoire. "Centuries ago, Adair and I studied under the same master. But Adair clings too much to hope. He is naïve. Sentimental. Weak."

"My master is many things. 'Weak' isn't one of them."

"Really? Adair did *nothing* when Science began stamping out the Art. The Inquisition. Salem. And so many other slaughters—that was the face Science showed to me, and to dozens of my apprentices. I resisted for as long as I could, but too many karcists followed Adair's example. All of them are dead now."

A derisive snort. "Along with most of your Thule minions."

"Yes, hundreds of promising new adepts—all murdered by you and your friends."

"You'll just make more. Unless we stop you."

Kein's eyes betrayed his frustration. "How many people in any generation do you really think are qualified to be karcists? It takes more than courage and basic literacy—though that seems to have done the trick for your Russian friend." A dejected sigh. "The truth, Herr Martin, is that the Art is dying, and this world with it. Unless *we* save it."

It almost had the ring of truth—but then the best lies often did. Cade laughed. "Nice try. Save it for the picture shows."

A ghostly murder of crows with tattered wings and rotted flesh sprang into being and set upon Cade, pecking at his ears, eyes, nostrils, and any soft spot he couldn't defend. Their beaks were sharp, and each savage thrust left him shouting in pain.

A clap of Kein's hands, and the birds dissolved into black smoke.

"It might have been foolish of me to hope you would see reason." Kein opened his grimoire. "Despite my regrets, I shall make the most of your defiance. Your blood will be the final ingredient in a ritual no one has performed in over seven centuries. When it is done, not only will I have rid the world of its last breathing *nikraim,* I will prevent your kind from manifesting on earth for three generations—or, to be a shade more precise, ninety-nine years."

He cast a handful of powder into the brazier between him and Cade. Purple smoke that smelled of lavender and sandalwood climbed into the blackness overhead.

Cade fixated on a detail from Kein's lament. "What the hell is a '*nikraim*'?"

The question halted Kein's preparations. "Are you serious? Has Adair not told you?"

"Told me what?"

"What you *are.*"

Curiosity collided with mistrust. Ever since Cade had awoken in Adair's custody, he had felt as if there was something the master was hiding from him, some vital truth being left unsaid. But could he really trust Kein, of all people, to show him the truth of his own existence?

He didn't have time to decide.

A blast of light and a ringing like tinnitus filled the conjuring room, originating behind Cade. His skin prickled and the hair on his arms stood up—magick was being unleashed on a horrifying scale. Bereft of defenses or the ability to join the fight, he did the only thing he could: he dropped to the floor.

Above and around him, the battle unfolded with such speed he could barely follow it. Kein, Briet, and Siegmar hurled demonic projectiles, torrents of red lightning, cones of fire. Charging into that mad barrage, Adair and Anja had come armed with nothing but blinding white radiance, a cold energy unlike anything Cade had yet seen in his studies of magick.

Briet unleashed a hail of knives at Anja, who parried them with a wave of light. Siegmar conjured the specter of a lizard-eyed, ram-horned Caesar riding a chariot pulled by winged lions. Holy fire from Adair's palm vaporized the beasts, rig, and rider.

Kein swung a semitransparent halberd at Adair. The master blocked it with his forearm, and a bright metallic *clang* resounded inside the stone chamber. Then Adair's jaw dropped open, and he let out a great roar: it was the crashing of the sea, the boom of an erupting volcano, a hurricane wind raging just inches above Cade and Stefan. The candles were snuffed and thrown aside; Kein's lectern and grimoire rolled away like tumbleweeds. His adepts staggered out of their circles. To hold his ground, Kein dropped to one knee.

The tempest ceased, and Adair shouted, "Anja! Get Cade!"

"But Stefan—!"

"Do as I say!" Blood spilled from Adair's nostrils, and trickled from his ears.

Anja ran to Cade, cut his chain with a beam of light from her hand, and helped him up.

Adair extended his arm. He coaxed Stefan's enchanted mirror to fly off of a table at the far end of the conjuring room and into his hand. His voice was a bullhorn: "Move!"

Anja pulled one of Cade's arms across her shoulders as Adair created an oval portal ringed in blue-white light. Through it Cade saw only darkness, but Anja pulled him toward it.

Behind them, the enemy karcists regained their feet. Before Cade could warn Anja, Adair fired from his eyes white jets of energy—not fire, not electricity, not anything Cade knew how to name other than to call it power. The twin beams slashed across Kein and his adepts, who cried out, stumbled, and scattered, all cowed behind their shields. At the same time, bleeding fissures spread across Adair's face and neck, then down his arms to his hands.

Adair pressed his attack as he levitated the barely conscious Stefan and sent him flying out of the fray, through the portal ahead of Anja and Cade, who stopped shy of its threshold.

Anja pleaded, "Master! Hurry!"

"Go!" He stumbled backward toward the portal as he filled the room with twisting ribbons of light and fire. He looked back with bleeding eyes. "Run!"

His tone left no room for debate. Anja pulled Cade through the portal.

They landed hard on the other side, in a place Cade didn't recognize. A sun-splashed room of pink tile, white stucco, natural wood and stone, with windows that looked out on red dusty hills dotted with scrub.

On the other side of the still-open portal, Adair faltered as he deflected three assaults at once. He backed toward the portal as he bombarded the enemy magicians with whirlwinds of fire. Then he leaped through the gateway—

Behind him, a pulse of indigo light from Kein's hand struck the portal as Adair passed through it. A spray of blood accompanied its collapse—and Adair slammed to the floor in front of Cade, his right leg severed two inches below the knee.

Anja wept tears of blood over Stefan, whose guts spilled through his ruptured sutures. Adair cursed and clutched at his amputated limb, desperate to stop his own bleeding.

Cade thought he might vomit; then he coughed up blood, and after it another mouthful, then another. His stomach churned, his head swam, and only then did he realize that whatever torture Kein had inflicted on him had shredded his insides.

He collapsed on the floor beside Stefan and Adair. His vision dimmed, and the edges of his world pushed inward. It dawned on him that he was dying.

I'm not ready! I have to fight . . .

He was in the ocean, being pulled into the cold, briny deep. The end was upon him, its attraction magnetic, and there was nothing he could do to resist it.

His soul raged in silent protest.

Can't let Kein win. . . .

The darkness drank him in.

I can't let—

The rest was silence.

Anja was light-headed from the brief but excruciating surge of angelic power the master had yoked to her. Standing in the main hallway of an unfamiliar rustic villa, above her wounded friends, she fought for calm and clarity, only to find them out of reach.

Stefan pawed with broken fingers at empty air, his jaw quivering. Adair groaned and trembled beside him on the tiled floor, blood spurting from the stump of his severed leg, his whole body ravaged from the strain of trying to contain angelic power. Cade's wet, bloody coughing ceased and his features took on a deathly cast.

Anja stood, frozen with indecision. *What do I do?*

Her mind clouded with panic. She had seen carnage before, worse than this, but time had dulled that pain. Cade and her friends were dying in front of her, and she felt paralyzed.

Stefan turned his head toward Adair. Remorseful tears rolled down his cheeks. "Sorry . . . Master. I was weak. Told them of the castle. And my mirror."

Adair reached out with a shaking hand. Brushed Stefan's face. "Not your fault."

Being absolved only deepened Stefan's sorrow. His voice broke as guilty sobs overtook him. "I doomed you all."

"None of us . . . could fight Kein alone." The master's desperate eyes found Anja's. His voice fell to an unsteady croak. "Lass . . . ?"

She kneeled and took his hand. "Master?"

He grabbed her shirt collar. His eyes bulged and his nostrils flared as he pulled her close to his fissured, bloodied face: "Help us!"

Shocked into clarity, she broke from his grasp and wreathed her hand in fire. She pressed her palm, hot as a branding iron, against Adair's leg stump and seared it black. His enraged bellows filled the villa; then he collapsed, gasping and spent. Stanching the bleeding was all she could do for him; his leg had been severed by magick, so replacing it was beyond Anja's talents. *He will learn to live with scars, as I have.*

Bullets of sweat rolled through his ragged eyebrows and his hedge maze of whiskers. After another breath he nodded at her. "Good." He looked toward Cade. "Now him."

Cade was unconscious and cyanotic. Stefan was awake and suffering. Anja's choice was clear. She shook her head. "Cade is gone." She turned to help Stefan.

The master yanked Anja away from the dying Dutchman. "Do as I say!" He shoved her in Cade's direction. "There's still time! Help him!"

She wanted to refuse, to ignore Cade and do all she could for Stefan—but Adair had been like a father to her since the day her mother disowned her. She couldn't refuse him.

Magick told her what she needed to know.

"Cade still has life," she confessed. "But Stefan has more."

"I don't care. Save Cade."

"But Stefan—"

"Without Cade, we've lost the war. Save him!"

Anja felt her strength ebb; her hold on Buer's yoke was slipping. Without the demon, she would have no magick for healing. She showed Adair her back and kneeled beside Stefan, who had always been patient with her, even when she had been a passionate but borderline illiterate novice. From his forehead she stroked a lock of hair that was damp with sweat and tacky with blood. "Have courage. I—"

"Let me go," Stefan whispered through cracked lips. "Save Cade."

"I am not strong enough."

"Take my strength. Give it to him."

She recoiled. "Kill you? For him?" Angry tears blurred her vision. "Never. I—"

He silenced her with the lightest touch of his fingertip to her cheek. "This is bigger than one life, Anja." He caressed her chin. "Set me free. Save Cade."

His request gutted her. She slumped to the floor between him and Cade, her breath stolen, her eyes brimming with grief.

Adair clasped her hand. "Please. I beg you. Before it's too late."

The master had never begged her for anything, ever.

A tragic memory tormented her—a vision of her younger brother, Piotr, dead in the snow, murdered by Kein. And herself, kneeling beside Piotr's body, grieving and powerless.

Her breaths grew quick and shallow as she struggled to fend off heaving sobs. She looked down at Stefan. "Forgive me."

A weak smile. "You do me no wrong. Call this a final kindness."

Her left hand she placed on Stefan's chest; she pressed her right hand onto Cade's. According to the grimoires she was working a healing charm, but she saw it for what it really was: a theft of one person's life for the benefit of another. It was all part of the universe's cruel sense of balance, its scales of injustice. Directing the powers of BUER, she shifted the last of Stefan's vitality—an otherwise intangible commodity—into Cade. To Anja it felt as if she were pilfering the last ember of a bonfire to rekindle a pile of ashes.

She watched life fade from Stefan's eyes, and a cold emptiness filled her as she accepted the truth that she had taken it from him, to give to a man she envied and resented.

Grave silence filled the villa.

Cade gasped; his eyes snapped open. He sucked in a greedy breath. As swiftly as he had roused, he slipped away, unconscious but no longer in the arms of the reaper.

Anja extended her senses once more, to confirm what she already knew. "Cade will live." She fixed Adair with an unforgiving stare. "Stefan is gone."

A sad nod. "Thank you."

She stood, filled with disgust. "Go to Hell."

"You think you're the only one hurting? Stefan was like a son to me. But I gave him up—because that's what had to be done. And he *knew* it! So don't you disgrace his courage by acting like his sacrifice was a waste. He died to give us a chance."

It took all of her willpower not to spit on the man she'd once called master. "He died because I tore out what was left of his soul"—she nodded at Cade as she continued—"and gave it to *him*. Stefan is dead because you needed him to die so your pet could live."

Anja walked away, her heart growing colder with each step. There was no path she could imagine for her life that would lead her to forgive Adair, or herself. But accepting that truth led her to another, even more sobering realization.

I have no place else to go.

The villa was smaller than Eilean Donan Castle. It was rustic—a more polite term than "dilapidated" or "ramshackle"—and located on a dusty hilltop accessed by a steep road of hairpin switchbacks that snaked down its southern side.

Faded pink tiles covered most of its floors, and the walls were made of off-white stucco. Open-frame ceilings betrayed the roof's history of neglect. The house was an oven at midday. It was populated with flimsy furniture, except in its first-floor great room, which had no furnishings at all, exposing its parquet floors. The pantry was half barren, the wine cellar empty, and Cade hated his bed's worn-flat mattress.

For all its faults, though, the house was not without its charms. Its windows' patinas filled the two-story dwelling with golden light in the afternoon. The patio looked out on foothills south of the Sierra Nevada range, between the towns of Orgiva and Lanjarón, about an hour's drive southeast of Granada, Spain. Fresh air, a property dotted with wildflowers, and plenty of exposed old wood filled the house with pleasant fragrances.

It had been five days since Anja and Adair had brought Cade here. Since the master had locked himself away in his master suite. Since Anja had buried Stefan or spoken a word.

Today marked the first time Cade had felt well enough to get out of bed and explore the villa. The only room in it that impressed him was its library. High-ceilinged, its walls were hidden by shelves packed with ancient codices and rolled manuscripts. Arranged on the library's central long table had been his, Adair's, and Anja's grimoires. Their leather-bundled tools of the Art were stored inside a majestic varnished oak wardrobe standing in a corner, along with their vestments. Seeing it all, Cade had wondered how it had got there.

The answer was obvious, of course: Adair had used magick to compel some demon to shift their personal effects and the library from Eilean Donan to this remote Andalusian hideout.

Desperate for open air, Cade wandered outside and found a patch of grass on which to stretch out, then lost himself in the sunset, which had turned the western sky a deep burgundy streaked with clouds of tangerine. Soon night would fall and salt the sky with starlight. Then the air would turn crisp, and it would be time to kindle a fire in the great room's hearth. Grateful for the solitude, he closed his eyes for a time and let his thoughts wander.

Night ascended and the heavens revealed themselves. Cade admired the stars until he tired of confronting his insignificance in the scope of creation; then he allowed his growing appetite to draw him inside the villa.

The house was preternaturally quiet. Night breezes moved through it, cool and silent.

At the risk of waking Adair, who had been sleeping almost around the clock during his convalescence, Cade called out, "Anja? You here?" No one answered.

She wasn't in the kitchen, or in any of the rooms upstairs. Cade ventured outside and circled the villa. There wasn't another soul for miles in any direction.

Dread led him to the library. Anja's grimoire was absent from the long table. He opened the wardrobe. Her robes and tools of the Art weren't there.

Without an explanation or a farewell, Anja had gone.

28

JULY

Fear and confusion, exhilaration and regret—was this stew of emotions what it meant to be free? All her life, Anja had been in the care of others. First her mother, then, since the age of thirteen, Adair. Now she soared alone, thousands of feet above the Mediterranean Sea, transformed by the charms of ANDREALPHUS into a peregrine falcon, while the duty of transporting her tools and other possessions had been delegated to DANOCHAR.

Beyond her left wing stretched the eastern coast of Spain; on the horizon to her right, the island of Palma. Her plan was to follow the coastline past France to Italy, then overland until she reached the Adriatic Sea, at which she would shift her course due east. Once she had the Black Sea in her sights, she could haunt its northern coastline until she found the mouth of the Peka Don. Tracing its winding path through the countryside would lead her to her destination: Stalingrad. There she would join the Red Army and honor her duty to defend Mother Russia, by standing with her comrade soldiers against Hitler's legions.

Yet as the world stretched out ahead of her, she felt her guilt pull her thoughts backward, to what she had left behind. To Adair. She tried to push him from her mind, along with the anger her memories evoked.

What made Cade's life more precious than Stefan's? That question tormented her. She had resented Cade for being Adair's new favorite, the one for whom the master was ready to sacrifice all his other adepts. *How long before he would have asked me to lay down my life for his American pet?*

As much as she wanted to hate Cade, she couldn't. He hadn't asked for the life Adair had thrust upon him. Even so, in battle he had been brave, and it had frightened Anja to see how swiftly he had mastered tasks and techniques that had taken her years to learn.

Despite her denials, she knew she would miss Adair. It filled her with remorse to abandon him while he was maimed and bedridden, but she had done all she could for him. The worst of his wounds she had tended; the rest could be healed only by time.

There was still the danger posed by the Thule Society's remaining covens, and by Kein and his apprentices. No doubt Adair and Cade had been counting on having Anja's help in those battles, but the time had come for her to answer a higher calling.

By her estimates, she would reach Stalingrad in another six days. Then she would embark upon the campaign for which, she now realized, she had spent the past seven years preparing herself in body and spirit: She would reclaim her honor as a Russian—and teach the Nazis new reasons to fear the heroes of the Soviet.

It had been days since Anja left the villa, but Cade remained unable to fathom her motives. He leaned against the bathroom's open doorway while Adair submerged himself in the claw-foot tub. When the master surfaced, Cade asked, "You don't think she went after Kein by herself?"

Adair swept his mop of wet gray hair backward. "I doubt it." He squeezed bathwater from his scraggle of beard and rubbed his eyes.

"But now that she's had a taste of angel magick—"

"It'd take more than a taste to beat Kein. Not that she'd be able to tap into it."

"But you used it at Wewelsburg—"

"Aye." Adair massaged his leg stump. "And nearly died for it."

"But why weren't we using angel magick from the start?"

Adair skewered Cade with a look. "Because I needed the Iron Codex even to attempt it."

"And now that you have it . . . ?"

The master pointed out the scabbed fissures that traced an atlas of pain from his head to his one remaining set of toes. "First, you might've noticed yoking angels takes a greater toll on the flesh than yoking demons. But the main reason is that angels can't be forced into service the way demons can. You can ask angels for help, but they're under no obligation to give it."

Cade filed that knowledge away, then turned his thoughts to more immediate concerns. "Any chance Kein and his adepts are still at Wewelsburg?"

"They're long gone by now. Could be anywhere." He extended a hand toward Cade. "Help me up."

Before Wewelsburg, Adair had seemed so imposing that Cade had thought him invincible. Now naked, wet, and teetering on one foot as he struggled to exit a tub without falling on his ass, Adair looked frail. Cade steadied the old karcist as he stood.

Despite having lost the lower part of one leg, Adair was still heavy as Cade lifted him out of the tub and set him on the throw rug. Before the master had to ask, Cade handed him his towel. Adair dried his chest, then draped the linen over his head like a hood. Cade held him steady as the master put on his robe, then sat on a stool next to the tub. "Thank you, lad."

The stump of bright-pink scar tissue below Adair's knee captivated Cade even as it repulsed him. "Does it still hurt?"

"Less than you might think." Adair examined the wound with cool detachment. "After Anja scorched it to stop the bleeding, I didn't feel anything. The pain came back after she fixed the burn." A deep frown. "Three hundred fifty-eight years and nary a scratch. Now this." His mood lightened. "Serves me right for charging in like a great pillock, all sound and fury."

Adair toweled his hair dry while Cade fetched his crutch. The master stood and tucked the padded support under his armpit, then hobbled from the bathroom to his bedroom. Cade followed him. "How long before you can work new magick?"

"Weeks. Maybe longer." He appraised Cade. "You?"

"I'm ready." It was a lie. Cade's insides felt as if they'd been boiled with acid and scraped raw by thorns, but he wore a stoic face for his mentor.

"If you say so." The master unfolded some underwear and a pair of pants. "Don't push yourself on my account. Whenever you go back in the circle, you'll be going alone." He seemed to sense the alarm Cade was trying to conceal. "Remember what I taught you: the circle's drawn for five, three, or one. Doesn't work with two. Now that Anja's gone, you're on your own."

"Not a problem." Another lie. The prospect of standing solo against a parade of demons chilled Cade to his core. He decided to shift the subject to one that had been bothering him for over a week, since his abduction. "I have questions."

"I'd be cross if you didn't."

He waited until Adair had pulled on his trousers before he asked, "What's a *nikraim*?"

The master sighed. "Told you, did he?" He frowned. "It's an old Hebrew word, one long gone from the common vernacular. It describes a person who's been spiritually bonded with an angel—and not the fallen variety, one of the true host of Heaven."

"I thought that was called a nephilim."

The master shook his head. "No, a nephilim is the hybrid offspring of a human and an angel made flesh, just like a cambion is the offpsring of a human and a demon incarnate. A *nikraim* is *not* a hybrid. It's two beings living as one, spirit fused to soul."

Cade was stunned by the implications. "How does that happen?"

"No one knows how or why Heaven chooses the souls it does, or why it sends spirits to meddle in human affairs. But *nikraim* wield great powers when they reach adulthood."

"And I'm one of them?"

A pained look passed over Adair, who gestured toward the dresser. "Be a lad—fetch my flask." Cade retrieved the master's tarnished steel hip flask, which sloshed half full in his hand. Adair unscrewed the cap and downed a swig. "Technically, yes, you're a *nikraim*." Another pull from the flask. "But you're not exactly one of God's chosen."

The more Adair told him, the less he understood. "Meaning?"

Adair hobbled on his crutch to a wardrobe, from which he plucked a wrinkled shirt. He put it on as he explained, "Your bonding was made by magick. Your father worked a grand experiment while you were still in your mother's womb. He made a pact with Heaven, called down one of the Celestial host, and offered to let you be its vessel."

"What're you saying? I'm some kind of puppet?"

The master paused buttoning his shirt. "No! You've got free will, always have. The angel's more of a passenger. You draw on its strength and talents, but you're the one in charge."

"But what talents do I—" Self-awareness came like a slap in the face. "*Magick.* Whatever my father did to me, it gave me a knack for magick."

A somber nod. "Aye."

"If I'm bonded to an angel, does that mean I can yoke angels?"

"As I said, true angels aren't like the Fallen. You can ask for their help, but they give it only at the whim of the Divine—it can't be compelled. Not even by you. And believe me, if you think yoking a demon's hard work, holding an angel in harness is ten times worse."

"But you're telling me I'm carting around an angel *all the time,* have been since before I was born. Why isn't that messing with my head?"

"Bonding and yoking aren't the same thing. Yoking a spirit ties its powers to your flesh. When your body weakens, you lose control of the spirit. But bonding—that's a fusion of a spirit's immortal essence with a human's mortal soul, and it lasts for life."

"But what's the point? Why did my father do this to me?"

Adair fastened his shirt's last button, then pivoted to face Cade. "Because Kein is one of the *nadach*—a man soul-bonded to a demon. It makes him a stronger karcist than I can ever be. It also means the only way to beat him is to find a magician who can be his equal. A *nikraim*."

"You mean me."

"Aye." Adair stared at the floor. "It's why I told Anja to let Stefan die—so she'd have the strength to save you. I loved Stefan like a son, but . . . he could never beat Kein." He looked up, his dark eyes brimming with tears, his voice breaking with grief. "So I had to let him go." With the back of his hand he erased the tears that fell from his eyes.

A wave of guilt flooded through Cade. "So many people have died for me. My parents; the passengers on *Athenia*; now Stefan. . . . How can I possibly repay all those lives?"

"By living one worthy of their sacrifice."

It was the simplest advice the master had ever given him—and also the truest, and the hardest. Cade tried to pretend he wasn't shaken. "Think you'll be all right getting downstairs?" The master nodded, so Cade slipped away from him. "Take your time. I'll make breakfast."

A day of mundane chores awaited Cade, tasks that had to be dealt with to make the villa not just livable but defensible against magickal assaults such as the one that had compromised Eilean Donan. Adair would be able to offer advice, but it was up to Cade to provide the elbow grease. It was going to be a very long day—but not nearly as long as the night that would follow it. Because once the sun was down and the hands of the clock turned toward the witching hours, Cade was determined to initiate preparations for his next experiment.

The time had come for Hell to bend to *his* demands.

New magick remained beyond Adair's reach, but he still had a few tricks at his command. In his study stood a large oval mirror mounted vertically by a central hinge on a heavy wooden stand, the last of his portal glasses in continental Europe. Without another enchanted mirror on the other side, it couldn't be used as a portal—but it could still serve as a scrying window.

Adair had seated himself in front of the mirror for days on end, reaching out through its watery, shimmering surface to find Niko, from whom nothing had been heard since before Stefan's capture. Guiding Adair were the clairvoyant talents of DEMOGORGON, with whose help Adair had narrowed his search to France, then Burgundy, and now the commune of Vitteaux.

At last he had found Niko, who regarded Adair from behind a swollen face that had been savagely bruised and lacerated. Adair summoned Cade from the next room: "Lad, it's him! I found him!"

Cade hurried in and joined Adair in front of the mirror, then winced at the sight of Niko. "Holy shit. Are you okay?"

"*I have looked better,* n'est-ce pas?"

Adair was agape. "Christ! How are you alive?"

"*I probably should not be. But this town's doctor is a stubborn man.*"

If not for the sarcasm in Niko's voice, Adair would not have recognized his once impetuous young adept. "Speaking of stubborn—you tried to save her. After I told you not to."

The mask of violence obscuring Niko's once handsome features failed to conceal his anger. "Oui. *She was my sister. I refused to let them take her without a fight.*"

"But at what price? God *damn* you, Niko! Bad enough you risked yourself, but you took Stefan with you. Thanks to you, Kein breached Eilean Donan. He killed Stefan, and he damned near took Cade and the rest of us down, too. All because *you* couldn't obey orders."

"*Maybe if you'd helped me save her instead of—*"

"Shut your bonebox! I told you one woman's life wasn't worth risking the war, but that's just what you fucking did! If we'd lost Cade, we'd all be as good as dead. You, me, the Resistance, the Allies, billions of fucking lives—all thrown away in the name of one."

Niko's fury turned to sorrow. "*She was my only family. I will not apologize for trying to save her.*" His grief became pleading. "*I had to try, Master. Please say you understand.*"

It was hard for Adair to bear witness to Niko's pain and not let himself empathize with it. "Just because I understand, it doesn't mean I approve—or that I forgive."

"*I asked for neither.*"

"What I need *you* to understand is how much damage you did. One selfish moment, and you nearly wiped us off the map. I need you back in the fight, lad. Back in Paris, hunting down that Thule coven before it gets any stronger."

"*The village doctor says it will be months before I can walk.*" A gleam in Niko's eye presaged the ghost of a smile beneath his blue-black wounds. "*But the Maquis still bring me news from Paris—news you need to hear.*"

"I'm listening."

A cough freckled Niko's fist with blood, which he wiped across the front of his shirt. "*The Resistance is using the old Catacombs to move men and supplies around Paris. They have detailed maps of all the tunnels, and where they reach the surface.*"

"Go on."

"*Last week, a team of Maquis gunrunners spotted strangers in the Catacombs. Not German soldiers. Civilians in robes. Including a red-haired woman. They followed them—and found a tunnel not on any of the maps. A path blocked by an iron grate with no door, and no other exit. But the intruders? Nowhere to be found. They had vanished . . .*"

". . . as if by magick," Adair said, finishing Niko's thought. "Did your Maquis have the presence of mind to note this mystery path on one of their maps?"

"Oui." He held up a folded document for Adair to see.

The master turned to Cade, pointed at the dresser. "Grab the camera."

Cade retrieved the camera and snapped pictures of several pages of maps. "I'll take the film into town. Get some blowups made." He headed for the door.

"Good work." In light of Niko's discovery, Adair felt embarrassed for having lambasted him so cruelly. He found it hard to face him. "Sorry I can't bring you through. I've got new portal glasses coming soon, but . . . they've been spoken for, I'm afraid."

Niko shook his head. "*It is just as well. It would raise too many questions among the Maquis, more than I can answer.*"

"True." From the shelf by the mirror, he picked up the enchanted mirror he had recovered at Wewelsburg. The steel-and-glass rectangle was shrouded in white silk. "This was Stefan's. I'll have a spirit bring it to you tomorrow at dawn, to replace the one you lost. In case you learn anything new. Or in case you need us."

The beat-up young man accepted the offer with a grateful nod. "Merci."

"Heal up, lad. We'll let you know what we find." He and Niko nodded in valediction; then Adair closed the scrying window with a wave of his hand.

He stood and pulled his crutch to his side, under his arm. Then he looked out the window and watched Cade bicycle down the twisting hillside road, on his way to town with the camera.

If the Catacombs were where Briet and her Paris coven had made their lair, it was going to be up to Cade alone to breach it, meet them in battle, and destroy them all.

Adair white-knuckled the grip of his crutch and bit down on his regrets. *God forgive me . . . what if I'm sending that boy to his doom?*

AUGUST

The moment had been weeks in the making. One step at a time, Cade had prepared the villa's great room for the conjuring. Every sigil, every line, every totem of Goetic significance had been placed, adjusted, and perfected in accordance with the grimoires of old. Adair had vetted the details and found no cause for objection—except for the entirety of Cade's plan, which Cade had decided wasn't up for debate.

He had clothed himself in ceremonial garb and taken up his tools, which he had exorcised and consecrated as prescribed by Honorius and Solomon. Cedar and sandalwood kindled in his brazier, stoked by splashes of oil and camphor.

Hell spewed its expected clamor of protest before producing LUCIFUGE ROFOCALE, whose arrival was marked by thunder, fire, sulfuric smoke, and putrid vapors. The horned abomination twitched its caprine tail and clomped its black hooves against the villa's parquet floor. Its yellow eyes fixed upon Cade with disdain and enmity.

The beast spoke in a roar like the sundering of mountains.

WHY HAST THOU DISTURBED ME?

"I come with a list of spirits subordinate to thee, and whom I mean to yoke into my service, in accordance with our pact. I command thee to compel those spirits I name to come forth when called and make themselves known to me, so that I might place them into bondage."

The demon rolled its eyes. Everything about this, Cade surmised, must seem mundane to it: the same demands, the same names, over and over again, ad infinitum.

Again, its voice boomed. ENUMERATE THOSE WHOSE SERVICE YOU DESIRE. THOSE WHO ART MINE TO PLEDGE SHALL BE THINE TO COMMAND.

At last the test of Cade's resolve had arrived. He recited the list from memory. "Great and powerful Lucifuge Rofocale, I command thee to call forth into my exclusive service Azael, Zocar, Xaphan, Vesturiel, Ariosto, Marchosias, Sathariel, Vaelbor, Jephisto, Sabaoth, Seir, Casmiel, Meus Calmiron, Aorotos, and Vermael."

The great spirit paused, as if taken aback by Cade's demand. Its grandeur diminished, as did the majesty of its voice, though it still rumbled like a gathering storm. Fifteen spirits? Never before hast thou asked to yoke so many.

"Wilt thou deliver them as required by the Covenant? Or must I punish thee?"

Lucifuge Rofocale curtsied and held its pose in a parody of deference. I think only of thy safety and well-being. Mortal flesh is not meant to hold so many of my kind.

Cade lowered his wand toward the smoldering brazier in front of him. "Mine shall hold as many as I choose. And if I desire thy counsel, I shall ask for it. Now produce those spirits I have named, and command them appear instanter before me, lest thou feel my wrath."

The spirit backed away and stood erect as it puffed its chest outward, projecting pride and haughty indifference. All those spirits thou hast named can I produce, save Zocar.

The tip of Cade's wand grazed the glowing coals in the brazier, producing growls of discomfort from the demon. "Why are you not able to deliver Zocar?"

Hatred burned in the demon's eyes. Zocar is for the moment yoked in good faith to another of my servants. If a gift for lightning is what you desire, I can summon Azaleth to thy service.

"To whom is Zocar yoked?" A long and sullen silence stretched on without a reply from the demon. Cade stabbed his wand into the reddish coals, kicking up a flurry of ash and unleashing a hideous noise from Lucifuge Rofocale. Its howls of unearthly suffering persisted while the wand remained in the embers. Cade felt no pity for the monster writhing and roaring before him. "Who has yoked Zocar? Tell me or I shall multiply thy pains a thousandfold!"

An anguished cry unlike any Cade had ever heard filled the villa. Then the spirit shook the rafters as it bellowed, Stay thy rod and I shall tell thee! Mercy!

Cade withdrew his wand from the brazier. "Speak quickly. My patience is spent."

THY RIVAL, KEIN ENGEL—HE HOLDS THE REINS OF ZOCAR'S YOKE.

Cade hadn't considered before then the role of the word "exclusive" in the demand for yoked spirits. It had just been one of so many words he had learned by rote. "So while Kein holds a spirit yoked, no one else can call it forth?"

LUCIFUGE ROFOCALE confirmed in a pained voice, VERILY, IT IS SO.

"Does the reverse apply, as well? When I yoke a spirit, does that bar Kein from calling it into his service?"

IT DOES. Brief as the answer was, it brimmed with contempt.

This was information Cade resolved to find a way to exploit—just as soon as he dealt with more exigent concerns. "I will accept AZALETH as a substitute for ZOCAR. Call forth AZALETH and all the others I have named, excepting ZOCAR, so that I may yoke them."

Hell's prime minister obeyed, just as the Covenant decreed he must, and summoned before Cade a parade of the unholy, each a unique abomination that filled the air with noxious fumes and horrid sounds. One by one, Cade called their names, and each appeared in turn, a procession of spectral forms that emerged from darkness to be absorbed inside Cade himself.

Every spirit he subdued brought new waves of pain, each multiplying the others, until he felt as if his body had become a gauze sack tasked to hold a pack of wolves.

As the last spirit disappeared inside Cade, yoked to his will, he felt a great sickness sweep through him, one more powerful than any he'd suffered before. His entire body was in revolt from the invasion he'd invited. His intestines churned; his stomach was racked by spasms. Bile crept up his esophagus. Pressure inside his skull made him wish he could crack open his head to let the pain fly out.

Warmth tickled his upper lip. He palmed smears of blood seeping from his nostrils, then felt a deep aching in his right eye.

Inhuman voices crowded his mind. They drowned out his own thoughts—a preview of the nightmare of demonic possession—until he forced them all into silence. It took all his concentration, and when it was done, his head swam and his gut begged to be purged.

When he looked up at LUCIFUGE ROFOCALE, he suspected the demon was chortling at his distress. He refused to give it any more free entertainment. "I thank thee for thy service, and I discharge thee by the terms of the Covenant, providing thou do harm to no person or beast in this place, nor to those I have named as my own. Depart in peace, and return when, and only when, I call for thee. Begone, spirit—in the name of ADONAY, ELOHIM, ARIEL, and JEHOVAM!"

A terrible boom rocked the villa. The interior of the circle that held LUCI-FUGE ROFOCALE vanished, revealing a chasm of swirling clouds, darkness, and stars, into which the demon fell. As soon as it was gone from the room, the floor reappeared with a peal of thunder that nearly extinguished the ceremonial candles placed throughout the conjuring room.

The ritual was over. The room was once again secure.

Cade fell to his knees, sick and spent. "Amen."

He had known that yoking so many demons at once would be dangerous, and that it would be painful, but until that moment, he hadn't understood the full extent of the torture he had chosen to inflict on himself. Learning to think, to hide his discomfort, would be a Herculean labor by itself. Being able to wield magick while under such duress . . . ? He had no idea how he would accomplish that. He only knew that he had no other choice.

In a matter of days, he was being sent alone into the land of the enemy. He had no desire to do so as a lamb to the slaughter. Cade was finished being the prey.

I'm done being afraid, he vowed. *It's time to make Kein fear me.*

⌘

Even with the aid of a cane, Kein winced with each step he took. All his joints felt as if they had been pulled taut with rusty wire. Friction burned in his shoulders, hips, knees, and elbows. Turning his head more than a few degrees to either side provoked jabs of pain between his cervical vertebrae. And those were the least of his physical complaints.

His headache was chronic, as were his diarrhea, blurred vision, and insomnia. Several days had passed since last he slept, but even that respite had lasted only a few hours, thanks to the plague of nightmares—endless visions of purgative fire and vengeful angels. Flagons of red wine and countless pipes packed with opiates had done nothing to assuage his ailments.

He had been trapped in this pitiful state for over two months, ever since Adair and his young female apprentice Anja had tracked him and his adepts to Wewelsburg—a feat Kein still couldn't explain—and blasted their way in with Celestial magicks. For centuries Kein had heard of such feats, but until then he had never witnessed them.

I did not think Adair had it in him to take the gloves off. Now I know better.

Siegmar and Briet flanked Kein on his long walk from the Auschwitz commandant's office to the camp's execution chambers. Siegmar wore a patch over his right eye, which had been cooked like a hard-boiled egg by a blast the Russian girl had unleashed at Wewelsburg. Briet's left arm was in a cast; an invisible blow from Adair had shattered her limb in three places, and there was no magick capable of fixing her humerus and tibia.

At least her arm will heal, given time. Siegmar will stay half blind unless we make this ritual work. Kein and his adepts passed the entrance to the cremation facility, a structure of cinder blocks and cement that housed ovens with cast-iron doors. Kein stole a look inside as they shuffled past. Only half its incinerators were active, but its blistering gusts tainted with human ashes were like the breath of Hell itself. Laboring inside, lit by the ovens' glow, was a legion of emaciated Jewish prisoners; under the watch of a handful of Nazi guards, they were tasked with cremating their slain fellows.

"Nothing like German efficiency," Briet said under her breath.

An evil snort of amusement from Siegmar. "Not on earth, at least."

"Quiet," Kein said, lurching forward, one awkward step after another. "We are almost there." He led them to a smaller building, one with a handful of entrances and no windows. Its roof was dotted with chimneylike portals, but Kein knew they were designed not for expelling toxins but for delivering them.

Waiting outside the closest entrance were three German officers. The two subordinates were unknown to Kein, but he recognized the camp's commandant, SS-Obersturmbannführer Rudolf Höss, whose uniform was as crisp as his greeting. "Herr Engel. We've been expecting—"

Kein interrupted the commandant with a raised hand, then said to his underlings, "This does not concern you." When they hesitated and looked at each other, whether for direction or for courage, Kein added with the suggestive influence of Esias, "Leave us. *Now.*"

Before Höss could protest, his men hurried away. Alone with Kein and his adepts, Höss maintained his hauteur. "I object to this inspection, Herr Engel. This camp is under my command, and you have no authority to—"

"Silence." Kein was reluctant to use magick on Höss. "I am not here to suffer your opinions or appease your ego. Return to your office and let us work in peace."

His order turned Höss apoplectic. "How dare you! You have no right—!"

The commandant doubled over as Kein pointed his right index finger at him. Kein was tempted to take the man's life out of spite, but he knew not to test the limits of the Führer's indulgence. He restrained himself to making a point.

"First, Obersturmbannführer, I have dispensation from the Führer himself to use your camp, your men, your prisoners, and *you*, as I see fit. If you make any note of this visit in your camp's logs . . . if you breathe a word of my presence to anyone, ever . . . I promise you an eternity of tortures worse than any you could ever imagine—even after lording over such a pit of despair as this." Kein half closed his hand and grinned at Höss's agonized expression. The Nazi officer fell to the ground, hunched into a fetal curl. "That pain in your chest? It is the invisible hand of a demon named ORNIAS. If I clench my fist, his hand will crush your heart like a rotten peach. When you die, he will devour your soul—and funnel your strength into me." He leaned down to whisper with exquisite menace, "Do not force me to make a fist, Herr Höss. Tend to your own affairs, and leave me to mine. Do you understand?"

Tears fell from Höss's eyes as he bobbed his head in a frantic nod. Kein relaxed his hand and pulled it to his side. Höss gasped, drew a few grateful breaths, then scrambled to his feet. He fled from the trio of strangers who had come without fanfare to inspect his camp's gas chambers. Kein motioned his adepts toward the open doorway. "Let us head inside."

The magicians entered the empty gassing structure. It was an ugly block of stained gray concrete, mostly open inside but punctuated by columns of wire mesh. A sickly sweet odor of chemicals leaked from every surface. Kein opened his senses to the reactions of his yoked demons. To the last, they reveled in the building's grim aura. He nodded. "This will do."

Siegmar wrinkled his brow. "For what?"

"We need new strength to destroy Adair and his apprentices. The Nazis are bent on genocide; it is time we turned their madness to our benefit. Camps like this will make the rites of blood sacrifice not just possible but more effective than they have ever been." He pointed around the interior of the building. "Briet, mark this structure and all the others like it with the invisible seals of our patrons—yours, mine, and Siegmar's. Consecrate each one as an altar to Hell. Siegmar, you'll do the same inside the crematoria—I want every corpse the Nazis incinerate to become a burnt offering to our Lords Below."

Briet seemed ill at ease with Kein's new directives. "Master, these are gas chambers. Goetic rituals demand *blood,* not just death."

For all her skill she was so young, so inexperienced. Kein traced the ragged stains on the walls with his fingertips. "Look closer, my dear. At the walls. The floors. The Nazis' instrument of murder might be gas, but when this chamber floods with poison, the Jews rip the nails from their fingertips as they try to claw through the walls. When that fails, they rip at one another, then at their own burning eyes." He scraped the toe of his boot across a dark patch on the floor. "In the end, most of them vomit blood as their lungs burn." He looked up at his apprentices. "Trust me—these rooms will yield more than enough blood to slake Hell's thirst."

30

SEPTEMBER

Chimes from the wall clock in the villa's second-floor hallway told Cade it was ten o'clock. He had spent the night with his nose buried in one of Adair's dusty references on the tactics and techniques of magickal combat. Much of it had been written in languages long dead and unreadable without magick, a fact that had compelled Cade to add a sixteenth spirit, CAELBOR, to his already cumbersome roster of yoked demons.

He shut the book and stretched his arms above his head. His muscles had become stiff despite his attempts at regular exercise, which consisted primarily of lonesome hikes through the surrounding hills. A steady diet of whisky, wine, and laudanum-laced absinthe had made his chronic headaches almost manageable, but he had traded demonic diarrhea for chronic constipation. It had been several weeks since his mass-yoking ritual, and he couldn't recall having enjoyed a decent night's sleep since.

Self-conscious about his appearance—the strain of the yoking had ruptured the capillaries in the whites of his eyes, turning them bloodred—he had avoided both his reflection and his master, in the hope that his injury would heal before it was noticed. That afternoon Cade had awoken to a note from Adair asking him to come to his study at 10:00 P.M. Now the hour had come, and Cade put aside his research to answer the invitation. Along the way he caught his warped reflection on the large pot of a polished silver tea service. His eyes remained noticeably red.

Maybe he won't ask. . . . And maybe I'll flap my arms and fly to the moon.

Cade knocked on the door of Adair's study. There was no answer. He tried the knob and found it unlocked, so he eased the door inward and peeked inside. The room beyond was dark as sin. Even late at night, its curtains were drawn; all its lights were off, its candles unlit.

"Master?" He edged past the door and closed it behind himself. The room was quiet—and then he caught a distant clamor of voices, ringing phones, and chattering Teletypes. He followed the sound to the oval portal mirror. The glass inside its dark oaken frame swirled with bluish gray clouds whose depths flickered with unearthly light.

As the maelstrom parted, the sounds from the other side became clearer. Cade recognized a variety of British accents—London, Manchester, Liverpool—and some American voices. The master's Glaswegian growl cut through them all. The mists dissipated to reveal Adair, perched on a pair of crutches. He stood close enough to the mirror's threshold that he obstructed most of the view of the other side, but Cade saw enough to deduce the master was visiting a military strategy room, with its plotting tables and manned banks of telephones, probably in some well-fortified bunker, though where he couldn't say.

One officer who wore a U.S. Army major's insignia saluted Adair, who responded with a jaunty wave farewell before he sidestepped through the mirror into the study, awkwardly shifting his balance from one crutch to the other as he navigated the magickal portal. As he cleared the oval frame, the mirror's surface reappeared behind him. He noted Cade's presence, checked his pocket watch, and smiled. "Right on time. Well done, lad."

Cade watched him hobble to his desk. "Nice to see you back on your foot." A scathing glare from the master made it clear jokes about his infirmity were still out of bounds, so Cade shifted the topic. "New mirror?"

"One of them. Currently in Gibraltar, en route to its new home." Anticipating Cade's next question, he added, "A new hand mirror's in the works for you, I promise."

"Yeah, sure, and the check's in the mail. How'd your meeting go?"

"Better than some." Adair settled into his chair and set his crutches aside. "The Allies are a month or two from invading French North Africa. After that, Italy."

"What about the Pacific?"

The master shook his head. "Not for us to know." He pulled a flask from inside his jacket, unscrewed the cap, and downed a swig. "Mission one is taking back Europe. The Allies are gathering, but if we don't knock out the last three Thule covens, it'll all be for nothing. So you and I need to get in gear, lad—and take down those bloody cockwombles as fast as we can. After that, we can focus all our efforts on Kein."

Cade couldn't help but look askance at Adair's crutches. "With all due respect, I don't think you're in any shape for combat."

"And you are? I've seen corpses with more vigor, and your eyes are redder than a gobbler's wattle." He studied Cade with suspicion. "How many spirits do you have yoked?"

"Enough to get this job done." He was in no mood to debate his condition or his choices, so he forced the conversation forward. "What do we know about the Paris coven?"

It was clear Adair knew what Cade was doing, but he moved on all the same. "More than we did a few days ago." He reached inside his coat again, this time to pull out a map, which he unfolded and smoothed across his desktop. It was an annotated guide to the Catacombs under Paris, based on the notes Cade had photographed. Appended to the map were a ton of marginalia, recent corrections and updates to the maze, and notations of new access points. "Niko's friends in the Maquis have been gathering new information."

The extent of the man-made caverns staggered Cade's imagination. "Jesus, who dug these tunnels, the Minotaur? I'm guessing it'd be easy to get lost down there."

"Damned right. It's why the Maquis started using them in the first place." He tapped an ingress point. "This is the entrance second-closest to the Thule coven's lair. Avoid the closer one, as that's the one they favor." His finger traced a path through the caverns that had been highlighted with dots of red ink. "This is the best route to the lair. It's not the shortest, but it offers some cover." His finger stopped where the dots ended. "This is the tunnel blocked by iron bars. The Maquis can't go farther without cutting the bars—which would tell the coven we'd found them."

Cade admired the simplicity of the coven's defenses. "It won't be a problem."

"Are you sure? Because unless that coven installed the best secret door ever made, it means the people on the other side of those bars aren't just dabblers—every one of them has to be a fully trained karcist with at least one yoked demon. They're the linchpin of Kein's defense of France. You'll be walking alone into the biggest fucking cross fire you've ever seen."

Cade cracked his knuckles. "I prefer to think of it as 'shooting fish in a barrel.' Just one question: How do I get to Paris?"

The master snapped his fingers, then pointed at the mirror behind Cade. Their reflections vanished. Green smoke churned, then yielded to reveal a dim space behind a towering curtain. Ropes dangled from above, and in the shadows Cade saw costumed mannequins, stacked crates, and mounds of bric-a-brac.

Adair gazed upon the mess with fond admiration. "Backstage at the Grand Guignol." He cracked a sly smile at Cade. "You're not the only one who's been keeping busy."

⌇⌇⌇

Five minutes before midnight, silence reigned on Rue de Sèvres. Dense mist choked the streets of Paris and blessed its streetlamps with halos.

Cade wore the fog as a cloak as he emerged from the shadows. In the middle of the street, where it met the Avenue de Breteuil, a cast-iron manhole cover protruded from the asphalt. He willed it upward; it rose from the pavement with a faint scraping.

Invisible hands supported Cade as he stepped into the manhole and controlled his descent into the sewers and tunnels below. As his head passed below street level, he guided the iron cover into place with a ponderous *thunk*.

Under the street, unbroken darkness. Cade looked through the eyes of SATH-ARIEL and saw the tunnel in gray-green twilight. It was mostly round and composed of bricks, but just as his map promised, there was a breach in the wall east of the manhole. Cade levitated himself above the muck, floated to the break in the wall, and stepped through it into the Catacombs.

Miles of claustrophobic passages, most not much wider than his shoulders, tiled from floor to roof with human bones and skulls, stretched away into endless shadow. No matter where Cade looked, Death gazed back at him. He checked his map of the centuries-old tunnels and followed the path of red dots through the subterranean labyrinth. In a place where most people would pray for the protection of guardian angels, he had only demons.

Time was hard to gauge in this dark world beneath the City of Light. Cade moved with haste, but his progress felt slow as he paused to verify every other step. The markings the Maquis had etched to guide their compatriots were subtle, so as not to betray their secrets to the Nazis should the Germans learn of the Resistance's movements through this sepulcher.

At last he found the tunnel the old maps said should not exist, the one Niko's allies had discovered by tailing the dabblers. Just as the Maquis had warned, the final downward stretch was blocked by a grate of iron bars. An inch thick and joined with solid welds, they stretched from floor to ceiling and wall to wall to form an impassable barrier. The shoulder-width passage of bones continued for a dozen meters on the other side before disappearing around a sharp turn.

Cade noted no wards on either side of the bars. Apparently, the Thule kar-cists considered the bars a sufficient deterrent for the curious. *Maybe they think this is all it takes to protect their lair. Or maybe this is just the outer defense.*

Only one thing was certain. He would learn nothing more from this side of the barrier. He shifted into the ghost form of VESTURIEL and stepped past the bars. On the other side he became corporeal again. No alarms sounded; no defenses rallied. Satisfied, he pressed ahead.

Bones and skulls, everywhere. There was an art to their arrangement. Some were sorted by color, darker bones around lighter ones; skulls scorched black were used to make geometric patterns. A thousand skulls formed a mosaic of one grinning specter.

He craned his neck to peek around the turn. He glimpsed a yawning space from which came ominous chants and shadows dancing in firelight. He stole around the corner to creep forward, only to halt when he felt the ground under his feet crunch ever so slightly. He looked down. In this unmapped passage, the path was paved with bones large and small, and the walls and ceilings were composed of skulls of all sizes. The lair was a house made of death.

He stalked to the edge of the pit and looked over its precipice. A few dozen yards below, at the bottom of a path that spiraled downward clockwise from his left, a circular platform of black granite had been laid. A grand circle of protection had been scribed upon it in limestone chalk, and at its northern point had been erected an altar of basalt.

Inside the circle stood three persons in hooded albs: an operator and two tanists. Facing inward along the spiral pathway were dozens of robed initi-ates, coven members invited to bear witness to that night's experiment, each inside his or her own pentagram of protection.

Based on the sigils and offerings he saw, Cade deduced that this hall was sworn to the service of ASTAROTH. The demon's seal was embroidered on all of the adepts' robes, no doubt as a sign of protection—one that Cade lacked and, by the rules of magick, could not appropriate simply by stealing one of the robes.

What if Adair was right? Maybe I'm taking on more than I—

His self-doubt ended as he saw one of the coven's adepts lead in the sacrifice: a young girl, a child of no more than five or six years of age. Barefoot, shiver-ing, clad in nothing but a white nightshirt. She was crying, terrified, and all too aware of where she was and what was happening. The adept laid her upon the altar, bound her, and set a crown of holly on her brow.

The choice before Cade was haunting in its clarity.

He could fall back and return later, better armed, perhaps with Adair at his side. His odds of survival would be better. But that would mean surrendering this child, an innocent, to a gruesome death at the hands of a demon.

Or he could enter the pit of bones, make himself the focus of the coven's attacks, and risk his life in a mad assault that had no preparation, no plan, and no exit strategy.

He remembered all the pain and tragedy that had come from Stefan and Niko's defiance of such hard realities. And he recalled all of the lives that had been lost because he'd failed to heed Adair's warnings in Oxford. Forfeiting the battle to win the war was the smarter tactic. And it was exactly what Adair would tell him to do: Sacrifice the child. Give up one life to save countless others. The sum of the moral calculus was clear—but not one Cade could live with.

Fuck it. I never liked calculus, anyway.

He leaped off the precipice, over the warded threshold, into the chasm.

All that he saw, all that he sensed, became his weapons. Flames from the circle's candles and the cavern's torches became tongues of hellfire lashing out at adepts on the walkways. Two dozen forks of red lightning sprang from Cade's open palms, linking dozens of Thule dabblers in a chain of lethal suffering. Necks snapped with wet sounds of splintering bone as Cade meted out merciless justice with the many hands of JEPHISTO. Shouts of fury and alarm filled the pit.

Then came a storm of retaliation.

Bursts of fire, bolts of electricity, cones of cold, swarms of shadows circling like raptors—all converging on Cade in a tempest as the ground rushed up to meet him.

This might have been a mistake.

He turned to smoke just before he hit the bottom, then resumed his shape standing on solid ground, bearing a broadsword in one hand and a trident in the other, both spectral and glowing with power. Demonic projectiles rained down on him from above and about, all deflected by his shield—until Cade turned his defenses reflective, turning the storm of attacks against their authors, who fell in droves.

Cade severed the young girl's bonds with a flurry of unseen demonic knives.

Bloodcurdling cries—men and demons charged toward him from several passages that radiated from the pit's killing floor. With a thought he surrounded

himself and the girl with his shield, then channeled the martial prowess of
CASMIEL and the strength of MEUS CALMIRON.

He swung his spirit sword and severed limbs and heads from torsos; he
thrust his trident to gut an attacker and break his spine. Foes behind him he
cut down with hellfire and lightning. Blood washed over the floor and sprayed
his face.

Automatic gunfire ripped through the din of magickal slaughter. Cade used
JEPHISTO's hand to hold the child down, for her own good. The gift of SA-
BAOTH meant metal couldn't touch Cade, but the girl needed him to be her
shield—he was her aegis against evil.

Demons poured from every crevice of the pit. Dozens of spirits spilled over
the ledges above, a torrent of evil raining down.

There was no stopping them all.

Cade could stretch his shield only so far. To protect the girl completely required him to risk the narrowest of gaps in his own defense—and the enemy
found that gap over and over.

Unseen blades slashed wounds into his arms and legs. Tongues of fire stung
his face and left him smelling his own singed hair. Needles of ice pierced his
back. A demon's hand closed around his throat until he cleaved it with
VAELBOR's blade, banishing it to the inferno. Burnt, bloody, and forced to his
knees, Cade locked eyes with the karcist who stood inside the operator's circle,
orchestrating the coven's Goetic nightmare.

Briet stared in fascination as her horde rained down on top of him.

Then Cade cracked a predator's grin—and unleashed utter mayhem.

All right, MARCHOSIAS—let 'em have it.

As promised by the grimoire of Honorius, the great duke had granted Cade
command over its Infernal legions: thousands of spirits, an army of fallen
angels—a release of power that overwhelmed the onslaught of shadows in
which Briet had taken such pride only moments earlier.

Her smirk contorted into a grimace. She disappeared in a blast of flames
and a pillar of ink-black smoke, leaving her minions to die without her.

Cade gathered the girl in his arms and soared upward. The coven's stragglers harried them with missiles in the shape of flaming skulls, storms of phantasmal arrows, spurts of chaotic magickal energy. Only a handful slipped past
Cade's shield, but they were enough to leave him coughing blood by the time
he reached the top of the pit.

Staggering toward the tunnel with the weeping child at his side, he answered the coven's parting jabs with a fireball brighter than the dawn. It rocked the Catacombs and shook the bedrock of Paris. Dust rained down as the bone pit and all its secondary passages caved in, erasing them not just from the map but from existence.

He knew Adair would not approve of this, but he no longer cared.

Three years earlier he had told the master, *This isn't my war.* Now it was— and he was determined to fight it his way.

He guided the girl down the tunnel to the iron bars, which he blasted into shrapnel with a thought. Then he slumped against the tunnel wall while giving her a gentle nudge onward.

"Go straight," he said. "Men from the Maquis. They'll take you home."

She trembled as she asked, "What about you?"

"Forget me. . . . Forget this place. . . . It was all . . . just a bad dream." Cade left a smear of blood on the wall of bones as he collapsed to the floor. "Run."

The girl disappeared into darkness.

Cade let himself do the same.

31

OCTOBER

After more than two months of urban combat, little remained of Stalingrad but a maze of ruins, yet the fight to control it slogged on. Everyone, including Anja, knew why: Not only was the city vital to the control of oil resources in the Caucasus, it had propaganda value because it bore the name of the Soviet premier. For the sake of morale, the Red Army couldn't let it fall to the Germans; for the sake of regional dominance, the Germans couldn't afford not to capture it. And so the battle dragged on, one building and street at a time, day after bloody day.

In spite of bombings and shellings, the skeletons of large structures towered over the devastation. Much of the city's street grid remained recognizable because buildings erected during the previous two decades tended to collapse inward on their own architectural footprints. Even so, heaps of rubble and debris littered the once wide-open boulevards, providing cover to guerrilla fighters and impeding the movements of the Nazis' feared panzer divisions.

Smoke often obscured the worst of the devastation, but there was no escaping it. Coated in a film of pulverized concrete, the German and Russian armies both had taken on the pallor of ghosts haunting the city's remains, distinguishable from rats and stray dogs only by their size and their infrequent habit of moving on two legs when the absence of sniper fire permitted it—which was not very often, thanks to Premier Stalin's long record of advocating that every Russian be, first and foremost, a sharpshooter.

It was an edict Anja had grown up with, and one she had taken to heart.

No one had asked her many questions when she'd volunteered for the Red Army three months earlier. The city had been in chaos. Civilians were being evacuated in droves as troops arrived in battalions, all of them underfed and poorly equipped. Everything had been in short supply, and still was: uniforms, boots, rifles, ammunition, food, medicine, shelter.

Survival hinged on adaptation. Soldiers who hadn't been given rifles followed those who had into combat; if an armed soldier fell, an unarmed comrade picked up the weapon and carried on. Troops traded clothing, mixing and matching uniform pieces until they found some that fit. Boots, though— the only way to get a decent pair was to take them off the dead. Now winter was imminent, which meant this Hell on earth was doomed to freeze over, and neither Anja nor any of her comrades could find a warm coat literally to save their lives.

That was a problem for tomorrow.

Anja was proud of what she'd done this night. While her comrades skulked through the shattered remnants of the city, she had soared above it, disguised as a humble pigeon thanks to the charm of ANDREALPHUS. From high overhead, a tiny speck passing through rising columns of smoke and ash, she had observed the latest round of Nazi troop movements. Three companies from the German Sixth Army were flanking wide to the south in search of a fresh angle of attack on the Russian commanders, while their slave laborers cleared a road that would let the Nazis move half a dozen panzers nine blocks north along the city's western periphery.

Her scouting mission accomplished, she alighted upon a half-collapsed rooftop that overlooked the current redoubt of the German command division. There was no way for one who couldn't fly to reach the upper floors of Anja's gutted perch, never mind its roof: all of its interior staircases had collapsed, making it little more than an obstacle to incoming fire.

Which made the Nazis' surprise all the more rewarding to Anja as she put a round from her Mosin-Nagant through the skull of an SS officer who doffed his helmet while passing through her scope's field of vision. Before any of the Nazis could pinpoint the shot's origin, Anja transformed into a sparrow and swooped away into the dark.

On nights when she was unable to sight a suitable target among the enemy officer corps, she satisfied her appetite for payback by summoning hordes of rats to infest the Nazis' food stores, spread disease in their camps, and chew the cloth coverings off the wires in the Germans' tanks. It made the rats happy, kept them away from Red Army positions, and provoked a slew of short circuits and power failures in the Nazis' armored units.

By necessity she had learned to be judicious in her use of magick. The battlefront offered little privacy and few safe places in which to conduct the rituals needed to summon and yoke spirits. Consequently, even with sparing use, her reserves of magick had waned rapidly.

Another reality Anja had come to accept was that surviving as a karcist in a war zone required subtlety and discretion, not firepower. She had learned to avoid being seen working visible magick. Unleashing miraculous powers in full view of civilians or her comrades would without a doubt get her arrested, sent to a gulag, and dissected by agents of state security. And no matter how much power she might wield, she knew from experience that one magician was rarely if ever a match for a large number of professional soldiers in open combat.

It was all just as well, in her opinion. The demons suited to high-energy magickal combat were hard to yoke and quick to slip away, while those that granted such talents as healing, transformation, and animal control could be yoked at lesser costs and held for longer durations.

It helped that the Nazi forces in Stalingrad lacked even rudimentary magickal wards for their men and equipment. Unfortunately, the Red Army was just as vulnerable. Anja hoped neither Kein nor his dabblers had focused their efforts against the city's defenders.

Anja glided through a concrete ruin. She reveled in the rush of air beneath her wings, her heightened awareness of direction, her sharpened visual acuity. Traveling as a bird was a pleasure of which she never tired. However, she had learned the hard way to fly only at night, and to be mindful of hungry Russian sharpshooters with a taste for poultry. The most dangerous moment of any nocturnal excursion came at the end, when she descended into a gap between two buildings so ravaged they resembled broken teeth. If she saw anyone within a block of that stretch of dirt and wreckage, she would climb away and keep flying.

Certain it was deserted, tonight she landed and resumed her human shape—a change she effected in midflight so that she hit the ground in a crouch, behind cover.

Back on two feet, she scouted the path to her comrades' underground camp. Distant cracks of rifle fire echoed, but nothing closer than half a kilometer. The machine-gun chatter she heard was even farther off. *So far so good.*

Caution, patience, diligence, suspicion: Those were the traits that kept Anja and her comrades alive. A soldier who didn't stick her head up was far less likely to have it shot off. It was an easy lesson to learn—all it took to drive the point home was being peppered one time with a friend's bloody brains, courtesy of a sniper's bullet.

She darted through the husk of an old theater that no longer had a roof, past its rows of scorched seats to a camouflaged trapdoor on what remained of its stage. She knocked twice, then once, then twice again. From below she heard bolts being retracted. The heavy plate was pushed upward, and she slipped under it and hurried down its stepladder into the network of tunnels and other excavations the Red Army had turned into a base of operations below the city.

Familiar faces noted her return. Some lifted their chins in greeting, others waved. A few pretended not to see her. She had learned not to take offense when that happened. Packed into close quarters, robbed of even the semblance of privacy, people did whatever they could to preserve the illusion of personal space. It was just part of surviving, a fact of life during wartime.

Everywhere Anja looked, people huddled for warmth under threadbare blankets, rubbed their palms in the smoke from twig fires, and filled their hours with busywork to fend off the cold and the boredom. She envied the lucky few who scrounged sips of vodka from unbroken bottles, an increasingly rare treasure. It had been weeks since Anja had enjoyed a drink, forcing her to contend with her yoked demons while sober. To keep control, she had released all except a few spirits, but even those were wearing her down, brittling her patience and sharpening her temper.

Almost at her bedroll, Anja felt relief at the prospect of sleep—only to see her tunnel neighbors shoot her fearful looks as she approached. Oleg and Anton averted their eyes, but Nadezhda—the bravest of the lot—opened hers wide, an attempt to warn Anja of danger.

Unable to imagine what had them spooked, Anja hurried to Nadezhda and gently took the young woman aside. "What's wrong?"

Nadezhda said in a terrified whisper, "Political officers!" She looked around, and locks of her unwashed blond hair fell into her eyes. "They asked about you."

"Why? What did they—?"

Nadezhda backed away while staring at something behind Anja.

Anja turned to see a pair of Soviet political officers. They were always easy to spot, with their crisp uniforms, clean boots, smart haircuts, and smooth faces. Neither one wore rank insignia, which were only slowly coming back into fashion in the Red Army as the war imposed its need for a clear chain of command.

Even bereft of rank, it was clear the older of the two men was in charge. He removed his hat to reveal his shaved-bald head. He tucked the hat under his arm, adjusted his round wire-frame eyeglasses, and stepped forward. "Comrade Anja Kernova?" He waited for her nod of confirmation, then continued. "We'd like a word with you. In private."

"And who are you?"

"Captain Misha Krezinskov, political officer." He indicated his younger, fair-haired subordinate. "This is Lieutenant Gogol." With a wave of his arm, he tried to coax her away from her fellow soldiers. "Shall we?"

Anja knew she had done nothing wrong, but she had heard horror stories of people escorted away by political officers, never to return. She stood her ground. "We can talk here."

"I'm not making a *request*."

So it was an order. Her options were to comply or be executed. She sighed. "As you wish. Lead on, Comrade Captain." Krezinskov led her deeper into the tunnel complex, and Gogol fell in behind her. They escorted her several minutes' walk through the underground passages, to a small room with a heavy door. Inside was a chair at a desk beneath a kerosene lamp.

"Have a seat," Krezinskov said. He set his hat on the table.

Anja sat on the chair as Gogol bolted the door shut and placed himself in front of it. She shifted her attention to the captain. "What can I do for you, Comrade Captain?"

He studied her. "I've been reading your service record. Barely three months since you enlisted, and already you've made quite a name for yourself. Did I read correctly you have *sixty-one* confirmed sniper kills?"

"Sixty-*two*. I shot an *SS-Obersturmbannführer* inside a Nazi command post tonight."

"Which post, exactly?"

"The one by the hospital."

Perplexed looks passed between the political officers. The captain regarded Anja with deepening suspicion. "You mean the one for which no one's been able to get a sight line?" He was not amused by Anja's faux-humble shrug. "This is the root of our concern, Comrade. You seem to have a knack for sniping targets in places no one else can approach. Not even Vasily Zaytsev has gotten so close to the enemy's command posts."

"He doesn't need to. And I'm not half the rifleman Comrade Zaytsev is."

"No, but you're also an accomplished spy. Your record says you've brought us more than two dozen tips about German troop movements, supply and ammo caches, and ambushes—and that every single one has checked out. If I didn't know better, I'd think you were in the enemy's headquarters when the Nazis made their plans."

She had been, of course—disguised as a rat, or as a mouse—but she knew not to admit the truth. Not to her comrades, and certainly not to political officers. Atheism was an official plank of the Communist Party platform; there was no way Anja could explain that her successes were made possible by Renaissance-era Goetic ceremonial magick. Either her interrogators would believe her and she would be locked away as an enemy of the state, or they would think her insane and lock her away as a menace to the body politic. There was no circumstance in which the truth could possibly set her free. In all likelihood, it would only get her killed.

She smiled at Krezinskov. "What can I say, Comrade Captain? I have rare talents. I'm just grateful I get to use them in service to Mother Russia."

"Perhaps you're a German spy. Sent to give us gifts so we'll learn to trust you—only to have you turn against us at a critical moment."

It was hard to mask her contempt for his paranoia. "Tell me you're not serious. Gifts? You really think the Nazis are so generous they'd let me shoot forty-nine of their officers and more than a dozen of their senior enlisted commanders? You really think them *that* cunning? Maybe they'll let me put a bullet between Hitler's eyes, just so I can win *your* trust."

He seethed. Had she pushed him too far? Was he about to reward her insolence with a beating? Or a bullet? His anger-hardened features relaxed, and he drew a calming breath. "Very well. Let's say for the moment I accept your reasoning. Can you teach your ways to others? If you could show Zaytsev how to reach some of the targets you have—"

She shook her head, resurrecting the captain's frown. "I'm sorry, Comrade Captain. But my methods aren't the kind of thing I can teach. At least, not here. And not to just anyone."

It was clear her answer had stoked their mistrust. Krezinskov shifted his hand toward the holstered pistol on his hip. That was Anja's cue to bring the meeting to an end—her way.

She looked up at Krezinskov until he met her stare—and then she channeled the mind-slaving talent of SICARIOS as she spoke in a low, calm register. "If you've read my file, Comrade Captain, you know I'm loyal to the Soviet

Union. It's too bad I can't help you teach others to do what I do, but Mother Russia needs me on the line. Don't you agree?"

The captain concurred with a slow, numb nod of his head. "I quite agree."

Behind him, Lieutenant Gogol stepped forward, abandoning his post at the door. "Sir?"

"It's been a pleasure talking with you, Comrade Captain," Anja added, "but General Khrushchev urgently needs you and Lieutenant Gogol at headquarters."

Krezinskov picked up his hat, put it on, and faced Gogol. "We need to go. The general needs us at headquarters." He breezed past Gogol, opened the door, and made his exit. Gogol started to follow him, but he paused to shoot a confused look at Anja.

She met his gaze with a sinister glare. "Better hurry, Comrade Lieutenant. Can't keep the general waiting." Gogol hurried out and jogged to catch up to his captain.

Anja sauntered out of the little room and plodded to her spot in the tunnel under the church. She'd had a long night and was ready to sleep. As she tucked herself inside her bedroll, Nadezhda rolled hers to face Anja. "What happened? Are you all right?"

"I'm fine, Nady. Go back to sleep."

The blond woman rolled away from Anja and sank into a troubled slumber. Anja, meanwhile, lay awake beside her, staring at the ceiling and regretting her lies.

We are not fine, Nadezhda. Nothing is fine. She shut her eyes and turned her last command of the day upon herself: *Go back to sleep.*

NOVEMBER

It troubled Adair how time's passage seemed increasingly fleeting to him as he grew older. After more than three and a half centuries, a week could slip by him unnoticed. A month could evaporate like dew on a windowpane at dawn.

Which is why it seemed to him that Cade had barely returned from his mission to Paris and now was packing his duffel, to venture alone once more into peril.

Adair hobbled through the open doorway of Cade's room. The young man had his back to Adair. Bathed in the dawn light streaming through the window, he stuffed his last few articles of clean clothing into his bag. His leather roll of magickal tools was tied shut and propped at an angle against the bed's footboard.

"You packed your grimoire, yes?"

"No, I burned it." Cade noted Adair's narrowed stare. "First thing in the bag."

"Good lad." Adair hop-stepped into the room. "Sorry I can't go with you."

"Don't be. Someone has to stay here to guard the wine." The young karcist zipped his bag shut, then rendered it into the unseen hands of his demonic valet.

"Remember to scout the Thule covens. Don't go bargin' in like a witless shitgibbon."

"Would you relax? I handled Paris on my own."

"From what the Maquis told Niko, you nearly got yourself killed."

The young man frowned. "I know what I'm doing."

"Aye. You do at that." There was no point seeding Cade's mind with doubts, and nothing to be gained by warning him that venturing into Germany, on a solo mission to destroy the last two great Thule covens, would be even more perilous than his mission to Paris had been.

This is why we bonded him. It's what I trained him for.

He hoped his air of nonchalance sounded more convincing than it felt. "You'll do fine. I wish I could be there, but I know it's time to let you walk alone."

Shrugging into his trench coat, Cade glanced at Adair's crutches. "Not much choice. I'm the only one of us who can still walk."

"You cheeky scullion! I'll have you know my old army mates are finding me a prosthesis."

"Great." Cade picked up his tools. "So you'll be running wind sprints by Christmas?"

Adair grimaced at the good-natured ribbing. "Sod a dog, you beetle-headed basket-cockle." He reached inside his pocket and pulled out a small rectangular steel mirror like the ones he had made for Niko and Stefan. "I had this made for you. So you can stay in touch."

Cade looked amused. "What, my birthday again so soon?"

"When is your birthday?"

The youth feigned offense. "Two years and you're only asking me this now?"

"I've had a bit on my mind."

Easing off the sarcasm, Cade said, "May ninth."

"So, I missed it, then."

"By about six months."

"And how old are you now?"

The lad pondered that for half a second. "Twenty-three."

"Well happy fucking birthday, here's a magick mirror. Know how to use it?"

"*Fenestra, velarium, discutio.*"

"Finally—proof that you've listened." He slapped the looking glass into Cade's hand. "But take care: the enemy knows how to use it now. Don't make the mistake Stefan did."

"I won't. But why don't we just change the command words?"

"Because they're not ours to change. They're set by the demon that makes the mirrors."

"Gotta love Infernal bureaucracy." The young karcist hid the mirror in one of his coat's inside pockets. "A shame we can't spare a large one for a shortcut into Germany."

"Sorry. Already put my last two portals into play. One got you to Paris before Kein broke it. The other's bound for safer shores." Adair pivoted to keep facing Cade, who circled him on his way out of the bedroom. "Kein's been beefing up his defenses on the German border. So if you're going into Krautland, you'll have to do it the hard way."

"I didn't think we *knew* any other way." Cade's affect turned maudlin. "Look, just in case I don't make it back—"

"Don't say it, lad."

"No, I need to. If I don't come back, I just want to say thank you, for everything you taught me. I'll try not to let you down."

"Aye, well . . ." What was there to say in response? Adair choked down his upwelling of sentiment and averted his misting eyes. "Remember where you're going?"

Cade nodded. "I hike from here to Carchuna."

"Right. Pick up your feet, you'll make it by sundown. What's the driver's name?"

"Esteban Alvaros. He has gray hair and his left pinky finger is missing."

"After sundown, he'll take you up the coast to Gibraltar. Where's the letter of transit?"

Cade patted his chest. "Shirt pocket."

"When you get to Gibraltar, show that to any man in uniform, and say you've orders to report to General Eisenhower. He'll get a plane to fly you into Germany as soon as he can." He set one of his crutches against the doorjamb. With his free arm he pulled Cade into an embrace. It was a gesture he hadn't extended to Stefan or Niko, or to any of the other young lives he had sent into harm's way over the years, and now his heart was full of regrets. His voice quavered with fear as he slapped Cade's back. "Come home safe, m'boy."

They parted, and in that moment Adair saw his raw emotions mirrored in Cade's eyes, and he remembered that the youth was an orphan, as much in need of surrogate kin as he was.

Cade banished his melancholy with a smile, then marshaled his humor to exorcise the moment of rank sentimentality. "Promise not to drink all the scotch before I get home."

"Ach. I never make a promise I can't keep."

"That makes two of us. And I promise *you*—" He clapped Adair's shoulder. "I *will* kick your ass if I come back and there's no single-malt."

Adair cracked a proud smile. "Understood."

"And if you think of it," Cade said, ". . . leave a light on for me."

"That I will, lad. That I will."

———

Little more than a bump on the southern coast of Spain, the British protectorate of Gibraltar swarmed with Allied troops. Cade saw Brits, Americans, Canadians, New Zealanders, Free French, and Greek partisans, all just during his ride to the headquarters, which was hidden deep underground, in a complex carved from the peninsula's bedrock. Every cubic foot of space he had seen inside the command center had been packed tight and stacked high with food, supplies, ammunition, and fuel. Every passageway had bustled with men and women in uniform, all moving with dispatch, soldiers anxious in the face of imminent deployment.

Nearly a dozen officers had checked and rechecked his letter of transit and verified his orders before he finally reached the one person who seemed to know what was going on. A tall and imposing man with crew-cut fair hair, features chiseled by wartime hardships, and four stars on his uniform's epaulets, General Dwight D. Eisenhower nodded as he reviewed Cade's documents. "So," he'd said. "You're the one." He handed back Cade's papers. "My men deploy two nights from now, on the eighth. Your flight'll go at the same time."

And that was all he'd had to say. A series of his subordinates had whisked Cade away, passing him down a chain of handlers marked by ever-decreasing rank, until a second lieutenant had shown him to a cot in a crowded subterranean chamber with five dozen strangers.

"We'll let you know when it's time to fly," the junior officer had said. He'd left before Cade learned his name or was able to ask what the fuck was going on.

Then the eighth of November arrived, and all Cade heard was chatter about that night's Allied invasion of French North Africa. Morocco, Algeria, Tunisia—they were all in the crosshairs. It was the "soft underbelly of the Mediterranean" to hear the Allied commanders describe it, and they were about to rip it out of the Axis's hands.

All except for the B-17 flight crew tasked to ferry Cade into Germany. He listened to the men of *Silver Sadie* complain and swear under their breath about him and his mission as they crossed the tarmac toward the aircraft, which stood separated from its squadron.

The flight engineer, Sergeant Ward, grumbled, "Six months of mission prep down the drain so we can ferry this shithead to Krautland."

"Good thing we're bomb-free on this run," said Corporal Trahern, one of the gunners. "Gotta make room for the general's luggage."

Cade admired the bomber. He loved the illustration adorning its nose: a zaftig platinum blonde in blue coveralls, her expression proud as she clocked a cartoon Hitler with a pipe wrench, sending the Führer's teeth flying. The dark green aircraft was silhouetted by a late-autumn sunset as Cade climbed the ladder into its midsection.

Inside the aircraft, Cade looked around. The lack of bombs made it feel strangely empty. Private Orson, the tail gunner, shouldered past and almost knocked him over. "Watch it, Meat."

Another gunner, Corporal Chao, muttered as he passed Cade, "Orson's an asshole. Ignore him." He did a double take at Cade. "Fuck—what happened to your eyebrows?"

"Occupational hazard." Cade turned away, ending the conversation.

The pilot and commander, Captain Gladwin, was the last man aboard. He raised his voice to fill the main compartment and address the entire crew. "Look sharp, guys. I know this isn't the mission we expected, but we have our orders. And look on the bright side—after we drop Mr. Martin behind enemy lines, we'll be continuing on to England."

No sooner was Gladwin ensconced in the cockpit than Ward snarked to Chao from the topside turret, "Oh, goody—England in November. I shoulda packed my swim trunks."

Silver Sadie was one of the last aircraft to take off, nearly two hours after sundown. Night fell while they traversed Spain, and darkness became their cloak as they raced over southern France, which was nowhere to be seen thanks to lights-out curfews.

It was freezing inside the bomber. Cade had expected to face wet cold in Germany this time of year, but he was unprepared for the sharp chill of speeding at two hundred miles per hour, ten thousand feet above ground. The ten-man bomber crew all seemed impervious to the frigid air, with their fleece-lined jackets, silk scarves, pullover caps, and thick gloves.

Worse than the cold, the drone of the propellers was deafening. Their vibrations permeated the bomber's hull and decks. Cade had hoped the sound might prove hypnotic after a few hours and lull him to sleep, but it was so loud it sounded as if a swarm of bees had taken up residence inside his skull.

Fucking hell. What I wouldn't do for a decent night's—

A nudge from a booted foot opened his eyes. He looked up into the scowl of Ward, who hooked a thumb toward the forward bulkhead. "Cap says we just crossed the Swiss-Kraut border, so get your shit together."

Cade checked his watch. It was just after 1:00 A.M. They had made exceptional time from Gibraltar, reinforcing his perception that the crew of the *Silver Sadie* wanted him out of their aircraft as soon as possible. The fact that the B-17 was carrying no heavy ordnance also had helped speed its progress on this night flight over enemy territory. While Cade fumbled in the dark to find his gear, Ward climbed into the topside turret.

Moonlight illuminated the rest of the crew as Cade looked fore and aft. Waist-gunners Trahern and Chao rubbed their eyes and seized the grips of their pivot-mounted M2 Browning machine guns. Far aft, tail gunner Orson swiveled left to right, anticipating trouble. As Ward rotated the top turret in a full circle while searching the skies for danger, Corporal Dominguez mirrored his actions in the bomber's belly-mounted ball turret. Through the open cockpit door Cade glimpsed the flight officers. The only member of the crew Cade couldn't see at all was Sergeant Rozansky, the bombardier and nose gunner.

The first thing Cade retrieved was his leather roll-up containing his tools of the Art. He strapped it diagonally across his back, as he always had while traveling.

Ward shouted over the roar of the propellers, "Hey, Meat! Are you fucking stupid? Strap that to your leg or it'll snag your chute!"

Cade wasn't sure he wanted to explain to Ward why he wouldn't need a parachute. He raised a hand to fend off further advice. "Don't worry about it," he hollered. "I'll be—"

Explosions filled the sky around the bomber with fire and flak.

Cade tumbled aft as the nose pitched upward and the engines buzzed with acceleration. All around Cade, each member of the crew pressed a hand to one ear as the copilot relayed information and orders over their headsets. Flames and shrapnel choked the sky around *Silver Sadie*. Captain Gladwin banked the bomber left and pushed it into a steeper climb as more flak harried the B-17.

Cade gripped the bulkhead, terrified. *So much for sneaking into Germany.*

Dominguez grinned up at him. "'Smatter, gringo? Don't like fireworks?"

Another cocky smile, this time from Chao. "Having fun yet?"

Ward looked down at Cade. "Hang tight, buddy! We're in for some—"

Pain knifed into Cade's ears as a jarring blast rocked the plane.

Silver Sadie's nose filled with orange fire and black smoke. Wind laced with oily spray and smoldering shrapnel roared from the cockpit into the main compartment. The aircraft bobbled and veered hard to the left, throwing Cade against the curved bulkhead.

The aircraft barrel-rolled twice, throwing Cade and the waist gunners into wild tumbles, human dice in a spinning cup. Another explosion tore through the starboard wing and blew its engines to bits. Then the bomber pitched into an uncontrolled dive as another hit tore off its tail, taking Private Orson's life in a storm of metal and smoke.

Fire and free fall, panic and bitter cold. Cade screamed, and so did the men around him. *Silver Sadie*'s midsection splintered as it twisted and rolled, ejecting him and the four surviving members of the crew into the night, where it was hard for Cade to hear anything but the rushing of wind past his soon-to-be-frostbitten ears. It was so dark he couldn't see the earth below. He remembered his briefing on Gibraltar: he had less than a minute before he hit the ground.

Plenty of time.

He engaged the Sight. The landscape below came into focus, a monochromatic sprawl of deep shadows and greenish highlights. Looking up, he saw the four survivors of *Silver Sadie* deploy their parachutes—then felt his stomach twist into a knot as fiery debris from the wrecked bomber rained down and set them all aflame.

The men released their reserve chutes, only to see them suffer the same fate as they were peppered with burning wreckage from above. Trahern, Chao, Dominguez, and Ward were plummeting to their doom.

Cade spread his arms to slow his descent, then reached out with the unseen hands of JEPHISTO, snared the men, and pulled them toward himself in midair. The first one he could reach was Chao. He took hold of the young Chinese American's sleeve and shouted, "Grab Dominguez!" As soon as Chao had his crewmate, the others got the idea, though they seemed confused as to what Cade was doing. They were seconds away from a fatal impact as Dominguez snagged Trahern by his collar, and Trahern gripped Ward's ankle.

That'll do.

He invoked Vesturiel's ghost form just before they met the ground. Arrested in midfall, they lingered like fog, gray wisps above a field of dead grass.

Then Cade breathed out, restoring himself and the survivors to solidity. They dropped to the ground, stunned and amazed. Their limp parachutes fluttered down and draped over them like burial shrouds. The four men scrambled out of their flight gear, then emerged from beneath the chutes and pawed at themselves, as if unsure whether they could trust their senses.

Dominguez wore a horrified look. "Are we dead? Are we ghosts?"

Chao punched him in the arm, eliciting a yelp. "Nope. Flesh and bone."

Trahern was at a loss to complete a sentence. "But I don't . . . But we . . . How did—? How are we—?" He finally strung together a complete thought: "How did you do that?"

The master had warned Cade against telling "the rabble" too much about magick, so he resorted instead to a convenient lie. "Sorry, it's top-secret. You weren't supposed to see it, but . . . I couldn't just let you guys fall."

Ward took off his fleece-lined leather jacket and handed it to Cade. "Take this." When Cade tried to wave off the gesture, the flight engineer insisted. "It's fucking freezing out here, and it's gonna get colder." He showed Cade its inner lining. A rectangle of silk was printed with a detailed map of western Europe. "If you get lost, it'll help you find your way."

"I can't. You'll need that to get out of enemy territory."

"Chao's jacket has the same lining." He pushed his jacket into Cade's hands.

Cade took off his less insulated coat and gave it to Ward. "Now you'll freeze."

"The boys and I can take turns trading coats. But you have to go on alone. Speaking of which—" He pivoted toward Trahern. "Danny, give him your Colt."

The corporal balked at the order. "What?"

"He's unarmed and marching alone into Krautland. Give him your fucking Colt." When the *Silver Sadie* gunner continued to resist, Ward added, "He just saved your life, you fucking ingrate. The least you can do is lend him your sidearm."

There was no easy way for Cade to explain to Ward that he was anything but unarmed, so he accepted the semiautomatic pistol that was grudgingly surrendered to him by Trahern. He received it and its holster with a humble smile. "Thanks. If I live, I'll try to get it back it you."

"Assuming I live," Trahern said. "If I don't make it, my wife and kid are in Secaucus. Give it to them."

"Will do."

Truck engines and voices barking orders in German began to echo in the darkness. From the east, bluish-white searchlights slashed over the top of a low hill. It was time to move on.

Cade shook Ward's hand. "Thank you, Sergeant. And good luck."

"Same to you, kid." He turned away and jogged past his men. "Let's go, ladies! The Krauts are coming, and Switzerland's calling!"

"Chocolates and milkmaids," Trahern said as he fell in line. "What's not to love?" Dominguez and Chao rolled their eyes and shook their heads as they hurried southwest, close on the sergeant's heels as they made their desperate bid to reach neutral territory.

Rendered invisible by Aorotos, Cade ignored the incoming German search team and walked north-northeast toward Frankfurt. In the morning, once he was someplace safe, he would contact Adair with the mirror to let him know he was on the ground in Germany, and that the survivors of the *Silver Sadie* would need transportation out of Switzerland.

Until then, he knew what mattered most was to keep moving and not look back, because that was where regret lived—and for Cade that was a burden already too great to bear.

———※———

There was no getting used to the stench in the infirmary. But then, calling this mess an infirmary struck Anja as a sick joke. It was little more than a crudely excavated tunnel, its roof held up by half-rotted timbers and the empty prayers of atheists. Every time a mortar shell struck within a quarter mile or a German tank rolled past inside half a block, dirt rained down on the wounded and dying, dusting them with the colors of the grave.

Anja tried to avoid this place, but her conscience had led her to it each night for over a month. Scores of maimed soldiers and civilians lingered here in need of attention, and more arrived every hour, adding to the ranks of the mortally wounded and the delirious.

The smell of blood was masked by a bite of disinfectant, but neither odor could compete with the miasma of human excrement that pooled on the floor. Dying patients voided their bowels with revolting regularity, as did those forced to endure amputations without the solace of morphine or even vodka. When one of the medical volunteers succumbed to the urge to vomit, no one paid attention anymore. It was just one more mess in the mix.

Anja walked between the rows of cots, dismayed by the bloodied and the burned. General Khrushchev and other Red Army leaders had promised the fighting would be ended by now. Long-overdue reinforcements had arrived the week before and crushed the Romanian and Hungarian forces defending the Nazis' flanks. It seemed then the battle was over; the Germans had lost. Everyone had expected them to wave the white flag. Unfortunately, someone forgot to tell the Germans, who had intensified their efforts, waging battles of attrition from one ruined building to the next, and sometimes even from one floor of a building to another.

It was insane. Anja didn't understand it.

What she understood was suffering. Sorrow. Loss.

There were so many children huddled under bloodstained sheets. Too many. Anja could tune out the plaintive cries of adult soldiers and spies, people who had gone to war knowing the cost it might entail. But the children. . . .

In every young boy's face she saw the dying grimace of her little brother, Piotr, his body cut in half by Kein's cruel magick, his lifeblood leaching into the snow. In the eyes of every wounded girl she recognized herself, grieving and alone, forever unredeemed.

Ash-covered fingers, small and trembling, reached out to her. Silent, she drifted past, a living ghost haunting those the Reaper had marked as its own.

Perceiving them through a lens of demonic sight, she knew which ones were too far gone for her gifts to save, and which ones might recover on their own in time. The ones she sought were those whose lives stood balanced on the razor's edge between life and death:

A boy of five or perhaps six years, shot through his abdomen. The bleeding was stanched, but it remained to be seen whether he would succumb to sepsis.

A girl of nine, comatose after falling from a collapsing building, struggling against a slow hemorrhage in her brain.

A teenage girl, clinging to life, written off by the medics—none of whom possessed the resources to realize she was nearly two months pregnant.

Anja paused beside each of them, pressed her palm to their chest, and channeled the healing talent of BUER, one of only three spirits she still kept yoked despite the discomfort they caused her and the risks that arose whenever she needed to renew their bondage.

After working her magickal therapy on each child, she dipped her index finger into a canteen of water she had exorcised and blessed. With her wet fingertip she scribed a cross in the grime coating each one's forehead.

When she turned away from the last of them, she nearly collided with Nurse Deshkin, a young woman who had volunteered to tend the wounded.

"If it isn't Saint Anja, making her rounds." There was no sarcasm in Deshkin's voice. She, like many of those who had observed Anja's visits to the wounded, had noticed that those whom she anointed always recovered.

"Just doing my best to offer comfort."

Anja started to leave, but halted as Deshkin called after her: "We could use your help. There are wounded coming in. Lots of them. From the battle out by the old grain silos."

"I don't come here for them." She quickened her retreat, eager to slip the noose of imposed obligation. Deshkin wasn't going to stop her.

A wave of wounded Red Army troops surging into the infirmary did.

Everyone was shouting, but no one knew what they were doing. Soldiers on stretchers gagged on blood so dark it was almost black, or clawed at torsos stained crimson. A dozen casualties raced past Anja missing limbs or extremities, or pawing at shredded eyes, or trying to hold severed ears against their heads in the hope that someone could sew them back on.

In the middle of all the mayhem was a lone surgeon, barking orders at anyone who might be able to help him, including Anja, who was too deep in shock to understand a word he said.

Nurse Deshkin grabbed Anja's wrist, put her hand to a wounded soldier's chest, and said with authority, "Press here, hard."

Blood pulsed against Anja's palm and oozed between her fingers, no matter how hard she pushed down. Panic bloomed inside her. Her heart raced, her breaths shortened, and she shook like a dog left out in the cold. Every nerve in her body told her to run, to escape this abattoir.

She looked down to apologize to her patient for being a coward—then froze. The face looking back at her was masked in blood and dirt, but familiar all the same: Nadezhda's eyes locked on to Anja's, pleading for life. The brave young sniper mouthed words, but her voice was gone. Anja leaned in, but all she heard were weak gasps passing her friend's lips.

Redoubling the pressure of her hand on Nadezhda's chest, Anja shouted over the clamor of the infirmary: "Over here! She needs the doctor! Now!"

The surgeon was wrist-deep in another soldier's mangled guts. "She'll wait her turn!"

It took no special sight for Anja to know her friend's life was expiring as she watched. Nady had at most a few breaths left before the Reaper struck.

She was nearly gone; Anja knew it would be a fight to save her—and if she did, how could she ever explain it?

A croak from Nadezhda's parched throat commanded Anja's attention. Anja lowered her ear to Nadezhda's lips and struggled to hear her friend's dying words.

"Anja?"

"It's me, Nady."

"I . . . I'm . . . scared."

The blood pushing against Anja's palm grew weak, the pressure behind it too feeble to force it past her fingers. The end was coming for Nadezhda; death was going to rip her from Anja's grasp just as it had taken her brother so many years earlier.

No. You cannot have her.

It was possible to heal a great many injuries and maladies through the power of BUER, but the greater the feat, the higher the cost it demanded from the karcist. Pulling Nadezhda back from the brink of death would push the limits of what Anja could compel from the demon. She felt BUER balk when she tried to focus it on restoring Nadezhda's tattered heart.

Do as I command, demon!

HER WOUNDS ARE TOO GREAT. DEATH IS TOO NEAR.

You will not let her die!

TO SAVE HER, YOU MUST LET ME GIVE HER SOME OF YOUR STRENGTH.

So mote it be.

YOU MUST ALSO RELEASE ME AND MY KIN FROM THY YOKE.

If thou swear one and all to depart in peace, I shall release thee.

BY OUR LORD AND PATRON ASTAROTH, WE SWEAR IT.

It was a steep bargain, but Anja had expected it. Even if BUER hadn't demanded freedom for itself and the others, sacrificing her own vitality to save Nadezhda was going to leave her weakened to the point that she would have to release them anyway. The worst part of the deal was that it would leave her bereft of magick indefinitely. In the tumult of Stalingrad, Anja had no way of knowing when she would have the strength or the solitude to conduct the ritual to bind more spirits into service.

BUER interrupted her musings: *I HAVE HEALED WHAT WOUNDS I CAN. PREPARE THYSELF. I SHALL GIVE THE WOMAN HALF YOUR VIGOR, AS THOU HAST COMMANDED. WHEN IT IS DONE, I AND MY KIN SHALL DEPART.*

Anja took a deep breath. *Do it.*

A profound emptiness struck her. It felt as if half of her blood had drained away in an instant. Balance abandoned her, and the world spun, a riot of color and sound. Then came the narcotic lightness of suddenly being free of demonic soul-passengers. Her knees buckled, and she collapsed on top of Nadezhda.

The wounded soldier snapped to consciousness with a gasp. "Anja? Anja!"

"It's all right," she whispered to her friend, relieved that this time she spoke the truth. She smiled and held Nadezhda's bloody hand. "We're all right, now, Nady. . : . We both are."

<hr/>

Rain drizzled from shallow eaves above Cade's head. Hunched against the cold, he stood alone in a sliver of darkness separating two buildings in central Frankfurt and surveilled the front doors of a Masonic hall across the street. A cigarette smoldered in his trembling right hand; his enchanted mirror shook in his left. "Fuck, it's cold. My fingers are going numb."

In the mirror, Adair reproached him with a mock frown. *"Toughen up, ye gobshite."*

"Easy for you to say. You're sitting by the fire with a glass of Garnacha."

"I'd prefer Glenmorangie. We all make sacrifices."

Four men holding tentlike umbrellas climbed the steps to the hall's front doors and tapped a once-thrice-twice pattern with its brass knocker. A gaunt, pallid figure dressed like a butler opened the doors. The men closed their umbrellas and handed them to the doorman as they entered. Seconds after the butler shut the doors, five more men in dark suits and trench coats, all hunched under umbrellas, hurried around the corner, climbed the steps, and knocked.

Cade took a drag off his cigarette. "Jesus, more of 'em? They're packing this place like a clown car. How many people are in this coven?"

"Our spy said thirty, give or take. Why?"

As before, the butler—who Cade suspected was a lamia of some sort—opened the doors, relieved the guests of their coats and umbrellas, then closed the doors behind them. Cade said, "I've counted more than twice that many in the last hour."

Concern creased Adair's careworn face. *"You're sure?"*

"Positive. There must be at least seventy people in there."

Adair stroked his beard, immersed in thought. When he looked at Cade, he seemed alarmed. *"Did you see a crazy tall bastard, bald head, dressed all in white, with a black cane topped by a golden wolf's head?"*

The description was uncanny in its specificity. "Yeah. About fifteen minutes ago."

The master winced. *"That's Ludwig Konig, leader of the Berlin coven. They must be holding a joint meeting. Everyone the Thule Society has left is in that meeting hall."*

"All of them?" Cade's imagination reeled. "You're saying we could wipe them out!"

"What? No! I'm telling you to walk away."

He recoiled. "Retreat? Are you crazy?"

"Are you? Attacking that many at once? It's suicide. Bugger off. Now."

The order was sensible, but still it rankled. Cade had spent weeks skulking through Germany. He'd slept in ditches, stolen food (and more than a few bottles of wine and liquor) from people's homes, and been forced to slay half a dozen Gestapo who'd had the misfortune of crossing his path. For the past four days in Frankfurt, he had haunted this and half a dozen other trash-strewn alleyways to spy on the Masonic hall and record the comings and goings of its coven members. He had come armed for a slaughter, not a stealthy escape.

Adair cut through Cade's brooding: *"Lad? Are you listening?"*

Cade took a pull from his cigarette. "I hear you." A disgusted sigh full of smoke. "So much for avoiding Berlin at Christmas. On the bright side, maybe I'll get a shot at Hit—" The Führer's name caught half-formed in Cade's throat as he watched a lone figure climb the steps of the Masonic hall. Even from a distance, Cade recognized him.

Lean of build and cruel of face, the Finn toted no umbrella but strode through the downpour untouched by the rain. The doors opened ahead of him before he knocked.

Cade flicked his cigarette over his shoulder. "Siegmar. He's here."

"Forget what I said. Don't walk away—run like hell."

"No." As the Finn strolled inside the coven lair, Cade's memory snapped back to Siegmar on the Liverpool docks, watching the *Athenia* depart so he could report it to his master. Kein had sent LEVIATHAN, but Siegmar had told him where to send it.

His heart full of wrath, Cade stepped out of the alleyway and marched through the rain, on a direct line for the Masonic hall.

From the mirror in his hand, Adair protested, *"Cade, stop! It's too many! You can't—"*

"*Velarium.*" Cade tucked the mirror into his coat pocket.

The stairs he took two at a time. As he passed the middle step, a pair of guardian demons swirled out of the mist on either side of the doors. They were chimeric horrors: one with a goat's head on a man's body, its flesh rotten and teeming with maggots, black talons curving from four-fingered hands; the other a desecration of the Blessed Virgin, her tongue a serpent, her billowing white robe stained with blood and shit.

Cade struck down the guardians with slashes of hellfire. The sentinels disintegrated as Cade reached the top step. In too great a hurry to knock, he magickally unlocked the doors and pushed them open at the speed of thought.

On the other side, the cadaverous demon butler reached toward a bell on a nearby table, to sound an alarm. Cade vomited hellfire, banishing the lamia in a cloud of sulfur and ash.

Ahead of Cade, wide stairs curved upward on either side of the empty grand foyer. Gilded double doors stood closed ahead of him, and to either side.

They didn't stay closed for long.

Doors to his left and right flew open toward him. From both sides charged half a dozen dabblers in ceremonial robes, most of them fumbling wands in unpracticed hands while their tongues tripped over curses in bastardized Latin.

The first six Cade skewered with VAELBOR's spears.

The next three he let JEPHISTO break like twigs.

The last three got shots off—hellfire, lightning, a swarm of wasps. Cade deflected the flames and turned them against the insects, which turned to dust. The lightning he absorbed, then threw back in a triple fork that left the last three dabblers twitching on the floor.

Through the open doorways he saw a library on his left and a sitting room on his right. Other doorways led out of those rooms, deeper into the hall's social areas. Might there be more dabblers lurking there, either cowering or oblivious? And what about the upper floors? He couldn't risk leaving his back undefended when he faced such overwhelming enemy numbers.

MARCHOSIAS, send your legions to search the rest of this floor. Tell them to slay any karcists they find other than me.

The demon's voice in his head had an old man's rasp.

SO SHALL IT BE DONE.

The great duke's legion of nameless spirits surged past Cade like a foul breeze. Curtains fluttered and papers twirled in the parlor and library as the invisible horde rushed through them.

Cade climbed the left staircase to the second floor. Scouting the path ahead with the Sight, he saw wards glowing in a chain across a middle step. He summoned a sword of fire as he stepped over the sigils.

A two-headed gryphon shimmered into view, charging at him. He leveled his blade and let the beast impale itself. The burning sword sank into its torso between its necks, and hellfire consumed the fiend from within. Cade wondered if this was the best the enemy had to offer.

At the top of the stairs, a hallway stretched in either direction. Both sides were lined with offices, smoking dens, and the like. All those doors were open, but there was no sign of action.

If anyone's there, they'd have heard my entrance. So either those rooms are empty, or someone is lying in ambush. He concentrated: MARCHOSIAS, *is the first floor secure?*

IT IS.

Send your legions upstairs. Bid them kill anyone other than me.

AS THOU WILT.

Another gust of cold stink blew past Cade and washed down the corridor to either side. If anyone was there, he would know in a matter of moments.

The demon was swift in its report. THE UPPER ROOMS ARE EMPTY.

Very well. Cade went downstairs. He stopped in front of the last pair of unopened doors. Guardians had been placed on them to keep the uninvited at bay. Against most intruders, that would be more than enough to guarantee the security of the hall's inner sanctum.

To Cade they were a formality.

He negated the door guardians and snuck into a dark antechamber on the other side. Voices echoed in what sounded like a large room ahead. Piercing the darkness with the Sight, Cade saw that a double curtain stitched with magickal sigils partitioned the antechamber from the space beyond. Unable to look past the curtain with the Sight, he crept forward and parted it just enough to peek through.

Then he laid eyes on the great hall.

Thirty yards wide. Fifty yards deep. A thirty-foot ceiling. Garish in its decoration. Gold leaf abounded, as did murals incorporating everything from ancient Egyptian hieroglyphs to Kabbalistic symbols and Goetic circles of protection. Also in evidence were classic Masonic symbols: the compass and square, and an unfinished pyramid topped by an all-seeing eye.

On either long side of the hall stood tiers of seats packed with the assembled members of both covens. The floor of the hall was mostly open, though a grand circle of protection, inside which had been scribed a complex seven-pointed star, dominated its center. Siegmar stood in the operator's circle. Two older men—including one whom Cade recognized as the man in white Adair had identified as the leader of the Berlin coven—occupied the tanists' positions. *If the Berlin top dog is a tanist,* Cade figured, *the other one's probably the Frankfurt boss.*

Seated at floor level on high-backed chairs inside other smaller circles of protection were men and women Cade presumed must be high-level members of the two covens. Everyone's attention was on Siegmar, who was addressing the room.

"For this reason, it is crucial we expand our ranks. Both your covens have excelled, far beyond the expectations of Master Kein. But our ability to defend the Fatherland has waned. So has our power to restrict access to the occupied territories of the west."

Listening to Siegmar, Cade pondered how he ought to attack this many foes at once.

"Starting over will not be easy," Siegmar continued. "But we must rebuild our lost covens—first, here in Germany, then . . . in France, and . . ."

Siegmar's voice trailed off as he squinted in Cade's direction.

What? I didn't make a sound. He can't possibly see me. Can he?

The Finn pointed at Cade: "Intruder! Kill him!"

Oh, shit.

The coven members turned toward the antechamber. Lacking a plan but determined not to get cornered, Cade charged into the main hall. *Time to improvise.*

Six dozen attacks rained down on Cade's shield, more than he could absorb at once, more than he could deflect with control. Hot and cold stabs of pain shot through his ribs, and an unseen hand clamped like a vise around his throat. Unable to breathe, barely able to keep his shield raised against an onslaught that seemed to fall without end, Cade started to panic.

Prismatic sprays of fire cascaded over his shield, but he felt their heat. Forks of lightning prickled his skin into gooseflesh. Galvanic tingling worsened into the stings of a thousand bees followed by agonizing spasms in his arms and legs.

Cade knew the legions of MARCHOSIAS couldn't help him here. The coven members, even the ones in the seats, were inside areas of protection.

From the pockets of his bomber jacket he produced a pair of fragmentation grenades. He pulled their pins and hurled them toward the tiered seats.

The grenades bounced across the parquet floor.

The barrage of magickal assaults on Cade's shield ceased. The Thule dabblers ran for the exit—which meant they'd left their scribed areas of protection.

With the omnidirectional perception of SATHARIEL, Cade watched the legions of MARCHOSIAS flense the retreating dabblers, even as he drew the Colt semiautomatic Trahern had given him weeks earlier and opened fire on the leaders. Three shots in Konig's center mass, and the Berlin coven master was down. A lucky head shot marred the great circle's outer ring of glyphs with a spray of the Frankfurt master's blood and brains.

Then the grenades detonated.

Explosions ripped through the dabblers who'd been too slow to get off the upper tiers, or who'd tripped over their own feet, only to get trampled by their fellows.

Thanks to the grace of unholy gifts, the blasts passed over Cade like a warm breeze. Shrapnel ripped through his clothes but passed through his body without harm.

On the far side of the cloud, Siegmar weathered the blast with the same sangfroid, clearly also impervious to metal and flame.

Behind Cade, a handful of stragglers limped toward the exit, or struggled to raise their wands in his direction to retaliate. He crushed one like a bug, decapitated another with VAELBOR's blades, and sent a wave of demons to devour the rest.

Flames roared up the curtains, and a stink of sulfur filled the great hall.

Cade faced Siegmar, his last foe standing.

The Finnish karcist was still inside the operator's circle. His alb was unblemished; his sword was in his hand. "If I'd had my way, I would have killed you years ago."

"Now's your chance, you son of a bitch."

A half-breath hang-fire—then they both unleashed Hell.

Lightning shot from Cade's hands, then slammed into identical salvos thrown by Siegmar. Violet light flared at the collision point, and the room reeked of ozone.

Dense trails of smoke transformed into serpents that lunged at Cade. He cut them apart with VAELBOR's ghost blades, then pressed his attack.

Siegmar deflected Cade's lightning, only to be knocked out of the operator's circle by a tempest wind. As Siegmar rolled to a stop, he hurled a venom-laced trident at Cade's chest. Cade dived to the floor as the gigantic weapon soared past him.

He and Siegmar regained their feet and came up attacking. A black cloud of spiders and scorpions shot from Siegmar's cupped hands and flew at Cade, who charged into the storm projecting white-hot hellfire from his palms, burning a path to his enemy.

Half-cooked arachnids scuttled over Cade's feet and up his legs under his trousers. Red-hot bites and stings peppered his calves, and then he felt the scratch of hairy legs on top of his head, followed by another vicious bite at the nape of his neck.

Primal instinct took over, arresting his charge while he stomped and swatted the crawling terrors from his body, but thanks to Adair's harsh training he kept his shield in place.

It did nothing to stop Siegmar's flamberge wreathed in emerald flames.

Cade dodged. The burning blade cut a smoking wound in the floor.

Siegmar hefted his two-handed, wavy-edged sword for another swing. Cade summoned a broadsword and parried Siegmar's next blow.

CASMIEL's prowess guided Cade's hands. The melee moved with such speed Cade barely registered what was happening: feints and parries, blocks and pushes, lunges and thrusts. Both spectral blades spat sparks and fire with each jarring impact. Cade pinned the flamberge to the floor, and MEUS CALMIRON put its strength in Cade's left hand, to deliver a punch that launched teeth from Siegmar's mouth in a bloody spray.

An unseen force threw Cade backward halfway across the great hall. As he struck the floor he called down colossal strokes of lightning, which smashed through the building's roof and upper floors, then through the great hall's mosaic-covered ceiling, to hammer Siegmar. When the conflagration ceased, Siegmar was on his knees inside a smoking crater in the floor, but still alive, protected by a sphere of defensive energy.

Walls of fire and smoke engulfed him and Cade. The entire building was aflame and collapsing. Blazing pieces of broken furniture tumbled through the ruptured ceiling and fell like meteors, exploding into sparks and cinders as they crashed to the floor, filling the searing air with millions of burning motes.

Cade swung his arm to hurl lightning—only to see the bolt fizzle in his hand. He tried to control the fire raging around him, but it resisted his commands. *Shit.*

Siegmar smirked as he stood. "Strength fading?" His burning sword reappeared in his hand. He strode toward Cade, his murderous intention plain.

MARCHOSIAS, your legions—

CANNOT TOUCH HIM. The demon sounded almost giddy over Cade's predicament. *HE IS WARDED BY VASSAGO. ONLY POWERS WIELDED BY YOUR HAND CAN DEFY VASSAGO'S SEAL.*

No fire, no lightning—Cade had lost his yokes on XAPHAN and AZALETH. He tried to pummel Siegmar with the fists of JEPHISTO, only to feel that demon slip from his control as Siegmar parried its assault and closed the distance to Cade in quick steps.

Need to buy time. Cade turned himself invisible and tried to flank left around Siegmar, only to have the Finn block his manuever with a singsong taunt: "I can see you!"

He was getting closer, and Cade was running out of options. He still had VAELBOR's broadsword, but it was growing heavy in his hand, which meant he had used up his quotient of strength from MEUS CALMIRON.

CASMIEL, you prick, you'd better still be with me.

Shedding his invisibility, he circled Siegmar, who charged, striking with a berserker's rage, his flamberge wreathed in green fire.

Each hit Cade blocked felt like a redwood falling on his blade. A crazy windmill-swing by Siegmar sent Cade sprawling backward, ass over elbows, out of control.

Siegmar leaped through the air and descended on Cade like a raptor on a field mouse, the tip of his flamberge plunging toward Cade's heart.

The demonic blade went through Cade's chest and sank three feet into the floor. Siegmar froze as he realized Cade had shifted into ghost form.

Intangible, Cade rolled clear of Siegmar's blade, drew his obsidian dagger as he solidified, and thrust the glass stiletto into Siegmar's chest.

A shudder racked Siegmar—Cade felt it through the dagger's grip.

The Finn coughed, spattering Cade's face with blood. Wet gagging sounds lodged in Siegmar's throat as he struggled to lift one hand toward Cade's face.

Cade twisted the glass dagger, then pushed and broke it at the grip, abandoning the splintered blade inside Siegmar's chest.

As the Finn collapsed, Cade scrambled out from under him. Siegmar slumped to the floor, expelled a gasp of bloody sputum, then went still. Cade stared at him, expecting to find satisfaction, but he felt gutted. Instead of exorcising his rage and sorrow, killing Siegmar had fed it, only to make it hungrier than ever before.

The vengeance Cade had sought for two years had left him empty.

Around him, the hall was an inferno littered with corpses to feed the blaze. The outer walls of the building toppled, revealing the city beyond, from which a chorus of sirens wailed. The fire would attract spectators—attention Cade couldn't afford.

He picked himself up and stumbled away, eyes burning, and choking on smoke. His every step summoned jolts of pain from deep inside his torso, harbingers of wounds unseen. On the far side of the hall from the entrance he shouldered through a pair of doors that led to a hallway. He sprinted to its end, then out of the building's rear exit.

The storm embraced him as he fled into the night. Each cool breath was a blessing, every drop of rain on his face a baptism—but he was wounded, alone in the heart of Germany, and, if his strength continued to ebb, soon to be without magick. Victory and vengeance had come at a cost, and his road home to Spain would be long and full of danger.

Yet even as he ran, hollow and hunted, he regretted nothing.

The Thule Society was gone.

33

DECEMBER

The louder Hitler yelled, the less attention Kein paid. Summoned by the Führer with a stream of invective delivered over the telephone, Kein had simmered with resentment for the duration of his train ride to Wolfsschanze. Now that he had arrived and been brought into the leader's presence, he wished he were still on the train.

Vulgarities mixed with insults and recriminations spewed from Hitler's mouth, and he pounded the top of his desk with his fist for emphasis. Or perhaps out of frustration. It was unclear, but Kein didn't care enough to inquire. He wasn't listening, anyway.

Outside the frost-covered windows of the Führer Bunker, all of which faced north into the Masurian woods, downy flakes took drunken paths to the snow-covered ground. Through the trees Kein noted several pyramidal bunkers topped with antiaircraft guns. Beyond those, the perimeter of the compound was ringed with land mines. Inside the camp, hundreds of soldiers stood guard day and night.

It would be a winter paradise if not for the Nazis.

After months of feeding on the stolen vigor of the Nazis' victims in the concentration camps, Kein had only recently begun to feel like himself again. Most of his chronic pain had abated, and now that his strength had returned, he had resumed yoking demons. He had harnessed twelve before Hitler's call dragged him from the Kehlsteinhaus.

If my recovery continues apace, I should be able to expand my repertoire to fifteen spirits by the New Year, and eighteen by Easter.

Eighteen would be a greater feat than he had ever achieved before, and it promised an array of new troubles—but as the slaying of Siegmar had so cruelly reminded him, this was war. Extreme measures were in order.

A scrape of boots on concrete, a huff of halitosis on the side of Kein's face.

He turned to see Hitler at his side, intruding into his personal space, his visage manic. "God damn you, Kein! Have you not been listening?"

"I gather it had something to do with Russia?"

"Stalingrad, you moron! We've lost over eight hundred thousand men! Now it's winter and our Sixth Army is trapped inside the city."

"I fail to see how this is my concern." Kein stepped away from Hitler and busied himself with a review of the record albums next to the phonograph.

"You what?" The Führer followed him like his shadow. "It's your concern, Herr Engel, because you were the one who advised me to launch Operation Barbarossa."

"Perhaps you misunderstood me. I advised you to take control of the Caucasus and its oil reserves. I never told you to waste blood or treasure on a street fight in Stalingrad." In truth, he had all but drawn the Führer a map leading him to Stalingrad. Bogging down the Nazis in a battle of attrition had prolonged the war and pushed Germany one step closer to its breaking point— which was precisely where Kein wanted them and every other player in this global mess.

Kein picked up a record. "Is this the only Wagner in your collection?"

"I'm trying to win a war, and you're asking about music?"

"Without music, life would be a mistake."

He expected Hitler's temper to snap at the invocation of Nietzsche. For once the Führer surprised him. The volcanic little man set aside his rage and restored his composure before he spoke again. "How we arrived at this juncture no longer matters. How we escape it does. My soldiers in Stalingrad are in need of your aid. What can you do for them?"

"Nothing." Kein returned the record to its place on the shelf. "I am not here to fight your war for you." He faced the dictator. "Do not mistake my aid for servitude. I answer to one patron only, and his dominion is much older and far greater than yours will ever be." He looked at the framed map mounted on the wall and noted the profusion of red pins in the southwest of the Soviet Union. "Stalingrad is lost. Order your men there to do whatever damage they can. In time they will disobey and surrender, but perhaps they can reduce the Red Army's numbers a bit before they fall. In the meantime, pull back your supply lines to fortify Kursk and Kharkov." Weary of the conversation, Kein headed for the door.

Looking at the map, Hitler fumed, "Then what?"

Kein answered on his way out, "Pray for an early spring, my Führer."

1943

FEBRUARY

Winter had left Normandy's coast not white but gray, and uniform in its gloom. There was no horizon Niko could see, just a slate-colored sea and a marble sky. Braving the wind at the cliff's edge, he squinted into the gale blowing landward from the English Channel. His hands he buried deep in his coat's pockets, and he tucked his scarred chin under his scarf.

Shivering at his side was Xavier Le Blanc, a short and wiry Maquis spy who had been Niko's main link to the Resistance during his seven-month convalescence in Burgundy. Niko turned a glum eye at his pencil-mustached ally. "What am I meant to see here?"

Xavier furrowed his brow in surprise. "The Atlantic Wall."

All Niko saw were empty beaches, breaking surf, and snow-streaked bluffs and cliffs. Baffled, he looked over his shoulder to see if he'd missed something. "What wall?"

"Not a literal wall." Xavier pointed at lumps dotting the cliffs. "Entrenched fortifications. Machine-gun nests." Shifting his gaze inland, he added, "Land mines. Antiaircraft guns. Heavy artillery." Once he saw that Niko recognized the camouflaged pillboxes dotting the coastline north and south of Caen, he continued. "It's been going on since last spring. Mostly near the ports—Cherbourg, Calais, Le Havre, Brest, Saint-Malo. But they've been digging in these guns anywhere the Allies might try to grab a foot of beach."

"Nazi radio has been boasting of this for months. If there's no good reason my toes need to be freezing right now, I'm cutting yours off." It was an obviously idle threat. Niko's injuries from the attack on the train had left one of his arms permanently crooked, his left eye half blind, and his stride hobbled with an exaggerated limp. He posed no threat to anyone in a fistfight.

Xavier motioned for Niko to follow him. "This way."

He led Niko away from the cliffs and two kilometers south along the coast, to an unfinished excavation. Surrounding it were snow-shrouded tools, buckets, and supply pallets. Xavier presented the scene as if he had just solved a capital crime.

An icepick wind stabbed at Niko's ears, prompting him to hunch his shoulders. After reviewing the scene, he turned in confusion to Xavier. "So?"

"This is the part that makes no sense."

"You showing me an empty hole in the ground? I agree."

Exasperated, Xavier pulled an oiled canvas tarpaulin off the pallet. Underneath were piles of cement predicate in sacks. "This is the point, Niko."

"What does any of this have to do with Briet?"

"She was here." Xavier pulled a folded, grainy photograph from his coat pocket. Despite the rough texture of the enlarged image, Briet's face was clearly recognizable. Behind her were a farmhouse and a silo that Niko recognized over Xavier's shoulder.

He pocketed the photo. "All right, she was here. So what?"

"She's responsible for this mess."

"What mess?"

Xavier kneeled beside the pallet, opened a folding knife, and stabbed a bag of concrete mixture. He showed the grayish white powder to Niko. "Quality cement from Germany. Came in by truck and train all last year, along with premium mix. But last fall the mix stopped coming, and work halted. Then Briet showed up." He kicked over a bucket and spilled wet sand across the snow. "Ordered the crews to keep working. Made them use beach sand to mix the concrete."

"Is this the part of the story where I slap you? Or the part where you get to the point?"

"Beach sand makes shitty concrete. Weak, prone to cracks. Salt rusts the rebars."

"Maybe she is not a construction genius."

"But the Germans are, Niko. And they told her, over and over. But she did something, scared them into doing what she said. Now they're using beach sand all up and down the coast, from Calais to Brest." He lowered his voice, as if afraid someone could eavesdrop on them out there, in the middle of nowhere, on a cliff overlooking the Channel. "If she works for the Nazis, why is she sabotaging their defenses? If this is what the Nazis want, why do they want it?"

Now he understood Xavier's dilemma. But he had no idea what to tell him. "When was her last visit?"

"About a month ago. She comes every few months."

"I need a place to hole up. A house. Something remote."

Xavier nodded and pointed west. "There's one in Meuvaines. Used to belong to a Jewish family before the Nazis ran them out. Been empty since."

"Isolated?"

"Very." The skinny Maquis kicked the pallet of cement. "What about this?"

"Keep an eye on it, but don't interfere. Whatever she's doing, I don't want her to know we've been here. Tell everyone: Hands off the Atlantic Wall until we know more. Understood?"

A reverent nod. "I'll pass the word."

"Thank you. Now take me to the house."

Months had bled away since Niko last wrangled demons. Months in which he had been afflicted with a surfeit of time to stew in grief and regret.

Tonight, in spite of his infirmity, he would summon his patron, rejoin the war effort, and take his first steps toward atonement . . . and revenge.

———

Few beasts of fact or legend were ever so ponderous as the Red Army on the move in winter. Thousands of troops trudged through knee-deep snow. Most of them toted overfilled backpacks and Mosin-Nagant rifles whose lubricating oil had been cut with gasoline to keep their bolts from freezing shut on the long march from Stalingrad to Kursk. Underfed and overtired, the comrades of the newly constituted Central Front plodded northwest, out of the shambles of Stalingrad, en route to a new battleground.

The monotony of the march and the desolation of the ruined urban landscape lulled Anja into a state of lightness. Freed from memories of what had been or expectations of what might come, she was content just to *be.* To breathe subarctic air; to hear the crunching of boots on snow ahead of and behind her; to taste the lingering bite of vodka on her own breath, and feel the ache of hunger in her belly. All of it simply *was;* it meant nothing, signified nothing, asked nothing. As one among thousands, anonymous in the ranks, she felt free for the first time in her life.

Still, a bowl of lamb stew would be nice. She pushed back against her selfishness. *Stop that. You think you are the only one who is hungry?*

She scooped a palmful of snow from the side of the path and stuffed it into her mouth. It was a temporary remedy, but what wasn't these days? The best she could hope for was a few minutes of relief from the emptiness in her gut.

After that, she would eat more snow, or chew on some bark, or—if she was lucky—find more vodka.

Ahead of her, the formation snaked across the winterscape, a dark line of ragged bodies cutting a path toward the gray horizon. Behind her, what remained of Stalingrad was roofless husks and mountains of broken concrete. Only a handful of the city's residents had persevered through the months of brutal urban combat.

Soviet political officers had called the Battle of Stalingrad a triumph—rightly so, now that the German Sixth Army had surrendered and been taken prisoner—but none of the propagandists had spoken of the cost the Red Army had paid for that victory. Anja had seen the streets littered with Russia's dead, its sons and daughters cut down, dismembered, paralyzed, blinded, reduced to horrors of scar tissue their own mothers would never recognize. She had watched the Germans execute Russian civilians while the Red Army did nothing, choosing instead to bide its time until it could act with the advantage.

A few were sacrificed for the many. There was no better way.

Anja repeated that to herself as she marched. She wondered if she might believe it by the time the Central Front reached Kursk.

Running steps, quick but still light, crunched in the snow behind her, drawing closer. Her mood brightened as she recognized their weight and cadence. Nadezhda caught up to her, rosy-cheeked and half winded. She served now as a spotter for Anja, who in the months since expending the last of her magick had earned her rations as a sniper-scout.

"Anja! Look what I found!" From inside her coat, Nady pulled a pair of golden-brown bread rolls. She handed one to Anja and grinned. "Only three days old."

The bread was tough. It was half stale now and likely had been as dry as a handful of dust when it first came from the oven. But it was food, and that was more valuable on the front line than anything except vodka or morphine. And maybe dry socks. Or a warm coat.

She hid the roll inside her coat and offered her friend a grateful smile. "Thank you. I'll soften mine in tonight's cup of broth."

Nadezhda ceased nibbling at the impenetrable edge of her own roll. "Good plan." She followed Anja's example and hid the roll under her winter coat.

Anja liked having Nady at her side. The young woman had shown her a sister's devotion after Anja saved her from death's domain in the infirmary.

Saving Nady's life had left Anja spent of magick, but the bond that had formed between them after Nadezhda's recovery had grown so powerful that it had taken Anja by surprise. Theirs was a friendship of unconditional loyalty, and it now was clear to Anja that Nady looked up to her. When she saw the innocent faith Nady placed in her, Anja remembered what it once had felt like to see her younger brother Piotr look at her that way: to be loved, respected, admired, and trusted.

I never knew how much I had missed that feeling.

From behind them came wolf whistles and catcalls. Three scruffy, filthy infantrymen—a description that Anja realized could apply to tens of thousands of her comrades in the formation departing Stalingrad—made rude noises at her and Nady.

A barefaced farmboy boasted, "Gonna be cold tonight! I can keep you warm!"

His bucktoothed buddy added, "Skinny little things like you need protection. I've got room in my bedroll for both of you!"

Their slope-browed friend chimed in, "I've got what you girls need."

Nadezhda linked her arm around Anja's. "Fuck off! She's mine, and I'm hers!"

Bareface leered harder. "Can I watch?" He and Bucktooth laughed.

Slope-brow refused to take the hint. "Do what you want to each other, as long as I get what's mine."

Petulance turned to anger as Nady glared at Slope-brow. "Fuck off or I'll cut what's yours into sausage and leave it for the dogs."

Jeers from Bucktooth and Bareface left Slope-brow flushed with embarrassment. "Tough talk, blondie. We'll see how tough you are when—"

He shut up the second he realized Anja had put the cutting edge of her bayonet to his crotch. She bared her teeth. "One more word and you're half the man you used to be."

During her months without magick, Anja had learned how to kill with a knife, up close and personal. Seven throats she had cut in the rubble of Stalingrad; she recalled each one in gruesome detail as she maintained eye contact with Slope-brow.

He raised his hands, backed off, and retreated with his pals into the ranks.

Anja sheathed her blade. She and Nady resumed their march.

Nady elbowed Anja and cracked a conspiratorial smirk. "Fuck them. We don't need men. We don't need anybody. Not as long as we stay together."

"I know we don't."

It was the right thing to say. But it was a lie.

Though she was full of sisterly love for Nadezhda, Anja harbored regrets for the way she had abandoned Adair. She still resented him for insisting she sacrifice Stefan's life to save Cade's. No matter how powerful the American was, he couldn't really be that important, could he? It was clear the master thought so, but what if he was wrong?

All Anja had wanted was to put some distance between herself and Adair, to have room to breathe, to think, to make sense of . . . well, everything.

But she'd found no sense to it, or to anything else. Nearly the entire world was at war, drowning in chaos. Everything was a mess; nothing was right. How could she sort out matters as irrational as love and grief when she had no idea if she'd live to see the next dawn?

The sun dipped low in the west. Soon night would bring her murky dreams of the man who'd been like a father to her. Or were they visions? Anja didn't know anymore. All she knew for certain was that she hoped Adair was all right, wherever he was—and that someday he might forgive her.

If only I deserved to be forgiven.

～～

Dusk painted the Sierra Nevada range a vivid fuchsia and outlined every rock and ridge with indigo shadows. In the west, the sky burned ruby about the sunset.

Cade climbed the winding road to Adair's villa. He had been walking for over twelve weeks, ten hours each night, through the harshest winter he had ever felt. He looked forward to sleeping indoors without needing to coerce, cajole, or bribe his way into a stranger's home or barn, even though quite a few lonely women in France had been happy to take him into their beds. Likewise, the promise of hot food he didn't have to steal called him onward.

He shifted the strap of his leather roll-up to a fresh part of his shoulder. The weight of swords, knives, and other metal tools of the Art was quick to cause him discomfort, despite the padding of his fleece-lined bomber jacket. If exorcising and fumigating his blades weren't so tedious, he would have let his demon porter haul them across Europe.

Drawing close to the top of the hill, he noted a jeep parked outside the front door. Its driver's-side door bore a simple emblem—the white five-pointed star of the United States Army.

Looks like we have visitors. There was no reason for Cade to think Allied military personnel would be hostile to him or to Adair, but he had been on the run for months, and he was loath to relax his guard around strangers, no matter who they were. *Better safe than dead.*

He slowed his pace. Voices carried from inside the villa, but there was no sign of anyone outside, on the grounds beside or behind the house. No one had been left behind in the jeep. He rested his hand on its hood. It was cool. Whoever was inside, they had been there awhile.

He climbed the steps, expecting to eavesdrop before he entered. Then the front door opened, and he froze on the top step as a pair of Allied military officers—one British, one American, both with their braided hats tucked under their arms—were escorted out by Adair. The master was his usual disheveled self.

"Thank you for making the drive out. Let me—" He beamed at the sight of Cade. "Speak of the devil! Gents, this is him! The man of the hour—Cade Martin."

There was admiration in the American's manner as he shook Cade's hand. "Captain Abraham Corey. It's an honor, son."

As soon as Cade's hand was free, the Brit seized it. "Major Bingham Wallis." He let go of Cade's hand. "Master Macrae tells us you've done a yeoman's job cleaning up this Thule mess for us, and in record time. Well done, young man."

"Yeah, well—beats working."

The officers donned their covers and faced Adair. The major did the talking. "We'll keep you apprised of any changes."

A nod from Adair. "Right, then. Cheery-bye." He and Cade watched the officers get in the jeep. The captain drove the vehicle, which rumbled down the dirt road.

Once the jeep had passed from sight, Adair took Cade by the shoulders. "Welcome home, lad!" The master's elation turned to alarm. "Christ, you look like shite. Smell like it, too."

"Maybe 'cause I just *walked* thirteen hundred miles, most of it with the Nazis on my ass."

Adair wrinkled his nose. "That's no excuse for stinking like low tide."

Pride demanded Cade change the subject. "Please tell me there's scotch."

"Aye." Adair led him inside. "But not 'til after you've washed up."

There was no need to convince Cade. He plodded to the second floor, dropped his gear in the room he had claimed months earlier, and retired to the bathroom to scrub the road off his skin. Submerged in the tub, he dismissed his yoked spirits, then exhaled a column of bubbles. When he surfaced, he felt lighter than he had in months. He could almost draw a deep breath without feeling his heart race or his head spin.

Naked in front of the washroom mirror, Cade stood dismayed by his own reflection. Demonic compulsions had driven him to rip out odd-shaped patches of his beard and whittle away the tips of his eyebrows. *It's like my face got attacked by hair-chewing moths.*

He took scissors from the cabinet by the sink, trimmed his beard down to whiskers, and sheared his ragged mop of hair to an uneven crew cut. Then he retrieved his shaving kit from his bedroom and slowly rediscovered the face he hadn't seen since the previous summer. There was nothing to be done about his eyebrows except hope that he could leave them alone long enough to grow back now that he was free of yoked demons.

Half an hour later, dry and dressed in clean clothes, he returned to the first floor. Adair sat awaiting him in the library. He smiled at Cade's entrance. "As promised." On an end table beside an empty armchair stood a tumbler two-thirds full of golden liquor.

Cade sank into the chair, picked up the scotch, savored its perfume for a few seconds, then downed half the glass in one swallow. "Damn. That's really good."

"Broke out the good stuff. You've earned it."

"Thank you. Got any cigarettes?"

Adair picked up a carton of Lucky Strikes from the floor beside his chair and lobbed it into Cade's lap. "A gift from our guests."

The cardboard box nearly fell apart in Cade's eager hands. He ripped off its end flaps, dug out a pack, tore it open, and tucked a smoke between his lips. By force of habit, he snapped his fingers, expecting to light his Lucky with a lick of XAPHAN's flame. Staring at his hand, he wondered what had gone wrong, then remembered he had just released all of his yoked spirits.

Pointing at the end of the cigarette, Cade shot an expectant look at Adair, who arched his brow and dipped his chin. A spark manifested inside the Lucky, which flared to life as Cade took a drag. The rush of nicotine was a balm for his nerves. "Thanks." He exhaled through his nose. "So is that why they came here? To bring you scotch and Luckies?"

"Hardly. Now that we've done our part, the Allies are gearing up. North Africa's theirs, and it sounds like Italy's next."

"Then France?"

The master looked uncertain. "Soon. But there's more to be done first."

"Like what?"

"Niko's hunting Briet. She's up to something in Normandy, but we don't know what." He fished a pack of cigarettes from a pocket inside his coat. "But the bigger issue is time. The Allies need to get their ducks in a row."

Smoke spilled from Cade's mouth as he spoke. "So what do we do until then?"

"Gird ourselves for a different battle."

"You mean Kein."

"Aye. He's gone to ground." Adair opened his pack of cigarettes.

Cade sipped his scotch and let the sweet burn linger on his palate. "You think he's training more dabblers?"

"I doubt he can find enough for a new coven."

"You sure? Germany's a big place."

"He can't teach magick to just anyone. Sure, any fool can learn the basics, but few have the nerves to put them into practice. It'll be years before he can build another army." The master put on a look of mischief. "It's our job to make sure he doesn't get the chance."

Another sip and a pull on the Lucky gave Cade time to think. "If he's in hiding, why don't we focus on bigger targets?"

His suggestion soured Adair. "Such as?"

"Hitler and his generals. Or even his armies. Give me half a chance, I bet I could lay waste to a panzer division without breaking a sweat."

Adair shook his head. "Absolutely not. I told you when we started: We aren't here to wage the Allies' war for them."

"It's a bit late for that. I mean, we're in this now. Why not go all in?"

The master sighed. "For one thing, Hitler and the other boss Nazis are guarded by demons Kein put in place years ago. Plus most of the field marshals, to boot. But even if they weren't, going after Hitler would be out of our league."

That made no sense to Cade. "Why? He's just a man."

Adair swept tangles of gray hair from his face. "This is what I get for glossing over the basics." He set his cigarettes aside and leaned forward, elbows on his knees. "The problem with what you suggest goes to the heart of what magick is, and how it works. At its root, magick is about exerting one's will over the forces and elements of the universe. Magicians use spirits as instruments to focus primordial energies and use them to shape this world to their desires."

The master levitated his pack of Luckies from the table by his chair and made it hover between himself and Cade. "Inanimate objects have no will of their own, and animals have only very little, so it's not that hard to turn lead into gold, or use a wolf like a puppet.

"But using magick against people . . . that's a different challenge." He guided the pack back to the end table, then continued. "Overcoming the will of one ordinary soul, a person not guarded by charms or spirits—that's easy for a trained karcist. But overcoming the collective will of thousands or millions of people at once—for instance, by trying to send a demon to kill a national leader, one invested with power, authority, symbolic importance—is difficult, costly, and bloody fucking dangerous. Heaven almost never meddles in human affairs, and Hell hates it nearly as much. So to go after a führer, or a president, or a premier, you'd need the power to overcome not just the will of the patient himself, but also that of his followers. The more powerful the figure, the harder they are to attack with demons."

Cade held up his hands to stop the lecture. "Hang on. I've used magick against dozens of people—no, hundreds. You're saying I couldn't do the same to Hitler? Or Mussolini?"

"You've wielded the powers of yoked spirits. That's different from sending a demon to do your bidding. If *you* could get close enough to Hitler without being gunned down by their armies and secret police, you might live long enough to take one shot at overcoming Kein's wards of protection to strike at Hitler from point-blank range. But if you miss, or even if you don't, his demonic guardians would tear off your limbs like wings from a fly." He lifted one brow into an inquisitive arch. "You sure you want to take that chance?"

Cade suspected there likely was no answer to Adair's question that wouldn't make him look like an idiot. He left it unanswered while he downed another swig of scotch. After a slow drag on the Lucky, he shifted the topic.

"If we can't go after the top dogs head-on, why not use magick against their troops? Nobody voted for them. Why not send a dozen demons to turn the Nazis' tanks to scrap?"

"Because you'll run out of magick long before an army runs out of fodder." Adair rubbed his eyes and groaned. "You're itchin' for a fight. I know the feeling, trust me. But I need you to heed me now. A battlefield is no place for a karcist. Used to be, our kind took no part in war. It's not what the Art was made for. And if Kein had respected that, we wouldn't be here now." He pulled a Lucky from his pack and stuck it in his mouth. "The only reason you and I are in this world of shite is because Kein threw in with the Nazis, for reasons I can't begin to grasp.

"Stopping Kein is something only *we* can do. So we can't waste our efforts on battles not our own." His cigarette lit as if of its own volition. "You and I need to track down Kein and Briet, and put an end to them, once and for all." Adair filled his chest with smoke, then vented it like a gray dragon. "The Allies have to fight their own war, lad. And *we* have to fight *ours*."

MARCH

It would come down to timing, just like everything else in life. Niko had insinuated himself into the ranks of civilians conscripted by the Germans as slave labor for the Atlantic Wall project. No one had asked him for papers or even his name. He had just showed up three weeks earlier—rumpled and unwashed—and queued up with the other workers near the cliffs north of Caen. A Nazi enlisted man had pointed him toward the work zone. The other workers covered for Niko's limp and bent arm by having him mix concrete. *They also serve who stand and stir.*

Most of the real work was going on inland, near bridges and crossroads, the choke points for an invading army. In spite of all the boasting the Organisation Todt had done about the Nazis' coastline defenses, the so-called Atlantic Wall was a relaxed front. Its beaches were empty, its cliffsides populated just enough to present the appearance of battle-readiness from the vantage of ships at a distance in the English Channel.

If only the Allies knew how vulnerable Normandy really is, Niko mused, *they might do more than sit in England with their thumbs up their asses.*

He had said as much to his superiors. First through the Resistance to the British SOE, and then to Adair, who insisted he had shared the information with top Allied commanders. Still the northwestern coast of France stood quiet, surrendered to German control.

It made Niko's blood boil. He had seen films of the Nazis marching under the Arc de Triomphe, parading up the Champs-Élysées. How could anyone see such an affront and not take up arms? How could the British and their allies not strike back?

I was born in Algeria, but my heart belongs to France. I will set her free or die trying.

He lingered on the periphery of the work site and pretended to tap a cigarette against the side of his hand. Out of the corner of his eye he tracked the progress of the foreman and the project leader from Organisation Todt. They had emerged from the command tent and were on their way to a chauffeured car that would take them to a bistro in Saint-Malo for lunch. The two Germans were escorted by an armed Wehrmacht soldier who had become so blasé with regard to his duties that his rifle was slung diagonally across his back rather than held at the ready. The boy-soldier didn't even tense as Niko pivoted into the path of the foreman and the project leader, held up a Gauloises, and asked with a disarming smile, "Can I get a light?"

Both bosses looked offended to be addressed with such familiarity by a mere worker, but the foreman, who still had the hand calluses of a man who had earned his place in the world, masked his disdain as he handed Niko his lighter.

Niko lit his cigarette with it, then returned it. "Thanks." He enjoyed a drag from the pungent cigarette, then continued as he exhaled. "Looks like rain."

"The forecast calls for snow," the foreman said.

"If it hits before sundown, do we quit early?"

The project leader shrugged. "Might as well."

Niko nodded. "Hope for the best, then." To the foreman he added, "Thanks again."

The Germans turned away and kept walking. Niko limped in the opposite direction, to the command tent. Two Waffen-SS soldiers standing outside intercepted him. The *SS-Schütze* raised his submachine gun while his superior, an *SS-Sturmmann,* set his hand on his Luger and called out in halting French, "Halt! This area is restricted!"

"Foreman von Gunsberg sent me." Niko invoked the suggestive force of DANTALION. "He wants me to get his new work orders for the teams on the north side."

He had made sure the SS guards had seen him talking with the foreman and the project leader. As powerful a force as demonic persuasion could be, it was doubly effective when there was other evidence that its targets could misinterpret in support of it—and seeing Niko talking with the bosses, and then nodding in response to whatever they said, fit that bill. It also helped that most soldiers were young, uneducated, and trained to defer to authority.

The *Sturmmann* waved Niko past. "Go ahead. Make it quick."

"I will, sir, thank you."

It was incorrect to call enlisted men "sir," but when it came from civilian workers the German troops seemed to thrive on the implicit flattery.

Niko shuffled inside the command tent. It was empty, as it often was at this hour of the day. Loose papers, maps, and schematics cluttered the worktables on either side of the tent's central support pole. Ancillary worktables stood to the sides. Kerosene lamps dangled from ropes strung between the center pole and the corner supports, filling the space with diffuse light. Niko moved to the center tables; that's where the valuable intelligence would be.

It took him less than half a minute to find plans and drawings that stopped him cold. He took his enchanted mirror from inside his coat and said in a low voice, "*Fenestra,* Adair."

Seconds later he heard the rough baritone of his master. *"What've you got?"*

He turned the mirror so Adair could see the drawings. "Plans for solid pyramids of concrete to be sunk into the paths connecting the beaches to the roads above."

"Tank barriers."

"*Oui,* but there are charms inside them. Magickal glyphs." He adjusted the mirror's aspect. "This sigil lies inside tetrahedrons buried from Cherbourg to Calais."

The master squinted. Then his eyes widened in horror. *"Demonic wards."*

"Powerful ones. And each adds to the next." Niko shifted the papers to show Adair a grid demarcating where the pyramids had been deployed. "If I am reading this map correctly—"

"There's no using magick anywhere on Europe's Atlantic coast."

Niko nodded. "I have tried to walk to the beach." He shook his head. "With demons yoked, I cannot come within a quarter mile of the cliff's edge. Until now, I did not know why."

The master buried his face in his hands. *"Bloody fucking hell."*

Eager to find reason for hope, Niko wondered aloud, "Would this not restrain Kein and Briet, as well?"

Adair lowered his hands, revealing his stricken expression. *"It might. But then what's the point?"* He shook his head. *"I can't square it. Why ward the coast from magick but force the Germans to build inferior defenses?"*

Niko had no explanation. "I don't know, Master."

"None of this makes sense," said the grizzled Scotsman. *"And in my experience, that's almost always bad."*

36

MAY

A thunderclap shook the villa, and the floor inside the demon's circle van-ished, revealing a vortex of fire. ABBADON plunged, its wings flailing. As soon as it was gone, another stroke of thunder marked the floor's instanta-neous return. A cold wind that smelled of rotten fish and a struck match rocked the flames on the ceremonial candles.

Calling up ABBADON had entailed weeks of preparation. Cade had spent days preparing the circle, the sacrifices needed to placate the spirit, and the quill made with a feather from a female dove. More trying had been the need for Cade to spend a week in mental preparation, followed by a fast that lasted three days. Thrice had he exorcised his tools in the name of safety.

Now it was done; the demon's name and seal were his to command. Yok-ing the King of the Abyss promised to be a grueling ordeal, but one that might give Cade a chance of surviving his next meeting with Kein.

Whenever the hell that happens.

Cade put the lid of the brazier into place to smother the embers inside, then left the operator's circle. He set his sword and wand on a worktable with his other tools. He removed his ceremonial garb. It all had to be washed and con-secrated before his next experiment, just as his tools needed to be fumigated and exorcised.

He returned to the circle, snuffed the tapers with pinches of their wicks, then collected his grimoire from the podium and put it in his wardrobe with his other effects. The rest of the cleanup could wait until the next day. *I never thought I'd miss the lamiae.*

His head felt light but his feet were heavy as he climbed the stairs to the villa's second floor. As he reached the top, he saw the clock on the wall. It was just after four in the morning. Living on Hell's schedule left Cade feeling out of sync with the rest of the world. It was becoming rare for him to fall asleep before sunrise, or to stir from his bed before midafternoon.

His only consolation was that Adair had slipped into a similar schedule, though the weeks of preparation had taken a toll on the master. The cycle of research, conjuring, binding, and banishing had become a slog for them both. They were grinding away in search of advantages for a battle they knew to be inevitable, but whose time and place remained unknown.

Cade did his best not to wake Adair. Padding down the hall in stocking feet, he passed the master's chamber on the way to his own. Adair's door was half open. The master lay hugging his own torso in his troubled sleep, his blankets in a pile on the floor at the foot of his bed. A cold breeze snaked through an open window and carried all the way to Cade in the hallway. When he looked closer, he saw the master was shivering.

I can't leave him like that. Cade slipped inside Adair's room, taking care to avoid floorboards he knew were prone to creaks. He gathered the blankets from the floor and pulled them over Adair, then eased them into place. After a few moments, the master's teeth ceased to chatter, and his shaking stopped.

Cade stood at Adair's bedside, disturbed by the damage the master had inflicted on himself in just the past two months. Not only had he been tearing at his beard and eyebrows, he also had plucked out almost a third of his eyelashes, and he had ripped enough hair from the top of his head to give himself an uneven tonsure, like that of a monk except grossly asymmetrical. There were scabs inside and behind Adair's ears, the result of incessant scratching.

Cade had wrought similar injuries on himself over the past couple of years, but not to such a degree. For the first time he understood how profound an advantage he had in the Art because of his nature as a *nikraim*. He had grown accustomed to holding nine yoked demons for extended periods. Protected by the angel bonded to his soul, he was sure he could handle up to a dozen for weeks or months at a time before succumbing to their insidious torments.

For all of Adair's experience, however, the master was still just a man. Holding eight yoked spirits for months on end was wearing him down, killing him by degrees. Cade had urged him to let some of his yoked spirits go, but Adair always refused. "I won't be caught with my guard down again. Not now, not ever." That was his refrain whenever Cade expressed concern. And so the master went on, driving himself beyond limits any sane man would respect.

No one can save a man from himself. It was a hard truth, one whose wisdom Cade had come to understand. He had done what he could for Adair. Now he had to tend to his own needs.

He escaped the master's chambers undetected, returned to his own room, and shut the door. When he switched on his bedside lamp, he was surprised to find on his end table a bottle of absinthe adorned with a silk bow. Next to it was a flat, slotted silver spoon, a bowl of sugar cubes, a low tumbler, and a vial. A tiny card was tucked under the ribbon. He plucked it free and read the message, which had been scrawled in the master's own hand:

> *Many happy returns, lad. Sleep well.*
> *—Adair*

He recalled the date and realized he had forgotten his own birthday. It was May 9, 1943. He was twenty-four years old. Smiling, he put the card on the table and picked up the vial. It was, as he'd hoped, laudanum.

The traditional method of consuming absinthe, as Adair had taught him, was to pour a small measure of "the Green Fairy," rest the slotted spoon across the top of the glass, set a sugar cube on the spoon, then pour water over it to dissolve it into the liquor. The sugar was useful for cutting the bitterness from the drink, but Adair had objected to diluting the beverage. Hence his compromise: dissolving the sugar with laudanum, a potent mix of opium and alcohol.

Maybe I'll get to sleep free of demons and dreams tonight.

A finger of absinthe, then a drizzle of laudanum over a sugar cube. The cloudy mixture in the glass promised Cade black slumbers. He downed it in one swallow, then reclined on his bed. In the space of two breaths, his coiled-spring mood unraveled, and he felt his mind sink into the drug's blissful fathoms.

Demonic whispers followed him into the deep.

YOU CANNOT ESCAPE US, threatened AZAEL.

VAELBOR's rasp haunted Cade's passage: WE ARE IN YOU, EVE-SPAWN.

Silence, Cade warned his yoked horde, and their susurrus abated. Then he submerged into the peace of oblivion, liberated from himself at last. . . .

Then came a rude awakening.

A callused hand gripped his arm and shook him like a tambourine. Sunlight streamed through the window, whose curtains had been pulled open.

Squinting into the glare, Cade recognized Adair only by his voice and brusque manner: "Up."

Cade sat forward and groaned. His stomach burned with acid, and his brain felt as if it had been smashed on a rock and shoved back inside his skull. "Jesus. What time is it?"

"Half noon," Adair said. "Chop chop. We have to go."

"What? Why? Go where?"

"We've been summoned to Washington," Adair said, his manner grave. "And when we get there, I need you with your wits sharp—because I've a job for you."

———✦———

Even before Cade had embarked on his latest mission to Germany, Adair had dispatched Hell's newest enchanted mirror to America. Though the looking glass wasn't breakable by conventional means, Adair had worried about it being lost at sea, collateral damage of the Germans' ongoing U-boat attacks on Atlantic shipping, so the U.S. Army had conceded to his request that the mirror be flown from Gibraltar to London, and from there to Washington.

The mirror had been expensive and hard to procure, and there wouldn't be another for two years, but the Allies had insisted Adair provide it to them. Now it would prove its worth.

Through the kitchen doorway, he saw Cade down a cup of tea in one grand swallow. The young man sleeved the dribble from his chin and dragged himself out to meet Adair in the study, where the master had set up his freestanding oval portal glass.

He checked his pocket watch. "Thirty seconds."

"I'm ready."

Attuning his thoughts to the vibrations of HAEL, Adair intoned, "*Aperite portam.*" Reflections faded from the mirror, giving way to a twisting gyre of smoke. He pressed his palms together as if in prayer. As his hands parted, so too did the churning vapors, revealing a dim but tidy office with a closed door.

He motioned Cade forward with a tilt of his head. The youth stepped through the gateway. When he was clear of its threshold Adair followed him.

They stood then in the office, its beige walls bereft of decoration and smelling of new paint, its furniture brand-new but also cheap and clearly mass-produced. Early-morning light bent through the window's venetian blinds.

Standing to their left was a trim American officer in his early forties. His

light brown hair was graying at the temples and shorn to a crew cut, and
his dimpled chin almost gleamed it was so cleanly shaven. He stepped forward, his hand extended. "Right on time! Welcome to the War Department,
gentlemen." He shook Adair's hand. "Mr. Macrae, I'm Colonel Jeremiah
Tolbert, United States Army." He turned and grasped Cade's hand. "You must
be Cade Martin."

If Cade was surprised to be recognized, he hid it well. He nodded once as
Tolbert shook his hand. "Colonel."

Tolbert released Cade's hand and faced Adair. "Thank you for coming on
such short notice." He gestured toward the door. "If you'll follow me, the others
are waiting."

"Others?"

"Secretary Stimson and the Joint Chiefs." The colonel walked ahead of them,
out of the office. "This way, please."

For once Adair felt the same astonishment as his apprentice. Stretching away
to either side of them was a corridor so long he strained to see its end. The
hustle of bodies coursing in crisscrossing paths, merging or diverging at in-
tersections, and flowing in and out of office doors on either side, left Adair
feeling like a leaf riding a river.

Tolbert seemed to recognize their reactions. "The Pentagon's the largest
office building in the world. Over seventeen miles of corridors on four levels above ground and two below. More than twenty thousand people work
here—" A quartet of women in military uniforms diverged in pairs around
the men and regrouped behind them without missing a step. Tolbert added,
"Most of them women." He led them down an intersecting corridor on their
right. "The whole thing was built in under sixteen months. Amazing the
kind of motivation a war can bring."

At an open passage to a broad concrete ramp they were met by a dark-haired
woman in a U.S. Navy uniform. Tolbert made the introductions. "Mr. Macrae,
Mr. Martin, this is Warrant Officer Ellen Gallo. Ms. Gallo, Mr. Macrae and I
have a meeting with the chiefs and the secretary. Please take Mr. Martin down
to the plaza. Mr. Macrae can collect him there when the meeting's over."

Cade resisted being led away. "Hang on, what gives?"

"It's nothing personal, Mr. Martin. The meeting Mr. Macrae is attending
is top-secret. Our invitation was for him alone. I apologize to you both if that
wasn't clear."

Adair set a calming hand on Cade's shoulder. "I'll be fine, lad."

The young man relented with a sullen glare. "All right." His affect bright-ened as he shook the naval officer's hand. "Hi, there. Cade Martin. Ellen, is it?"

She deflected his come-on by ignoring it. "'Warrant Officer Gallo' will do just fine. Follow me, please." She led him down the ramp.

Tolbert beckoned Adair to accompany him to another part of the second floor. Adair fell in beside him and hooked a thumb over his shoulder. "A ramp?"

A shrug. "No elevators."

"Why?"

"Same reason the building's only four stories tall: to save steel. We couldn't build up, so we built out." He led Adair to a door guarded by a pair of armed soldiers. "Here we are."

Tolbert opened the door. Adair stepped inside a long room. Seated farthest from him at the head of the conference table was Henry Stimson, the secre-tary of war. Except for Adair himself, Stimson at seventy-five was the oldest man in the room. Nature had graced him with a prominent, almost Gallic nose. His years had left him portly, but experience had given him serious eyes and an unforgiving frown capped by a snowy mustache.

The other men were all in their fifties or sixties, Adair surmised. As he stepped toward the table and Tolbert closed the door with himself on the other side of it, Stimson and the others at the table stood in greeting. Stimson's cul-tured voice filled the room. "Gentlemen, allow me to introduce Mr. Adair Mac-rae from the British Special Operations Executive."

Nods were made in Adair's direction.

The secretary gestured at the square-jawed man to his left. "Mr. Macrae, Admiral William Leahy, the ranking officer of the Joint Chiefs."

Stimson faced the man opposite Leahy—an army officer lean in features and physique, with eyebrows that peaked like tents. "General George Mar-shall, chief of staff, U.S. Army."

Beside Marshall sat another navy man, a proud-looking fellow with a long face, rudder nose, and cleft chin. "Admiral Ernest King, commander in chief of the United States Fleet."

Last to be introduced was the officer next to Leahy—a diminutive man in army colors whose balding pate was ringed by a white tonsure, and whose eyes had a surprisingly gentle quality for a man of war. "General Hap Arnold, chief of the Army Air Forces."

To one and all Adair said, "Good day, gentlemen."

The secretary sank into his chair, tacitly giving everyone else permission to sit. Adair chose a seat at the near side of the table, opposite Stimson and as far from him as possible. "So, Mr. Secretary. How can I be of service?"

Stimson slid a manila folder down the table. It slid to a graceful stop in front of Adair. "Plans are afoot."

Adair opened the folder and thumbed through the papers inside. The top page stopped him cold. "Is this right? North Africa's under Allied control?"

"As of yesterday," General Marshall said. "A quarter million Axis troops surrendered after General Eisenhower took Tunis."

Adair flipped through more pages. "Invasion of Italy by July. Bombing raids on Germany." He paused, skipped ahead and checked the last page. "And the Pacific?"

"That's being handled on a need-to-know basis," Admiral Leahy said.

There was something sinister lurking in the admiral's demeanor, but thanks to anti-magick safeguards the U.S. military's contractors had built into the Pentagon—on Adair's recommendation, and in accordance with his specifications—he was unable to peek into the man's thoughts to suss out the truth. He closed the folder. "Ambitious."

Stimson smiled. "You don't know the half of it." He tapped the ash off the end of his cigar. "One year from now, we want our boys on the ground in France." He pointed at Adair with his stogie. "I'm told that's where *you* come in."

"I'm sorry, but you were told wrong." He pulled a page from his folder, one that featured a map of the coastlines in the North Atlantic theater of war. Tracing the shorelines, he continued. "The Germans' Atlantic Wall isn't anywhere as tough as they say it is—but it lives up to its billing in one respect: No magick can work within half a mile of these beaches."

General Arnold suppressed a derisive snort. "I could've told you that."

It was easy for Adair to read the mood in the room. Except for Stimson, these men all thought him a charlatan. "You men have something you'd like to say?"

Admiral King's reply was cool and measured. "We agreed to meet with you because Prime Minister Churchill insisted we do so. But we're under no obligation—"

"Gentlemen," Stimson cut in, "need I remind you General Eisenhower *himself* vouches for this man? As does the president?" The secretary's warning was met with silence. He caught Adair's eye. "Mr. Churchill is in Washington, meeting with the president, even as we speak. They're hoping to nail down a date for the invasion of France. What should I tell them?"

Adair opened the folder again, flipped to the page headlined "OPERATION OVERLORD," and skimmed its top-level objectives. "Tell 'em they're in for a bloody hard fight."

Leahy cocked one bushy eyebrow. "Is that all? I'm so glad we took this meeting."

"Don't blame me, Admiral. I didn't sign on to fight your war for you."

Stimson leaned forward and steepled his fingers atop the table. "Then what about *your* fight? You've eliminated the Thule Society."

"Isn't that enough?"

"What about this Kein Engel person?"

Adair grew annoyed. "What of him?"

The secretary shrugged. "Does he still pose a threat?"

"He does."

Admiral King chimed in, "Where is he?"

"No idea." Adair's honesty was rewarded with frowns.

Stimson resumed his inquiry. "What about his lieutenant? A woman named Briet Segfrunsdóttir. Are you aware of *her* current whereabouts?"

A shake of his head. "Afraid not. She and Kein are in the wind."

General Arnold's genial manner turned confrontational. "Do you have a plan for finding them? Or for dealing with them when you do?"

"Not as such. Not yet, anyway."

Marshall's visage darkened. "You're far from the wonder Mr. Churchill led us to expect, Mr. Macrae. You seem unwilling to assist our plans, and even those objectives we all agree are within your sphere of responsibility appear to confound you. The War Department has spent a significant sum on your Midnight Front. Tell me, if you can: How are we to justify your group's continued funding with the money of American taxpayers?"

"Remind them we've kept the host of Hell from killing you, your president, these gents, and Generals Eisenhower, Patton, and MacArthur. And I swear, we will hunt down Kein and Briet." Adair closed the folder and slid it down the table to Stimson. "It's just a matter of time."

He got up, walked to the door, and opened it. Tolbert waited there in the corridor. He fell into step beside Adair as the master left the meeting room. Adair retraced his steps from earlier and snapped an order with the confidence of a man who expected it to be obeyed. "I'm done here. Let's collect my man so I can go home."

⌇⌇⌇

Not a word passed between Cade and the master after they left the central plaza of the War Department. All the master had told him before their jaunt to America had been, "Stay alert, and notice everything." And that was exactly what Cade had done, every step of the way.

Adair had traded a few pleasantries with Colonel Tolbert on the return to his office, and he had shaken the man's hand before motioning Cade through the portal mirror.

Cade emerged from the looking glass in Adair's study, stepped out of the way, and waited until the master returned. As soon as Adair was through the portal, it reverted to its mundane form behind him.

The master walked to a hutch and retrieved a pack of Lucky Strikes. He stuck one in his mouth and lit it with a snap of his fingers. As he inhaled, he lobbed the pack to Cade, who lit a smoke of his own. Then the master blew a series of smoke rings, nesting each new one inside the others. Cade just enjoyed his cigarette. They relaxed into armchairs facing each other.

Adair took another drag. Smoke curled around his every word. "Tell me: Did you notice anything odd about the War Department?"

"You mean aside from the fact they built it in the shape of a pentagon? Which happens to be the same shape in the middle of a grand circle of protection?"

"Aye. Aside from that."

"There's residual demonic energy in its plaza. I might not have noticed it if the rest of the building wasn't as cold as an Eskimo's ass. But once I set foot outside—it was like that tingle you get when you yoke a lightning spirit, or when you close a thaumaturgic circle. The hairs on my neck stood up." He watched the master, hoping to read his reaction, but Adair's face remained a blank slate. "What was that? Part of their defense system?"

The master shook his head. "Not one I devised. This is something worse, I think. I told them how to defend the building from magick—but I *never* told them to make it a pentagon."

"Maybe it's a coincidence."

"Not likely. I know these varlets. They don't do shite by accident." He fixed Cade with a grim, conspiratorial look. "They've set up a magickal warfare program under their War Department. Or they mean to. Either way, it's not good." A heavy sigh. "This is why I wanted no part of the war. Limited to a few, properly trained karcists, magick can be a force for good. For insight. Wisdom." A long slow pull on his Lucky, then a despondent exhalation. "The world had forgotten us. Now it wants us to drive its war machines. This is everything I'd hoped to avoid."

Cade hoped he might salvage some excuse for hope from the master's news. "It didn't feel active, if that's any consolation. And who knows? Maybe they built it for you."

That drew a mordant chuckle. "Oh, I doubt that. I told those bum-biters years ago they could chew ma banger before I'd ever be their knife-in-the-dark. And if that didn't take me off their short list, I'm fairly certain I just burned whatever bridges I had left."

"Maybe you're assuming too much. I mean, if they didn't ask you to run a project like that, who else could they get?"

That question stymied Adair. "Buggered if I know. Not many karcists in America. There's a Salem-style coven down in New Orleans, but they've no love for the government, and they like to keep to their own. I knew a karcist who tried to make his name out West when it was still the frontier . . . but he died in some Nevada shithole."

"If they won't ask you," Cade said, "would they ask me?"

"If we're lucky, maybe." He snuffed his cigarette butt and lit another. "I know as much as I need to for now. We'll follow up on this when the war's over."

Something in the master's tone troubled Cade. "You don't sound optimistic. You really think this might be a problem?"

"Magick in the wrong hands? It could be a right fucking disaster."

37

JUNE

All of the conjuring room's details had been prepared in accordance with the Covenant. Tapers of beeswax from a new hive stood atop stands of unalloyed gold, their flames populating the walls with erratic shadows. The flayed skin of a newborn lamb was staked with spruce to the floor beyond the northwest quadrant of the double circle; its entrails bubbled in a pot of brandy and magpie's blood, above coals taken from a priest's funeral pyre.

The ritual's key component dangled from the ceiling, suspended above an iron brazier filled with myrrh and camphor: an eighteen-year-old boy, unsullied, naked but for the bindings about his wrists and ankles. Two silken cords—one white, one carmine—restrained his extremities. His hands flailed through the smoke rising from the brazier as he struggled.

He gazed at Kein with frightened, desperate eyes. "Why are you doing this?"

"Because I must." It was true, and Kein didn't wish to belabor the proceedings with mawkish sentiment. But when he looked down at the man-child, he had to admire him.

His hand stroked the youth's cheek. "You look so much like Sabine. You have her eyes. Her hair." He gestured toward his own face. "But my nose, I think." He caressed the teen's earlobes. "And a few of my other features." Noting the youth's confusion, he couldn't resist the temptation to confess. "Forgive me. Did you really think Herr Lohmann was your father? How sad you should learn of your mother's indiscretion in this manner."

Tears ran from the young man's eyes; sobs racked his chest. Kein stroked the youth's cheek, then purged himself of pity and cleared his own mind for the ritual at hand.

He had taken many lovers over the centuries, most of them by dint of his own charm and good looks, and only a rare few—those who existed at the intersection of great beauty and intractable refusal—by sorcery. Never had he seduced a woman out of love or affection. A few he had enjoyed for recreation; others he had conquered in the name of spite. But a special few he had chosen to serve as vessels for his offspring.

His decision to spawn progeny had stemmed not from some illusion of legacy through his descendants, but from a pragmatic need for sacrifices born of his own blood.

When he opened his eyes, all was in order. The hour had come for his experiment to commence. His sword was balanced atop his toes, his athamé was tucked against his left hip, and his wand was ready on his right. He reached into a pocket on the front of his alb, clutched a handful of sulfur and powdered wormwood, and cast it into the brazier at his feet as he spoke:

"Havoc! Havoc! Havoc!"

Green sparks jetted from the brazier and rebounded off the ceiling. Moans and cries from Hell's depths drowned out the youth's screams inside the conjuring room, which was hidden underground, deep within the Wolfsschanze complex.

Kein lifted his voice to break through the unholy clamor: "I invoke thee, LUCIFUGE ROFOCALE, by virtue of my lawful pact with thee, and by the names ADONAI, EL, ELOHIM, JEHOVAM, TETRAGRAMMATON, and by the names ALPHA AND OMEGA, by which Daniel destroyed BEL and slew the Dragon; and by the whole hierarchy of superior intelligences, who shall constrain thee against thy will: *venité, venité, submirillitor,* LUCIFUGE ROFOCALE!"

Thunder shook the room. Blue fire and noxious smoke manifested outside of the circle, then dissipated to reveal Hell's prime minister. It took stock of its circumstances, then showed Kein a fanged grin. YOU'VE BROUGHT ME A SWEETER GIFT THAN I NORMALLY DEMAND. It sniffed the air. A VIRGIN SON. ONE BORN OF YOUR OWN SEED. YOU MUST WANT SOMETHING SPECIAL.

Kein drew his athamé and slashed the young man's throat. Blood rushed out, drawn by gravity into the brazier. "LUCIFUGE ROFOCALE, as prescribed by the Covenant, I give you the blood of my own virgin son as a sacrifice, so that I may ask of thee a boon of prophecy."

The boy's death jolted the beast into ecstatic spasms. Its forked tongue flicked in and out, as if it were lapping up the sweet wine of slaughter.

When the sacrifice's veins ran dry, the demon ceased its convulsions and leered at Kein like a whore ready to serve. WHAT TRUTH DO YOU WISH REVEALED, MY FAITHFUL SERVANT?

"The Allies gather strength. It is only a matter of time before they try to land a major expeditionary force on the European mainland. I want to know precisely *where* and precisely *when* that assault will occur."

His question sent the demon into a trancelike state. Its eyes fluttered shut, and its hands fell still at its sides. When its jaundice-yellow eyes snapped open, they burned with madness. WHAT WILL YOU DO WITH THE KNOWLEDGE I GIVE YOU?

"That is none of your concern. I have abided by the terms of the Covenant. Answer my question—" He drew his wand and poised it over the brazier. "—or feel my wrath."

A growl from the beast, then sullen compliance. THE ALLIES WILL STORM THE SHORES OF NORMANDY, FROM BARFLEUR TO LE HAVRE, NEXT YEAR, ON THE MORNING OF JUNE THE SIXTH, THIRTY-TWO MINUTES AFTER THE SIXTH HOUR OF THE DAY. It leveled a withering stare. KNOWING THIS WILL NOT ENABLE YOU TO CHANGE WHAT IS TO COME.

"I think not to change it," Kein said, "but to usurp it . . . in the name of Hell."

JULY

No journey had ever been so tedious to Briet as the one she had just made from Cherbourg to the compound known as Wolfsschanze, the Führer's military headquarters in the Masurian woods of northeastern Poland.

Despite the urgency of Kein's telegraphed summons, he had forbidden her to hasten her journey by magick. He had ordered a moratorium on portals of fire and shadow, on account of the enemy's seeking his whereabouts with the same fervor that he sought theirs.

So it was that Briet had bid a reluctant farewell to her *amoureux* Victor and Sandrine, to endure nine days on three trains, each a sadder rattletrap than the last, all of them crowded and stinking of sweat and dirty clothes.

Europe was caught in the grip of a miserable summer. Across the continent, temperatures soared and potable water grew short. German propaganda had repeatedly forecasted rain and relief from the heat, but its last half dozen predictions had gone unfulfilled.

There had been little for Briet to do during her journey but read the stacks of newspapers the conductor brought to her sleeper car. Each day had brought fresh reams of bad news. In recent months, she had been skeptical of the Nazis' efforts to conscript foreign nationals to serve as labor in German factories. Today she was dismayed by reports of the ease and rapidity with which the Allies had invaded Italy and forced Duce Benito Mussolini into retreat.

The Devil take the fucking Italians. First they lost North Africa, now they can't even hold their own country. Useless.

Steel shrieked and the train stopped with a shudder. Vapors spewed from its undercarriage as Briet looked out the window to see they had reached Wolfsschanze. Outside, German troops manned defensive posts or assembled to meet the train.

Standing among them but palpably separate from them was Kein Engel.

In spite of the swelter, the creases of his suit looked crisp, and the man him-self was impeccably groomed. His composure filled Briet with admiration and envy.

She gathered her sole piece of luggage, a long leather bag in which she car-ried her grimoire and her tools of the Art. The rest of her belongings—all the mundane necessities of daily life—she had foisted upon DANOCHAR, her hellbeast of burden. With her tools over her shoulder, she got off the train and was met trackside by Kein.

"Master."

"Welcome to Wolfsschanze. I trust your journey was tolerable."

"It was nine days in hot metal cars with the rabble."

He almost smiled. "My apologies, then." He motioned toward a nearby structure. "Do come inside. A chilled bottle of Gewürztraminer awaits us." What the master lacked in emotional warmth he had always made up for with generosity and taste.

They retired inside his guesthouse, whose interior, to Briet's relief, had been cooled and dehumidified to levels that approached comfortable. Its appoint-ments were simple but of quality, and had been chosen for comfort as much as for aesthetics. There was a minimum of decoration; the walls were mostly bare but had at least been painted and, in a few places, paneled to help one forget that the building was little more than a cement box.

The house comprised an office, a bedroom, a lavatory with a shower, and a small kitchenette. A trapdoor in its central hallway appeared to lead to a basement level, which Briet surmised must be where Kein had established his conjuring room.

He walked to his desk, on which a pair of tulip glasses stood beside a slen-der bottle drenched with condensation. Briet set down her tools and relaxed onto the room's sofa. The master uncorked the bottle and half filled the glasses before handing one to her.

"To victory," he said.

She clinked her glass against his. "Victory."

The wine was tart, with notes of apple and green pear, and its acidity made her mouth water. She liked that it was less sweet than some Rieslings she had found cloying. She guzzled the rest of the glass, hoping to shed the stresses of travel and dull the pain of dragging nine yoked demons. Then she set the glass aside and regarded her master. "You didn't bring me here from Normandy for a wine tasting. Why am I here?"

"As ever, straight to the point." He set his glass on his desk. "I have received . . . a *revelation* from Below."

"Of what?"

"Things to come. Inevitabilities we can turn to our advantage." He paced while folding his hands one over the other, massaging the knuckles. "For months I have had you seed the Atlantic coast with Enochian wards. And you have done an exemplary job. But now I know where and when the Allies will strike when they invade France, and I mean to prepare something special for their arrival." He stopped and faced her. "Something never seen before."

His penchant for drama vexed her. "Am I meant to guess what it is?"

"A trap—one that will change the face of the earth, leave the Allies and the Axis in ruins, and force both sides to pursue the kinds of desperate measures that will turn the people of the world against them and their precious Science once and for all."

Had the master finally gone mad? The gleam in his eyes suggested the possibility. Briet kept her tone neutral. "What kind of trap, exactly?"

"One that can unleash a legion from Hell, without instruction or restriction, to wreak havoc on the earth until I am satisfied it has laid waste Science's decadent modern world." Perhaps noting some hint of alarm in Briet's gaze, he added, "You and I will have nothing to fear. Knowing the day and the hour, we will be protected by circles and wards greater than any that Solomon or Honorius ever dared to conceive."

"Putting aside the logistical hurdles to crafting such a trap, why do it at all? Unleashing that many demons on the earth, without commands or control, would almost certainly herald the coming of Armageddon."

"Ridiculous. The Seven Seals are unbroken, the Antichrist has yet to appear—"

"You're quite certain of that?"

He inferred her meaning at once. "The Führer is many things—a megalomaniac and a small-minded worm of a man, for starters—but I assure you: He is not the Antichrist. At any rate, my point stands. The prophecies remain unfulfilled. Judgment Day is not upon us, no matter what we do. And I will make certain I can rein in the mayhem when I have had my fill."

"How?"

"By being the one to mold the trap. I am going to compose a seal of bondage that will put Solomon's to shame. He became a legend for trapping seventy-two spirits in his vessel of brass. I will imprison a thousand and one inside slabs of stone—which I will put squarely in front of the Allies' invasion. However they break them, once the seal is shattered, the Allies will be the first to feel Hell's fury. And when their armies are vanquished, the demons will turn on the Germans. And then on anyone and anything else they find." A malevolent smile gave him the affect of a madman. "It will be glorious, my dear."

Was there any reason left in him? She had to try to find it. "How does destroying the world benefit us? Would it not be prudent to leave some of its technologies intact?"

He refilled his glass, then hers. "Technology gave us industrialized warfare, Briet. This slaughter that engulfs the globe—where will it end? Can it end? The Chinese flooded the Yellow River valley in a failed bid to halt the Japanese army, and ended up killing half a million of their own people. Defenseless civilians, most of them women, children, or the elderly, all drowned without warning because war drives men to madness. Now, thanks to Science, governments can eradicate entire populations in the blink of an eye." He spread his arms in a dramatic flourish. "Man has used Science to make a vision of Hell on earth. I plan to give them the real thing, and to make sure Science takes the blame."

"And a night of demonic carnage accomplishes that . . . how?"

"By forcing all sides to the ends of their desperation. The Germans have built rockets that will let them bomb London and eventually America's east coast, without risking any pilots. The Russians have already sacrificed the better part of a generation, and I have no doubt they will push their own people to extinction in the name of pride. And the Americans . . ." He pressed a finger to his lips, then shook his head. "Let it suffice to say Hell gave me a taste of what the Americans have in store for the world. If I can push them far enough— say, by sinking their attack fleet and sending their invasion force to the bottom of the English Channel—they will have no choice but to unleash their nightmare masterpiece. First on Germany. Then, I suspect, on Japan. Compared to that, a night of a thousand demons will seem like a pale prelude."

He stood at his desk and set his hands on a map of Normandy. "When we are done, Briet, humanity will swear off Science for at least a century. Only then, when the world lies in cinders, will we be able to begin the long work of remaking the world—this time, in *our own* image."

AUGUST

Machine-gun fire ripped through the streets of Kharkov, a city of ruins shrouded in dust and the smoke of burning tanks. Russia's dead here outnumbered German casualties by a ratio of five to one, a number that was growing daily thanks to the Red Army's tactic of throwing lives and resources at its enemies until it wore them down by the weight of numbers. It was a wasteful, stupid strategy, but an effective one.

Piercing whistles announced incoming mortar rounds—Anja's cue to dive for cover with her comrades. A shell dropped in the street ahead of them. Its detonation shook the earth and scoured her with grit and shattered glass.

It was impossible to see the sky through the brown haze choking the city, but it didn't hide the drone of Stuka bombers making another run. The Luftwaffe had run out of its usual ordnance and so had been hitting Red Army positions in Kharkov with the sorts of bombs it normally used to punch holes in battleships and aircraft carriers.

Her platoon leader barked, "Get down!"

Anja, Nadezhda, and the rest of their unit scattered in a race to shelter as falling bombs screamed down from above. Booms ripped through the stifling air and turned hollowed buildings into storms of pulverized concrete. Cracked cement poured into the streets from all directions, followed by the chatter of the Stukas' machine guns strafing the rubble.

Down the road, through a curtain of smog and fumes, Anja picked out the silhouettes of an advancing line of German Tiger tanks. She shouted to her comrades, "Heavy armor! Rolling in from the west!"

The platoon leader yelled back, "Who still has tank-shredders?"

Anja's hand moved to the RPG-43 handheld antitank grenade slung from her belt. A few other voices returned confirmations to the platoon leader before Anja added, "I have one!"

"Shredders, move up! Flank the street! Hit the lead vehicles to block the others. Everybody else, dig in and lay down suppressing fire! Go!"

There was no time for debate or questions. Anja sprinted toward the approaching panzer column, hoping the dusty churn from the tanks' treads would hide her from their gunners until she could find cover from which to strike.

A staccato buzz of machine guns filled the streets as the tanks' crews fired blindly into the haze ahead of them. Two of Anja's comrades twitched and fell, torn to shreds, as she darted off the street and took shelter in a heap of broken stone and steel.

She and the rest of her unit went quiet as the tanks drew near. The street trembled before the sheer mass of the Nazi juggernauts and the power of their engines. Crawling like a spider, Anja ascended the mound of debris shielding her from the Germans. At its crest she paused to unclip her antitank grenade from her belt; then she clambered forward.

Sighting the first tank, she armed her RPG-43. Landing the grenade on target would be tricky. It had a shaped charge on its end, and it had to strike at the perfect angle or else the force of the explosion would be deflected with minimal damage. Of course, taking the time to aim and set her stance would make her a prime target for the tanks' gunners.

I did not come home to die a coward. She stood and aimed.

Below her, the panzer column rumbled past.

She planted her foot and threw. As her grenade sailed toward its target, she saw more thrown by her comrades from the other side of the street.

Fiery tracer rounds from the tanks, a thudding percussion of automatic gunfire. White heat lanced through Anja's side. She fell, delirious, suddenly cold in spite of the summer heat, disoriented as explosions rocked the street and turned the sky above black with oily smoke.

Awareness came back to her in flashes.

The grind of dirt against her face.

Her own ragged breathing.

Sick pain welling up inside her.

Then she was in motion, the street drifting past her, the earth tugging at her dragging toes, her arms almost yanked from their sockets. Short of breath, barely able to focus, she struggled to understand what was happening. She lifted her head to see Nadezhda pulling her by her wrists, towing her up the street, away from the blazing husks of Tiger tanks heaped one upon another in the middle of the street.

"Nady? What . . . what are you—?"

"Saving your life," Nadezhda said between grunts of effort. She wasn't strong enough to heft Anja over her shoulder in a proper carry, so instead she was endangering herself and Anja with this foolish attempt at pulling her to cover.

Anja croaked through a mouth caked with grit, "Leave me."

"You didn't leave me in Stalingrad, or in Kursk."

A month before, on the ugliest day of the battle to liberate Kursk, Nady had been pinned down by German sniper fire. Their platoon leader had written her off as a loss, but Anja had refused to accept it. She had skulked into the ruins under cover of darkness and outwitted a German sharpshooter in a sniper battle that had lasted nearly until dawn.

I should have known Nady would make me regret—

A burst from a German submachine gun.

Bullets slammed into Nadezhda's chest and gut. Red mist filled the dust cloud behind her. Her hands went slack and lost hold of Anja's wrists.

Red Army soldiers charged past Anja and Nady, returning fire on the German troops, the cracks of their rifles crisp and precise against the chaos of the Nazis' automatic barrage, but all Anja heard were her own anguished cries as she watched Nady collapse in a bloody heap.

Other hands took hold of Anja: two male soldiers each grabbed one of her arms. They hauled her away from the tanks and left Nadezhda's tattered corpse behind. Remanded to the care of medical volunteers, Anja kept her eyes fixed on her friend's lifeless body until the fog of war, the sting of a needle, and the shadow of morphine stole Nady from her for the last time.

Twists of smoke rose from unsteady flames. Incense smoldered in brass cups Adair had placed within the chords of the six-pointed star he had scribed around his operator's circle. On an altar inside the triangle situated northwest of the top of the circle, a live young goat hung trussed to a spit, its coarse white fur painted with violet Enochian glyphs.

The kid bleated twice in fear, and with good reason.

Adair raised his wand. In his left hand he clutched a handful of finely ground herbs and flammable powders, a well-tested recipe from an ancient grimoire. "I invoke and summon thee, Great King of Hell—appear or feel my wrath, PAIMON!" He threw the dust into the brazier at his feet. Violet sparks geysered from the pot and scorched the rafters above his head.

Sickly yellow fog rolled around the outer circle. An atonal keening: faint at first, it grew louder and more shrill as, in the northwest, a parade of shapes appeared. All wore the garb of medieval troubadors. They emerged from the swirling vapors, revealing their true natures—ghouls with glowing embers for eyes, all reeking of putrefaction.

With them came a horrible music never meant for mortal ears. Some of the horde played long trumpets festooned with tattered banners. Others strummed mistuned lyres, crashed rusted cymbals, or blew conflicting melodies through steel flutes or wooden panpipes. It all combined to fill the conjuring room with a dissonance that made Adair's skull ache.

In the center of their formation was a lone figure mounted on a colossal dromedary. The steed wore a crown of gold attached to its bridle, and a blanket of Persian design was draped across its back, under its saddle—upon which sat the terrifying majesty of PAIMON, Adair's patron spirit.

Its imposing frame was garbed in robes of black and vermeil. A mane of sable framed the demon's effeminate face and reptilian eyes. It wore a jeweled gold crown, around whose ten spires writhed a serpent ever in motion. A diaphanous veil billowed behind it, as if caught in a perpetual gale. The demon's long, ratlike tail twitched to and fro.

As always, PAIMON took its place astride the triangle without delay, then shook the bedrock with a voice that married a tsunami to an earthquake. STAY THY ROD, EVE-SPAWN, I AM HERE! WHY HAVE YOU DISTURBED MY REPOSE?

"To invoke my rights as per the terms of our compact. I need to know where Kein Engel and his apprentice Briet are, and where they're going to be—and I command you to tell me."

PAIMON reached toward the altar, extending one of its arms as if it were made of some forgiving elastic, and snatched up the bleating kid. The demon's jaw gaped open and its face stretched into a horror as it devoured the animal in a bite of sharklike teeth.

Once the sacrifice was consumed, the demon's face returned to its previous aspect, but now its fangs were stained vermilion, and dribbles of dark blood ran from the corners of its mouth. Its voice boomed again in the close quarters.

YOUR SACRIFICE PLEASES ME, ADAIR! I WILL BE GENEROUS AND NOT REPEAT THE ANSWER I GAVE THE LAST TWO TIMES YOU ASKED ME THIS.

Twice before PAIMON had failed to locate Kein, both times for the same reason: Kein's wards against scrying and divination were too powerful for

PAIMON to overcome. Encouraged that something seemed to have changed, Adair became impatient. "So? Where is he?"

I NEVER SAID I COULD ANSWER YOUR QUERY, ONLY THAT I WOULD NOT REPEAT WHAT I HAVE ALREADY TOLD YOU IN THE SIMPLEST POSSIBLE TERMS. BUT I CAN TELL YOU THIS: YOU ARE ASKING THE WRONG QUESTION.

Adair was tempted to stab his wand into the coals to punish PAIMON for taunting him, but he knew from centuries of experience that there were harsh consequences for karcists who abused their patrons. He curbed his wrath, cleared his mind, and considered the demon's counsel. "What do you know about Kein's actions that might be relevant to my quarrel with him?"

A diabolical smirk tugged at the demon's delicate lips. HIS ACTIONS ON EARTH ARE WELL HIDDEN—BUT HE CANNOT CONCEAL THOSE PARTS OF HIS LABORS THAT AFFECT HELL. HE HAS RECEIVED AN UNHOLY DIVINATION FROM HIS PATRON, LUCIFUGE ROFOCALE.

"What kind of divination?"

A PROPHECY. OF WHAT, I KNOW NOT. WHAT MATTERS IS HE HAS RESPONDED TO THIS VISION BY EMBARKING ON A WORK UNPRECEDENTED IN THE ANNALS OF HELL. HE HAS CALLED MORE SPIRITS INTO ITS SERVICE THAN ANY KARCIST HAS EVER DARED BEFORE.

It was an outrageous claim that left Adair doubting his patron's veracity, which was always a wise policy when dealing with demons. "I've tracked the signs, watched my Lull Engine. There's been no uptick in demonic activity. In fact, it's been falling off for weeks."

YOU HEAR BUT YOU DO NOT LISTEN. KEIN IS NOT CALLING UP SPIRITS TO SEND THEM ABROAD, NOR IS HE YOKING THEM. HE IS BINDING THEM TO A UNIQUE WORK OF UNKNOWN INTENTION. THE SIGNS AND PORTENTS ALL POINT TO A DISASTER ABORNING.

"That's all you can tell me? Can you say where? Or when? Or anything that might actually help?"

His plea seemed to amuse the spirit. I DOUBT HE COULD EXECUTE SUCH A GRANDIOSE EXPERIMENT ALONE. KEIN CAN WORK FROM THE SHADOWS— BUT HIS APPRENTICE CANNOT.

All at once, Adair remembered Niko's warnings of Briet directing the installation of anti-magick defenses along the Atlantic coast. *If Kein's working up a doomsday plan,* Adair reasoned, *that's where it will be.* "Thank you for this insight, Great King. Is there anything else I should know before I give thee license to depart?"

THIS CHALLENGE WILL BE UNLIKE ANY YOU HAVE EVER FACED—AND THE PRICE OF ITS DEFEAT MIGHT BE MORE THAN YOU ARE WILLING TO PAY.

"We'll see about that." He dismissed PAIMON and its band of music-mangling demons, who vanished in gouts of green fire.

Alone in the smoky aftermath of the conjuring, Adair stripped off his robes and put away his tools. Until that moment, he had dismissed Niko's hunt for Briet as the product of vengeful obsession. Months of near misses by Niko had made the search start to seem futile.

Now Adair saw it in a new light: Finding Briet was the Allies' only chance of uncovering Kein's latest scheme and putting an end to it while they still had time.

He could only hope it wasn't already too late.

40

SEPTEMBER

Death's stench greeted Anja as she fought her way to consciousness. It was a fetid odor, with metallic undertones of dried blood and tangs of disinfectant overpowered by sepsis. It was rotten meat and the vinegary stink of vomitus. The closer Anja came to recovering her faculties, the less she wanted to. Fearing she might find herself lying among the fallen in the streets of Kharkov, she opened her eyes.

The cots in the Red Army field hospital stood in rows and columns. All were occupied by maimed or dying soldiers of Mother Russia, each lying head-to-head with a fallen comrade. Anja winced at the bloodied sheets draped on top of her before she realized the stains were old and dry. Holding the frayed hem of her sheet, she lifted it to inspect her wounds.

Her abdomen was a mess of crude stitches and bright pink scar tissue. She probed it with her fingertips. Some of the wounds still felt raw and wet. A bit of pressure provoked deep echoes of pain, a warning of how extensive her wounds were. Against her better judgment she tried to sit up. Agony knifed through her and left her sweating and short of breath.

A nurse—or perhaps a medical volunteer in a nurse's uniform—hurried to Anja's bedside. The woman was rail-thin, with wide-set dark eyes and hacked-short black hair. "Comrade Kernova? It's good to see you awake. How do you feel?"

"Terrible."

"That's to be expected. You're lucky to be alive."

"How long have I been here?"

The nurse lifted a sheaf of papers from an envelope hanging at the foot of Anja's cot and paged through them. "Just over three weeks."

Anja struggled to spy a familiar face in the legions of wounded. "Did anyone bring in Comrade Nadezhda Proschkeva?" She parsed the nurse's lack of recognition from her expression. "Small, blond hair. She was part of my unit, the Central Front."

"We don't have any patients here by that name."

Despair settled over Anja. She knew it had been too much to hope for. Her hands still felt the strength vanishing from Nady's grip as the Germans' bullets ripped into her; her memory was seared with the image of the light going out of Nady's fierce eyes.

What was I thinking? Russia has no place for miracles—especially not in wartime.

Noting the nurse's discomfort, Anja changed the subject. "My gear—I had a leather tool roll. Where is it?"

"Under your cot, with your rifle and pack."

"Hand it to me. The tool roll, I mean."

The nurse reached under the cot, retrieved the bulky, heavy leather roll-up, and set it gently into Anja's arms. She wore a curious expression as she watched Anja embrace the bundle of tools. "Prized possessions?"

"Something like that." It would have been difficult for Anja to explain the value of the tool roll to a non-karcist. To most people, the hand-fashioned implements would be little more than a curiosity, objects of no particular value aside from their metal content. But to Anja, these would all be costly and difficult to replace. She smiled at the nurse. "Thank you."

"Let me know if you need anything"—she rolled her eyes at the tragic absurdity of the filthy, understaffed setting—"not that we're likely to have it."

"I will. Thank you again." As soon as the nurse moved on to tend to another patient, Anja unwound the tool roll to inspect its contents. To her relief, everything was in its place, and nothing appeared to have been damaged or tampered with. She rolled it up and tied it shut.

The next part, she knew, would be harder.

She turned slowly onto her right side, which hurt a tiny bit less than trying to turn to her left. Perched at the edge of her cot, she reached under it and found her pack. She dragged it out from under her, untied its flap, and rooted inside it until her hand found her grimoire. Its silk binding was still in place, its warding seal unbroken. She breathed a sigh of relief.

Deeper inside the pack, she found a small aluminum canister in which she had stored a smidgen of enchanted unguent. Its most common use was to focus magickal healing on particular wounds while protecting the patient from any of the side effects of contact with a demon. On this occasion, Anja had other plans for it.

She set the canister at her side, pushed her pack under her cot, then put her tool roll on the floor before nudging it underneath, as well. After checking to make sure no one was watching her, Anja pried off the canister's lid and scooped a dollop of unguent onto her right index finger. She lifted her sheet over her head and scribed two ancient Enochian wards on her ravaged torso— the first beneath her breasts, but linked by an elegant S to the other above them. The former was a symbol to keep demons at bay; the latter was an appeal to the healing powers of Heaven—not that the Celestial powers owed her any favors.

She wiped her finger clean on the cot's top sheet, then closed the canister and hid it among her other possessions. The wards were feeble gestures in comparison to her wounds, but it was all she had the strength to do. It might be weeks or even months before she could conjure her patron and resume yoking spirits.

Until then, whether she lived or died would depend on the healing prowess of human doctors and so-called modern medicine.

In other words, Anja brooded, *I am at Fate's mercy.*

It was a troubling thought for Anja—not because she harbored any fear of Fate, but because life and war had taught her never to believe in mercy.

Under a sky bruised with dusk, Niko prowled Bayeux's cobblestone alleyways. Deep shadows stretched down the nooks of the old coastal city. Niko limped toward a V-shaped intersection that birthed a new alley at its junction. He took such pains to draw no attention to his own passing that he barely noticed his man Xavier until he was almost on top of him.

The Maquis spy was wedged into a tight gap between two old brick buildings. His hair was a mess, his face gaunt. "You're late."

"One of those Vichy pricks spotted me in town. I had to shake him."

"Did you?"

"Of course." Niko felt no need to explain he had misled the Vichy agent by transforming himself with the talent of GAMIGIN into the guise of a teenage girl and directing the French traitor into a large building he would no doubt spend hours searching to no avail. He mirrored Xavier's suspicion. "You said you had a lead on Briet."

"You said you'd pay me."

Niko reached inside his jacket with his good hand. Xavier started to draw his knife. The blade was half out of its sheath when Niko froze and told his twitchy colleague, "Relax."

"How much did you bring?"

"It's not money."

"Then we're done." Xavier tried to sidestep Niko, who showed him the paper bag he'd hidden under his coat. "Fresh baguette. Two sausages. And a wedge of triple-cream Brie."

The spy's eyes widened as if he'd been offered the fortune of Midas. "How? From where? All the food is rationed! The Germans haven't left us a bite in weeks!"

"From the best charcuterie in Bayeux."

Xavier looked stunned. "Monsieur Delacroix? How?"

There was nothing for Niko to gain by explaining his magickal powers of suggestion, so he evaded the question with a euphemism. "I appealed to the better angels of his nature."

The young Maquis opened the bag, stuck his beak of a nose inside it, and breathed deep its savory perfumes. "Most excellent. Truly splendid." Another deep huff, then he rolled the bag closed and relaxed his defenses. "Briet has been visiting the new fortifications on the cliff at Pointe du Hoc a few times each week for the last month. She is supervising the construction of a new Nazi artillery bunker overlooking the beach."

"Why that bunker? What's so special about it?"

A shrug. "Who knows? The Nazis won't let anyone near it."

Footsteps echoed from farther down the alleyway. Xavier pulled Niko down a shaded street from which more narrow passages branched. Hobbled by his gimp leg, it was hard for Niko to keep up with him. Hidden once again, Niko whispered, "Tell me all about her visits. Anything you remember. Even the smallest detail might help." Without asking permission, he invoked the memory-enhancing gifts of VERMIAS to improve Xavier's recollection.

"She tends to come in the late afternoon," Xavier said, his often lax focus honed by the memory charm. "Never alone. Usually with a few Waffen-SS guards, but sometimes up to half a dozen. Most times she stays late into the night, or even until the wee hours."

Niko committed the details to his own demonically enhanced memory. "Good, good. How does she arrive? On foot? In a truck?"

"Chauffeured car, German military registry, French driver. He usually waits near the car until she returns."

"Do you know where they come from? Or where they go after they leave?"

Xavier shook his head. "No. It never comes up. No one asks."

More steps nearby. They ducked around a corner into another maze of narrow alleys flanked by high walls. Once more out of sight, Niko listened until he heard no sounds of pursuit. "Do the Germans building the bunker get any advance notice of her visits?"

"I don't know. We've intercepted no phone calls, telegrams, or radio signals announcing her visits. If they were scheduled, it was done by secure post."

"Who has access to this special bunker?"

"So far? Only a few high-level engineers, a handful of workers, and Briet."

"All right." Niko considered all that Xavier had told him. It was a good start, enough on which to formulate a plan. He dispelled his demonic enhancement of the other man's memory. "You've done well, Xavier. Can I ask you to keep eyes on the bunker? I need to know if Briet comes back, or if the work is ever halted long enough for me to sneak in and get a look."

The Maquis turned a skeptical look at Niko, but his loyalty to Free France overcame his doubts. "That can be arranged—for a price, of course." He started walking, and Niko followed.

"Trust me, Xavier. I'll make it worth your while."

"So you say. I'm pretty sure you still owe me a bottle of Pinot Noir."

"Like hell I do, you—" Niko and Xavier rounded a bend in the alleyway and came face-to-face with a pair of street urchins: a boy and a girl, neither older than ten years, both emaciated, victims of long neglect. They recoiled from the men until Niko tipped his beret to them. "Good evening. Are you two lost?"

The children seemed paralyzed by fear. Tiny shakes of their heads indicated they were not lost. Softening his tone, Niko continued, "Are you all right? Where are your parents?"

Anxious looks hinted at the children's silent exchange of fears. Then the girl spoke. "Gone. The Nazis. Killed Papa. Took Mama."

Niko kneeled to bring himself down to the children's level. "When?"

"July," the girl said. "Before Bastille Day."

The boy added, "Shot Papa in our house."

"Put Mama on the train," the girl continued. With wide, pleading eyes, she implored Niko and Xavier, "Can you spare any money? We're hungry."

Xavier started to turn away. "Beggars and hustlers. I should've known."

Catching the other man's arm, Niko asked the children, "How long since you've eaten?" He listened to their replies with the discerning ear of AMON.

"Six days for me," the girl said. She nodded at her brother. "Five for Marcel."

Xavier grumbled, "What a load of—"

"They're telling the truth," Niko said.

"How can you tell?"

"I just can." He reached into his pocket and fished out a few francs, the only currency he had on his person, and gave it to the girl. Then he nudged Xavier and shot a prompting glare at his bag of foodstuffs.

The spy was appalled. "Why would I?"

"To serve the better angels of your nature."

"I haven't any."

Marshaling the mind-altering powers of NEBIROS, Niko instilled a deep seed of primal terror into Xavier's psyche. "Shall I help you *discover* them?" It was a cruel way to motivate someone, but the situation called for it.

Fearful, Xavier thrust the grease-stained paper bag into the boy's hands. The children tore the bag open and marveled at its contents. Beaming with joy, they scampered into the shadows with their bounty. The men watched the children retreat into the twilight.

Xavier grimaced at Niko. "You are a bad influence, *monsieur*."

It was hard for Niko to feel sorry for a rank opportunist such as Xavier, so he cracked a mischievous smile instead. "What can I say? I've the Devil in me."

OCTOBER

More than seven weeks in the Red Army field hospital had driven Anja to her wits' edge.

Time spent in forced convalescence was, she noted, much like time spent in prison. It moved with maddening sloth and was full of strangers who wanted to stick her with sharp objects to take some of her blood. The food was bland and horrid. Each day was a refrain of the one before and an omen of the one to come. Fellow patients asked one another, like inmates trading secrets of guilt, "What are you in for?" And all that the nurses or doctors cared about when they spoke to her was whether she was sufficiently rehabilitated to merit her release from the institution, to return to the meat grinder of the war.

Anja was done waiting for their permission.

She rolled from her cot to a floor of bloodstained planks atop packed dirt. With stealth and dispatch she dressed and gathered her belongings: coat, pack, rifle, tool roll. The dated notes on her chart told her it was October 7. A wristwatch looped around the frame of her neighbor's cot showed the time was just after four in the morning, which meant the witching hour, when demons sent abroad were at their most potent, was passed.

Time to go.

There were no guards posted on the field hospital. In the wee hours the handful of nurses, doctors, and volunteers tended to steal naps before sunrise roused the patients, who would fill the dawn with pitiful cries and complaints.

Anja skulked past the rows of cots. The only person who seemed to note her departure was a soldier with a throat wound and no voice with which to betray her. She nodded at him on her way past and whispered, "Good luck, Comrade." He half raised one hand in a meek wave of farewell, then went back to sleep.

Anja stopped at the exit, which was just three blankets draped in front of an arch whose door had been blown off years earlier. She pushed aside the woolen layers and peeked outside. There were few signs of life, just deserted streets of rubble. She parted the blankets and passed between them with as much speed as her atrophied limbs could bear.

To conceal the extent of her recovery from the doctors she had feigned weakness and an inability to stand on her own. The cost of her deception now came due: her legs, after weeks of disuse, trembled under the burden of her pack, rifle, and tools.

Just keep moving, she told herself. Through will alone she impelled her body into motion. She couldn't afford to be seen or stopped, not now. When she was found to be missing, she would be declared absent without leave. In a matter of days she would be charged with desertion. It was imperative she be as far away as possible by then. Her life depended on it.

The landscape around her was jarring in its bleakness. Where once Kharkov had stood, nothing remained but the husks of buildings—sometimes as little as a single wall, or a lone doorway propped up in a field of bricks. Jagged like broken teeth, they stood in the footprints of a city laid waste. Smoke twisted from empty stretches of debris and wrecked tanks; fires burned in oil drums pockmarked with bullet holes.

A few foot patrols were out and about, usually no more than three or four infantrymen each. They all seemed more interested in their rambling conversations and idle boastings than in policing the smoldering corpse of the city, which made it easy for Anja to evade their notice and slip by them. In less than an hour she was on the outskirts of Kharkov, heading alone into the countryside, which tank battles and artillery fire had reduced to a cracked wasteland.

She turned her steps north-northeast, in the general direction of Moscow. Passing so close to the capital would be dangerous, but she had little choice: there were no direct routes from Kharkov to her native village of Toporok in Novgorodskaya Oblast. Even more perilous, she needed to make her trek on foot while avoiding any Red Army personnel who might come looking for her. She also had to hope the Germans made no late-autumn pushes into Russia before winter arrived. As for the coming cold and snow, those were hazards she would face one night and one step at a time, until she completed this long-overdue journey.

She'd had enough of war and enough of magick.

Desperate for sanctuary and absolution, Anja was going home.

～～～

Viewed through binoculars, the world was narrow and always in motion. As hard as Niko tried to hold them steady, the field glasses shook in his one good hand.

Tonight he blamed the cold that had frosted windows on the Normandy coast. He was hunkered in a ditch set back from the cliffs of Pointe du Hoc, not far from the bunker his contact Xavier said Briet had been frequenting since summer.

Why she had visited was still unclear. Neither Xavier or his source could confirm what part of the multi-battery artillery emplacement had been of interest to her. All he could do for the moment was hope tonight would be the night she showed her face here again.

Damn you, Xavier. Three weeks I have spent my nights in this hole.

He made another survey of the cliffs overlooking the beach. Only a handful of German soldiers patrolled there after dark. This night's sentries looked no more vigilant than usual. Despite the proximity of England and the Allied forces, Normandy remained a relaxed front.

For Niko, the stakeout of the bunker had proved a mixed blessing. Because it was located inside the half-mile-wide zone within which no demon could enter and no magick would work, Niko had been forced to release his yoked spirits and venture into enemy territory with only a semiautomatic pistol, a knife, and his wits for protection. Out of habit he always carried his enchanted mirror, though it too was unable to function inside the "dead zone."

Stripped of magick, he felt impotent, vulnerable. However, he'd enjoyed the freedom from nightmares that came with being rid of demons. Without spirits to vex him, he had cut down on cigarettes and wine, consuming them now more for enjoyment than for relief.

A far-off rumbling of engines turned Niko's gaze inland. Distant headlights pierced the dark. A small convoy was approaching the work site. Niko lay low in his ditch and steadied his binoculars on its edge.

Three vehicles were waved through the security checkpoint. In the lead was a black Mercedes-Benz convertible with a long front end. Behind it were two German military trucks. They parked near the chief architect's tent.

From one truck poured a platoon of Waffen-SS troops armed with submachine guns; out of the other climbed a team of civilian workers Niko had not seen before. The soldiers assumed protective formations on either side of the Mercedes-Benz, while the workers unloaded a six-foot-long, weighty, linen-wrapped wedge from the rear of the second truck.

Briet got out of the car. She stepped through her line of defenders and snapped orders at the workers who labored to carry the mystery wedge to the bunker.

What have we here? Niko focused his binoculars on the workers. *Tell me that's not some avant-garde coffee table or—*

A man exited the car. Tall, handsome, and tailored: it was Kein. He interrupted Briet's shouting to whisper in her ear. She nodded, then resumed her tirade at the workers.

The Waffen-SS troops moved with Kein and Briet as they followed the workers to the bunker. The magicians entered the fortification; the soldiers halted outside its door. No one acted as if this was the least bit suspect or out of the ordinary.

Niko noted the bunker's position on his map. Over the last few weeks he had updated it to record the point's warren of trenches, which linked the bunker to neighboring fortifications. Tucking the map away, he fantasized about lobbing a grenade inside the bunker, a nasty surprise for Kein and Briet. Only cold blue reason and the memory of Adair's unequivocal orders—*Observe but do not engage; gather intelligence, but don't risk capture*—stayed his hand.

As keen as Niko's appetite for revenge had become, he remembered Adair's warning that Kein was on the verge of unleashing something unprecedented in its destructiveness, a threat about which the Allies had no actionable intelligence. More than anything else, they needed to know what Kein was planning—and whatever it was, this was where it was being prepared.

The bunker's door opened with a scrape of metal on stone. Briet emerged first, followed by Kein, and then the civilian workers. The Waffen-SS regrouped. One squad escorted Briet and Kein toward the chief architect's tent, while the others herded the workers toward the trucks—then, without warning, mowed them down in a blaze of rifle fire. As the workers fell, neither Kein nor Briet spared a glance for the condemned. Their indifference told Niko the mass execution was no surprise to them, just another mundane atrocity on their path to victory.

The SS men chortled over the carnage. Niko seethed. *If they were not inside the dead zone . . .* He wished he could send a demon to gut the Nazis like trout, or crush their skulls like rotten fruit, or dismember them alive while he cut their throats with his athamé—

Stop. Keep control. It was painful to put aside his anger, to bury his lust for vengeance, but it was necessary. He needed to be calm now.

He crouched as he shuffled toward the bunker, sheltered by the deepening twilight. No one had been left inside or at its entrance. He stole down its concrete steps, past a murder hole to a covered area that led to the bunker's main entrance. Mindful of the armored portal's loud scraping, he pulled up on its handle to lift it off the ground, then opened it just enough for him to slink past. He breathed easier once he was inside, hidden by the bunker's shadows.

The interior was pitch dark. Niko dug his lighter from his pocket, opened the cover with a jerk of his wrist, and thumbed the flint. A tall flame danced on the lighter's dense wick, throwing weak darts of illumination into the blackness that surrounded him.

He stood in a narrow passage. Directly ahead was another armored door, half open. Open doorways to his right and just ahead on his left. He crept forward, spooked by the shadows his own flame tossed onto the walls.

The chamber on the left was a guardroom, the space behind one of the murder holes. Through the other door he found a long windowless room fitted with a small cooking stove and four bunk-bed frames attached by chains to the walls and ceiling. An alcove on his left stood empty, but pipes, wires, and a round duct dangling from its wood-frame ceiling suggested it was meant to house some kind of machinery, either a heater or a generator, or both.

He returned to the passage inside the main door and ventured left, into a large open room. On its far wall, opposite the entrance, another armored door was propped open, admitting fresh air and reflected light from the fading dusk. The large room was devoid of furnishings. But before he progressed more than two steps inside . . . he saw it.

A demonic sigil adorned the floor. It was composed of eight wedges of marble, all of equal size and identical shape, but each unique in its engravings. Arcane glyphs had been carved into them. Some Niko recognized as Enochian wards, or as ancient Hebrew letters forming sacred names, or as seals representing specific demons. Others he couldn't begin to identify. With all eight wedges in place, he saw that they and their markings fit together with precision. He saw no gaps; the seams between the wedges were barely visible.

As he stepped closer, a bloodcurdling fear shot through him, in spite of the magick-suppressing countermeasures with which the enemy had blanketed the coastline.

I don't know what this is, but I know Adair must see it.

Mounted on the walls were four kerosene lamps. Niko closed the door to the observation room, then used his lighter to kindle the lamps. They filled the room with honeyed light.

He took out a miniaturized camera he had acquired from a British SOE agent. Niko photographed each wedge, pivoting atop the center of the seal and checking his focus before each shot. The lines cut into the rock were so minuscule that he knew every detail in his photos would matter. After he documented all eight wedges, he realized that alone would not be enough.

A search in some adjoining rooms yielded simple tools left behind by the work crews. He found a meter stick. *Yes, this will do.*

Back in the sigil room, he took a small compass from his pocket. He opened it and set it on the floor in the center of the eldritch seal. He rotated it toward magnetic north and was not surprised to find it aligned perfectly with one of the seams between wedges. Next he laid the meter stick beside the compass, for scale. Then he stood, held his camera over his head, and pointed it at the floor as he snapped multiple reference shots. After he put away the camera, he used the meter stick to measure the room's dimensions and jotted them in his annotated notes about the bunker complex, with a second note indicating that the center of the sigil and the center of the room were one and the same.

Niko snuffed the kerosene lamps, then returned to the bunker's main entrance. It was still unguarded, so he slipped outside into the trenches. Three limping steps away from a clean escape, he halted. A dark impulse took shape in his heart—a will to revenge, an urge to deliver justice on Kein and his apprentice. Niko's hand seized the grip of his pistol.

Here in the magickal dead zone Kein and Briet had created, they were just as vulnerable as he was. Without yoked demons, they were nothing but flesh and bone, blood and breath.

I could take them out, here and now. I could end this.

Driven by a dream of violence, Niko sneaked through the trenches and behind the chief architect's tent, where Kein and Briet sat and conversed with the project leader over glasses of wine. Most of the SS men lingered in pairs or small groups, chatting or smoking cigarettes.

If I can find one of the guards alone . . .

Cut his throat, take his submachine gun . . .

And strafe this tent . . .

Through the canvas wall, he overheard the magicians and the architect talking. Without a demon to translate for him, Niko's understanding of German was halting at best. He concentrated on their voices, and on making sense of what he heard.

"So, naturally, we've been pressing for more resources," the architect said. "Of course, Berlin is loath to spend the money we need, as usual. But if you could talk with—"

"Forgive me, Herr Bader," Kein interrupted. "But the hour grows late, and my associate and I have other business to attend."

The project leader struck an apologetic note. "Of course, Herr Engel."

Briet asked, "How soon can you finish hiding the floor in the map room?"

"First thing in the morning," Bader said. "We'll melt down the beeswax you brought us, and pour that over the stone to protect it. Once it hardens, we'll lay wood and then cement on top of it. Thirty-six hours from now, your marble masterpiece will be safe from everything except a bomb or a naval artillery round. Of course, I'm curious: Why cover something so beautiful?"

Kein's tone conveyed both courtesy and menace. "Remember my advice, Herr Bader: Tend to your own affairs, and leave me to mine."

"Of course, Herr Engel. I did not mean to pry. My apologies."

Niko felt his own confusion deepen. Why were they planning to hide the floor? And why under beeswax and then cement? Something strange was afoot, and Adair had to be apprised of it—which meant Niko couldn't afford to risk being captured or killed before delivering this information, no matter how desperately he wanted to gun down Kein and Briet.

For once, be ruled by your head and not your heart.

Resolved to seek his vengeance some other day, he skulked away from the architect's tent—only to meet with a young SS man walking alone. The German fumbled to lift his rifle as he hollered, "Alarm! A—" Niko slashed the young Nazi's throat with his athamé before he could repeat his warning, but the damage was done.

Sirens wailed from loudspeakers mounted on bare poles. Around the work site, the SS platoon snapped into action. German troops raced to defensive positions around the architect's tent. Niko knew he would have only seconds before he was surrounded.

He grabbed the dead man's submachine gun. Doddering toward the vehicles, he peppered the converging German troops with burps of gunfire. Ricochets pinged off the trucks, and wild shots kicked up dirt around the Germans' feet as they scrambled for cover.

Niko fired his last few rounds at the tent, on the off chance that he might kill Kein or Briet by sheer luck. The weapon clacked empty; he threw it aside, climbed inside the black Mercedes-Benz convertible, and started its engine, which roared to life. With effort his left foot pushed in the clutch; he shifted the car into gear and stepped on the gas pedal.

The car leaped forward, a powerhouse unlike any he'd ever driven before. Before he had time to admire its acceleration and handling, bullets shattered its windows and cobwebbed its windshield, stinging his face with glass shards. White heat—a bullet tore through his right shoulder and spattered the car's dash with his blood. Another hit sent a jolt of agony through his left rib cage and left him gasping for air.

Need to get out of the dead zone—just a quarter of a mile . . .

The car barreled toward the checkpoint. Barely able to see or breathe, Niko stomped on the gas and gripped the steering wheel with his one good hand. The sentries leaped clear as the car broke through the gate, scattering wooden pickets and metal wires.

Niko swerved onto the main road, only to lose control of the car. It fish-tailed and hurtled over the shoulder into the woods. Branches lashed at the windshield—then a bone-shaking jolt of impact pinned him to the steering wheel, and everything went dark—

Niko jerked awake from a momentary blackout. Steam rose from the car's crumpled front end, which was wrapped around a thick tree. Blood seeped from Niko's side and pulsed from his mangled shoulder. Fighting for clarity, he pushed open his door and fell out of the car. Crawling over frozen ground, he heard German voices in pursuit.

No time left. I pray I'm far enough from the beach . . .

Drenched in his own blood, Niko propped himself against a tree and pulled his enchanted mirror from a coat pocket with a quaking hand. "*Fenestra, Adair.*" He was shaken by a hacking cough full of blood while he awaited the master's reply. Searchlights slashed through the trees as the Germans followed his swath of destruction through the woods.

Adair's face replaced Niko's reflection. "*Christ, lad, what—*"

"No time, Master." He propped the mirror on his leg, then used his good hand to pull the map and camera from inside his coat. He pushed them one at a time through the mirror to Adair. "Kein . . . built a trap. . . . In a bunker. At Pointe du Hoc."

"*Niko, I—*"

"They will cover it with wax and cement. It will be hidden. But destroy it you must." Tears fell from his eyes. He croaked out his last words. "*Bonne chance, Père.*"

Shadows converged upon Niko. Kein shouted, "Take him alive!"

Niko put the barrel of his pistol into his mouth.

I will not be used against my friends, as Stefan was.

SS troops surrounded him, submachine guns at the ready.

In the name of love, Niko pulled his trigger.

———

Briet followed Kein through the cluster of German troops gathered in the woods. When they reached the front, she frowned at the spectacle of blood and brains scattered in the dirt.

From the steel mirror in Niko's lap she heard the voice of Adair bellow, "Confringes longius speculo!" The mirror exploded into dust.

A pall settled over the woods. Kein told the soldiers, "Go away." No one questioned him. Seconds later, he and Briet were alone with Niko's body.

"We have to assume Adair knows," she said.

"Unlikely." Kein appeared unconcerned. "How much could Niko have told him in the seconds he had? We don't even know what Niko saw or didn't see."

Was he willfully obtuse? His nonchalance infuriated her. "This is no time for overconfidence. Niko was no amateur. We should assume he knew about the seal."

"And if he did? What of it?"

"Then Adair and the Allies know, as well."

A shake of his head. "It no longer matters."

"I disagree. Our chief advantage was the element of surprise. If we've lost that—"

"They will still have no defense against this."

Her temper boiled over. "You weren't the one tasked with overseeing its construction. You didn't spend months out here, attending every detail—"

"No, I was the one who spent half a year conjuring and imprisoning a thousand and one demons in slabs of marble I had to carve by hand. I was the one who had to craft the containment glyphs to negate the magickal suppression field at the moment of its breaking. And I was the one who had to placate an increasingly neurotic Führer. But please, tell me again how difficult *your* role in all of this has been."

Kein had been an excellent teacher in the Art, but he was also the most vexing soul Briet had ever met. She reined in her dudgeon, but refused to relent on matters of fact. "If the Allies have been warned, we need a response."

"There is no response. The seal is whole and in place. It cannot be moved without being broken, and we cannot break it without becoming its victims. Just as important, we must not do anything that might warn the Nazis how dangerous the seal is to them."

"So we do nothing?"

"The seal is secure." A sigh. "For the sake of argument, let us presume you are correct, and Adair knows everything. So what? He is hobbled, and the Atlantic coast is a death trap for karcists and rabble alike. Even if Adair has a plan to contain the seal, the only agents he can send are his last two adepts—the Russian girl and the American. Neither of whom can bring their magick to bear—they would stand alone against an army." He cocked an eyebrow. "Let the whelps try their luck. If they do, it will be the last that we—or Adair—ever sees of them."

His point made, Kein strode away from the smoking wreck and the dead magician. Briet watched him leave, at a loss for a retort—and wondered, for the first time without hyperbole or jest, whether her master had, in fact, gone mad.

⌘

Grief crushed the air from Adair's chest. He had watched as Niko turned his pistol on himself, thrust its barrel inside his mouth, and fired. Now Adair wanted to cry out in fury and pain, to howl until he shook dust from the rafters, to fill the world with curses that could never express the true depths of his rage. Strangled by sorrow, he dropped to his knees. Then he saw Kein and Briet through the mirror, and he knew what he had to do.

"*Confringes longius speculo!*" On the other side of the magickal link, Niko's seeing glass shattered. As the remote image vanished from Adair's mirror, the master expected to confront his reflection—but like the Fool gazing upon Lear, he saw only his shadow.

He pounded the floor with the sides of his fists. *How could I have doubted that lad? Loyal to the end. Braver than I knew.*

Tears streamed from Adair's shut-tight eyes. Niko's last words haunted him. *Bonne chance, Père.*

Adair's chest heaved with painful sobs for which he had no breath, so his body shook in near silence as he surrendered to his heartbreak. *He called me Father.*

Minutes melted into hours as Adair sat alone in the dark, enveloped in mourning. When at last he arrived on the far shore of his despair, he was left with a great emptiness, a hunger for meaning. He picked up the blood-spattered camera and the map Niko had rolled into a skinny tube. The camera's film he would have developed at Gibraltar. The map he unfurled.

It was a detailed study, complete with latitudinal and longitudinal coordinates down to the arc second, of a fortification atop the oceanfront cliffs at Pointe du Hoc, in Normandy. Niko had drawn corrections to its chart of the trenches that surrounded the observation bunker, and he'd made special notes concerning its interior, including a glyph that in the Art was a warning:

Demons here.

Intuition struck Adair: This was what PAIMON had warned him about. Whatever diabolical scheme Kein had set in motion, this was its trigger.

No time to waste, Adair told himself. He stood. Dried his eyes. Downed a shot of whisky. Lit a cigarette. Walked downstairs and radioed a coded message to his contacts in Gibraltar, to ask them to send a car for him at once. Then he sat down to wait.

Niko, lad . . . you honored me today. I swear to fucking God, I will honor you. He closed his hand around the camera. *And I vow: Kein will pay for this in blood.*

NOVEMBER

A simple but unexplained message from Adair—*Bid your spirits depart*—had been Cade's first warning their plans had changed. Weeks had passed since Niko's death in France. The master had spent more than half of each week since then at Gibraltar, while admonishing Cade to stay inside the villa and abstain from magick. Even the use of a Lull Engine—a divination tool that could be called upon without invoking any Presences—had been forbidden.

Divested of demonic riders, Cade had grown edgy. He was accustomed to a steady regimen of cigarettes and alcohol—balms for his nerves when he was contending with the mental and emotional toll of holding malevolent spirits in bondage. But just as Adair and the other adepts had warned him years earlier, even after the demons were gone, their appetites remained. His mind craved the solace to be found at the end of every bottle, the soothing rush of a chest filled with tobacco smoke, the bliss of veins coursing with opiates.

Worse, satisfying his desires did nothing to save him from the obsessions with which the demons had trained his hands. When his thoughts wandered, or his mind fell idle, his fingers plucked out beard whiskers, eyebrow hairs, even eyelashes if that was all they could find. Denied easy targets, his hands resorted to scratching at phantom tingling; he often failed to notice until long after he had broken skin and drawn blood. His wrists and ankles bore the scars of those mishaps. At other times, despite thinking himself at peace, he became fixated on trimming his fingernails and toenails, only to wind up ripping them down to the quick.

He lifted his cigarette in trembling, scarred fingers. Took a drag. Half the Lucky had burned down while his imagination had run wild. An inch-long column of ash fell away and smeared as it struck the floor between his feet. He almost laughed at himself.

The glamorous life of a karcist.

He sat alone at the kitchen table, nursing a glass of neat whisky and watching late-afternoon shadows creep across the Sierra Nevada range. The master had sequestered himself since the previous night in the villa's conjuring room, hidden behind closed doors and drawn curtains. He had refused to tell Cade what he was working on, but Cade had a feeling it was connected to whatever Niko had found in France before he died.

Just as Cade started to wonder if he should scrounge up something to eat, the door to the conjuring room was pulled open from inside by Adair. "Join me." The master retreated with hobbled steps into the shadows.

Anxious but curious, Cade followed Adair inside the conjuring room. A ring of kerosene lamps hung from ceiling hooks above the middle of the room. On the parquet floor, Adair had inscribed in fine white lines of chalk the most Byzantine conglomeration of glyphs Cade had ever seen. Nothing in his studies of ancient grimoires had been as intricate as this.

He was mystified. "I'm guessing this isn't a new needlepoint pattern."

"This . . . is what Niko died to show us." Though Adair wore a brave mask, Cade saw through it, to the still-raw grief the master concealed. As angry as Adair had been at Niko after the fiasco with the train, it was clear to Cade the master had forgiven his rash adept. Now he would need to make peace with the young man's grisly self-sacrifice.

Adair beckoned Cade with a tilt of his head. As Cade sidled over, Adair unrolled a map atop a worktable at the side of the room. "The pattern on the floor is a copy of the one Niko found in the map room of a German bunker on the Normandy coast." His finger stabbed a red dot. "Here. On top of Pointe du Hoc." He handed Cade an unsealed envelope.

From it, Cade took a slew of black-and-white photographs—detail shots of the complex magickal seal, one wedge at a time, plus a few including a compass and a meter stick for scale and directional orientation. "What is this thing?"

"The biggest devil's trap ever made." The master pointed out details as he continued. "There's a thousand of these scribbles—each one a seal representing a demon trapped inside these blocks of stone. This is what that git Kein was up to. Chaining up a legion of spirits so that the first fool who breaks the stone sets them all loose."

To Cade it looked to be both a masterpiece and the work of a madman. "All right, it's a trap. But why put it there? What if the Allies enter Europe through Italy? Or land at Calais?"

The master frowned. "Because Kein knows where the Allies will strike." His anger turned to dismay. "What I'm about to tell you is top-secret. The Allies are planning an attack." He tapped the map of the French coastline. "Here. In Normandy. Next summer."

"When?"

"I don't know. But Kein does. If he didn't, he wouldn't dare unleash a disaster of this magnitude. A thousand and one demons running amok? He'll be sure to put himself and his ginger witch inside a circle of protection to ride out *that* storm. Because anyone outside a circle is as good as dead. And that means Kein knows the place, the day, and the hour of the attack."

Cade studied the map, which showed only pockets of German tanks and infantry on the Normandy coastline. "But if Kein knows the Allies' plans, why aren't the Germans moving more forces into position? Why are they still building their bunkers with that shitty weak concrete?"

A shrug. "Because Kein doesn't want the Nazis to know."

The more Cade learned, the less he understood. "If he isn't telling the Germans what's coming . . . and he's making them build weak bunkers . . . it's because he wants the Allies to bomb or shell that bunker and break the seal." He looked up at Adair. "And he wants both sides to get hit by the demons." When his master didn't correct him, he asked, "Is this part of that war on Science he was babbling about in Wewelsburg?"

"We'll have to ask him—right before we cut off his head." Adair's sadness darkened, tinged by simmering rage. "But first we need to unmake this seal and banish its spirits, before some damn fool sets them loose."

"Unmake it? We can do that?"

Uncertainty colored Adair's reaction. "Maybe. It would be like the seals you changed in that demonic cathouse in Caen, just a lot more complicated. I've been studying this for weeks. It's a work of evil fucking genius—but I think it might be possible to negate it."

"Like cutting the fuse off a bomb."

"If only it were that simple." Adair limped on his prosthesis and Cade walked beside him, out on top of the great seal, which was twelve feet in diameter. "If you add exactly the right lines, glyphs, and letters—in the right languages— at exactly the right places and in the correct order, you can turn the seal from a prison to a banishing ward. You can use it to command every spirit trapped inside back to Hell." A grim sigh. "But there's a catch."

"Of course there is."

"For a few seconds after you make the last change, a guardian spirit Kein placed on the seal will be loose—and you won't have any defense."

"I've fought demons before."

"Not without magick of your own, you haven't." He pointed out more minutiae in the seal. "These symbols, inside the third and sixth wedges, are designed to negate Briet's anti-magick wards when the seal breaks. That's so the demons aren't forced out of the combat zone. But you'd be neutralizing the seal intact, which means no magick within half a mile of shore."

Cade almost wished he hadn't asked. "Anything else?"

"Aye. There's another wrinkle."

"I figured there would be."

Spreading his arms in an expansive gesture meant to encompass the entire seal, Adair said, "When you reach the room with the seal . . . you won't be able to see it."

"Excuse me—what?"

"Something Niko said when he gave me the map and the camera. Kein's hidden the seal under wax from a new hive, and a layer of cement. To keep the Germans from setting it off too soon, I suppose. At any rate, your challenge is to find the room's center, use a compass to gauge magnetic north, then add your symbols on the cement above the seal without being able to see it. You'll have no margin for error—and every change has to be placed perfectly."

"On top of something I won't be able to see."

"Aye."

"That's impossible."

"Damn near. But the hardest part might be getting you inside the bunker." The master noted Cade's bewildered stare. "The Allies won't alert the Nazis to their planned invasion of Normandy by sending an advance team to Pointe du Hoc."

Cade mustered his bravado. "Then I'll go alone."

"Without magick? Against a division of Wehrmacht and a panzer group? You'd be dead before you got within a quarter mile of the bunker door."

"What other choice do I have?"

A growl rattled deep in the master's throat. "General Eisenhower wants you to land with the troops, as part of the assault. They'll get you to the bunker. After that, the rest is up to you." He shook his head. "It's a shite plan. Totally fucked. I said as much, but do they listen?" He began to pace, visibly desperate for a way to vent his agitation. "It's just what Kein wanted. We're playing right into his hands!"

"How? What do you mean?"

"You! Charging into the jaws of death!" Adair shook with indignation. "You're the only one I can send—" He lifted his pants leg to show the crude wooden prosthetic that had taken the place of his lower right leg. "—thanks to *this*. A fucking gimp, Ike called me. Unfit for war, he said. So I have to send you—my last apprentice, my fucking ace in the hole, my one hope of stopping Kein—and I have to risk your life on a fucking suicide mission!"

Cade regarded the seal with apprehension. "I get why you're upset. But this has to be done, and I'm the only one to do it." That garnered a wide-eyed stare of shock from the old man. Cade pushed past his fear and found his courage. "More to the point, I *want* to do it."

"But going into a war zone, onto the front line—?"

"When my best friend asked me to join the army with him, I told him, *This isn't my war.* Because that's what my dad always told me. But the truth is, I knew I should've signed up with Miles. I was too scared to say it, but I should've listened to him that day. Or hell, even to you. If I had, maybe my parents would still be alive. But now I know for a fact what I always felt to be true: This *is* my war. And it always has been."

Adair looked sad but resigned. "Then you've just one more choice to make: Would you rather hit the beach in a boat? Or jump out of a perfectly good aircraft?"

Painful memories—of the cold bite of seawater, his parents' anguished cries, the stink of LEVIATHAN—pushed Cade toward a decision. "I think I'll go with a plane."

"Are you sure? Remember—no magick anywhere near that drop zone. And all it takes is a few bullets to turn you and your parachute into confetti."

Cade remembered falling through the dark with the flight crew of the *Silver Sadie*. He wondered how that night might have ended if he had been without magick when all else failed.

After careful consideration, he nodded at Adair.

"Right. . . . Boat it is."

DECEMBER

Freighted with more yoked demons than he could reasonably bear, Adair endured a headache so brutal he feared it would outlive him.

His and Cade's mirror-jaunt to England had gone without incident. The army had tracked down Adair's old friend Denton Crichlow, an occultist who lived outside Bristol, and compelled him to exhume one of Adair's first enchanted mirrors from storage and see it delivered to an SOE safe house in the south of England, near Weymouth. The coded message confirming the mirror's delivery had arrived just before midnight, and Adair had wasted no time hustling himself and Cade through the portal, to a land they both had come to think of as home.

A cold fog haunted England's southern shores. Though it was only half full, Cade's ruck slowed the young man enough that Adair was able to keep pace beside him, despite the gait imposed by his prosthetic leg. Adair had donned a long trench coat and a scarf in anticipation of facing a typical English winter; Cade wore his bomber jacket.

The young karcist shifted his ruck from his right shoulder to the left. "What's the point of coming back in the middle of the night, *after* all the pubs are closed?"

"It's how the army does things," Adair said. "'Hurry up and wait.'"

"What does that mean?"

"You'll see."

No light escaped from the buildings on either side of the road, thanks to the blackout curfew in effect throughout Britain, as a defense against German bombing raids. Muffled laughter spilled from the houses, however, hinting at the camaraderie of the troops inside them.

Cade looked anxious. "Wish I could've brought my tools. I feel lost without them."

"You won't need them." Adair handed him a fat grease pencil. "Just this." He almost laughed as Cade scowled at it. "Don't fret. I'll keep your tools safe."

He tucked the grease pencil into his pocket. "The thought of weeks without magick—"

"Months, more like."

Horror and dismay: "*Months?*"

They stopped and faced each other. "Lad, you're about to start the hardest days of your life. Come tomorrow, you'll be grateful not to have a demon in your head when the army kicks you in the bollocks. You hear what I'm saying?"

A resigned nod. "I hear you."

"Good. Because now I want you to hear this." He shed his anger. "I'm sorry. For all of this." He read Cade's confusion in the wrinkling of his brow. "For dragging you into my war."

"It's not your fault. I'd have joined anyway."

Adair shook his head. "Not *this* war—the one against Kein. I saw it coming decades ago." He mustered courage to speak the rest of his truth. "It wasn't just your father who made you a *nikraim*. He never could have done it alone. I pushed him to it. Helped him with the magick." He hung his head in shame. "I cursed you with this destiny the day I bonded an angel to your soul. I had no right to ask it of your parents, no right to force it on you. But I knew the world would need a karcist strong enough to stop Kein." He favored his last apprentice with a kindly smile. "And I knew Blake and Valerie Martin would raise a smart, decent child. One who could be trusted with power."

Cade seemed thunderstruck by Adair's revelations. "You went to all this trouble to bond me with an angel. Are you saying I'm some kind of chosen one?"

"No, there were six others. . . . Kein killed them all." He turned an apologetic look at Cade. "You were not our only hope—but you are the only one we have left." He clamped his callused hand on the back of the young man's neck. "That's why I'm sorry, lad. I put all this on your shoulders. The world doesn't know it, but it's counting on us. . . . It's counting on *you.*"

Cade exorcised the fear from his eyes. "I won't fail them, Master. Or you."

Adair gathered his apprentice in a hug, the kind he wished he'd given to Stefan and Niko before sending them to their deaths. His eyes misted and his voice trembled. "I know you won't, lad. I know you won't."

They parted as Cade said in a low voice, "Someone's coming."

"Our welcoming committee, no doubt." Adair composed himself, then shuffled forward. "Dry your eyes, lad. Time to meet your new master."

Farther down the road they were intercepted by a man in a U.S. Army officer's uniform. He greeted Cade and Adair with polite nods and firm handshakes. "Gentlemen. I'm Major Paul Abell, battalion command." To the master he added, "You must be Mr. Macrae, SOE." Then he eyed Cade's bomber jacket. "And you are—?"

"Uh . . . Cade Martin, karcist."

"Not anymore. As of now, you're Private Cade Martin—U.S. Army."

1944

JANUARY

"Again." The master clicked the fob on his stopwatch. Seconds were burning.

Cade could barely keep his eyes open. "I can't."

Adair snapped his fingers. "If you're this slow in Normandy, we all die."

"Fuck. Off." The grease pencil fell from Cade's weary, cramped hand. The dull glow of kerosene lamps filled the sixteen-foot-square training shed. "Don't you understand I've been up since five in the fucking morning? Some sergeant came into the barracks banging a trash can with its own lid. Made me put on a forty-pound pack and run *ten fucking miles* before breakfast. Have you ever run ten miles in your entire fucking life?"

"Not without something chasing me." He tapped the stopwatch. "Time's wasting."

Cade splayed himself, spread-eagled, across the floor inside the simulated bunker, atop the replicated demonic seal. "You don't get it. They put me with the Fifth Rangers. They're insane. They've been training forever. And they want me to catch up. You know how long they spent in basic? Four months. Guess how long they're giving me. Two fucking weeks."

"You learn fast. Already you cuss like they do."

Hysteria overtook him. "Christ, give me a break, will you? After breakfast I do more push-ups than I can count, then I run again, usually 'til I puke. I spend lunch reading manuals, and regulations, and learning how to take apart weapons I can't reassemble yet. Then everybody yells at me, and I do more push-ups, and they make me run some more. After dinner I get an hour to polish my shoes and press the wrinkles out of my clothes. Then you drag me out here to this shotgun shack to practice drawing a thousand squiggles from memory on a blank floor." An imploring look at Adair. "Fuck me—what time is it?"

The master checked his watch. "Half one."

"Goddammit! I have to get up in less than four hours, and do all this shit *again*. Let me go. I need to fucking sleep!"

"You need to learn how to unmake this trap, or billions of people die."

"And I *will*—but not all in *one night*! Fuck!"

There was no hiding Adair's disappointment. "We've been working on this for weeks, and you've barely mastered one of eight wedges. We don't have much more time."

"I thought you said the assault wasn't until summer."

"It's not, as far as I know. But your unit's heading north soon, for special training. And in case you haven't noticed, this thing isn't exactly fucking portable."

That was no exaggeration. To train Cade in modifying the glyphs, Adair and a team of military engineers had crafted a full-scale replica of it, then put it under a sheet of high-tech safety glass, on which Cade drew his practice markings with a grease pencil.

For the first two weeks, Adair had let Cade rehearse with an unobstructed view of the seal beneath the glass. Now he had inserted a retractable mask of black cardboard between the glass and the duplicated seal, to let Cade experience the disorientation of trying to revise sigils he could no longer see.

Cade sat up and rubbed his eyes. His face felt numb from exhaustion. "I've got the first wedge figured out."

"Not quite. Remember, one mistake—"

"And we all die. I know." A plaintive look up at his master. "The first few weeks were the hardest, learning the whole seal. I'll have wedge one perfect by tomorrow night. If I keep at it, I can have the whole thing worked out by April."

"You might not have that long."

"Then work your magick to get me more time." He raised a hand to cut off Adair's protest. "I can rehearse without the shed. Just copy the template and give me some onion paper, or something else semitransparent, and I'll keep practicing after my unit goes north."

Adair nodded. "Aye. That could work."

"Great. So can I go back to my bunk now?"

"Aye." Adair reset the stopwatch and poised his thumb over the fob. "Just as soon as you prove to me you've got wedge one down cold." *Click.* "Go."

Cade picked up the grease pencil, then glared at Adair. "I hope you know the Devil has a cock waiting with your name on it."

"Chop-chop."

———

After learning to yoke demons, Cade had thought nothing on earth could break him. The U.S. Army was determined to prove him wrong.

The rope was three inches thick and hurt like a fistful of razors, but Cade didn't dare let go. It chewed into his hands, which were bloody from climbing it and the wooden obstacles the Rangers had set up in the woods outside Leominster.

His legs snaked around the rope. He clenched it between his booted feet and pushed upward toward a tape mark still far out of reach.

His training buddy, Private First Class Carl Pinchefsky, a wiry young Jewish man from New York City, had already reached the tape marker on his rope and was working his way back down. Below them, their section leader, Staff Sergeant Tom Dale, an athletic Texan, barked orders. "What's your problem, Martin? Got lead in your ass? Faster!"

Cade wanted to let go, fall to earth, and maybe break his own neck if he was lucky. Instead, he reached higher, clutched the rough strands, and pulled.

He was one hand shy of the tape when Pinchefsky reached the ground. Dale snapped at the rifleman, "What's his beef, Pinch? A possum could run circles around this guy."

"Beats me, Sarge."

"Does it? Way I hear it, Dunce Cap doesn't spend much time in his sack at night." He raised his voice at Cade, who at last reached the tape marker. "That it, Dunce Cap? Got a bimbo wearin' you down? Maybe you ought to get more sleep!"

"Sounds good to me, Sergeant!" Wincing at the pain biting into his hands, Cade descended the rope. He'd learned on day one not to slide down—and spent the rest of that day picking sisal fibers out of his palms.

The moment Cade's feet touched dirt, Dale was shouting again. "Double time! Pick up your feet!" Dale kept pace beside Cade and Pinch, who as training buddies were ordered to remain within arm's reach of each other at all times, whether they were running, crawling, or climbing. As they jogged to the next section of the confidence course, Cade was dismayed to notice he was the only one of the three who had broken a sweat.

After a couple of minutes, they arrived at the next obstacle, which consisted of parallel shallow trenches filled with cold water, then capped with perpendicular strings of barbed wire every couple of feet. There was barely enough room under the wire for a man to crawl and not be completely submerged in the mud.

"In you go!" Dale blew a whistle, his signal for Pinch and Cade to start their crawl. As soon as they dropped to their knees, Dale bellowed, "On your backs! Feet first! Hands on your chests! Keep your heads up, and pull yourselves forward with your heels! Move!"

Cade did as ordered, but he shot a stunned look at Pinch. "Is he serious?"

"Yup. And this is gonna hurt."

They sat in the six-inch-deep mud, reclined, and set their hands on their midriffs. For Cade, just keeping his head raised was torture; he felt himself straining core muscles he hadn't known he possessed. When he started the labor of pulling himself forward through the mud using only his heels, his head swam. *I'm gonna pass out for sure.*

Pistol shots cracked in the biting morning air. Bullets peppered the trenches on either side of Pinch and Cade, kicking up mud that spattered the two soldiers until the sergeant's .45 semiautomatic clicked empty.

Clarity restored by terror, Cade scrambled faster. His heart slammed inside his chest; his breathing sped and shallowed. In his haste to reach the end of the trench, he lifted his head a half inch too high and felt the sting of a steel barb slicing his crew-cut scalp.

Another shot, a fresh geyser of mud in his face. "Keep your goddamn head down, Dunce Cap! And pick up the pace!"

The motivational salvos continued until Cade and Pinch scrambled over the trench's far side, got on their feet, and sprinted to the next section of the course. Cade heard the sergeant's running steps behind them, catching up.

Every nerve in Cade's body wanted to collapse, to let fatigue claim him. He forced himself to keep moving. Then his limbs betrayed him. His legs felt like rubber, his feet like lead. He began to stumble.

Pinch grabbed Cade's shirt and propelled him onward. "Don't you die on me, pal! Sarge says if you die, I'm on KP 'til the war ends."

Cade gasped in reply, "Wouldn't that be a shame?"

The skinny Ranger let go of Cade's shirt. "Buck up, bud. All we gotta do is make it over the wall, and then we hit the mess for chow!"

"*That's* my reward? Fuck. The army needs better incentives."

Pinchefsky belted out a laugh, then stifled it before the sergeant heard. "Shit. You're all right, Dunce Cap." He weaved in closer to add in a confidential register, "You're doin' better than you think. Find me after chow, I'll show you the trick to putting your M1 together. But no kidding, bud—you gotta score more sack time, or you're not gonna make it."

All Cade could do was nod and keep running. He couldn't explain to his section mates what he was doing every night. Defusing a magickal bomb? One that would explode with demons instead of fire and shrapnel? He abandoned any notion of coming clean.

One whiff of that, and they'll Section Eight my ass in a heartbeat.

He and Pinch drifted apart to arm's length as Sergeant Dale caught up to them. "Don't let me interrupt your grab-ass, ladies! You two enjoying this morning's run?"

In unison, Cade and Pinch answered at the tops of their lungs, "Yes, Sergeant!"

"Prove it! Hit that wall! Up and over! Like you mean it!"

They sprinted and charged the twelve-foot-tall wooden barricade, from whose top dangled several ropes. Cade matched Pinch's stride and kept the Ranger in the corner of his eye as they leaped up the wall and each took hold of a rope.

White heat raged through Cade's shredded palms. He blocked it out, just as he would bury the torments of a yoked demon, and reached higher, one hand over the other, as his mud-slicked boots scrambled against the wooden planks. His vision reddened with pain, he grasped the wall's apex. Then he vaulted over and enjoyed half a second of falling.

He landed on his feet beside Pinch, who slapped his back. "Well, fuck a duck! You made it, Dunce Cap!"

Stunned and silent, Cade looked at the wall. More than two dozen times before he had charged that wall and failed. This was the first time he had made it over.

Sergeant Dale stepped around the barrier, looking as stern as ever. "I'll be damned, Dunce Cap. There might be hope for you yet. Hit the showers, then fall in for chow. Move!"

"Yes, Sergeant!" Cade ran for the barracks, desperate to enjoy a shower and a meal before Dale changed his mind.

The Rangers had overwhelmed him, mentally as well as physically, since the start of his training. After two weeks, he still spent most days feeling as if he were drowning. When the sergeants weren't running him ragged or making him memorize military regulations, he was quizzed on the army's jargon and its alphabet soup of acronyms. The more he learned, the more he discovered how much further he had to go to catch up to these men. There were dozens of weapons on which he had to qualify, and he was expected to learn to scale cliffs, perform combat first aid, and do so much more—all while keeping his boots polished and his bunk tautly made.

Compared to this, wrangling demons was nothing.

He and Pinchefsky cleared the woods. Down a short slope, the barracks were in sight. Warm water and hot if barely edible food were in sight.

Pinch grinned. "Sorry you volunteered?"

A derisive snort. "*Volunteered?*" He thought of Adair. "Fuck, man. I was *drafted.*"

FEBRUARY

There was no hero's welcome for Anja Kernova.

One heavy step after another, she defied the Russian winter. Half-healed wounds plagued her from within as she trudged through knee-deep snow that numbed her feet. After weeks of icy weather and empty roads, she had returned for the first time in over a decade to the place of her birth: the isolated village of Toporok.

Tucked against the south bank of the River Msta, the village had never been much to see. More than five hundred kilometers inland from the eastern front, Toporok was a lumber town that tolerated just enough farming to feed its handful of permanent residents.

Anja glimpsed its ramshackle houses and its patches of clear-cut woods, and she felt comforted to see little had changed in the decade she had been away. The sharp tang of smoke from dozens of chimneys perfumed the wintry, twilight air.

Ghosts born of her memories fleeted through dusk's lengthening shadows. She had been thirteen years old the last time she had seen this place.

Will anyone recognize me now?

Many times in recent years, she had felt confounded by her own reflection. The rigors of learning the Art had taken their toll on her youth, and whatever shreds of her innocence magick hadn't stolen had now been ripped away by the Great Patriotic War.

Unfamiliar faces squinted at her through grimy windows. Her former neighbors looked at her as if she were a stranger.

I've been away so long. Maybe I am.

She adjusted her ruck and tugged the strap of her tool roll, which bit into her shoulder. After she had passed a dozen houses, she noticed that nearly every face she saw was female. She had spied only two exceptions: one a young boy, no more than three or four years of age; the other an old man, his hair white, his face a deep-creased map of life's heartbreaks.

In all of the places Anja expected to see boys committing a day's final mischief before dinner, her searching gaze found only empty silences. Toporok, as small as it was, had given the Red Army its every man and boy who could hold a rifle or die to stop a German bullet.

Mournful winds whipped up snow devils between dilapidated houses. Anja pushed herself toward a destination that filled her with hope and fear.

She stopped a few paces shy of the closed door. The house looked as she had remembered it. Its paint had faded, but it was still the blue-gray of a late-winter sky. Behind its shuttered windows dwelled a glow of firelight. But there was no music now, no tunes plucked by young fingers from her family's old balalaika.

Intimidated by the house's silence, Anja stood frozen in front of its door. Once she would have pushed it open and charged inside without a thought. Now, dancing shadows hinted at a blaze inside the hearth where once she had soothed her cold hands, but her guilty conscience warned her she would find no comfort within these walls.

But I don't know where else to go.

Dread paralyzed her. If she left without knocking, no one would ever know she had been here. She would be free to vanish into obscurity and anonymity. There would be no questions to answer, no lies to tell. All she had to do was turn away and keep walking. The night would swallow her as it always had. As it always would.

An insatiable emptiness inside her made her step forward, lift her hand, and rap her knuckles against the weathered wood and blistered paint. Then she waited.

From the other side came the slow, muffled scrape of a body in motion. Tired steps on a wooden floor. The knob creaked as it turned, and the hinges shrilled in protest as the door was cracked open. Anxious eyes peered out at Anja. Impatience added an edge to her mother's rasp.

"What do you want?"

"Mama? It's me. . . . Anja."

Galina Kernova opened the door wide enough for Anja to see her face. It felt to Anja as if she were peering at a mirror from the future. She and her mother shared the same pale cast, raven hair, gray eyes, and elegantly arched eyebrows. They might have been twins but for their difference in age and the irregular, Y-shaped scar that dominated the left side of Anja's face.

Her mother scowled. "What do you want?"

"Can I come in?"

"No." She started to shut the door.

Anja struggled to keep it open. "Please."

"You let Piotr die." Galina pushed her away and spat at her. "You're dead to me."

She slammed the door. Heavy clacks of turning locks resounded through the thick wood. In all the years since her mother had cast her out to fend for herself, Anja had never felt so alone.

There was little point in seeking shelter from anyone else in the village. No doubt her mother's bile had long since poisoned them all against her. *Why did I come here? Why did I think she would forgive me? That any of them would?*

Mired in loneliness, she could think of only one place to go, and of only one soul in Toporok who would receive her without judgment.

Bereft of hope or purpose, Anja left home for the second and last time.

⁓⁓⁓

Piotr's headstone stood entombed in ice. Anja knelt in the snow and chipped with the pommel of her knife at the marker's frozen shell until her younger brother's name was visible. She sheathed the blade and pulled off one of her gloves. Her fingers traced the roughhewn letters of his name. *You didn't deserve this, little brother.*

She couldn't silence her memory's litany of regrets.

If only we hadn't blundered into the middle of a wizards' duel.

If only Adair, dying at Kein's hand, hadn't pleaded with his eyes.

If only you hadn't tried to interfere.

She remembered watching Kein's magick cut Piotr in half—just as she recalled taking up the rifle her brother had dropped, and putting three rounds through Kein's back. It should have been enough to kill the bastard, but thanks to magick he'd escaped with his life.

Thus it had fallen to Anja, with Adair's somber aid, to take home the two halves of her brother's corpse. It was a failure for which her mother had never forgiven her, and never would.

She felt ashamed, not for the unwitting role she had played in Piotr's death, but for indulging in the sentimental folly of thinking he could hear her lament. *He is dead and gone. It is too late to ask his forgiveness. All the regret in the world cannot change that.*

Her memory of that night remained vivid and terrible. It hadn't mattered to Galina that Anja hadn't done the deed, or that Adair had vouched for the truth of her account, or that she herself had been wounded. All that Anja's mother had cared about, then or now, was that her only son was dead, and Anja was the one she had chosen to blame.

Anja rested her head against the stone and let the night settle over her. After all she had done and suffered, she had hoped for a warmer homecoming than this. She had nearly died of her wounds in Kharkov. As soon as she had been strong enough to walk again, some inchoate need inside her had turned her path homeward.

Where else can I go?

The war had engulfed the globe, leaving few civilized places untouched. In the neutral countries, a Russian woman alone would attract suspicion as a possible spy; she'd find no peace there. She could only hope the Red Army considered her missing in action rather than AWOL. And even if she knew where to find Adair, she couldn't go back to him now, not after the cruel way she had abandoned him and Cade.

She wanted to believe she could make things right with Adair, but her heart was too raw to face him. *How can I atone for leaving when he needed me most?* She decided the notion of redemption was folly. *Is there anything left in the world worth fighting for?*

Anja had seen too much, suffered too much, to believe in illusions like love and hope—yet she couldn't bring herself to exorcise their fading light from her soul.

The road ahead was long and dark. Anja set her eyes on the future and kept walking. The night received her with open arms, as it always had.

As it always would.

MARCH

Everything the Rangers demanded of Cade was hard as hell. That was the point. Every single thing they asked of every man under their banner was damned near impossible. They wanted to know now, while they were still in Britain, which men would break under pressure, who would fold when the pain cut too deeply, who would run when the bullets flew. Better to break the weak links here than lose the entire chain on the battlefield in Europe.

Eleven weeks. That was how long they had held Cade in their grip. For close to three months they had carved every ounce of fat off his body, chiseled away every bit of him that didn't fit their vision of a soldier. Eleven weeks, and he was still here.

He had made what felt like amazing progress. He could keep up with the Rangers on their daily runs and their turns through the confidence course, and he was no longer always the last to finish reassembling his rifle. He had even qualified on all of the unit's weapons except the mortar, bazooka, and flamethrower.

The rest of the unit still called him "Dunce Cap," of course. That nickname had stuck since his first day, when his section leader had found out Cade needed a full remedial training regimen. It often felt to Cade as if the only smart decision he had made since his arrival was not protesting his unit moniker. The only thing the Rangers hated more than a green recruit was a complainer— and that was a sin he refused to commit.

At least, not within earshot of Sergeant Dale.

He and the rest of Dog Company's First Platoon were jolted awake by the lurching halt of the locomotive that had carried them north into the Scottish Highlands. No one had seen fit to tell them where they were going or why. All that had mattered was that they had their rucks packed, their socks and ammo dry, and their asses in formation at 0430 to board their transport.

Late-afternoon sunlight slanted through the windows, making it hard for Cade to see where they were. Before his eyes adjusted, the sergeants of First Platoon marched down the aisle thundering overlapping orders: "On your feet!" "Grab your gear!" "Muster in formation!" "Get your asses off this train!"

Chaos ensued, a scramble to comply and escape the wrath of the sergeants. Cade and the Rangers leapt from their seats and fell over one another on their way to the exits. Each man hit the ground with both feet after a leap from the train's elevated ladder-steps, then scurried to his place in the ranks. In less than two minutes, the entire Fifth Ranger Battalion—more than 450 men—was off the train and assembled by company, platoon, and section.

Platoon sergeants and officers stood in the front ranks, and the company commanders and first sergeants stood with their respective HQ formations. Inspecting them while passing in a slow march were several British army officers. On the return leg of the review, the British officer in charge paused to trade words with each of the company commanders, and then with the battalion commander, while the assembled troops stood at attention and kept their mouths shut.

At last, clear orders came down the line: "Right face! Double-time, move out!"

Each company turned as if with one mind, like a flock of birds changing direction, then advanced down a tree-lined dirt road, past a sign that identified their location as the Spean Bridge railway station. In a steady rhythm, the battalion marched behind the British officer, who led them down a series of tree-lined roads that cut through an otherwise desolate parcel of the Scottish Highlands. In the distance rose rugged snowcapped mountains draped in tattered shawls of mist. Cade pulled a pack of Luckies from inside his coat, tucked a smoke into his mouth, and fired it up with his lighter.

He offered the pack to the men on either side of him. "Wrench? Professor?"

Privates Calvin "Professor" Dalto, the section's know-it-all, and Walter "Wrench" Mikalunas, its top fix-it guy, both waved off Cade's offer, but the corpsman, Private Alvin "Butterfingers" Kimball, reached over Cade's shoulder. "Spot me one?" Cade handed him a cigarette, then passed him the lighter. After Kimball lit up and returned the Zippo, he took a drag, then smiled as he exhaled. "Thanks, Dunce Cap."

"Any time."

Cade finished his Lucky long before the battalion finished its eight-mile hike, which halted on a dirt road. He drank in the landscape of rolling hills beside a loch of dark water, all lorded over by a modern-looking fortified residence.

Learn magick at one castle; learn war at another. Full circle.

A British officer sporting a pencil mustache and a beret of hunter green met the Rangers with a tirade almost theatrical in its gruffness.

"Gentlemen! Welcome to Achnacarry. I am Lieutenant Colonel Charles Vaughn. Over the next month, you men will be subjected to the most arduous training in the history of warfare. Any man who fails to keep pace will be returned to his unit."

Cade wondered what that would mean for him, a man with no previous unit who, as far as the United States was concerned, was already dead.

Vaughn prattled on. "During your time here, you will live like soldiers: outdoors, in tents. We will teach you to storm beaches. Scale cliffs. Climb mountains. Defuse mines. Control occupied towns. You will learn to kill with bayonets, knives, stones, your bare hands."

The Brit walked at a leisurely pace in front of the battalion. His keen eyes searched the ranks, as if to ferret out any sign of weakness. "Your training will include exposure to live rounds and full-strength ordnance. You will learn to distinguish the sound of Allied weapons from those of the enemy. You will train by day, and by night. We will afflict you with every hardship and danger at our disposal. Not all of you will pass this training; some of you might not survive it. Those of you who do . . . will one day thank us for the hell you are soon to endure."

There was no mirth in Vaughn's demeanor, only the pragmatism of a man tasked to build living weapons out of the crooked timber of humanity. As the battalion's companies each were directed to their campsites, Cade had no doubt that Vaughn was serious about putting the Rangers through hell. The only part of the British commando officer's speech Cade found hard to believe was his claim that the Rangers would thank him.

He must know I've gone by now. Soon he'll come looking for me.

Trust never came freely to Briet. With her it was hard to earn and easily broken. She had convinced herself Kein had a plan. But the longer she had borne witness to Kein's singular preoccupation with seeing the world burn, the more she realized she had let herself become swept up in his cult of personality, in a quest as grandiose as it was misbegotten.

A full moon inched above the horizon, its silver light casting a path across the Baltic Sea. Briet lurked in the forest that bordered the rocky beach. She had traveled lightly, with only the clothes on her back; a coat with her rat familiar Trixim tucked in one of its pockets; a ruck that held her grimoire, cash, and a few personal effects; and her tools of the Art. Now she awaited the boat whose owner she had hired, through an intermediary, for passage out of Germany.

If he cheated me, I'll be in great danger.

Thanks to her NSDAP credentials, Briet had been able to travel throughout Germany at will. No one had questioned her when she had withdrawn tens of thousands of reichsmarks, or when she had converted them, at a loss, into gold coins. But the last thing she had wanted was to be recognized during the last leg of her journey—or to be tracked down by Kein, either in person or by one of his demonic agents sent abroad to corral her into compliance.

She had taken pains to foil her pursuers by effecting her disappearance in Hamburg, far from her planned point of exodus. There, a goodly sum of her gold had been spent on two sets of new identity papers—one identifying her as a German, the other as a citizen of neutral Sweden. Letters she had sent to her lovers Victor and Sandrine had implied she was bound for India.

Her least costly preparation, but the dearest blow to her pride, had been her hair. Briet had worn her coppery tresses long most of her life. But they made her stand out in crowds, and that was something she could no longer afford.

Briet still winced when she recalled the chirps of the shears slicing through her locks, or the sight of them falling to the floor of her hotel room in Hamburg. After she had given herself a sloppy crew cut, she had collected her cut hair into a braid, bound it with threads of white silk, sprinkled it with holy water and magpie's blood, then doused it with brandy and camphor before setting it aflame in her brazier while dedicating the sacrifice to her patron, ASTAROTH.

Even more than the ward permanently scribed between her shoulder blades, her burnt offering would shield her from Kein's scrying gaze for the next several months. After that, she would, if all went according to plan, be sequestered somewhere far from the war, far from the affairs of the rabble, far from every other living soul on earth.

She shivered in the ocean breeze, then adjusted her black wig. *At least this thing is warm.* Submerged into her new persona, she had traveled incognito from Hamburg to Stralsund, and from there to Sassnitz on the Jasmund Peninsula. She had booked a room for a month in Sassnitz, an unassuming seaside village, knowing full well she would be leaving it all behind in a matter of hours. Just before sundown, she had walked four kilometers up the beach, to its easternmost point. Then she selected a spot in which to wait, one partially sheltered from the wind, with a view of the waves shredding themselves across the boulders just offshore.

Every precaution she could have taken, she had. She had created false trails and used magick to plant false memories in people traveling west from Hamburg. There were more than enough decoys to lead any hunter astray. Yet paranoia nagged at her.

He'll know. He'll find you.

The last thing she had abandoned to effect her escape had been her yoked spirits. Without their strengths, she felt vulnerable and alone. But with them, she would be a beacon to Kein's allies from Below. Worse, because of the Atlantic Wall defenses she herself had helped create to guard the Reich's borders, she couldn't approach the coastline while holding spirits in thrall.

I built my own prison. But then, doesn't everyone?

From the sparkling darkness of the sea appeared a silhouette. A small boat piloted by a lone figure cut through the waves, its outboard motor a low purr beneath the wind. The pilot carried no lantern, no light of his own. Only the lunar glow set him apart from the night.

Briet remained under cover until the boat was almost ashore. She emerged from the trees and walked to the beach as she heard the craft's keel scrape against the stony sand. The pilot climbed out and dragged the boat aground from the shallows. He was dressed for a cold night at sea: a long hooded jacket, heavy boots, rugged trousers. His hood was cinched so tightly she didn't see his face—only fleeting glimmers of reflected moonlight in his eyes.

Under her coat, she gripped the handle of her athamé, ever alert to the risk of betrayal. "You're here to take me across?"

The pilot nodded and held out an open, gloved hand. Briet counted out five gold coins and pressed them into the stranger's palm. He pocketed the fee, then beckoned her to follow him aboard. He steadied the boat with both hands on its port gunwale as she stepped over it and found a seat on the middle bench. After she settled, he pushed the boat into open water, then climbed aboard. He settled into the rear of the boat, fired up the motor, and steered them into the night. They picked up speed and cut through the waves. Seawater crested the bow and doused Briet in icy sprays. She winced in the face of her salt-water baptism.

By the time she looked back, Germany had sunk beyond the horizon. The pilot showed no interest in talking, so Briet kept silent. Around her yawned the mystery of the sea at night, one darkness upon another. She hoped that in Sweden she could slip into obscurity, fade away, and be forgotten—as if the Baltic Sea were her Lethe, one in which she could drown all memory of her former life, and from it be born again unknown.

It was a beautiful dream, but a foolish one. If Kein won his war, he would not forget Briet's desertion, nor would he forgive it. If his foes proved the victors, she had no doubt they, too, would someday seek her out on a mission of vengeance.

I can hide until the war ends. After that, I will need sanctuary. But who has the power to shield me from Kein? Or from Adair? The Covenant says the Synod has the right to keep them at bay, but why would the Vatican help an unrepentant karcist like me?

She found no answers in the darkness, or in the pitching and rolling of the sea. Only the emptiness of a future unwritten, and the promise of escape.

For now, that was enough. The rest would have to wait.

<hr>

Cade set aside his manual and sat up. He was awake, but he felt as if his brain would pop like a balloon if he tried to stuff one more fact into it before he slept. *Gotta clear my head or I'll never sleep tonight.* He dug his Zippo and a pack of Luckies from his ruck, pulled on his boots and jacket, and crawled out of his tent.

The night greeted him with cold air and a sky peppered with stars. He lit a smoke and headed for the perimeter of the campsite. Few others were out and about, except for a circle of NCOs gathered around the embers of a cooking fire in the middle of camp. Cade drifted away from the tents, hoping for a moment of solitude.

He followed the dirt road toward Achnacarry Castle. Nearby woods resonated with the hoots of owls, and the highland hilltops were limned with moonglow. Taking in the serenity of the location, Cade found his thoughts harkening to his first days at Eilean Donan Castle. The loneliness. The confusion. The anger. How lost he'd been, in the depths of his grief; how empty he'd felt, unable to slake his thirst for revenge. He watched reflected moonlight stretch across the black water of the River Arkaig and remembered LEVIATHAN's tentacles rising from the sea and dragging his parents to their deaths.

All I've learned . . . all I've done . . . what difference has it made? He quashed his doubts as quickly as he'd summoned them. *Don't be stupid. Taking down the Thule Society mattered. And that bastard Siegmar deserved what he got. Don't go second-guessing your—*

A pistol's hammer cocked behind his ear and silenced his thoughts. "Halt," said a man with a Mancusian accent. "The main building's off-limits. What's your business here?"

Fuck.

Cade's opened his hands and raised them slowly in surrender. "Just stretching my legs."

Another voice, this one Glaswegian: "Turn around." Cade turned to see he had been intercepted by a pair of British commandos in camouflage and night-ops blackface. The Scot toted a STEN submachine gun, whose distinctive long magazine jutted from its left side. His partner kept his large-caliber revolver trained on Cade's face.

The Scot shook his head. "Bloody Rangers. Think they own the place."

A grim nod from Pistol Man. "Drinkin' all the beer, takin' all the birds. Fuckin' Yanks. Overpaid, oversexed, and over here." His index finger curled around the trigger. "Too bad we're on the same side, or I'd teach this one a—"

"What's all this?" said a baritone from the dark.

Cade knew that voice, though he'd never thought to hear it again. Ignoring the weapons aimed at his face, he turned to face his old Oxford cohort, who aside from being leaner, more weathered, and decked out in camouflage, looked just as he had four years earlier. "Miles!"

Miles Franklin paused, squinted, then beamed. "Cade?"

The Scot sounded disappointed. "You know this man, Sergeant?"

"What do *you* think, you stupid sod? This man and I were at Oxford together!" He took Cade by the shoulders. "I'd never thought to see *you* here!" To the sentries he added, "He's with me, gents. Back to your posts." He tilted his head and confided to Cade, "This way."

They passed the main building of Achnacarry Castle, then descended a slope to the riverside. Once they were away from eavesdroppers, Cade nudged his old friend. "Sergeant? I thought you wanted to be an officer."

"Not all it's cracked up to be. But never mind me! I thought you were going home to your life of Connecticut luxury."

Cade shook his head. "Never got the chance." He met Miles's questioning gaze. "We were on the *Athenia*."

Shock and sympathy. "Oh, *no*. Mate—your mum and dad?"

"Lost at sea. And officially? So was I."

"What are you telling me? You're legally dead? Then how are you here?"

He wondered how much he could tell Miles without sounding insane. "I've spent the last four years with a top-secret warfare program."

The taller man's proud brow creased in amazement. "Secret? You're with the SOE?"

"Something like that." Hoping to shift the subject, he asked, "What are *you* doing here? And why the hell haven't I seen you until now?"

"The brass keeps my unit out of sight, for the most part. Technically, we're not even supposed to be here. We're not regular commandos, you see. We're the auxiliary."

"Meaning . . . ?"

"We're not being trained for Europe. Our mission is a bit more pessimistic. If you lot bungle the French invasion and the Jerries wind up on English soil, the commando auxiliary has orders to shed its uniforms and go underground in the cities, to organize an armed insurgency."

"Sounds like a hoot."

"I assure you, it's anything but." Miles looked across the river. Cade tried to find what his friend was staring at, only to realize there was nothing to see but the curtain of night. Dejection crept into Miles's deep voice. "Vaughn and the others say they need men like me in the auxiliary, men who can blend into 'urban communities' undetected. But I think the real reason I'm not going to Europe is your Yank pals."

"What do you mean?"

"Are you blind? Because of my skin, old boy."

"I know the American forces are segregated, but—"

"And that doesn't strike you as ironic? That the world is counting on a racist country like yours to save it from a racist lunatic like Hitler?" Dim moonlight traced the edges of his frown. "You know what a Ranger once said to me? I was a trainer when some of your lot came through last year. During a live-fire exercise, I stopped some young chap from Alabama from dropping a mortar round on his command company. He turned and told me to shut my 'nigger mouth.' When I informed that buck private he was addressing a sergeant, he replied, 'Stripes on a zebra mean more than stripes on a nigger.' Had he been a British commando, I could've put him in the stockade for a month. But we've been asked to 'tolerate' the Americans' . . . *special needs* with regard to separating white and colored personnel. And so . . . I find myself in the auxiliary."

All Cade could feel was deep, abiding shame. For his country, for his fellow Rangers, for himself for not having spoken up against it. An awkward silence freighted with guilt and quiet resentment stretched out between them while Cade searched for anything to say that didn't threaten to add insult to injury. At last he sighed and stuffed his hands in his pockets. "I'm sorry, Miles, for all of it. But it could've been worse. Imagine if they found out you're a poof."

Miles almost laughed. "You really are an ass."

"As advertised." A brisk wind whistled through the trees. Cade tilted his head southward. "I hear there's a pub in Spean Bridge. Want to pop down for a pint?"

Miles threw an arm across Cade's shoulders. "I thought you'd never ask."

APRIL

There seemed to be no limit to Hell's ignorance. For over a month, Kein had petitioned his patron for any clue to the fate of his last remaining apprentice. He had sent half a dozen demons abroad with the simplest of missions: *Locate Briet and report her condition and whereabouts to me.*

All had returned, none the wiser.

Even a Lull Engine, despite being notoriously difficult to deceive, had yielded inconclusive results. Fearing she might have been captured by his rival, Kein once again resorted to the simplest and most direct method available.

He stood in the operator's circle of his conjuring room, beneath his Wolfs-schanze bunker. Red flames hugged the coals in his brazier. From his pocket he pulled a wad of Mercurial incense wrapped in virgin gauze. Crystals of rock salt crunched in his fist. The pressure of his hand released the floral scent of powdered black dianthus.

He dropped the incense into the brazier.

Orange sparks shot up from the coals, scorching the ceiling and raining phosphors onto the floor, where they skittered off to fade away and die. Kein extended his hand into the geyser of fiery motes and intoned, "*Exaudi. Exaudi. Exaudi.*"

In his imagination he held an image of Briet. If she was alive, even if behind a magickal barrier, she would hear his summons and be able to conjure a flame of discourse in her palm.

Kein repeated his incantation. No answer came, nor any vision of his lost adept. The jet of sparks from the brazier petered out, and the flames licking the coals shrank to nothing.

He withdrew his hand.

He snuffed the brazier's coals and opened the circle. The last time he had seen Briet had been in Normandy, months earlier. They had spoken briefly in

January, but not since then. None of her bodyguards had seen her leave; all they knew was that one morning in February they had gone to fetch her—at Kein's telegraphed request—only to find her Berlin apartment abandoned. All her possessions had been left behind, with the notable exception of her tools of the Art.

Some reports suggested she had been seen in Hamburg, and that she had purchased a ticket for a midnight train to Düsseldorf—a ticket that was never redeemed, and a passage that, as far as Kein could tell, she never made.

Beyond that, all attempts to track her movements had failed.

The uncertainty of the matter vexed Kein. Had Briet been killed? Captured? Could she have deserted him? Or, worse, defected to the enemy?

There was nothing left to be done. He had to let it go for now. As far as Kein was concerned, Briet was dead.

But when this war is over, if I find her alive, she will not remain so for long.

———

Between the road and the river, the Fifth Ranger Battalion fell into formation for the eight-mile march to Spean Bridge, where, they had been told, a train stood waiting to take them to their next training site.

Cade was checking his pack's straps and accounting for every last bit of his gear when a firm hand closed on his shoulder. He turned to see Miles smiling at him.

"Thought you could break camp without a good-bye, did you?"

"Wouldn't dream of it." He and Miles clasped each other's forearms in an aggressive parody of a handshake. "They say we're off to Braunton, then Swanage."

"Assault training. Keep your head down and your eyes open. You'll do fine."

Cade nodded toward the castle. "How about you? Staying here?"

"Someone has to train your next batch of wankers." Somewhere down the line, sergeants started shouting men into motion. "You'd best get going, old boy."

The month at Achnacarry had gone by so quickly, and Cade had had less than two weeks to catch up with Miles. His whole life seemed to be racing past before he had time to breathe. Now, saying farewell to Miles once again, he remembered feeling as if he'd failed him in the recruiting office by leaving him to crack on alone. Now he was the one being asked to march into Hell while Miles stayed behind to keep the home fires burning.

"We'll meet again," Cade said. "After the war."

"You know how to find me, mate."

Sergeant Dale's shout split the morning air: "Dog Company! First Platoon! Move out!"

The ranks ahead of Cade started to march. He turned a mischievous look at Miles. "Hey! You got that ten pounds you owe me?"

An ivory grin. "Sorry, mate. We're not flush like you Yanks. Settle up next time?"

Following his section on the march out of Achnacarry, Cade answered Miles over his shoulder: "Count on it."

48

MAY

"Lad, we're running out of time. Come have another go." Adair lagged behind Cade, who walked faster now than he ever had before. Striking a plaintive note, Adair added, "One more go-round, then we'll call it a night."

"I've had enough." Cade quickened his pace. The barracks he shared with his Ranger cohort on the outskirts of Dorchester—their latest staging point, following whirlwind rounds of training in Braunton and Swanage—lay just a short ways up the dark road. As with most other military sites in the south of England, there were no lights on in the wee hours, a precaution against Luftwaffe bombing sorties. Cade, like most other Allied soldiers training for the European campaign, had learned to navigate by compass and starlight.

Adair did his best to keep up with Cade, but after nearly six months in the Rangers' care the youth was a changed man. Matching his pace left Adair winded. "Cade, please. Convincing the army to move the practice bunker from Leominster wasn't easy. They won't move it again. We need to use it while we can."

"And we will. Tomorrow, when I'm better rested."

Why is it so hard to talk sense to him? "You think you'll be well-rested for the real thing? You'll spend a night crossing the Channel; then you'll have to storm a beach, scale a cliff, and attack a bunker—all under fire. Even if you reach the seal intact, you think you'll be daisy-fresh? You'll be lucky to catch your breath and not heave your guts out."

Cade stopped and confronted his master. "Get off my back. I've spent months studying that thing. I know every goddamn mark on it."

"Not from what I saw tonight."

A sharp intake of breath telegraphed Cade's mounting frustration. "I transposed two out of a thousand glyphs, and missed a dot on one. I'll remember next time."

"You'd better. Botch even one on the real thing and those demons fly free. You get sloppy, the rest of us see Hell on earth."

"The rest of us?"

"Aye. You'll be dead the moment you bollix it up. It's the other two billion sods on this planet that'll have to suffer."

Those numbers sobered Cade in an instant. He let go of his defiance, nodded, then met Adair's searching look with humility. "I'll go over the glyphs again in the morning."

"Why not now?"

Cade checked his watch, then jogged toward his section's barracks. "Sarge wants me back by midnight, didn't say why." Adair trotted a few paces behind as Cade added, "I hope it's not another screening of *Girl Crazy*. I like Judy Garland, but if I have to watch that flick one more time, I'll blow my brains out."

Under his breath, Adair cursed the passion and energy of youth, then rebuked himself for his envy. *The world is new to him. Let him savor it.*

He followed Cade down narrow lanes steeped in darkness until they approached his barracks. An armed sentry, more a voice in the dark than a person, blocked their path.

"Halt! Identify yourself."

"Martin, Private Cade. Fifth Rangers, Dog Company, First Platoon."

"And who's that behind you?"

Cade answered, "That's Adair Macrae, British SOE. He's with me."

The sentry snapped on a flashlight, aimed it into their faces for a few seconds, then turned it off. "All right, get inside. Sarge is waitin' for you."

"Thanks." Cade and Adair climbed the steps to the barracks door. At the top, Cade knocked twice, then waited for a single knock in response—a signal that the lights inside were out, for safety—before opening the door and leading Adair inside. As soon as the door clicked shut behind them, the lights snapped on, and the duo found themselves facing the entire First Platoon of Dog Company, who had gathered for Sergeant Dale's announcement.

Dale nodded at Adair. They had met a few times before, to speak briefly about Cade's need for separate, specialized training after lights-out. Unlike the enlisted men in Cade's unit, the NCOs and officers all had been briefed regarding Cade's singular mission in the upcoming attack. So far as Adair could tell, none of them had let anything slip to the rank and file.

The sergeant stepped forward to meet Cade. "Son," he said in his Texas drawl, "I've got a confession to make. When the army dumped you in my lap five months ago, I didn't think you were gonna make it. You didn't know shit about soldierin', and you could barely find your ass with both hands, never mind field-strip your M1. So when the army said I had to get your sorry ass up to speed and make you ready to hit the beach, I was not what you would call optimistic."

Dale looked around at the other members of Dog Company, many of whom were struggling and failing to suppress knowing smiles. "But I'll be goddamned, son. You proved me wrong. You learned faster than anybody I've ever seen. And last week, in Braunton and Swanage . . . well, shit. You showed real grit, boy. Ain't a man in this company who'd think twice about goin' into battle with you. Myself included." He looked over his shoulder as someone else stepped forward. "So we all chipped in and got you a little somethin'. Hope it fits."

Out of the ranks stepped the burly platoon sergeant, Staff Sergeant Gordon Speath, and the platoon's commanding officer, First Lieutenant Francis Dawson, whom Adair had glimpsed only once before, in passing. He noted that Cade looked upon the man with genuine awe and respect.

Dawson held out his open hand to Cade. In it was a diamond-shaped shoulder patch: a navy-blue field with a gold border and gold type that read, in capital letters, RANGERS.

"Take it, son," the lieutenant said. "You've earned it. You're one of us now."

Cade stared in shock, then accepted the patch. "Thank you, sir."

Private Pinchefsky gave Cade a friendly punch in the shoulder. "Fast learner, huh? Guess we can't call you 'Dunce Cap' no more." He smirked at Dale. "What's his new nick, Sarge?"

"Well, everybody loves an underdog, right?"

The cluster of soldiers broke up and flowed past Cade like a river breaking around a stone, all of them patting his back or his shoulders as they passed: "Way to go, Underdog." "Good job, Underdog." "Kickin' ass and takin' names, Underdog!" "Way to do it, Underdog."

Dawson raised his voice. "Now the bad news." He handed Cade a folded paper. As Cade opened it, Dawson said, "You've been transferred. Second Rangers, Easy Company." A disappointed frown. "Sorry, son, the order came from Eisenhower himself. There's a jeep waiting to take you to Braunton. Report to First Sergeant Lang, he'll get you sorted out."

A pall fell over the platoon. It was clear from the stunned look on Cade's face that he didn't know how to process the news. He folded the paper, nodded once. "Understood, sir."

The other men gathered around to shake Cade's hand, bid him farewell, wish him luck, and encourage him to keep his feet dry, his head down, and his ass attached. The last man to face him was Pinchefsky. "Take care of yourself, Underdog."

"Same to you, Pinch."

"And if any of those Second Ranger pricks gives you shit—"

"I'll send 'em right to you."

"Fuck, no," Pinchefsky said. "They're nuts. I was gonna say smile and keep walkin'."

The men of First Platoon went on lobbing jokes and good-natured barbs at Cade while he packed his duffel for the midnight trip to the Second Ranger Battalion.

Watching from a respectful distance, Adair felt a swell of reflected pride in Cade's achievement, and at the bonds the young man had so quickly forged. Adair had feared his push to see the lad integrated into the army's ranks might fail or backfire. Instead, Cade had succeeded beyond all of Adair's expectations. It was a hopeful sign. If the other Rangers believed in him, perhaps Cade might be ready to face the horrors of war.

But seeing his apprentice bask in the praise of his brothers-in-arms, Adair couldn't deny his own mounting fears—because humanity's survival hinged upon Cade enduring what Adair knew would be nothing less than a one-way ticket into the maw of Hell.

JUNE

The HMS *Amsterdam*, a Channel steamer converted into an infantry transport for the Royal Navy, was a cramped can of a ship, stripped of comforts and reduced to bare necessities. Suspended over its sides from hydraulic hoists, level with the main deck, were a dozen LCAs, flat-bottomed amphibious landing craft. Not long after the Second Rangers had arrived in Weymouth on June 1, they were transferred across the harbor on barges to the *Amsterdam*, into which they had been jammed like rounds into a rifle's magazine.

Hidden away in the bowels of the ship, the Rangers had been berthed by platoons and sections, told to stow their gear anywhere they could find space, and to make themselves comfortable. That instruction had struck Cade as a sick joke. There was more than enough room for the men. Finding space for all their gear, on the other hand, had made for tight quarters.

There were few portholes below A Deck, and the only source of light in his platoon's compartment was a bare bulb that dangled from a frayed cord in a haze of cigarette smoke. Huddled under it, Cade and a few of his new buddies from Easy Company's Second Platoon sat in a loose huddle around a creased deck of cards and wrinkled wads of cash.

Dutch flicked the corner of one his cards. "Bet's to you, Martin."

"Really? And I thought you were all staring at me 'cause I'm so damn handsome." Cade pondered his hand: two pair, queens and threes. It wasn't a bad hand for five-card draw poker, but the way Dutch and Paddy had been betting, he was sure at least one of them had three of a kind. And Rooster never started the betting, but he had called even after two raises, which left Cade suspecting the barracks lawyer of setting a trap for the rest of them. Folding was probably the smartest call. Problem was, they were threatening to change Cade's nickname to "Yeller" because of how often he folded before the showdown. Pride was a bad reason to call a bet, but Cade had nothing else to spend his money on, so why not?

First Lieutenant Leagans pushed open the compartment's door and leaned in just far enough to fill the space with his voice: "Martin! Front and center!"

Relieved to have an excuse to bow out, Cade feigned disappointment. "Shit, just my luck." He mucked his cards, stood, and brushed off his pants. "Look sharp, Dutch." Hooked a thumb at Rooster: "Keep this one honest."

The game continued without him as he walked past fellow Rangers and side-stepped out the door, which could be opened only halfway because of the human cargo blocking its inward swing. In the corridor, he snapped to attention in front of Leagans. "Sir."

"At ease, Private. Follow me." The lieutenant offered no explanation, and Cade knew not to ask. An officer had given him an order; that was all he needed to know.

They climbed a ladderway to the main deck, then walked aft on the port side to a hatch that led to a transverse through the ship's superstructure. Inside, a door on the forward bulkhead was ajar. Leagans pushed it open and walked inside. Cade followed him, noting a placard beside the door designating this as the ship's wardroom.

Unlike the accommodations belowdecks, the wardroom was spacious and lit with warm light. Gathered at the conference table were the senior NCOs of Easy Company, Second Platoon: Technical Sergeant Elliot Mann, platoon sergeant; the assault section leaders, Staff Sergeants Jerry Sykes and Sam Kelly; and Sergeant Michael DeStefano, head of the mortar section.

Leagans pointed Cade toward the open chair next to Mann. "Take a seat, Private." The platoon leader sat opposite Cade, next to Sykes. Then everyone waited. A clock on the bulkhead crept with maddening sloth toward the top of the hour. Cade wondered, as the hour hand snapped into place, whether that would herald some dramatic—

The door was thrown open as if by a storm, and a tall, thin four-star general entered the room and strode to the head of the table, his braided hat tucked under his arm, a young female army officer trailing him toting a briefcase. Leagans and the NCOs sprang to their feet, so Cade did the same, a fraction of a second behind them. No one saluted, since neither the general nor his aide were wearing their covers. Easy's commander, Captain Richard Merrill, and its top kick, First Sergeant Bob Lang, followed the general inside and flanked him.

The general smiled. "At ease, gentlemen. Be seated."

As soon as the general spoke, Cade recognized him from their brief meeting on Gibraltar years earlier: He was Dwight D. Eisenhower, Supreme Allied Commander Europe.

The Rangers dropped into their chairs and did a fair approximation of sitting at attention. Eisenhower set his hat on the table and remained standing, while his adjutant opened her briefcase and handed manila folders to the men around the table. As soon as she had finished, she left the wardroom and closed the door behind her.

"Gentlemen," the general said, "our invasion of France is imminent. Twelve days ago, you were told Pointe du Hoc is your target. Now it's time you knew the rest of your mission. If you'll open the folders you've been given and look at the first page—" He waited while the Rangers complied. "You'll see that credible intelligence from the French Resistance suggests the Germans have moved the six artillery pieces inland. You are not to share that information with your men. The observation bunker atop Pointe du Hoc is your chief objective. On page two—"

Papers rustled as Cade and his fellow Rangers turned pages.

Eisenhower resumed, "—you'll find aerial and ground recon photos to help you identify the most direct approach to the bunker. It is imperative you eliminate all enemy forces defending this facility, without damaging its map room." A genial half smile tugged at the general's mouth. "Now, to answer the question that I know is on all your minds: Why did I ask a private to attend this meeting?" He fixed Cade with a look that seemed equal parts admiration and pity. "For the same reason I transferred him to your unit: he's the key to your entire mission."

That declaration raised the sergeants' eyebrows and triggered surprised looks that lasted until Eisenhower continued. "I've briefed your battalion command, as well as Captain Merrill, First Sergeant Lang, and Lieutenant Lapres of First Platoon. What you men need to know is this: In the observation bunker's map room is a unique type of bomb, one that requires a rare and special expertise to defuse. And our only man qualified to do it is Private Cade Martin."

Sykes leaned forward. "Pardon me, General. What kind of bomb is it, exactly?"

"That's classified, Sergeant."

Kelly was the next to give in to curiosity. "And what qualifies Martin to defuse it?"

"Specialized training he received prior to joining the army."

"What kind of training?" asked DeStefano. "Received where?"

Cade wondered how much the general intended to tell the Rangers about the Midnight Front and Adair, and of what they were really up against. Eisenhower looked again at Cade, then said with a perfect poker face, "Those details are top-secret. All you men need to know is that Private Martin was educated at Oxford, and for the last few years he's been serving behind the lines with British SOE. He has the full confidence of our British allies, and mine as well." He planted his knuckles on the table. "I'm putting his life in your hands. Make clear to all the men under your command that getting Private Martin into that bunker, alive and preferably in one piece, is your only imperative after you hit the beach. You are to consider any previous orders you have in hand, and any contradictory directives you might receive in the future, null and void, on my personal authority. When it comes to getting Martin into that bunker, all of you, and every man in your unit, should be considered expendable. Do I make myself clear?"

Merrill nodded and spoke for the group. "Perfectly, sir."

"Good. One last thing. Your mission is classified top-secret. Do not discuss it with anyone outside your unit, *ever*. Even after this war is over, as far as all of you are concerned, this meeting never happened, I was never here, and you've never heard of this operation. Clear?" Silent nods of affirmation drew a satisfied smile on the general's lean face. "Good." He picked up his hat and tucked it under his arm. "Ready to hit the beach?"

"Do or die, General," Leagans said. "Just give the word."

"Gentlemen . . . the word is given. Now, if you'll excuse me, I have to get back to Southwick House before anyone notices I'm missing."

Eisenhower pivoted toward the door. On cue, Leagans and the NCOs bolted to their feet, with Cade emulating them a split second behind. They watched at attention while Eisenhower made his exit. As soon as the door clicked shut, their collective bated breath escaped in a great gasp. DeStefano glowered at Cade. "Goddamn, Private. What the fuck did you get us into?"

"It wasn't me." Cade shrugged, palms up, signaling surrender. "If I could've gone in alone, I would've. But the army had other plans."

"It usually does," grumbled Sergeant Mann, whose deep-set eyes gave him the affect of a cadaver. "Most of which involve us going home in boxes."

There had been no chance for Adair to say good-bye. Not that he had been of a mind to say much to his last apprentice beyond "good luck" before chiding him not to transpose tau and rho when he altered the glyphs inside the bunker, but it would have been good to see the lad's face once more. Just in case it proved to be for the last time.

Can't think that way. Chin up. He'll do you proud.

It had been four days since Cade and his battalion had embarked on barges to the ships awaiting them in the harbor. Four days since the HMS *Amsterdam* and dozens of other vessels had churned away under cover of darkness, to the fleet's rendezvous point off the Isle of Wight.

Adair turned a worried eye skyward, toward the starless heavens. Overcast weather had settled over England and the Atlantic coast of France, and the leaden clouds refused to budge. Eisenhower had already postponed the attack once, at the last possible moment the night before, on account of foul weather over the English Channel.

Tonight, another stormhead had threatened to halt the invasion force—a disaster that would likely have exposed the Allies' attack plans to the enemy. After Eisenhower was assured that the weather would break in the Allies' favor—courtesy of Adair's pact with MERCAEL—it had fallen to the general to decide whether to cast the die of Fate.

With characteristic brevity he'd set history in motion: "Okay. Let's go."

The concision of the order garnered Adair's admiration.

He stood now on the end of the quay, staring into the night toward Weymouth Harbor, imagining thousands of ships, more than 150,000 men, and a fleet of aircraft, all racing toward what he was certain would become a turning point in human history.

And swept up in its inexorable tide was one young man whose success or failure would determine whether all this effort had been made in vain.

God be with you, lad.

SUPREME HEADQUARTERS
ALLIED EXPEDITIONARY FORCE

Soldiers, Sailors and Airmen of the Allied Expeditionary Force!

You are about to embark upon the Great Crusade, toward which we have striven these many months. The eyes of the world are upon you. The hopes and prayers of liberty-loving people everywhere march with you. In company with our brave Allies and brothers-in-arms on other Fronts, you will bring about the destruction of the German war machine, the elimination of Nazi tyranny over the oppressed peoples of Europe, and security for ourselves in a free world.

Your task will not be an easy one. Your enemy is well trained, well equipped and battle-hardened. He will fight savagely.

But this is the year 1944 ! Much has happened since the Nazi triumphs of 1940-41. The United Nations have inflicted upon the Germans great defeats, in open battle, man-to-man. Our air offensive has seriously reduced their strength in the air and their capacity to wage war on the ground. Our Home Fronts have given us an overwhelming superiority in weapons and munitions of war, and placed at our disposal great reserves of trained fighting men. The tide has turned ! The free men of the world are marching together to Victory !

I have full confidence in your courage, devotion to duty and skill in battle. We will accept nothing less than full Victory !

Good Luck ! And let us all beseech the blessing of Almighty God upon this great and noble undertaking.

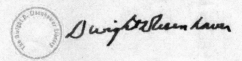

JUNE 6, 1944
D-DAY

50

There was sick, and there was two-days-of-stormy-seas-inside-a-tin-can-without-windows sick. It was worse than any illness Cade had ever known; he was cold sober but staggered like a drunk as decks, bulkheads, and overheads seemed to tumble around him. His head ached, his vision was blurry, and any food he dared send down to his stomach came right back up.

The decks inside the *Amsterdam* were slick with vomitus. An hour earlier the Rangers had been fed pancakes and coffee, a meal intended to reduce the effects of seasickness. As far as Cade could tell, it hadn't worked.

Desperate for air and feeling another surge from his belly, Cade struggled up steep, puke-covered steps to a watertight door that opened onto the main deck. He lurched through it into a wall of bodies. At least half of the Rangers on board had crowded the deck in search of relief from the seasickness. Wind gusted through the ranks; sea spray crashed over the bow and doused the huddled men. The lucky ones had staked their claim to spots along the railings, so they could heave their guts into the ocean with some bit of their dignity intact. The rest, like Cade, were left to paint one another's boots and apologize between hurls.

Every time Cade thought he was done shouting his intestines onto the deck, someone else near him started to retch, and his misery began all over again.

Above the roars of wind and engines, a deep and ominous droning permeated the night. Sleeving spittle from his lips, Cade looked up. Against a bank of clouds lit by moonlight, he saw the silhouettes of more aircraft than he could count. Bombers, fighter escorts, paratrooper transports, all lined up like great black serpents stretched across the sky, reaching from one end of the horizon to the other. If all went to plan, the bombers would soften up the coastal defenses while the paratroopers would strike inland, creating pockets of resistance behind enemy lines and cutting off the Germans' avenues of retreat.

As if they'd even think of falling back. We couldn't be that lucky.

A shift began in the bodies around him; some of the men abandoned their places on the railing to stagger belowdecks, perhaps in the hope of stealing a moment of sleep before the order came down to man the Higgins boats. Cade stole a spot near the bow. He was rewarded by a stinging mist of seawater in his face.

He winced, then wiped the water from his eyes. It was cold at the bow, but it beat being cooped up belowdecks, mired in a swamp of stink. At least up here he could strain to see the horizon and recover his equilibrium. All around the *Amsterdam*, the Allied armada cut through the winedark sea, thousands of ships cruising in close formation. The HMS *Ben-my-Chree*, which carried the rest of the Second Ranger Battalion, was so close off the starboard side that Cade imagined he could leap across the divide.

Pulses of red light in the sky, just beyond the horizon ahead of the armada. The bombers were doing their work. It wouldn't be long now.

Cade tried not to imagine what would happen if one of those bombs went astray and hit Kein's trapped bunker on Pointe du Hoc. Instead he cast his thoughts backward, to the last time he had traveled the open sea on a steamship such as this: the night the *Athenia* had gone down, victim of a U-boat's torpedo, its sinking a prelude to his parents' demise and the start of his own mission of vengeance. He knew now he had grown beyond that shallow aim. For months he had brooded on his reaction to killing Siegmar—how empty it had felt. How pointless.

My parents don't need me to avenge them. They need me to honor them.

Piercing whistles shrilled. Staff Sergeant Sykes moved up the port side of the main deck, and Staff Sergeant Kelly shadowed him to starboard.

"Everybody, get below!" Sykes barked. "Hustle, dammit!"

Kelly shouted, "Back to your berthing compartments, on the double!"

Sykes snapped, "Any Ranger on this deck in one minute gets my boot up his ass!"

Cade followed the rest of the Rangers into the bowels of the ship. The sergeants hounded the men all the way to their quarters, where they bellowed new orders.

"Grab your shit and get ready to roll!" Sykes said. "Buddies, check each other's gear! Keep your weapons clear and your ammo dry!"

Chatter dwindled as the Rangers rounded up their equipment, then tied condoms over the barrels of their rifles, carbines, and pistols to guard them from sand and seawater. Unlike most troops hitting the beach that day, the Rangers of Force A were traveling without heavy combat packs, to facilitate the scaling of the cliffs at Pointe du Hoc. The unit's best climbers, or "top monkeys," weren't even toting M1 rifles; they were armed only with pistols and carbines.

Cade and Dutch checked each other's gear, then found their places on the ready line.

A soul-shaking boom rocked the ship, followed by another, and another. Within moments a devil's drumbeat resonated through the hull—the Allied naval batteries had begun their bombardment of Normandy's coastline.

Sergeant Sykes moved down the line, checking each man's gear, delivering slaps on the back, and telling each man some variation of, "Relax, those big guns are doing our work for us." One blast dimmed the lights inside the berthing compartment. Sykes patted Cade's shoulder as he passed. "Keep breathing, it's supposed to do that."

Cade closed his eyes and tried not to let the tooth-rattling concussions of the artillery break his nerve. He drew a deep breath and pictured his parents smiling down upon him.

Mom, Dad . . . give me the strength to make you proud.

They seemed to go on forever, those bone-rattling cannonades, merciless godhammers from which no one could escape, endless salvos of deafening violence. They were overpowering. Cade found them impossible to block out; he couldn't think of anything else. All he could sense was his own body shaking before the might of the navy's big guns.

Just before 0400, another shriek of the sergeant's whistle. "We're moving to the boats! Do it like we practiced! On me!" Sykes blew his whistle again and led Second Platoon out of its berthing area, through the passageways, and up the ladders to the ship's main deck.

With every step the Rangers took toward topside, the guns grew louder. When the men charged two-by-two onto the main deck, Cade couldn't hear the sergeant's orders anymore. All he could do was follow the men in front of him. Then he looked up.

The sky was burning.

Fire jetted from hundreds of naval guns on and around the *Amsterdam*. Gold and orange streaked across the dome of night, lighting up shredded veils of smoke through which the Allied fleet surged. Each earsplitting blast of artillery lit up waves kicked into frothy peaks by the armada's passage.

Oiled tarps were pulled off of the LCAs, which had been made ready for troops to board while they were level with the main deck. British coxswains settled in at the controls of the assault craft, to conduct final equipment checks before deployment.

Sykes stood next to LCA 862, barking Second Platoon over its gunwales and into position. "Pack 'em in! Nuts to butts! Move!" The boat was wide enough for four men to stand shoulder-to-shoulder if they held their breath. Cade and Dutch were in the middle of the LCA, next to Paddy and Chapeau. Ahead of them were Rooster, Bandit, T-Bone, and Hopalong. At their backs were NCOs—Sergeants Waldman, Sykes, and DeStefano, and Corporal Brett. Assault Section Two filed in behind them, followed by Lieutenant Leagans.

The sergeants gave thumbs-up to Leagans, who relayed the signal to the boat's coxswain. The Higgins boats were lowered into the black and choppy surf between the massive transport ships. Overhead, another fusillade of naval artillery rent the sky and shook the sea.

As soon as the guide ropes were cleared, the pilot gunned the LCA's motor, and the landing craft lurched and rolled through waves that seemed to batter its hull from every direction. Less than a minute after getting under way, every man in the boat was sopping wet and bailing water from the deck with his helmet.

Hunkered down in the middle of the boat, his shoulder to its outer bulkhead, Cade caught only glimpses of the sea ahead, whenever the LCA's nose dipped. Above its sides he watched the capital ships fall behind, their crew-served deck guns pummeling the coast with steel and fire.

Then there were no more behemoths flanking the LCA. Just a dozen or so other small boats coursing through a terrifying yawn of open water.

Someone at the front of Cade's LCA threw up. In seconds half of the platoon was doubled over and painting the deck. Dry heaves left Cade coughing and spluttering—and grateful his stomach was already empty. The only man who seemed unaffected was Leagans.

Cade sleeved the bile from his chin and hooked a thumb over his shoulder. "I guess Lou's too good to hurl with the rest of us."

Dutch spit out bits of puke. "Must have gravel in his guts."

"Good for him. Ask if he can spare any."

The flotilla raced toward shore with the rising tide. A steady barrage of Allied naval artillery fire soared over and ahead of them, hammering enemy emplacements. Ever-present behind the shelling were the purr of the LCA's engine, the gray roar of wind, and the sharp slapping of waves against the hull.

Cade might have found the LCA's slalom through the sea mesmerizing if it hadn't been so jarring. He tried not to fixate on the dangers awaiting him and the others, but it was all he could think of—until a cry of alarm went up from the port side.

Chapeau pointed: One of the supply boats had swamped. Before Cade could wonder what might be done, the craft sank. Staring at the empty space from which it had vanished, he hoped to see its crew surface, but none of them did.

Haunted by the speed at which the supply boat had foundered and disappeared, Cade felt that the waves spewing over his LCA's bow had taken on a new degree of menace.

Minutes later another shout went up, and more fingers pointed, toward the starboard bow. This time one of the LCAs had swamped. Neither the lieutenant nor any of the NCOs in Cade's boat acknowledged the sinking assault craft, or voiced any thought of stopping to render aid. Cade watched the commander of Dog Company and more than twenty of his men flail in the freezing water as the rest of the flotilla left them behind.

Dutch nudged Cade. "What's takin' so long? Shouldn't we be on the beach by now?"

"How the fuck should I know?"

A rifleman at the front of the boat peeked over the bow and complained to Sergeant Waldman, "That ain't Pointe du Hoc."

Worried murmurs traveled through the ranks. One of the medics, Corporal Larry "Pow-Wow" Pawlikowski, leaned over the starboard gunwale just long enough to steal a look, then dropped back into ranks shaking his head. "Something's fucked. That's Pointe de la Percée."

Slick, one of the sergeants, sounded worried. "Force B's target? Fuck, that's three miles from du Hoc. Where are these Limey assholes taking us?"

The men looked to Leagans for answers, but he was busy covering his conversation with one hand while he groused over the radio handset to someone— maybe fleet command, maybe Colonel Rudder in the lead boat, there was no way for Cade to know for sure. But while the lieutenant argued with the coxswain and whoever stood on the other end of the radio frequency, the predawn twilight that had been meant to cloak their landing at Pointe du Hoc gave way to the flat illumination of a gray dishwater dawn.

So much for the element of surprise, Cade brooded.

Less than a thousand yards from landing on the wrong beach, the nine LCAs, their remaining supply boat, and their four DUKWs, or "Ducks" in GI jargon, all made a sharp right turn and charged westward parallel to the Normandy coastline.

"This ain't good," Rooster grumbled to Bandit.

"No shit," the corporal said.

Immediately, Cade understood their trepidation. LCAs were sluggish and hard to maneuver under the best of conditions. The Ducks, heavy amphibious vehicles that had been fitted with turntable-mounted extendable ladders acquired from the London Fire Brigade—an innovation that the army hoped would be the Rangers' secret weapon, by enabling a swift ascent of the cliffs—were even slower and harder to control in rough seas. Now they were all driving against the current, which would make them slower still. In other words, prime targets for German troops to harass with sniper fire and mortars from the cliffs above.

Less than three minutes later, the Germans did exactly that.

Precision shots from high-power rifles punched through two men at a time, spraying the other men in the LCA with their blood. T-Bone died before he hit the deck, but Hopalang, one of the platoon's top monkeys, clasped his hand over his bloodied flank. "Medic! I need a patch-up!"

Chapeau scrambled over with his medical kit as more enemy fire pinged off the LCA's front ramp. The boat shook as mortar rounds detonated in the water close by. Then a boom rattled Cade's teeth, and he looked over the side in time to see one of the Ducks belch fire and smoke before it vanished under the water.

The gray ghost of Pointe du Hoc hove into view, a forbidding V-shaped mass jutting into the Channel. It was just as the landing plans had described: steep cliffs above an exposed strip of beach. Except now all of it was concealed by morning fog and a pall of smoke that made the surrounding terrain nearly unrecognizable.

"Jesus Christ," said Private William "Hillbilly" Hillman. "Look at those fucking cliffs. Three old ladies with brooms could knock us offa there."

Cade frowned. "Then we better hope the Jerries didn't bring their grandmas."

On either side of the boat, mortar rounds and shells from inland artillery rained down like divine retribution. All Cade could do was watch Hell open up before him. One minute stretched into two, but time felt slow, almost elastic, stretched by his adrenaline and fear.

German bullets raked his LCA.

Machine-gun and small-arms fire pelted the boat's hull with an unholy percussion, a staccato of pings and thuds. Ricochets pealed off the bulkheads, and passing shots buzzed like insects as they tore past over the Rangers' heads.

A stray round caromed off Bandit's helmet, provoking a mumbled curse and a deeper bending of the boyish private's knees. "That was close."

Paddy grinned. "'Swhat you get for not keeping your—"

Paddy slumped to the deck at Cade's feet, blood sheeting over his face. Cade knew at a glance the man was dead, just as he realized he'd never heard the shot that took him.

Falling screeches followed by deep booms: mortar rounds. Shells slammed down amid the incoming boats. Explosions from inland artillery shot up geysers of water between Cade's LCA and the beach. Sykes marched forward and aft in the middle of the boat, shouting over the wind, waves, and engine. "Clear the ramp! When it drops, haul ass. Don't bunch up! Scatter and go forward. Three men make a target. One man's a waste of ammo. Don't get pinned down! If you stop moving, you're dead."

Bullets pattered against the LCA's hull like lead popcorn. A mortar round kicked up a blast wave and a jet of water off the port side, dousing the sodden Rangers in numbing-cold salt water. Cade suppressed a shiver as the wind cut through his sopping-wet uniform.

Beside him, Chapeau evacuated one last bit of bile from his stomach onto Cade's boots. "Sorry," he said with an abashed shrug.

"It's fine, I had to polish 'em later, anyway."

At the back of the boat, the coxswain lifted his fist. "One minute!"

"Okay, boys," Leagans said, doing his best to project confidence. "Look sharp!"

The chatter of the Germans' MG-42s and the roars of detonating mortar shells was overwhelming. Cade could barely hear the boat through the hellish clamor.

An off-white flutter of motion—a blood-spattered seagull landed on one of the LCA's bulkheads, opposite Cade. It looked him in the eye and shrieked like a banshee.

The men around Cade noted the seabird's arrival with confusion.

Sykes muttered, ". . . the fuck?"

Dutch squinted at the bloodied gull. "Does it have a death wish or something?"

The others tried to shoo it, but the bird held firm, and never took its eyes off Cade as it loosed another bloodcurdling screech.

Cade stared in wonder at the seagull—and remembered Adair's raven familiar, Kutcha, trying to warn him of the attack on the *Athenia,* seconds before the torpedoes struck.

The gull shrieked a third time, blood dripping from its curved beak.

Cade abandoned his grenades. "Drop your gear! Get over the side!"

Sykes grabbed Cade. "The fuck are you doing?"

"If we stay in the boat, we die! We gotta bail! Now!"

The pilot shouted from the rear, "Thirty seconds!"

"We're almost on the beach!" Sykes said.

Cade looked his section leader in the eye. "Sarge, trust me!"

Sykes shot a look at Leagans. The lieutenant nodded and dropped his own gear. "Follow Martin! Drop your gear! Over the side!"

The Rangers snapped into action, tossing rifles and heavy ordnance. Even as Dutch shed his gear, he asked, "What do we fight with? Dirty words?"

Sykes snapped, "Grab what you need on the beach! Go!"

The seagull took off and retreated seaward as Cade scrambled over the side of the LCA. Behind him followed half a dozen other Rangers. He splashed into the shockingly cold water and sank like a stone, his breath stolen by a gasp of panic.

Submerged, all he heard was the droning of LCA engines and the thuds of mortar rounds detonating. Then he caught the whoosh of bodies falling into the water, and through the stinging-cold murk he perceived fuzzy shadows, blurs of motion—

Pain knifed through his ears as everything flared white. Water rushed away as a blast wave hurled Cade and a dozen other Rangers away from their boat, whose twisted husk rolled over like a burning coffin. Broken bodies and orphaned limbs tumbled from its open deck, pouring blood into the sea. The shattered LCA splashed down with a groan and pinned half a dozen Rangers beneath its smoking bulk as it sank.

Machine-gun fire strafed the sea around Cade. Bullets cut through the water in lazy, drooping arcs, slow enough to see with the naked eye.

He fought his way to the surface. Breaking free of the water's embrace, he gasped for air as the sounds of battle, briefly muffled, returned with a vengeance. Officers and sergeants bullied the men to advance, to get to the beach. Cade's feet scrambled for purchase until they struck a corpse. He couldn't see the body through the swirling sand; the water was murky with blood and fuel, but he felt a man's neck under his boot. He had no time to feel guilt or shame; he pressed ahead and pushed through the water, grateful for each inward surge of the tide, which offered him brief moments of concealment as well as pushing him a few yards closer to shore.

Waist-deep in crashing surf, he could see barely ten feet ahead through drifting banks of smoke that hid the beach. Mortar rounds detonated on the stony shore, hurling corpses and fouling the air with the bite of gunpowder. Machine-gun fire raked the water's edge with dogged persistence, shredding men and boats. Cade strained to see where the fire was coming from, but all he saw was an endless gray curtain.

Looking seaward, he saw that the Ducks had failed to mount the beach. They were unable to get traction on the muddy spoil—not that it would have mattered. A slope of rocks and muddy debris had collected at the base of the cliff, making it impossible for the Ducks to get close enough to deploy their ladders. The secret weapons had just become useless.

Most of the LCAs had halted shy of the shingle, and Cade could tell a few had fired their grapples too soon, because they had bounced off the cliff and now lay on the beach. Several others, however, were already in position, and Rangers were scrambling through the water and across the narrow beach— some to take cover at the base of the cliff while setting up manually fired grapples, others to start their ascent in the face of enemy fire and grenades.

Bullets eviscerated a Ranger to Cade's left, spilling the man's guts into the breaking waves, which stank of shit and ran red with blood twenty feet out from shore. A mortar round struck to Cade's right, knocking him flat as it filled the air with carnage, smoke, metal, and fire.

Ankle-deep water. Cade spat out brine as he ran, his heart pounding, his breathing fast and shallow as he sprinted toward the cliff's base. A German MG-42 peppered the sand around him with an angry rip he had learned to fear during his training at Achnacarry.

He stumbled down the slope of a crater. Three Rangers lay dead at its nadir. He set upon on them like a scavenger, snapping up an M3, a full spare magazine for the compact submachine gun, and another man's bandolier of smoke and fragmentation grenades. Enemy fire chased him out of the pit and dogged him to the base of the cliff. Bullets pelted the fragile rock above his head, showering him in dirt. His entire body started to shake.

Fuck, I'd give anything for invulnerability to projectiles. Or protection from fire. Or immunity to metal. Anything to get off this fucking beach.

Twenty yards west down the heavily cratered shore, LCA 861 fired its grapples at the cliff as it plowed ashore over sharp rocks. The cumbersome hooks failed to reach the top of the cliff and tumbled to the beach. The LCA's ramp dropped, and MG-42 rounds tore apart the men in its front ranks as they stormed out.

Cade drew panicked breaths but felt as if he were suffocating. He knew he had to move, but his hands shook and his feet felt like bricks. He recoiled from screams, rips of automatic gunfire, gut-quaking blasts of grenades dropping into the middle of Rangers setting up rocket-propelled grapple launchers. In the haze shrouding the beach, soldiers staggered and fell, or struggled to hold in their mangled viscera.

A grenade's blast kicked sand into Cade's face—and flayed two men next to him with shrapnel.

A bloodied hand clamped on to Cade's shoulder. He blinked until he could focus on the man's face. It was Dutch. He was shouting. Cade heard his voice, but words had no meaning, they were just more noise in the midst of bedlam. Then Dutch seized Cade with both hands and shook him, hard. "Get up, you prick! We gotta climb!"

Cade shook his head, trapped in denial. "Can't. Can't move."

"Bullshit! You're not hit! Stop fuckin' around!" Dutch seized Cade by the front of his jacket and pulled him to his feet. "Let's go, Ranger!"

Dragged into motion, Cade felt his muscle memory take over. He and Dutch scampered up the muddy slope of rubble and spoil, toward dangling knotted climbing ropes. A dozen Rangers were scaling the cliffs, and others were launching more grapples from the beach.

Explosions overhead—grenades dropped from above detonated against the cliffs, sending hunks of rock and wounded Rangers plunging to the beach. Cade ducked a falling body, which rolled down the debris pile to the surf. He froze until Dutch pushed a rope into his hands. "Cheer up, Underdog! This shit takes thirty feet off our climb!"

Too rattled to laugh, Cade started climbing. Bullets from small arms caromed off rocks by his head. To his left, a rope with four Rangers on it went slack, and they plummeted to the beach and landed in a groaning heap.

Ahead of him on his right, without missing a step, a sergeant deadpanned, "Somebody at HQ fucked up, boys. They issued the enemy live ammo!"

It was gallows humor, but it did the trick. Cade and the other Rangers grinned as they continued climbing, pulling themselves up a cliff toward a hostile welcoming committee.

Thunderous booms shook the bedrock as Allied naval artillery dropped a fresh round of ordnance on Pointe du Hoc. The distance between Cade and the top of the cliff shrank with each agonizing step and pull. His hands bled on the wet rope; his shoulders and hips ached, and it felt as if every muscle in his arms and legs was on fire. Icy wind dried the sweat on his face and neck. The only reason he was able to breathe was that he kept reminding himself to do it.

He looked up to see a German soldier staring at him, down the rope.

The German fumbled a pair of cutters as he raced to sever the barbed wire in which the grapple for Cade's rope was snagged.

Cade snaked his left arm around the rope, braced himself with his feet, and drew his sidearm. The Colt 1911 .45 semiautomatic felt heavy in his hand as he tried to aim.

One length of wire broke; the grapple slipped, and Cade held tight until it caught again. Senses sharpened by adrenaline, he raised the pistol and fired.

The German's forehead erupted in a crimson splash.

Cade holstered his weapon and kept climbing.

A grenade exploded and peppered him with splinters of rock. He felt the right side of his face warm with fresh blood. Machine-gun fire sent him scrabbling across the cliff into a crevice, a natural defilade. He winced as bullets chewed up the rock inches from his chest.

Wild sprays of suppressing fire raked the clifftops, forcing the Germans to duck for shelter in their trenches and resistance nests. Cade looked over his shoulder for the source of the fire support. His jaw fell open as he watched a Ranger from Fox Company ride the top of a fully extended ladder as it swung like the needle of a metronome, swaying as its Duck rolled in the rising tide far below. The Ranger held on to the ladder with his legs and focused all his attention on swearing at and strafing the German troops, who for him were almost at eye level, and who found this bizarre moving target hard to shoot.

Never question a gift. Cade put one hand over the other and fought his way up the rope. Six meters from the grapple, the almost vertical slope gave way to a traversable rocky path, where he quickened his pace to a jog. At the top

he saw Rangers who had arrived ahead of him. They had breached a path in
the barbed wire, so Cade sprinted through it even as he cocked his M3, extended its stock, and braced it against his shoulder.

He looked for Dutch, but the other Ranger was nowhere in sight.

Keep moving, get cover. Instincts and training dictated Cade's actions. He
leaped into a five-foot-deep German trench. Its walls were reinforced with
wooden planks, and thick beams supported its corners. The dirt floor was
packed solid.

Someone moved near the corner ahead. A flash of gray—

Cade fired as the German rounded the turn. The M3 kicked hard into Cade's
shoulder as he put three bursts into the German's center mass. As the enemy
soldier fell, another pivoted into view, hoping to even the score, only to have
Cade gun him down. Neither man moved as Cade hurdled over them, following a path through the trenches that hugged the cliff's edge and led to the
observation bunker the Germans had built at the tip of the point.

More naval artillery rounds screamed past overhead and slammed down a
few hundred yards away, in the midst of the Germans' extended fortifications,
the ones made to house a sextet of heavy artillery pieces. Cade poked his head
above the trench wall to get his bearings.

Aerial and naval bombardment had reduced the flat sprawl atop Pointe du
Hoc to a smoldering moonscape. On his left, German soldiers who had abandoned their posts retreated through tattered curtains of gray smoke, fleeing
inland, pursued by groups of Rangers. To his right, other German forces remained inside their machine-gun nests and rifle pits, from which they cut down
a wave of Rangers who had just reached the clifftop.

Movement, left—Rangers, men from Cade's unit. Sergeant Sykes, Corporal Brett, and two privates, men Cade knew only as Clover and KZ. Sykes beckoned Cade into their huddle. "Good to see you breathin', Martin."

"Good to *be* breathing, Sarge."

"Okay, listen up. Clover, KZ, stay here and watch our six. Martin, you and
Brett flank left behind that MG. I'll go at 'em straight." He paused as more
naval artillery hit and rocked the point. "When I hit 'em with smoke, you light
'em up. Clear?" Everyone nodded. "Move!"

Cade followed Brett. They climbed out of the trench, stayed low as they ran
a few steps, then rolled into a different trench.

As they skulked behind the *Widerstandsnest,* Sykes crawled toward it, heed-
less of the MG-42 fire blazing from its narrow slit facing the sea. From a slop-

ing patch of dirt, hidden only by a bit of scrub, Sykes rolled a pair of smoke grenades toward the nest.

The charges went off with loud pops and clouded the nest in thick smoke. Cade and Brett sprang from cover, lobbed fragmentation grenades through the nest's open rear, then sprinted away from the blast. German sharpshooters in the pits beside the nest turned in time to see Cade and Brett open fire and mow them down. East and west along the cliffside, other small teams of Rangers did the same, flushing out pockets of German resistance, clearing the way for the rest of the men on the beach to make their climbs.

Men from Dog and Fox companies pressed inland, toward the villages and hedgerows of Pointe du Hoc. The men of Easy Company, Second Platoon regrouped. Half of them were absent—dead, wounded, or missing.

Lieutenant Leagans surveyed the grimy, bloodied group. "I know we look like shit, boys, but the worst is yet to come." He pointed toward the observation bunker, at the northernmost edge of the point. "We still need to get Martin in there, alive and kicking, and we need to be quick about it. Move out in twos and threes, and form a cordon around Martin. Understood? All right. Let's go."

Like wild animals on the hunt, the Rangers climbed out of the trench, split into small packs, and fanned out for their prowl across the open flat top of the point. Leagans snapped his fingers to draw their attention; then he directed them with hand gestures toward targets ahead.

They were a dozen meters short of the next warren of trenches and tunnels when the buzz of an MG-42 sent them diving for craters, debris, and any other shelter they could find.

Bullets chewed up the ground between the Rangers as small-arms fire picked off a few unlucky men who had been too far from cover when the shooting started.

No one had to tell Cade or the other Rangers to start lobbing smoke grenades; they just did it. A baker's dozen of the nonlethal charges detonated in the space of a few seconds, shrouding the area ahead of their position in gray smoke.

As soon as the clouds merged into a single obscuring wall, the Rangers pulled on their gas masks and pressed their attack. The moment the smoke enveloped Cade, he lost sight of the men around him, but he kept moving toward the observation bunker. Alone in a gray mist, he dropped into another trench. Advancing with his weapon ready, he listened for anything other than his own footsteps and ragged breathing, any sign he was about to encounter the enemy.

A flare of small-arms fire—bullets pocked the wooden planks of the trench wall to his right. He ducked left, fired his M3. Pained grunts behind the fog, then a wild spray of automatic fire into the air. Cade pushed ahead and found a dead German on the ground. He stole one of the dead man's potato-masher grenades and continued forward.

Smoke rolled through the trenches and bunched up at the corners. Another shadow in the gray—Cade fired, but missed. Growls of submachine-gun fire hounded him, forced him behind a corner. Then he heard the scrape of boots on dirt, getting closer. Cade pulled the cord at the base of his stolen grenade's handle, triggering its friction igniter and five-second fuse. He counted to three, then chucked it around the corner, down the trench.

German vulgarities and running steps were drowned out by the blast, which launched a fireball into the air, along with a pair of Nazi soldiers.

Cade dashed around the corner, only to find the trench blocked by smoking debris and caved-in walls. He scrambled over them, onto the flat ground above, and sprinted toward the next open length of trench between him and the observation bunker.

Red-hot and sharp as a scalpel, a bullet ripped through Cade's right side, below his rib cage. He felt another searing bite as he fell, this time grazing his right trapezius. He landed facedown as more rifle fire zinged by above him. Lying prone, he sighted the muzzle flash of his attacker's weapon and emptied his M3 until he heard the German drop.

Incoming fire from the Allied fleet howled overhead and detonated far beyond the smoke. Energized by the shock of his injuries, Cade got up and ran. Motion to his right—he pivoted, fired, saw the shapes of men fall. He tried to eject the empty magazine from his M3. It jammed.

No time. Cade tossed the M3, drew his Colt, and advanced, steadying the pistol with both hands. He dropped into the next trench and continued his push toward the bunker. He turned a corner and almost collided with a German rifleman.

The frightened youth hefted his rifle, and Cade put a bullet in the kid's throat. The German dropped his weapon and collapsed, clutching at his ruptured carotid artery.

Cade was close enough to smell the coffee and cigarettes on the dying man's breath, count the flecks of mud on his youthful face—and watch his eyes dim and fade forever.

He reloaded his Colt and kept moving.

Around him, submachine-gun fire mixed with the cracks of M1 rifles. The barks of German machine guns were answered by the bangs of grenades. Lording over it all, the piercing shrieks and tooth-rattling blasts of naval ordnance. Cade tuned it all out and watched the trench ahead of him while constantly checking his flanks for rude surprises.

Above the trenches, Germans abandoned their posts and ran inland, toward the coastal highway and the next line of German defenses. Seconds after Cade spotted them, a barrage of rifle and submachine-gun fire mowed down the retreating Nazis, to the last man.

All was quiet ahead of Cade, but he kept his Colt raised and ready. Then he turned the last bend in the trench. Ahead of him was the entrance to the observation bunker designated H636A. A dozen dead German troops littered the ground near it. Emerging from the smoke with Cade were Lieutenant Leagans, Sergeant Sykes, and most of the other men from Second Platoon. Standing outside the bunker were Lieutenant Lapres, the leader of First Platoon, and a handful of his men, whose boat had landed directly beneath the observation bunker. They waved in Second Platoon. When the two groups of soldiers converged, they squatted into a large huddle.

"Nice of you gents to join us," Lapres said. He nodded at Cade. "We cleared the bunker but stayed clear of the map room, like the general said."

"Thanks."

Sykes pointed at the blood on Cade's uniform. "You okay?"

"Nothin' a year in the tropics won't fix."

Leagans smirked. "Don't let the brass hear that. They'll send you to fight the Nips."

Cynical chortles filled the circle.

Leagans lowered his voice to ask, "Son? You sure you're good for this?"

It was a time custom-made for a lie. "Yup."

Sykes remained doubtful. "It's just . . . once you head inside, we can't go with you. The general's orders say we need to stay out here."

"I know. Somebody wet a cloth and clean my hands, please." Noting their reluctance and confusion, he explained, "My hands need to be clean before I . . . defuse the bomb." It was the simplest explanation he could give them—far easier than explaining that he couldn't risk contaminating the floor of the bunker's map room with his blood or anyone else's, lest he foul up the sigils he needed to draw, or add marks that rendered his efforts invalid.

The medics dampened a cloth with water from a canteen and quickly scrubbed the dirt and blood from Cade's hands. He approved their efforts with a nod. "Good. Now patch me up. If I bleed on this thing, it might kill us all. So wrap my ass like a mummy."

Chapeau started cleaning the wound on Cade's shoulder. "Whatever you say, Underdog."

The other Rangers fanned out into a defensive perimeter while the medics packed, patched, and taped Cade's wounds as quickly as they were able.

He confirmed that his grease pencil, compass, and tape measure were still in his pockets, then suppressed a wave of pain as he smiled at his Ranger brothers. "Okay. I'm going in."

"Good luck, Martin," Leagans said. "We'll be here when you get back."

Cade saluted his lieutenant, then did his best to conceal his pain and fatigue as he plodded inside the charred observation bunker. He hugged the wall on his way down the stairs to the bunker's entrance, and to the mission he had to face alone.

———∼∼∼———

After months of study, practice, and rehearsal, Cade had thought himself prepared for whatever awaited him inside the map room. He had memorized every glyph he couldn't see and every mark he needed to make, and he could execute each step of his protocol for the alteration of the devil's trap with his eyes closed.

None of them had included moving furniture.

The map room, the bunker's nerve center, was dominated by a huge plotting table with a map of the coastline and grid references for the section of the English Channel for which its crew had been tasked with directing artillery fire. Two wooden desks and chairs sat against the east wall, between the steel doors at the northeast and southeast corners.

Every last piece of it had to go before Cade's work could begin.

Tides of pain rolled inside him as he struggled to clear the room. The chairs weighed the least, so he removed them first, hurling them out the southeast door, into the communications suite. Next had gone the two desks—one with the chairs, the other through the northeast door, into the officers' quarters.

That left only the plotting table—a hulking slab nearly ten feet long, over three feet wide, and twice as solid as Fort fucking Knox.

I'll never get this thing out of here. He considered the room's dimensions, and where the demonic sigil sat within it. *I don't need it out—just out of the way.*

He crouched and braced his left shoulder under the table's edge.

A grunt of effort turned into a roar of agony as he tilted the plotting table onto its edge. Once gravity took over he dodged clear and let the table fall against the wall.

If my calculations are correct, the table is off the seal.

Its thick legs still protruded enough to interfere with his work. He stomped the two closest to the floor until they splintered and broke free. He tossed the table legs into the officers' quarters, cleared the last bits of detritus from the floor, and prepared himself to work when all his body wanted was to sink into unconsciousness.

He opened his water-resistant pouch and took out his tools.

A compass. A tape measure. Four pieces of twine, each thirteen feet long, inked with guides at eighth-of-an-inch intervals, and attached at either end to small, flat stones. A small tube of resin adhesive. And a grease crayon.

With shaking hands he pulled the tape measure along the bottom edge of each wall, confirming the room's dimensions. Just as Niko's notes indicated, it was precisely 4.2 meters wide and 5.2 meters long. He marked the center point of each wall for reference.

He set the tape measure along the room's north-south axis, just right of the center line. Using it as his guide, he stretched one piece of twine beside it. Then he repeated the process along the room's east-west axis to locate its center point. There he set the compass and aligned its needle with magnetic north. *Step one of the protocol, complete.*

He adjusted his first piece of twine to match the compass's north-south orientation. Then its partner was shifted to lie on the east-west parallel. The third piece of twine he placed from northwest to southeast; and the last he set from northeast to southwest. After a final check that the lines were precise and correct, he used the resin to affix one of each string's end stones to the concrete floor outside the bounds of the devil's trap. The adhesive dried quickly, so that by the time he had fixed the first stone of string four, he was ready to pull string one gently taut and fix its second stone into place. And so it went, until all four strings were locked down.

Step two of the protocol, complete. End of the easy part.

Grease crayon in hand, he stepped inside the circle of the trap, taking care not to disturb the strings as he squatted and pivoted. He knew the order of the symbols he had to draw, their shapes, every last detail. He had practiced it so many times that he had dreamed this part in its entirety. Yet now, with his wounds on fire, his muscles cramping, and his stomach in rebellion, he couldn't see it. He forgot all the rehearsals as he faced the blank slate of the bunker's floor. Now, the only time it mattered, he felt paralyzed with dread.

You know the first glyph. One at a time. Do it.

A check of his coordinates inside wedge one. He found the familiar mark on the twine, and trusted his hand to remember the curve of the arc and the curlicue at the end.

Adair's voice haunted his thoughts. *One mistake and all the demons fly free.*

The first glyph led his hand to the second, which flowed into the third. In his mind he saw the symbols and characters hidden beneath the concrete. It was painstaking work, superimposing hundreds of arcane shapes over others hidden from sight, but he was sure he could do it—if only his strength would last until he finished.

It has to. It has to, or the world dies.

One part of his labor bled into another as he submerged into his task. The further into the process he continued, the more he recognized the mental echoes of demonic taunting. Their voices were little more than whispers at first, easy to mistake for tricks of the wind, their suggestions of surrender possible to write off as his own faltering confidence.

Then he caught their stink in the air.

"I know your lies," he said as he worked, knowing the spirits would hear him. "And I know your tricks. Save them for someone who fears you."

Cade caught his breath and wiped sweat from his eyes. Looking down, he saw he was more than half finished. He had superscribed the first four wedges without incident, and half of the fifth wedge was complete. He tried to take a deep breath, only to feel his lungs resist the effort. He coughed into his sleeve; when he finished hacking like a consumptive, it was soaked with bloody sputum. The sigil's guardian was already starting to strike at him.

Fuck, that's not good.

He settled into place and forced himself to continue.

By the end of the fifth wedge he felt the demons' revolt swelling around him. Their malevolence clouded his thoughts with fear and doubt. They blurred his vision, their ancient cruelty amplified the pain of his wounds, and they made his hands shake as if from a palsy—all as he struggled to work blind magick with a grease crayon. He could glimpse the spirits on the edges of his perception, but they vanished when he tried to look at them.

"I know what you're doing," he said, defiant. "You think if you make me hurt, I'll try to work faster. You think . . . you can trick me into making a mistake." He caught his hand a fraction of a second before he did just that. Lifting the crayon from the floor, he forced himself to breathe and clear his mind. "Not. Today."

When his superscription of the seventh wedge was complete, a horrible crushing sensation took hold of his head. Spots swam in his vision, and he felt vomit course up his esophagus. He pulled off his helmet and shouted it full of blood and stomach acid. *Can't get any on the seal.* When the retching stopped, he hurled his helmet aside, well clear of the circle.

Time to finish this.

He knew the worst was yet to come. The scribing of the penultimate glyph would fully release the trap's guardian spirit, one whose remit no doubt included tormenting and slaying whoever set it free. Unless he finished the last mark and banished the spirits of the trap in a matter of seconds afterward, this was all going to end badly.

Four symbols from the end, blood ran from his nose. He sleeved the first drops away, but it rapidly grew worse. He tore two small strips of fabric off of his already ripped jacket and packed them into his nostrils.

As he finished the third-to-last symbol, the wounds in his side and shoulder bled through their bandages. He felt his blood soak through his uniform.

He couldn't feel his hands as he drew the next-to-last symbol. His vision blurred then doubled, and his fingers twitched. When the symbol was complete, a seizure racked his body, and the grease crayon fell from his hand.

Everything was spinning—

No, Cade realized. *The room's not spinning. I'm spinning.*

His body had risen from the floor. Now he was turning, revolving facedown above the devil's trap like the hand of a clock spinning in reverse. He couldn't breathe, and as a kaleidoscope of horrors manifested around him, he saw it was because a spirit, one whose burning skull was crowned with ram's horns, was choking him to death.

The beast's exquisite torments had only just begun, but even seconds in the hands of a demon felt like an eternity. Cade knew he had only seconds in which to act.

Barred from bringing yoked demons within half a mile of Normandy's coast, he had been given no choice but to come without magick in his hands or imbued into a weapon. But he hadn't been foolish enough to come this far unarmed.

He pulled out his canteen. Unscrewed its cap.

And flung a streak of holy water into the demon's face.

It roared like all the guns of war—but it let go of Cade long enough for him to fall to the floor. He dropped the canteen. Grabbed the grease crayon. Set it to the floor—

The demon's hand plunged inside Cade, through his back. He felt the monster's talons close around his heart. Panic overtook him, afflicted him with violent shakes—but he forced his hand to scribe the final mark.

From beneath the concrete, the trap's intricate design flared, described now in fiery strokes that set Cade's own vandalizing marks aflame.

Cade spent his last breaths on a command: "I banish thee! By the . . . Covenant! And the . . . names . . . most holy! OPHIEL, MICHAEL, TETRAGRAMMATON, ADONAI, JEHOVAM! Amen!"

A cyclone of fire raged inside the map room. With it came a terrible shrieking of wind and the fury of the unholy host plunging into the Flame Everlasting. Cade feared the conflagration was about to consume him, body and soul—

Silence.

Wisps of red mist snaked upward from the concrete floor, only to dissipate halfway to the low ceiling. The four lengths of twine smoldered, then collapsed into lines of black ash, which scattered as a sea wind swept over them.

Coughing blood, barely able to see, Cade staggered out of the map room, then out of the bunker. He squinted, expecting to meet daylight, but found a hazy sunset instead; time's passage had gone strange while he was locked in the embrace of demons. Across Pointe du Hoc he saw no trace of his brothers-in-arms—only the corpses of friend and foe, and a landscape devastated by bombs and artillery. The air was heavy with the tang of scorched metal, the stench of dead bodies left in the sun, the acrid smell of burnt hair.

He didn't know what drew him toward the cliffs. Perhaps it was the sight of the Allied fleet, thousands of ships crowding the English Channel; maybe it was the view of beaches lined with slain Americans and the burning wreckage of boats and tanks, the tide dimmed red with the blood of the fallen, the sand littered with thousands of dead fish and fowl. Everywhere Cade looked, he faced a spectacle of carnage unlike anything he had ever thought possible.

He turned. Took two weak steps toward the bunker.

His legs buckled. For a second it felt as if he were flying.

Someone far away called his name, but by then his sight had gone black. He heard another voice shout for a medic, but by then it was too late.

Cade surrendered to the darkness, and all he felt was relief.

His fight was over.

"Appear, damn you! I command thee, appear instanter, or feel my wrath!"

It was hard for Kein to stand composed inside the operator's circle. He trembled with a rage that almost shook the wand from his hand, and he felt the quaking of his fury deep in his core. His outrage threatened to consume him like a fire with an appetite of its own.

Foul vapors roiled outside his circle. The demon was here but refused to show itself. Kein grazed the coals in the brazier with the tip of his wand. He was rewarded by a murderous roar, followed by the tenuous apparition of Hell's prime minister manifested in the outer ring.

Yellow eyes full of hatred blazed from the smoky darkness.

WHY HAST THOU DISTURBED ME AGAIN SO SOON?

"You know why, damn you!" Kein wanted to rack LUCIFUGE ROFOCALE with torments, but the Covenant required that he give the spirit a chance to answer. "I set the stage for a global holocaust! But morning has come and gone, and my labors have yielded only silence! Where is my black dawn? My heaven aflame? My sea of blood choked with wormwood?"

ALL UNDONE BY THE *NIKRAIM*.

"How?"

THY SNARE WAS NEGATED GLYPH BY GLYPH, AND ITS LEGION BANISHED BACK INTO MY CARE. The demon *tsk*ed. A PITY. I WOULD HAVE SAVORED YOUR DAY OF CHAOS.

"At least tell me the *nikraim* perished in the effort."

A grin of fangs. THE COVENANT DOES NOT PERMIT ME TO LIE TO THEE.

Bad enough to be beaten—I will not be mocked, as well. "I banish thee and command thee depart in peace, back to the Flame Everlasting!" Kein shouted the holy names to finish the ritual, his hoarse cry buried beneath LUCIFUGE ROFOCALE's gales of cruel laughter.

Thunder rocked Kein's conjuring room, and the demon vanished—but its sinister chortling echoed in the shadows. Bitter tears of shame stung Kein's eyes.

Half a century of planning . . .

Nearly two years of work . . .

. . . all for nothing.

Kein's self-control faltered. Then it disintegrated.

Abandoning centuries of discipline, he let slip a scream of frustration, then another. He swatted aside his lectern and grimoire, then sprang from the operator's circle, a berserker on a rampage. He picked up one of the room's shoulder-height candelabra and swung it like a quarterstaff at the others. Brass stands clanged across the cement floor. Fragile, hand-cast candles smashed against the walls and broke into bits.

Kein hammered the floor with the candelabrum until it bent, and then he flung it away. It crashed into his workbench, shattering handblown glass decanters and drenching the table and floor with inks, oils, and exotic chemicals.

He dropped to his knees in the middle of his now-marred circle of protection. Fists balled, he raged in wordless howls at the ceiling until he gasped for air.

Spent and humbled, he returned to his senses with a jolt of self-consciousness.

It cannot end like this. I cannot allow it.

The master karcist closed his eyes and took slow breaths. In his ears he heard the beat of his pulse slow and soften. He knuckled the tears of rage from his eyes.

I've lost a great battle. But the war is not over yet.

Kein stood and cast off his ceremonial robes. He brushed chalk dust and motes of glass from his trousers, then smoothed the wrinkles from his shirt. Purged of his imbalancing fury, he took a moment to adjust his cuff links and straighten the knot of his necktie.

That's better.

He collected his suit jacket from the hook by the stairs and pulled it on as he climbed the steps back to his private bunker. Upstairs, a chilled bottle of Riesling awaited him.

In a few hours he would return to clean the mess he had made. The broken glass he would dispose of; the spilled liquids he would mop up. Tomorrow he would bleach and repaint the floor. The day after that he would begin the tedious work of replacing the laboratory glassware, the candelabrum, and the candles.

That would be his penance for a moment of unshackled temper.

And when my atonement is done, he vowed to himself, *I shall summon the spirit I set to guard my trap—and make it reveal to me exactly how my apocalypse was unmade.*

51

Neither warm nor cold, wind washed over Cade and coaxed him from the arms of oblivion. He remembered falling to the ground, but now he hovered above it.

He drank in the desolation of Pointe du Hoc, mystified by its surreal quality of light and shadow. What he had thought was wind seemed not to affect the dust in the air or the leaves on the trees, but it streaked the world's details into chiaroscuro blurs, as if the earth were a watercolor painting exposed to a tempest. Where wind would have howled, this storm cried like a choir out of tune; the sky resonated with minor-chord lamentations. Stray thoughts circled the earth as if from an endless spring of consciousness, a fountainhead of dread and desire.

Below him lay a face at once strange and familiar: his own. Not the one he knew from the mirror, but the one he more rarely glimpsed and sometimes failed to recognize in photographs. Sprawled on the ground. Eyes open but sightless. Bruised, bloodied, filthy.

Like a magnet reacting to its opposite, he sensed another presence. Turning in place, he saw no one at first—and then there was something at his side. A mist, or a shadow. Vapors tenuous and pale. They coalesced and took on a form not unlike that of a man, but without definition, as if an artist's mannequin could shape itself from fog. Despite its lack of eyes, it seemed to regard him with a reflection of his own curiosity.

"What . . . who . . . are you?"

It answered in whispers of smoke and song, with a voice Cade felt more than he heard.

I AM YOUR BOND-SPIRIT, GESHURIEL.

The claim struck Cade as improbable. Adair had told him he was bonded before birth to an angel, yet this creature was drab, like exhausted wash water. "You're an angel?"

I AM A SERAPH, THE HIGHEST ORDER OF ANGEL.

"No offense, but I expected something a bit more . . ."

GRANDIOSE? MY KIND AND I HAVE, IN THE PAST, EMPLOYED SUCH DECEP-TIONS WHEN NECESSARY. BUT I AM BONDED TO YOUR SOUL AND THEREFORE ENJOINED FROM LYING TO YOU. YOU SEE ME AND MY KIND AS WE ARE, NOT AS YOUR ROMANTICS WOULD HAVE US BE.

More entities became visible around them. A handful were ashen shadows that lingered without apparent agenda or urgency. Others, though smaller, blazed with white light so intense it seemed as if it should hurt to look at them, yet Cade felt no need to avert his gaze. He faced GESHURIEL. "Those gray shadows? More angels?"

WATCHERS. MINOR SPIRITS OF LITTLE IMPORT.

"What about the others—the walking bonfires?"

DO YOU NOT RECOGNIZE YOUR FELLOW MEN?

The angel's reply compelled Cade to look again with new expectations. Piercing the auras he saw the faces of men he recognized—Sergeant Sykes, Lieutenant Leagans, Corporal Pawlikowski. He remained perplexed. "Why don't angels shine like men?"

IT HAS EVER BEEN THUS. SUCH IS THE WILL OF THE DIVINE.

Below them, the Rangers huddled around Cade's unresponsive body. The medic worked like a man possessed, and the lieutenant and the sergeant got their hands into the mix. From his elevated vantage, Cade thought their efforts looked nothing less than heroic.

Another question returned his focus to the angel. "Why am I seeing you now?"

BECAUSE YOUR SOUL STRAINS ITS TETHER TO YOUR DAMAGED FLESH.

"No—I know my body's dying. What I mean is: Why didn't I see you *before*? When I spent sixteen months lying in a bed in Scotland. Where were you then?"

AT YOUR SIDE, AS I AM NOW. AS I WILL REMAIN UNTIL YOUR END.

"But why didn't I see you?"

YOUR SPIRIT WAS SET IN STASIS BY MAGICK, AS IF SEALED IN AMBER. IN THAT STATE NOTHING COULD YOU PERCEIVE—NOT EVEN MY PRESENCE.

On the ground, the medic grew visibly frustrated. Reading the grim expressions on the faces of Sykes and Leagans, Cade asked GESHURIEL, "I'm gonna die, aren't I?"

IT IS THE FATE OF ALL THINGS UNDER HEAVEN. ONLY THE EMPYREAN IS ETERNAL.

"When I die, will you bring my soul to Heaven?"

THAT IS NOT MY PURPOSE.

"But could you take me there?"

IF THAT IS YOUR COMMAND.

"My command?" Cade pondered the implications of the angel's statement. "You have to obey my commands?"

UNTIL DEATH SEVERS OUR BOND, YES.

Temptation harrowed Cade's thoughts—there were so many questions he wanted to ask his parents, so many things he wanted to tell them, not least of which was good-bye. Could it really be within his reach? He had to know. "I want you to take me to Heaven."

I THINK YOU ARE MISTAKEN.

"I'm not asking your advice. I'm making this a command. Take me to Heaven."

AS YOU COMMAND, SO MOTE IT BE.

Together they ascended, leaving behind Cade's ravaged meat on the dusty ground of Pointe du Hoc, climbing instead through the invisible maelstrom, into an endless silver sky. Pale clouds gathered behind them, stealing the earth from view, until the two of them were all that seemed to exist in an ethereal realm of alabaster mist and ivory shadows.

"Why did you accept bonding? To me, specifically, I mean."

IT WAS THE WILL OF THE DIVINE.

"That's the only reason?"

WE ARE MESSENGERS AND SERVANTS. WE OBEY THE WILL OF THE DIVINE.

"And you're okay with that?"

THE ANGELS WHO REBELLED WERE CAST DOWN INTO THE FLAME EVER-LASTING. THEY ARE THE FALLEN. THE SCORNED. AFTER THEIR FALL, THE DIVINE STRIPPED US ALL OF FREE WILL.

Without warning they pierced a pearly veil and left behind the blank void of eternity for a realm of sallow shores beneath a platinum dome of sky. A dim orb of light perched on the wide horizon, casting its pale glow across a becalmed sea the color of pewter.

Ashen shadows wandered the shoreline and floated in droves overhead, all droning the same monotonous but mellifluous song, their voices melodic but bereft of inspiration. It was a realm of cold beauty and devotion devoid of passion.

As Cade and GESHURIEL flew inland, over broad plains swaying with cinereous waves of grain, all Cade saw were endless legions of gray presences serenading the stark, distant sun.

"Is this a trick?"

THIS IS HEAVEN.

"Then where are the souls of the dead?"

THERE ARE NO HUMAN SOULS IN HEAVEN. The angel's reply was so flat and matter-of-fact that it filled Cade's essence with dread. Then it asked, WHAT DID YOU HOPE TO FIND?

"It doesn't matter. Can you take me to Hell?"

THAT WOULD BE UNWISE.

"Answer me: Can you bring me safely into and back out of Hell?"

I AM CAPABLE OF SUCH A JOURNEY.

"Then let's go. Now."

The angel offered no further argument. It extended its wing of pallid smoke around Cade and carried him upward, away from the monotony of Heaven, into the blanched ether between realms. Forever they seemed to beat on against an unseen current, tiny vessels fighting against an upswell of darkness that resisted their approach.

In time Cade noted the darkening of the void. Dolorous cries rose up on chilling tides. It took Cade a moment to realize it wasn't a physical sensation of cold—it was a manifestation of despair, of hopelessness, and of utter seething contempt.

Before he realized they were there, sooty clouds engulfed him and GESHURIEL. Cade imagined it was like diving into the tower of smoke crowning a wildfire.

The longer they fell, the louder and more dissonant became the music from below. Cade recognized the hideous mockery of melody: it was the Infernal orchestra of PAIMON, a great king of Hell, an angel fallen from the Order of Dominations—and Adair's demonic patron.

GESHURIEL parted the ebon clouds, revealing the dark majesty that sprawled across the scorched, cratered landscape below. The city of Dis, the metropolis of the Fallen: nine concentric circular tiers cut into the black rock of Hell, the outermost ring level with the surrounding charred plain, and each successive inner tier set miles deeper than the last. The city was hundreds of miles in diameter, and its tiers were spiked with marvels of demonic architecture. Rivers of sludge flowed in endless circles within the top tier; the next level sported rivers of blood. Beyond that, Cade was unable to pierce the under-gloom's shadows—though the ring-shaped lake of fire at the pit's nadir was impossible to miss.

"Closer," Cade commanded, and again GESHURIEL complied. He wanted to see the souls trapped in the city. If it was to this forsaken place that his parents' souls had been condemned, Cade had to see it for himself. He needed to know.

Speeding as one, he and GESHURIEL raced over the capital of Hell.

The only denizens Cade saw in its pits of torment, in its boulevards of shadow and regret, were the shades of the Fallen, whose hues were darker than those of the angels but otherwise not substantially different. Nowhere did he see the luminous shimmers he had glimpsed on the battlefield of Pointe du Hoc. Not a single human soul.

Cade hovered silently, in shock, above the center of Dis. Stricken, he faced GESHURIEL once more. "Where are they?"

WHO?

"The souls of the damned."

THERE ARE NONE.

"What do you mean?"

THERE ARE NO HUMAN SOULS IN HELL.

Cade's imagination reeled. "What about Limbo? Or Purgatory?"

THERE ARE NO SUCH REALMS, EXCEPT IN HUMAN FICTIONS.

Staring down into the Flame Everlasting, Cade felt the first stirrings of true despair. "I . . . I don't understand."

YES, YOU DO, the angel said, its tone now one of pity. BUT YOU DO NOT WANT TO.

JULY

Wet wood smoked inside the iron stove, stubborn in its refusal to catch fire. Outside the window of Anja's lakeside cabin, rain fell in silver whispers. A chill crept under the front door in spite of the rug she had piled up against it. Against her frugal instincts, she baptized the damp log with a few of her last remaining drops of kerosene. At last the fire took hold. The black wood reddened, and a minute later its sodden core let out a snap, the sound of winter's embrace being broken. She warmed her hands and looked forward to a warm night's sleep.

She stood, turned, and recoiled at the sight of an intruder—

"Hello, lass. Long time." It was Adair. Or, rather, a shade of him, an astral projection, shimmering and translucent, standing in the center of her abode in the middle of nowhere. The sight of him rekindled all her feelings of shame for having abandoned him.

"How did you find me?"

"How do you think?" A prankster's grin. "Magick."

She shook her head, refusing to believe. "I'm warded."

"Lass, I put that ink on your back with my own hand."

It made sense: Who better to circumvent a charm than its maker?

She feigned nonchalance and went about preparing a mug of tea. "So . . . you could have found me any time you wanted? Congratulations. It took you over two years."

"Only because I wasn't looking." He cast appraising looks around her abode. "Rustic. I approve. Where are we, exactly?"

"About a mile outside Nikkaluokta." Noting the master's interrogative glance, she clarified, "Northern Sweden. About thirty miles from the Norwegian border."

"Ah. I'm guessing you're not here for the nightlife."

"In fact the northern lights are quite beautiful, but it is not the season for them." She picked up a bellows and used it to breathe life into her fire. "Why were you not looking?"

"Pardon?"

"For me. You said you were not looking. Why not?"

Adair shrugged. "I assumed you had your reasons for leaving." He wandered the cabin's main room and pretended to take an interest in its knickknacks—snowshoes, fishing gear, skis, Anja's military ruck, her Mosin-Nagant rifle. "I respected your right to be left in peace."

"Does that mean you forgive me for leaving?"

"A conversation for another time."

She regarded her feet to avoid Adair's eyes. "Then why are you here?"

"I need your help." When she looked up, he continued. "It's Cade. He's dying."

Cade's memory still filled Anja with resentment. "What happened?"

"He landed with the troops in Normandy."

"Why?"

"Because he *fucking had to,* that's why. The rest doesn't matter." The master calmed himself. "Army docs patched him up on the beach, then shipped him back to England. He's in the Royal Victoria Hospital, in Netley, near Southampton Dock."

She framed her concern as curiosity. "How bad is it?"

Adair was despondent. "A coma. A real one, this time."

"Prognosis?"

"Not good. Not fucking good, at all." He tried to take her hand, but his passed through hers, an illusion without substance. He settled for looking her in the eye. "He needs you."

"No. He does not. He has you."

"Lass, I've done all I can, but healing was never my forte. Not like it is for you." Sorrow shone in his eyes. "It's not just Cade who needs you. I need you, too. Please come back."

It was a greater burden than she was willing to bear. "Master . . . I cannot." She turned a desperate eye toward the hills and mountains outside her window. "It took me a long time to find a place where I could be at peace."

"You can have peace when the war's over."

"But the war never ends. That is what you always taught me." She fixed him with a hard look. "I have been free of demons for months. I almost feel sane again. Some days I make it from dawn to dark without taking a drink." She went to the stove, where steam jetted from the spout of her kettle. She lifted it from the cooktop and filled her mug, then sank a steel tea ball into it. The aroma of the steeping tea was at least a partial balm for her anger. "I am not sure I want to take up the Art again so soon—or maybe ever."

He was horrified. "Don't say that! To lose a karcist like you at a time like this—"

"You lost me two years ago."

"You can come home."

"Home." His saccharine platitude dredged up memories raw and painful. "I tried to go home. . . . It was no longer there."

His entreaty took on a note of desperation. "You don't have to stay. Just help me bring him back to the land of the living. After that? Fall off the face of the earth if that's your wish."

She let out a derisive bark of a laugh. "You make it sound so simple! And how would I get to you? It is not as if I can travel freely. The Swedes *hate* Russians. So unless you have one of your precious mirrors somewhere nearby—?"

"Afraid not. But even if I did, we couldn't use it. Kein's watching for that, now. And I can't take a chance on leading him straight to Cade, not when the lad's this vulnerable." His brow crinkled. "Can't you fly back?"

"I have not agreed to come."

"But if you did? Humor me."

The prospect of resuming a magickal regimen dismayed Anja to her core. "I would have to check my ephemeris for the best date and hour. Fast and meditate for three days. Scribe my circle. Exorcise my tools." She sighed as she pondered the labors involved in the step known as "the preparation of the operator." "Can the doctors keep him alive another two weeks?"

"I fucking well hope so."

She hid her face in her hands, unable to believe she was letting herself be dragged back into a world and life she thought she had escaped. Then her conscience nagged: *Not escaped—abandoned.* She lowered her hands and faced Adair. "The stars permitting, I will join you at dusk in ten days. Two weeks if the planets are unfavorable."

A grateful nod. "Ten days, then. I'll await you at sunset, in the gazebo on the hospital's pier." His astral shade vanished. Anja wondered how long it would take her to regret her decision; then she laughed at herself with contempt.

Who do I hope to deceive? I regret it already.

53

Moonlight slashed bright and argent through the windows of Royal Victoria Hospital's eastern corridor, opposite a row of recovery suites. A breeze perfumed by lavender and roses wended down the passage, which embodied a uniquely British fusion of dignity and simplicity.

Adair and Anja's footsteps disturbed the hospital's late-night quiet as they hurried from one section of its south wing to another. He led the way while she pushed a wheeled hospital cart draped with a sheet. With a scowl of discomfort, Anja tugged at the hem of her borrowed nurse's uniform. She glowered at him. "Is this disguise really necessary?"

"We can't risk drawing attention." They passed through another set of double doors into a section of single-occupant dormitories. "He's down here. I pulled a few strings at Allied command, got him a private room, like they give the officers."

The cart's wheels squeaked as Anja sped up to keep pace. "I doubt he cares."

"It's for *your* benefit, not his. Can't have witnesses, can we?" He stole a look through an open door as they passed and marveled at the machinery that had been hooked up to the soldier inside. "Amazing, isn't it?"

His reluctant accomplice seemed oblivious. "What is?"

"This. The hospital. New drugs, new surgical techniques. Medicine's come a long way in the last hundred years. Imagine where it'll be in a hundred more."

The young Russian woman was unimpressed. "It will be where it is now. Lagging behind war and every other way men hurt one another."

Adair had no antidote for her cynicism, only the distraction of mission. "In here." He entered Cade's room, then stood aside and held open the door while she pushed the cart inside. She parked it at the foot of Cade's bed as Adair locked the door.

Once their privacy was assured, Anja tore the peaked white cap from her head and cast it aside. Her black hair tumbled free as she leaned over Cade. She pressed her left palm to his chest and her right to the side of his face. Then she shut her eyes and concentrated. There was nothing for Adair to do but await Anja's diagnosis.

She removed her hands from Cade. "There is damage inside him. Bleeding, metal the surgeons missed. But that is not the cause of his coma. His soul still lives, but is not here."

"He's astral-projecting?"

"I think so. But he must be very far away. The link to his soul is almost gone."

It was both better and worse news than Adair had expected. He had hoped that Cade's mind was present and merely in need of aid regaining awareness. The worst-case scenario would have been to learn Cade's soul was already expired, his body just an empty vessel, but the lad's current predicament was nearly as dire.

Adair didn't try to hide his fear. "Can you bring him back?"

"I do not know." She removed the sheet from the cart at the foot of the bed. In place of its usual freight—clean sheets, bedpans, and the like—they had loaded it with her grimoire, her tools of the Art, and a collection of arcane powders, unguents, and oils. "First I must fix the wounds to his flesh. When that is done, I can try to coax his soul back into his body."

"How long, you think?"

She unfurled her tool roll on the floor. "I will finish by dawn. If I succeed, his soul will return at sunrise. If I fail, and sever the bond between body and soul, he will die."

It was a grim prognosis. In the face of it, Adair felt helpless and small. He watched her pull the blankets off of Cade. "Can I help?"

Anja removed Cade's pajama shirt. "Spare me from interruption." She cast the flannel top aside and pulled down Cade's pajama pants. "Guard the door."

He unlocked the door, opened it, then paused on his way out. "Thank you."

Her mood was dour as she scribed eldritch symbols with holy oil on Cade's forehead. "Thank me if he lives."

<hr />

Anxious and spent, Anja sat beside Cade's bed. And she waited.

After so many months free of demons and their torments, the past several days had been a whirlwind of exhilaration and disgust, one after the other. Every moment of narcotic delight she had enjoyed at the return of power, at the ability to see the unseen and sense the unknown, had come at a cost measured in blood and pain.

Food hadn't tasted right since she yoked BUER for its healing gifts. BELIAL always fouled her digestion, but she needed its talents in the astral plane. Yoking ANDREALPHUS for the ability to fly as a bird had cursed Anja with unpredictable nosebleeds. RAMIEL, her hellbeast of burden, was tame by demonic standards; it restricted its harassment to nightmares. And though she would not have found her way to Southampton so quickly without the unerring directional sense of NUMORIS, its penchant for driving karcists to chew off their fingernails and scratch through their own flesh had led her to free it and compel its peaceful departure as soon as she had reached the hospital's pier the night before.

Was it worth it? Or did I do all this for nothing?

The clock on the wall seemed frozen. Anja swore its hands had been locked forever just shy of quarter past five.

Faint smudges of diluted ink stained Cade's flesh. Anja's ritual had required drawing dozens of Enochian symbols on various parts of his body, in order to recall his wandering soul and restore his battle-ravaged flesh. After the ceremony was over, she had done her best to erase the marks with a cloth and a bowl of warm water Adair had fetched at her request. Most of the glyphs were gone, but ink-stained water had pooled along the edges of Cade's fingernails, in the creases where his limbs met his torso, and at the corners of his mouth.

His chest rose and fell in a slow rhythm, his breathing almost too faint for Anja to discern. If she didn't know the depths of his wounds, she would have thought it possible he was merely sleeping, lost somewhere in the uncharted fathoms of dream.

Outside the door, heavy steps. She imagined Adair pacing in the corridor as the predawn sky blanched before the rising sun. *The master needed me to return. But does he want me here? If Cade hadn't been hurt, would Adair ever have tried to find me?*

Questions impossible to answer. She could ask Adair, but he had a gift for replies that shed more heat than light. *It makes no difference,* she decided. *Why I left, why he asked me to come back. None of it matters now. Home, family, country—none of them mean what I thought they did.* She remembered the carnage of Stalingrad. The tragedy in Kharkov. The betrayal at Toporok. *Everything I thought I was fighting for turned out to be a lie.*

But not Cade. He had tried to be her friend, no matter how many times she had pushed him away. The American had been a fool. Probably still was. And for many reasons, not all of which Anja could explain, she still disliked him. But he was, if nothing else, genuine. Naïve and too earnest for his own good, but never duplicitous.

"I know it is not your fault you are 'special,'" she whispered to him. "Adair told me it was something he helped your father do to you, before you were born." She took his hand. "I was unfair to you. The truth is . . . you are a decent man. And I do not hate you."

He gasped. She recoiled and let go of his hand as his back arched off the mattress and his eyes opened. His face was a mask of wonder—or perhaps terror—for a few seconds, until he exhaled and relaxed, sinking onto the bed.

Anja stood over him. "Welcome back."

As he saw her, strange emotions glimmered in his eyes—but like dying embers they faded. A shadow of despair fell over him. He rolled away from her. "Get out."

"Cade, you were right. We do not need to like each other to be allies. I am sorry."

"It doesn't matter." His voice quavered with grief. "Nothing matters. Just go."

She circled the bed to confront him, only to see tears fall from his closed eyes. Perhaps feeling the weight of her concern, he pulled his pillow over his head, then cocooned himself under his bedsheet. His physical injuries were healed—Anja knew that beyond a doubt. But now she understood he had suffered spiritual wounds beyond her ability to salve.

Something in him had changed . . . and not for the better.

⁂

Kein awoke to muffled thunder, followed by the keening of sirens. Outside his guesthouse in the Wolfsschanze compound, the afternoon came alive with soldiers scrambling in multiple directions to guard posts, all of them shouting in panic and confusion.

I know this music—this is no drill.

He rolled out of bed, dressed in a hurry, and raced out his front door into the midst of bedlam. Armored cars sped past in either direction. Alarms wailed from the compound's PA system and merged with those of medical trucks and fire engines into an earsplitting din. Kein tried to halt a trio of SS officers sprinting past, only to be knocked aside. Then he saw the source of the camp's hysteria: A black cloud twisted upward from the conference building three hundred meters away, on the other side of the train tracks from Kein's private house.

Then he was running with everyone else.

He reached the scene long after the firefighters and members of Hitler's elite bodyguard unit. High-ranking officers staggered out of the smoke-filled conference building. Four others were carried out, burnt and bloody. The Führer was nowhere to be seen.

Kein stopped a passing firefighter. "What happened?"

"Somebody bombed the Führer's meeting with the generals!"

Ignoring the warnings of the firefighters and the SS men near its entrance, Kein ran inside the building, trusting ANDRAMELECH to shield him from fire.

Moving against the line of wounded men being assisted out of the wreckage led Kein to the main meeting room. Its conference table had been reduced to splinters and fractured planks. All the chairs had been thrown against the walls with such force that not one was still intact. The ceiling had fallen in, leaving wires with half-melted insulation dangling from exposed joists.

Officers and medics surrounded the Führer, whose trousers were tattered and blackened. Soot smeared Hitler's face and coat. He was standing and impatiently answering the medics' questions, which Kein took as a hopeful omen.

Then the Führer looked up. When he recognized Kein, his face contorted with rage. "You!" He pointed at Kein. "This was your fault!" Everyone in the room and the corridor outside stared at Kein, who preferred to go unnoticed during his sojourns at Wolfsschanze. The officers and medics attending Hitler retreated as he waved his arms and ranted, "You said you'd protect me! That I'd be safe! You call *this* safe? What are you doing to find the traitors?"

Kein answered the Führer's fire with ice. "Everyone . . . get out."

The others moved to comply with Kein's order, then froze as Hitler bellowed, "He doesn't give orders here! Only I give orders here! You people obey *me*!"

Kein infused his voice with the suggestive force of ESIAS: "*I said get out.*"

Even the Führer stood shocked as his underlings scurried out of the meeting room, then cleared the corridor outside. Marshaling every ounce of menace invested in him by the powers of Hell, Kein confronted the suddenly cowed leader of the Third Reich.

"You seem to enjoy hearing yourself talk, my Führer. Now you will listen to me. In case it escaped your notice, you just survived a front-row seat to an exploding bomb. Do you think that was luck? I assure you, it was not." He moved closer to Hitler and met the shorter man's glare with his own. "If the demons I tasked to defend you had not been here, you would now be little more than bloody confetti in this pile of kindling you used to call a conference room. Make no mistake: You are alive and drawing breath right now only *because* of my precautions." He brushed a bit of ash off of Hitler's shoulders. "But if you doubt that, you need but say the word, and I will revoke my protections without delay."

Hitler shook with righteous indignation. "Is that a threat?"

"Of course not, my Führer. I am just reminding you that without my hand to guide them, those demonic bodyguards you take for granted will make a sport of driving you mad. A few days at their mercy, and you will be ready to eat a bullet to escape their tortures. So, for your own sake, spare me your threats, and do everything in your power to make certain nothing happens to me. Because if *I die*—" He emphasized his parting thought with a firm poke in the center of Hitler's pigeon chest. "—*you die.*"

AUGUST

A river black as coal flowed past the Royal Victoria Hospital's pier, its surface rippled by a breeze. Cade watched the water slip past. Once he might have seen poetry in it. Now all he saw was liquid obeying gravity and being disturbed by air that moved because the earth turned. Even the moon was nothing more than a ball of rock reflecting sunlight, an orb as bereft of romance as it was devoid of air. They were all just gears in a clockwork universe long deserted by its maker.

Footsteps drew near across the pier's groaning planks. Their cadence Cade knew well. Unwilling to invite conversation, he kept his eyes on the river as Adair sat beside him on the wrought-iron bench inside the pier's gazebo.

A rustling of papers. Adair pretended to read them, then feigned a reaction to a question Cade hadn't asked. "These? These are your discharge papers." He folded them and tried to hand them to Cade, who ignored the gesture. Adair continued as he tucked the orders inside his own coat. "Your doctors say there's nothing wrong with you. Not physically, anyway. They want your bed for someone who really needs it. Can't say as I blame them."

The silence between them drew out like a blade.

Adair took out a pack of cigarettes. Lit one. Offered it to Cade, who took it and filled his chest with a long drag. His head swam from the nicotine rush, a sensation he hadn't felt in months. As he exhaled through his nose, Adair lit another Lucky, then set the pack and his lighter on the bench between them. "You haven't said a word in weeks. Not since Anja brought you back. Have you gone mute, or are you just being a cunt?"

Cade blew smoke into Adair's face.

"Right. Cunt, it is." Another drag. "If we had years to burn, I'd say 'Go with God' and leave you to it. But we don't have time for this shite. The war's not done, and neither are we."

"Speak for yourself."

"He talks! Halle-fucking-lujah! It's a miracle! Now that the ice is broken, maybe you can tell me what your problem is, you scabby bastard."

Cade pulled on the Lucky until it burned nearly down to his fingertips; then he flicked its smoldering end into the river. "My problem is that none of this matters."

"None of what? The fuck are you on about?"

"*This.* The war. The world. *Life.* It's all pointless. All of it, all of us. Everything we do. Everything we care about. None of it means shit."

Adair watched him with paternal concern. "What happened to you out there?"

"In Normandy? Nothing. Just the mission."

The master discarded his own expired cigarette. "After that. Anja says you did some astral projection, took a long holiday. Where'd you go?"

Cade stared across the river, into the darkness. "I met my bonded spirit. He took me up to Heaven. Then into Hell." He aimed an accusatory look at Adair. "Ever seen them?"

"I've had a vision or two."

"They're wastelands. Bleak, eternal, and completely barren of human souls." He studied the guilt and regret that played across Adair's craggy face. "But you knew that, didn't you?"

A sad nod. "Aye."

"Where are they, Adair? Where are all the human souls?"

He shot a sidelong look at Cade from beneath an arched gray eyebrow. "Where do you think they are?"

Dredging up the truth freighted Cade's words with sorrow. "They're gone."

Sympathy softened the master's rough baritone. "Aye. Our souls are as mortal as our flesh. No afterlife for us—no eternal paradise, no Flame Everlasting. Just oblivion."

It was still impossible for Cade to wrap his mind around it. "But . . . why?"

"It's the way the world was made. We all shine with Empyrean flame, each of us blazing a billion times brighter than any angel ever did . . . but we don't last."

"But the scriptures go on and on about the glory of the angels, about how beautiful and powerful they are."

Adair nodded. "When they're reflecting the light of the Divine, they can be the most amazing things you'll ever see. But that's not *their* nature."

"So those boring gray shades I saw—"

"Are their true essences. They don't dazzle on their own, but they were never meant to. That's why the Divine made us." Reading Cade's perplexed reaction, he added, "The angels were made in the image of God, as we were. But each of us represents only one aspect of the Divine. Angels were cast in the mold of God's eternal form, but after SATAN's lot rebelled they all lost their free will. Humanity was made to reflect God's creative force—but like sparks cast off a bonfire, we're only meant to burn for a moment in the darkness before we fade away."

It was a strange and chilling vision, one that to Cade seemed designed to deny the human race even a glimmer of hope. "But if our souls die with us . . . what difference does anything make? Who cares if we're good or evil? Kind or cruel?"

"It makes as much difference as we decide it does."

"But if we don't go to Heaven or Hell—"

"Then so what? So there's no endless garden of treats for the good boys and girls; no eternity of getting rogered by demons for the miscreants. Just the same empty silence at the end of the line for each and every one of us. But why does that change anything? Morality that has to be bought with bribes or coerced with threats is just shite. The one is nothing but greed, the other just fear. Truly *moral* behavior comes from a place of love. It's about empathy. Compassion. Mercy. Seeing the Other in yourself, and yourself in them. We all have to serve something in this life, but we get to choose what it is. For some, it's love; for others, country. But *we* choose."

Cade remembered a conversation years earlier, when Stefan had told him much the same thing. Without asking, Cade pulled another Lucky from Adair's pack and lit it. "If there's no afterlife for us, why do all the religions promise it?"

"Salesmanship, mostly. Makes the rabble easier to control. After all, if a million starving people knew there was nothing waiting for them but the grave, that this one life was their only shot at being happy, you think they'd let the rich and powerful walk all over them? Fuck, no. Heads would roll. And the elites can't have that, can they? So they force-feed the masses bullshit by calling it sugarplums. . . . That's the way it's always been. And very few people ever see the truth with their own eyes the way you did."

Nettlesome questions still nagged at Cade. "I see what you're saying, and I understand why most people don't know better. But the angels all know the truth, don't they?"

"Of course."

"Even the Fallen?"

A derisive snort. "Especially the Fallen."

"Then why do demons make deals for human souls they can never collect? I mean, they let us summon them. They grant us powers and knowledge. They even let us yoke them. And all they ask in return is that we promise to let them roast our eternal souls for a thousand years here, ten thousand years there. But if our souls are mortal, and they know it—what's the goddamned point? What do they get out of all of this, if not souls?"

Adair chortled with genuine amusement. "Congratulations, lad. You've just discovered the great cosmic joke of magick. There have been karcists who lived hundreds of years and went to their graves without the truth you now possess." He paused to light a new cigarette. "At heart, all angels and demons want the same thing: to increase the quotient of human suffering, misery, fear, and anxiety. But they go about it in different ways.

"Thousands of years ago, the angels concocted a message of repression and spoon-fed it to us. Made us believe God would punish us if we indulged our desires and enjoyed the physical pleasures of this world. But they knew not to take something away without promising something better in return: freedom from suffering, and eternal life in the world to come, if only we deny ourselves all the joys and beauties of this one.

"The demons? They love to stir up chaos. To them, mucking with God's universal order is an end in itself. But they come into their own when they deal with karcists. They bully us into making pledges of eternal suffering and damnation—not because they could ever make good on their threats, but to ensure that people like us don't fully enjoy the time we have or the power we wield. They'll extend our lives for centuries and let us shape the primal forces of reality—as long as they think they've tainted our every moment with fear."

Cade's mental picture of the cosmos felt as if it were coming into focus for the first time in his life. "Angels and demons . . . resent us. Because we have free will."

"Now you're getting it."

"They hate us because we imagine. Because we create and reshape reality." More pieces of the puzzle revealed themselves. "And demons don't *let* us summon them, or command them, or yoke them. They submit because they have *no choice*—because they have no free will, but we do. Our spark—it's what gives us the power to control them. And that's why they despise us."

"*Good.* Keep going."

"The angels are still loyal to God. That's why we can't compel their service, because they answer to Him alone. But they and the demons exact their grudges against us by playing on our fear of death . . . and our envy of the one thing they both take for granted: *immortality.*"

Adair rewarded Cade's summary with mocking bow. "And there you have it, lad. The secrets of magick and the universe, in a nutshell."

It seemed to Cade a perverse vision, a cruel way to order the cosmos. Thinking of himself as being complicit in its amorality left him queasy.

Smoke spilled from Adair's mouth as he said, "I'm glad you're talking again. It's been good to hear your voice." He snuffed his Lucky on the side of the bench and stood. "But, if you'll excuse me, I've a war to finish."

Cade stood and faced his master. "What about me?"

A mocking lilt: "What *about* you?"

"Knowing what I know . . . what do I do now?"

Adair locked his callused hands on Cade's shoulders. The master beamed with pride and courage. "You get up. You go on. And you *burn brightly.*"

55

OCTOBER

As heavy as the table in the villa's study was, it shook like a leaf in a gale when Adair pummeled it. "This is fucking hopeless. We've dug through this shite for weeks." He gathered up a fistful of telegrams and transcripts from the Allied intelligence services. "It's all dead ends, the fucking lot of it!" He hurled the crumpled pages aside.

Cade looked across the table at Anja, to see if she was as ready as he was for an end to the master's nightly tirades. She gave him a subtle nod to proceed.

He cleared his throat to draw Adair's attention.

Looking up, the master cocked an eyebrow. "Aye?"

"Permission to speak freely?"

"This isn't the army, you prat. Speak your mind."

Another glance at Anja steeled Cade's courage. "We've been talking . . ." The master's mood soured with every word Cade spoke. ". . . and we think we're going about this all wrong."

"Do you?" Adair leaned away from the table. Lit a cigarette. "Well, don't keep me in suspense, lad." He added with a theatrical flourish, "*Elaborate.*"

A nervous swallow, then Cade gestured at the avalanche of paperwork they had been scouring for weeks in search of clues. "We knew most of this would be useless. But the problem isn't the intel. It's that we're up against someone who's just as good at hiding as we are."

When he paused, Anja carried the argument forward. "Kein could never have breached the wards on Eilean Donan had he not tortured Stefan. By the same logic, Kein will not be able to find this villa—or us, so long as we remain inside it."

"The problem," Cade interjected, "is that Kein can set up the same kinds of defenses. We've been looking for his new stronghold ever since you forced him to abandon Wewelsburg. But wherever he is, he's invisible."

Adair rubbed his bloodshot eyes. "Christ, wake me up when we get to what I don't know."

His jest sharpened Anja's tone. "Unless we draw him out, we will never find him. He knows the same is true of us. It is why he took Niko's sister. We cannot wait for him to force our hand again. We must be the ones to set the trap this time."

That refreshed Adair's interest in the conversation. "What kind of trap?"

"Something that lets him think he has the element of surprise," Cade said. "We haven't worked out all the details yet, but the idea is to dig in somewhere, then compel him to attack us."

Adair waved off the proposal. "Are you mad? Give him the initiative?"

"In combat," Cade said, "the attacker is the one most likely to be exposed and off-balance. If six months with the Rangers taught me nothing else, it was that defending a fortified position is almost always easier than attacking one."

Anja nodded. "My experience with the Red Army was the same. Better to defend."

The master wore a frown of doubt. "I still don't like it. Setting traps means putting ourselves at risk. If he sees us coming, strikes before we're ready—"

"We can mitigate the risk of detection," Cade said. "Personal wards, minimal use of magick before the ambush. But doing it right means taking it slow—and choosing the right place and time for the ambush. Somewhere Kein would expect to have the advantage, on a night when he'd think the stars favor him."

A disbelieving shake of Adair's head. "Fucking hell, lad. You're talking about going into Germany! Facing him on his own ground. Tell me I'm wrong!"

"You're not wrong. That's *exactly* what I'm saying."

Adair's hand trembled as he lifted his cigarette to his lips and took a clumsy drag. He sat down, then heaved a smoke-filled sigh. "Fuck me."

Anja moved to stand beside the master's chair. She set her hand on his forearm. "I know it seems we have a death wish, but we are sure this is the best plan."

Cade moved to the other side of Adair. "*We* pick the battleground. *We* set the terms. We lure him to us when *we're* ready. Then we *destroy* him—once and for all."

He met their proposal with a chuckle.

"God help me. I've created a fucking monster."

56

NOVEMBER

To walk the streets of Dresden was to step backward in time. With its rococo architecture and quaint side streets, the city was steeped in quasi-medieval ambience. Intricate stonework covered entire blocks of façades and dozens of lofty cathedral spires. If not for the fact that it was blacked out after dark and teeming with Allied prisoners of war during the day, Cade might almost have been fooled into thinking it had been spared the horrors of war.

Adair had chosen Dresden as the place where they would lay their great trap for Kein. Whenever pressed by Cade or Anja to explain why, the master had resorted to arcane mumbo jumbo about the alignments of stars and planets. Cade hadn't pretended to understand. Like Anja, he had faith in Adair, and that sufficed.

There were enough German troops in the city to make it dangerous for him, Anja, and Adair to move about, even after dark. One of them was always on watch, listening for signs of approaching patrols. In the dead of night, the enemy was more often heard than seen.

The trio had stuck to the city's outskirts since their arrival. Encounters were less frequent the farther one was from the city's center, making their halting German and foreign accents less likely to be detected. Under Adair's direction, they had worked counterclockwise around Dresden, starting from Räcknitz in the south. After more than a week of nightly forays into the city, they had made their way to Blasewitz, near the southern bank of the Elbe. If all went to plan, they soon would be in Neustadt, on the other side of the river.

The trio scurried across a deserted street into a warren of alleyways. Adair checked his compass, then the folded map in his other hand. "This way," he said, leading them deeper into the shadows.

If not for the Sight, Cade was sure he'd long since have lost track of Adair in the dark. Anja, however, lagged a few paces behind on purpose, to make it easier for her to hear if they were being followed.

They stopped at an intersection of several alleyways. Adair nodded. "This is it. Here."

Cade dropped to one knee, shrugged off his ruck, and dug into it for supplies. An ivory horn brimming with black powder. A vial of holy oil. Blessed chalk. And a leather pouch of ashes taken from the brazier in which they had cremated crow feathers with the finger bones of a dead child and a crucifix carved from a single oak branch.

He looked up at Adair. "Whose sigil?"

Adair consulted his map. "LILITH."

Cade sketched the demon's seal in chalk on the pavement. It was one of many Adair had planned. According to the master, the pattern of seals, placed in the correct positions throughout the city, would create a massive lens to focus their powers against Kein, while simultaneously stripping the dark master of his own yoked spirits, leaving him defenseless. It was a complex scheme, one that would take months to execute—and, in a stroke of irony, it had been inspired by the devil's trap Kein himself had created to unleash mayhem in Normandy.

When LILITH's seal was done, Cade traced the design with holy oil. Twice he paused at the touch of Anja's fingertips on his shoulder, a warning they might have company; both times the threat passed without incident and he continued. When the seal was traced, he put away the oil, pulled the stopper from the horn, and poured black powder into the center of the seal.

Adair grew impatient. "Is it done yet?"

"Almost." Cade put away the horn. He dug a match from his coat pocket, struck it on the ground, and dropped it onto the black powder. A pop of combustion echoed off the brick walls, and sparks shot into the air. Flames consumed the gunpowder and ignited the oil on LILITH's seal, burning it into the asphalt and activating it as a permanent glyph.

The black powder ceased sparking, but the oil still burned.

"Kill it," Adair said.

Cade upended the pouch of ashes onto the burning sigil, dousing the flames. Somewhere nearby, large dogs filled the night with furious barks.

Adair hustled Cade and Anja down another alley, away from the approaching canines. "We're done here. Let's go."

Their retreat was quick and calm, aided by their individual powers of magickal silence, intangibility, or flight. Soon their pursuers were far behind them, and the trio regrouped in the darkness of a side street in the Striesen district.

The master pressed his large hands onto Cade's and Anja's shoulders. "Smartly done, both of you. Now back to the cellar."

Anja deflated. "Already?"

Her protest didn't sway Adair. "We're walking a tightrope here. No way we'll make it to Neustadt before morning." He resumed walking. "Onward. Miles to go before we sleep."

There was no more discussion on the walk to their hideout. They had set up camp in a steam-choked cellar beneath an administrative building on the campus of the Technische Universität Dresden. Wards, illusions, and demonic guardians served to keep them safe there from Kein's scrying and other magicks of clairvoyance, as well as to fend off unwelcome visitors who might happen into the building's basement.

Anja had converted a janitor's neglected quarters into their new dormitory and base of operations. She had draped wool blankets—borrowed by Cade from the campus laundry—from pipes that ran along the ceiling, to create corners of privacy for each of them. They shared the table and chairs in the middle of the room, but Adair had taken over one entire wall with his annotated maps, photographs, calculations, and notes.

While Cade and Anja shed their coats and gear, Adair moved to the wall, found the red dot he'd inked for that night's step in the building of the trap, and put a check mark through it. "Making progress," he said. "A few more weeks, the outer ring will be complete."

Cade took a bottle of vodka from their provisions. He poured a few fingers into a dirty glass, then sipped from it as he eyed the map. "At this rate, we'll be working through the winter. Can't we pick up the pace?"

"Not unless you feel like giving away our position to Kein. And this won't take as long as you think. The inner circles get smaller as we go."

Cade studied the snare's design. "How many circles do we need?"

"Four, I think." Adair dug out a pack of cigarettes, took one, then offered it to Cade, who snagged a smoke. The master lit his, then Cade's, as he continued. "Not sure yet where they'll go. We need to pick a killing field before we can drive Kein into it."

Anja emerged from her corner-tent in stocking feet, shaking loose her black hair. "This is taking too long. I came here to kill Kein, not spend my nights playing lookout."

"Patience, my dear." Adair puffed smoke rings against the map, as if they might direct him where to set the next nodes of his trap. "I know this is slow, but it's for our protection. It's also the only way to build the trap that keeps the whole thing passive until we trigger it—which means Kein won't be able to sense it until it's too late."

She plucked the cigarette from Adair's hand and the vodka from Cade's. She downed the booze in one tilt, then took a long drag off the Lucky. As she exhaled, an illusion disguising the left side of her face vanished, revealing her Y-shaped scar. "Fuck careful. I want his head."

"We all do," Cade said, "but none of us is strong enough to take him alone. Hell, I doubt we'd have much of a chance even if we ganged up on him. Gotta neuter him first."

She pushed Cade's empty glass to his chest. "Then I need another drink."

"If this trap works," Cade said, "we can banish most of Kein's yoked demons before we throw the first punch. I know it feels like we're wasting time, but this is the smart play." He refilled the glass and handed it to her. "Trust me."

"Trust is for children and fools. But you are right. I have waited this long for revenge. I can wait a few months more." She downed her second shot, then trained her stare on Adair. "It would be a shame to squander such an opportunity, no?"

Adair lit another cigarette and enveloped himself in a gray shroud as he exhaled. "It'd be a fuck of a lot worse than that. If Kein finds out we're here before we finish the trap? . . . We're all as good as dead."

1945

JANUARY

Mornings, Adair had found, were the best times for working complex math based on the various ephemerides he relied on to track and predict celestial events. Though his labors in the streets of Dresden were committed at night, as were the majority of his recent experiments, the hours when Cade and Anja slept were the only times he could count on peace and quiet in the lair.

He didn't blame them for it. They had to eat sometime, and plans for the trap needed to be coordinated with everyone alert, but their waking presences made concentration difficult. And these numbers had to be precise.

Popular astrology was hokum. At least, the common variety peddled to the masses in newspapers and gaudy shopfronts was. Adair had seen enough bastardized astrology to know it from a distance. All it took for charlatans to make a living as "astrologers" was a knack for reading the unconscious physical and verbal cues of the gullible, and a bit of practice at asking leading questions. It was so simple, Adair was sure he could teach a monkey to do it.

Real astrology, on the other hand . . . that was a tricky business. It was more art than science, but some of its elements were the mechanisms of the universe. Unlike its watered-down popular form, it never promised truth or predicted anything with certainty. Its chief purpose was to expose propensities and potentials. To show the trained eye what might be, or what was possible, in the right place at a specific moment in time.

The language of astrology was one of geometry and trigonometry. It spoke of a sky divided into twelve houses. It defined stellar and planetary influences by their relative angles: the beneficial trine, the baneful square, the gentle sextile, the vexing quincunx, or the energizing clash of opposition. Every detail mattered; not only did Adair need to know in what zodiacal sign each planet and major celestial object resided, he had to know where it would be in relation to all the others. Then he had to account for the specific latitude and

longitude of Dresden, for times of day, and for precession—periodic varia-
tions in the earth's axial tilt.

Every time he thought he had found an optimal night to spring the trap
upon Kein, he began the tedious process of checking the ephemerides and ferreting out any sign of a possibly dangerous or disastrous planetary configu-
ration that could backfire upon them. He had learned to pay close attention
to two vital harbingers of peril: Mars and Pluto.

Lastly, as if his task weren't complicated enough, he had to weigh any pro-
posed date against what he knew of Kein's horoscope, based on information
he had cobbled together over the past two centuries. The sheer volume of the
calculations was enough to drive a man to madness, or at the very least to drink.
Fortunately, vodka had proved abundant in Dresden.

With painstaking care he scribed planetary symbols and their degrees and
minutes of arc within their respective signs onto a wheel-shaped chart. When
they all were in place, he used a red pencil to note planets aligned in opposition; green lines to expose the trines; blue for the squares; and black for the
ever-irritating quincunx. Then he laid Kein's chart atop it, and held both sheets
of paper together as he lifted them in front of the room's bare, dangling bulb.

Planet by planet, angle by angle, he compared the two charts.

When he set them on the table, he was sweating. His heart hammered inside his chest as he bellowed, "Up! Both of you."

The young magicians groaned and cursed before they rose to answer his
summons. Cade reached the table first, yawning and knuckling sleep from
his bloodshot eyes. He squinted at Adair. "Fucking hell. What time is it?"

"Half nine."

"In the morning? Shit, this better be good."

Bleary and groggy, Anja bumped into the table before she stopped next to
Cade. "If this is not vital, I will kill you both."

Adair hunched over the chaos of grids, graphs, calculations, and horoscope
charts. "I've got it. The perfect date and time for the attack." He slammed his
latest chart onto the table in front of Cade and Anja. "The night of February
thirteen, at ten o'clock."

The young karcists blinked and eyed the chart.

Cade looked dubious. "The night before Ash Wednesday?"

"Exactly," Adair said. "Ash Wednesday is a terrible date for magick, but we'd
strike just before it begins." He pulled forward more pages of calculations and
excerpts from ephemerides. "On its face, the night itself looks common. Even

if Kein reviews the charts before taking our bait, nothing here should give him reason for concern." He pointed at Kein's estimated natal horoscope chart. "It would take a detailed cross-reference to see the threats this chart poses to him. It's the night when most of his strongest planetary influences will be in opposition to themselves, thanks to their upcoming transits over Europe." He stabbed at the papers with his index finger. "This is it. The night and the hour. Now we need the place."

"We have it," Cade said. "We were waiting for you to pick a date before we told you."

"Fucking hell, lad. Don't keep me in suspense."

Off a cue from Cade, Anja said, "The Zwinger grounds, in the Altstadt."

"Why there?"

"It's a large enclosed area," Cade said, "and off-limits to the public after dark. We can scribe our last ring of glyphs on its outer walls. After we get Kein inside, we seal the gate."

"If we contain the duel inside the Zwinger," Anja added, "we will reduce the risk of civilians seeing the battle or coming to harm."

Their proposal troubled Adair. "Breaching the Zwinger might be harder than you think. And we could reduce civilian risk by confronting him on the Augustusbrücke."

Cade shook his head. "We considered that. The bridge is guarded at night, probably to prevent sabotage. Even if we could burn a few nodes into it, the really effective ones can't be set over running water, and we'd be in full of view of at least half the city." He pointed at the Zwinger on the wall map. "This is the best option. A contained killing field. Limited collateral damage. And enough room to set nodes to make sure Kein never walks out alive."

Still uncertain, Adair looked to Anja. "I presume you have a plan for how to get near the Zwinger to set the last circle of the trap?"

A devious smirk. "Of course."

That was good enough for Adair. "Then it's settled." He lit a cigarette in celebration. "Three weeks from tonight, we lure Kein to the Zwinger. And we kill him."

FEBRUARY

Voices rose to meet him in the ether, arriving before his destination came into view. That was typical during astral projection; thoughts and ideas often carried beyond the physical plane, impelled by their own creative force into the spaces between dimensions.

There was no confusing the voices; each had its own inimitable character.

President Franklin Delano Roosevelt's arch tenor faltered beneath the twin burdens of age and illness: "You asked for a second front in Europe. That's what we've given you."

"After how many millions of Russian soldiers died?" It was vintage Premier Josef Stalin: gruff and curt. "We press our attack from the east while you dawdle in Italy."

"Perhaps you've forgotten this war is global." Prime Minister Winston Churchill—as imperious as he was ponderous, with a growl of a voice. "America has waged our war against Japan in the Pacific all but single-handed, since nearly the beginning."

"I have pledged Russia's support for the Pacific war—"

"Only after the war ends in Europe," Roosevelt interrupted.

The scene came into focus as his consciousness migrated out of the astral plane, back into the material world and its assault on the senses. Though his mind was only a projection into the room deep within Livadia Palace, outside Yalta, he savored its mingling smokes: the acrid bite of American tobacco from Roosevelt's cigarette; the pungent perfume of Churchill's cigar; and the rich aroma of burning oak from the crackling blaze in the fireplace.

Stalin sipped from a glass of clear liquid that was most likely vodka, then palmed droplets from his bushy mustache. "If you want our help in the Pacific, don't—" He startled a bit as he noted their meeting had been intruded upon.

Roosevelt and Churchill pivoted away from the comfort of the fire. The

American president smiled, and the prime minister got up to greet their guest. "Master Macrae, welcome! Premier Stalin, I don't know that you've met our resident sorcerer. Allow me to present Adair Macrae." Stalin stood, joined Churchill, and extended his hand.

"Forgive me, Premier Stalin. I'd shake your hand if I could, but I'm not actually there." To illustrate his point, he let his astrally projected hand pass through one of the room's sumptuously padded and upholstered sitting chairs. "I'm more of a waking dream, or a living ghost, if you prefer."

Churchill took the news with steady composure. "Marvelous, sir!" He beckoned the shade to join him and the other leaders. "Tell us, old friend: What news?"

"Good tidings, I think. Four days from now, at ten P.M., in the Altstadt section of Dresden, my adepts and I will draw the Nazis' top karcist into a trap. If all goes to plan, the magickal defenses that have thwarted your efforts against Hitler will be gone. With luck, the war in Europe can be over by spring."

His news kindled new life into Roosevelt's tired eyes. "You're sure?"

"Quite sure. After we take down Kein Engel, the spirits he set to guard Hitler will become the Führer's worst nightmares. He'll be dead, mad, or both in a matter of months."

Stalin bared a shark's grin. "Good. Very good. The German high command already tried to oust Hitler once. Once he's gone, they'll crumble into factions."

"This calls for a toast," Roosevelt said. He lifted his glass, and Churchill followed suit. "To the death of Kein, the fall of Hitler and his Reich, and the end of this war."

"Hear, hear," said the prime minister, and the three heads of state drank.

It seemed an opportune time to depart. "Good luck with the rest of the war, gentlemen. I shall look forward to celebrating Kein's demise with you in five days' time."

"Indeed," Churchill said. "Godspeed, Master Macrae."

"And to you, Prime Minister."

✎

The astral projection faded from the room, and a pensive silence fell upon the Allied leaders. They settled into their chairs. Stalin swilled his vodka, Roosevelt sipped from a tumbler of bourbon, and Churchill tipped back a lowball of gin. Deeply troubled by all he had heard, Roosevelt broke the verbal stalemate. "How do we like his chances?"

Churchill's doubts were evident. "Against a monster like Kein? Abysmal."

"He and his adepts will have the advantage of surprise," Roosevelt offered.

Stalin said, "We should not gamble the war's outcome on one man's promises."

The prime minister asked accusatorily, "Meaning what?"

"We should remove the element of chance," Stalin replied.

Bolder now, Roosevelt nodded. "I agree. Historically, mages have always been wild cards. In a modern world like ours, they constitute a threat, one that could disrupt the balance of powers. I should not enjoy trusting my fate to their whims or mercies."

"My point exactly," Stalin said. "If this Master Macrae is correct, then we know exactly where all of the last living sorcerers will be in four days' time. We could rid the human race of their kind in one blow. We might never have another chance to do the world such a service."

"You mean bomb Dresden," Churchill said. He harrumphed. "It would serve the Germans right, after what they've done to London. But Adair has been a friend to us—"

"Not a friend," Stalin interjected. "An asset. And an unpredictable one. Will you still call him friend when he and his kind turn against us? When they put their devils and demons above duty and country?"

"He has a point," Roosevelt said. "But I don't like the idea of bombing a city with few if any valid military targets. Especially not on the scale that would be required here."

Churchill gnawed the end of his cigar. "Now is not the time to get squeamish. We didn't push for total war, Hitler and the Axis did. At any rate, your Pacific forces are already bombing Tokyo without discretion. I see no reason Dresden should be spared."

The American president shook his head, and he feared his sagging features betrayed the ravages of his long illness. "It could be seen as a war crime."

Stalin dismissed Roosevelt's sincere concerns with a callous wave. "Let history call it what it wants. What matters is striking while we have the chance. If your armies will not do what must be done, *mine will*."

"Then we're agreed," Churchill declared. "Come the night of the thirteenth . . . we bomb Dresden until nothing remains but rubble and ashes."

Night fell on Dresden. It was only a few days past the new moon, but even that sliver of reflected light was long gone, having made its transit in daytime. It had chased the sun over the western horizon hours earlier, leaving the city as dark as the core of a fist.

Adair stood in the center of the Zwinger grounds, surveying its perimeter with the Sight. The palace's double-spired cathedral stood to the north; to the northeast stood the open main gate, beneath a majestic double arch supporting a dome painted the green of oxidized copper and topped with a golden crown. Hundreds of well-groomed topiary trees, their bare branches frosted and drooping, bordered the snow-covered lawns between the grounds' pedestrian paths. Gas-fed lamps that lined the walkways stood cold and dark.

Nothing moved. Not even the freezing winter air, which smelled clean but for a faint tang of woodsmoke curling from the palace's chimneys.

About a dozen meters away on either side behind him, Cade and Anja watched the other corners of the Zwinger, their own senses magickally keen, alert for any sign of Kein.

Anja masked her anxiety with impatience. "Are you sure he's coming?"

"Aye," Adair said. "I had a demon bring my portal glass from the villa. There's no way Kein could have missed that. He'll come tonight, for sure."

"Or perhaps he is already here," said a voice that chilled Adair's blood.

He spun to see his nemesis standing between him, Cade, and Anja.

Kein's sense of style remained unimpeachable. His hair was trimmed and his shave was as close to perfect as the marriage of steel and flesh allowed. His open trench coat and Burberry scarf fluttered in the wind, revealing his three-piece suit and polished shoes. "Hello, Adair."

Anja tensed. "Where is your ginger bitch?"

"You mean Briet? I have not seen her in months." Kein acknowledged Cade with a half nod. "I had assumed you killed her. Now I know she deserted me." A casual shrug. "No matter. I will deal with her soon enough. After we finish here."

It was time to erase Kein's smug look. "*Infirmitas!*" Adair channeled the vitality-draining talent of ARAMAEL to trigger his trap and humble his nemesis for the first time since—

The bastard shook his head. "Oh, Adair. My old friend . . . did you really think I had blundered into your net? That I was just prey for your snare?" He flicked his hand, a backhand swat through open air—and a freight train of force bashed into Adair and laid him out on the frozen ground. Kein prowled toward him.

Cade and Anja unleashed fire and lightning at the dark master, who deflected it all without seeming to pay it any mind. He kept his eyes on Adair, who struggled to his feet and scrambled to draw his wand. At a gesture from Adair, Cade and Anja ceased fire but kept their attention on Kein.

"I love this plan of yours," Kein said, waving his hand at all of Dresden. "It is based on my devil's trap, yes? If imitation is the sincerest form of flattery, I should be touched by your scheme, despite its intent. But did you really think you could craft something of this magnitude and not attract my notice?"

Horror spilled the words from Adair: "You knew?"

"Of course I knew. For months have I watched you. I sabotaged every seal you made, sometimes mere hours after you made them." Kein shot a look at Cade. "I got the idea from you. After I learned how you unmade my trap in Normandy, I vowed to master this new trick. And then you handed me the perfect opportunity. You built a killing jar with my name on it"—he spread his arms wide—"and I turned it into a lens that serves only me."

His implicit promise of slaughter was answered by air-raid sirens.

Cade looked up as the warnings resounded through the city. "The fuck? Is it a drill?"

The faint drone of distant aircraft widened Anja's eyes. "It is no drill."

Adair turned toward the sound of bombers but couldn't see them—just a moonless black sky. He wheeled toward Kein. "What've you done?"

"It is not me, old friend. Thank your precious Allies for this. You see, after you—terribly sorry; after I, *posing* as you—told Churchill, Roosevelt, and Stalin about your plan to ambush me here, they reacted most predictably: by deciding to kill us all. In so doing they will bring my masterpiece to fruition—by inaugurating the greatest burnt offering in the history of the Art."

"You're mad!"

"Mad?" Kein shook his head. "No, my friend. *Prescient.* I knew your leaders would raze this city, just as I knew you"—a look at Cade—"would bring me the sacrifice I needed."

Panic flooded Adair's thoughts. His careful scheme had imploded; he'd played straight into Kein's hands. He drew his white-handled knife and lunged at Kein, who caught Adair's wrists. As they grappled, Adair bellowed at Cade and Anja, "Run!"

For once, bless them, they obeyed.

Anja transformed into a hawk and launched herself into the dark. Cade sprinted toward the main gate then vanished into thin air, perhaps by invisibility, maybe by shifting into a gaseous or spectral form. Outside the Zwinger, the outskirts of the city flared gold and crimson as falling bombs filled the night with hellish thunder and searing flames.

Kein kneed Adair in the groin. Adair doubled over, and met Kein's knee again with his chin. He landed on his back, spread-eagled on the cold ground.

His adversary smirked. "You think running will save them? I am bonded to a demon, old friend." In a sickly green pulse, there were three of him.

They all said in unison, "And my name is LEGION."

Three bodies, one mind—a power Kein had taken decades to master. Now he was hurling fire and forked lightning at Adair across the Zwinger grounds; soaring through the dark as an owl, in pursuit of the Russian woman; and hurling spectral missiles as he chased the young American *nikraim* through the Zwinger's main gate into the streets of the Altstadt.

Gray armies of nameless demons poured from every shadow of Dresden— some under Kein's command, the rest answering to his foes. Endless ranks of the Fallen crashed against one another in waves, breaking around their summoners like a sea swallowing islands.

Adair punched forward with ORCUS's disemboweling claws, only to have Kein block his attack with his shield. Kein retaliated with lightning that sent the grizzled Scotsman diving for cover while it ripped a steaming scar into the snow-covered lawn.

Half a mile away, the talons of Kein's owl form dug into the back of Anja's borrowed hawk body and dragged her flailing toward the rooftops. In the northwest, explosions marched across the city, silhouetting buildings as they fell.

In the narrow streets of the Altstadt, Cade ceased his retreat, spun about, and hurled a green fireball at Kein, who deflected it. The burning orb crashed through a window of a nearby building, whose interior was consumed by a blast of emerald flames. Kein answered the youth's clumsy strike with GŌGOTHIEL's fist. The impact batted Cade through the air and slammed him against a brick wall.

Inside the Zwinger, Kein harried Adair by vomiting flames into his face, forcing the hobbled old mage to his knees as the blaze bent around his unseen shield. Kein swallowed the rest of his firestorm, then taunted his rival. "You should have stayed out of this war, old friend."

"And let you murder humanity's future? Not fucking likely."

Owl and hawk crashed together on a rooftop, tumbled over eaves in a flurry of claws and feathers. A hair shy of the pavement, Kein and Anja rematerialized, crouched and facing each other. "Walk away, girl. You have done it before. Do it now."

"Never." A ghostly whip took shape in her hand. She snapped its barbed tip inches from his head, mussing his hair and kissing his face with violence. The whip struck a steel lamppost behind Kein and broke it in half with a shriek of sheared iron.

The streets of the Altstadt shook under Kein's feet as if the city were in the center of an earthquake. Across the cityscape behind Cade, columns of fire climbed into a sky whose thin blanket of clouds turned red reflecting the inferno's light.

Cade manifested a burning broadsword in his right hand, a short sword glistening with poison in his left, and charged. Kein tasked a hellhound to meet him. With superhuman agility, Cade sidestepped the monster's ravenous jaws, severed its forelimbs, and stabbed it in the heart. Then, with both blades, he scissored off its snarling head.

Adair deflected a surge of Kein's lightning, cutting a red-hot wound across the palace's inner walls; then he hurled blue fire from his palm. Kein swatted away the flames, igniting a stand of bare-limbed trees—only to be nicked on the back of his head by the scythe of Azazel.

Kein smirked at Adair. "You almost had me, old man."

"I'm not done yet."

"Yes—you are."

In the Zwinger, he skewered Adair with Savnok's fetid spear.

In an alley of Friedrichstadt he cracked a reptilian whip at the girl.

In the Altstadt he throttled Cade with tendrils of smoke.

Thunder and flames advanced across the city, toppling buildings and erasing entire streets beneath storms of fire. Crowds of fleeing civilians erupted into flames as incendiary charges detonated in their midst.

Kein gloated over Adair, who twisted on the end of his demonic spear. "The rabble and their love of Science brought you to this."

The dark master laughed at Anja, who clawed at the pair of hissing asps coiled around her throat. "You came all this way for revenge, only to die a failure. How tragic."

Adair melted into mist and escaped the backward teeth of the spearhead. Anja freed herself of the reptilian whipcord by incinerating it with her hands. Cade severed Kein's smoky coils usin swords ablaze with Infernal light.

Overhead, arcs of tracer fire lit up black bellies of cloud, scouring the heavens for the Allied aircraft that were turning Dresden into a crucible. Trailing tongues of flame, a bomber plunged from the sky and slammed into a cathedral's spire, toppling it in flaming shards onto the panicked masses below.

Cade charged at Kein, swinging his blades with uncanny skill. Kein summoned a pair of falchions and parried the hotheaded young karcist's whirlwind attack, filling the air between them with showers of sparks and a song of clashing steel.

Anja ran toward the train tracks. Falling munitions leveled entire city blocks on either side of her and Kein. A bomb landed in the street ahead of her. Its shock wave launched her through a wall of fire and engulfed Kein in smoke and dust.

Adair called up tentacles of fog to snare Kein's limbs. Kein cut himself free with a demon's rapier, then shot petrifying beams from his eyes to chase Adair to cover behind the base of the statue in the center of the Zwinger grounds.

Tired of Cade's berserker assault, Kein swatted the young karcist aside with the hand of GŌGOTHIEL. Cade flew through the crumbling brick façade of a building gutted by bombs.

On either side of Kein, civilians fled from burning apartment buildings, their hair and clothing aflame. A woman whose flesh was seared almost to charcoal collapsed in the street, the charred corpse of an infant fused to her breast. Mother and child dissolved into black grease. Terrified throngs trampled their neighbors, only to suffocate as the fire ate their oxygen.

Anja limped out of the maelstrom of fire, wand in one hand, athamé in the other. Blood ran from her nose and ears, and her tattered clothes smoldered on her slight frame. "Now you die," she rasped at Kein. Behind her raged the hellscape of what once had been a city of art.

In the Zwinger, Adair threw disintegrating pulses and tempests of white light, only to see Kein swat them aside, punching more holes in the palace walls. No longer amused by the exercise, Kein took away his foes' principal defenses with the might of KERAVNOS—the spirit known in Hell as "shield-breaker."

Adair's shield crumbled. Kein lashed his serpent-whip around the Scot's throat. The girl was a petty distraction, one best dispatched quickly; Kein shredded her defensive barrier, then put her down with a pair of deadly thunderbolts. He seized the American in the paralyzing grip of LEVIATHAN and used the strength of GŌGOTHIEL to drag him toward the Zwinger.

On the edge of Friedrichstadt, Kein's first avatar flinched as a barrage of demonic arrows plowed into his back, forcing him to his knees. Dazed, he twisted around—and saw Anja, bloodied and caked in soot, her hand outstretched toward him. Kein buried her in a cyclone of dust, shattered concrete, and fire.

Outside the gate of the Zwinger, Kein's second avatar faltered as the first collapsed. His concentration on Cade lapsed for only a fraction of a second—but it was enough for the *nikraim* to squirm free and regroup as bombs leveled the city on either side of him and Kein.

Inside the palace's killing grounds, Adair lashed out with a desperate invisible-hand attack, but Kein reflected it back at him. Adair mustered an iron-skin charm in time to survive what would otherwise have been a fatal error.

Cade tried to take down Kein with a rudimentary strangling hex. Kein broke the demonic chokehold, then turned the pall of smoke over the city into a rack of pain for the arrogant young karcist. "Playtime is over, boy. Now we finish this."

Kein's two wandering bodies returned to the Zwinger, whose walls shattered before the holocaust unleashed by the bombers overhead. One explosion after another rocked the ground, to the point that Kein expected the bedrock to crack open below his feet. All around him, blasts leveled the Zwinger palace. Its walls fell to reveal the nightmare of the Altstadt—dozens of square miles reduced to skeletons of gutted brick an an inferno worthy of the Abyss.

Fire above, fire below: It was Hell on earth—all Kein had hoped and more.

His old rival lay on his right, stunned and bleeding. His new rival lay on his left, paralyzed and in shock. Adair and his adepts had played their parts to perfection.

A shame they will all be dead before I can thank them.

He drew his wand and athame, then declared in a mighty voice, "Hear me, great minister LUCIFUGE ROFOCALE! By the holy names GABRIEL, RAPHAEL, ZACHARIEL, NURIEL, SAMAEL, TETRAGRAMMATON, and JEHOVAH, I command thee! *Aperire portam inferni!*"

A thirty-meter-wide circle yawned open in the center of the Zwinger grounds. The great statue and dozens of lampposts, trees, and shrubberies were consumed by a fast-growing, swirling vortex of fire and shadow, pulled down into the Pit.

For the first time since the dawn of man, the gateway to Hell was open.

Strength and focus were only memories now for Cade. Pain and delirium had become his whole world. Curled on the ground at Kein's feet, he was racked with agonies inside and out, as if he were meat turning on a barbed spit. He sensed only six spirits he still held in yoke; nearly two-thirds of the demons he'd harnessed had escaped his control in just the past few minutes.

Mere feet away, a funnel of smoke and fire entranced him with its spinning as it drilled into the bowels of Hell. Lightning danced in its walls. From its depths roared a chorus of nightmares soon to rise and prey upon earth's billions of unsuspecting souls.

All around the ruins of the Zwinger, the city of Dresden burned. Gutted brick façades broke apart. The spires and domes of great cathedrals vanished into the firestorm that engulfed the heart of the city—a hurricane of fire with the palace's now-barren grounds as its eye.

Just out of Cade's reach, Adair lay on his side, blood seeping from his jaw, his whole body shaking with the tremors of the mortally wounded.

Between them, lording over them, was Kein. He raised his arms to the burning sky and basked in the moment. Then he beamed at Cade and shouted over the firestorm, "Beautiful, is it not? Your leaders gave me all I needed to bring the modern world to its end. Ere the sun rises, I will lay their lands and armies waste—and tomorrow, mankind can start over, free of the horrors it made but cannot control." He mocked Cade with an insincere, overly formal bow. "And I owe it all to you, Herr Martin. Because after I sacrifice you, the hell-mouth will be locked open—and earth will be closed to the angels forever."

The dapper fiend extended one hand toward Cade, closed his eyes, and concentrated. "Still clinging to a few yoked spirits, I see—including GADREEL: defense from projectiles and immunity to metal. Most impressive." He reached inside his trench coat and drew out a dagger with a blade of yellow-tinted quartz. "Fortunately, I came prepared."

Kein lifted Cade by the front of his shirt. "*Nikraim* or not, you were never going to beat me as a karcist." He raised his blade and struck—

—only to have Cade block and seize his arm: "Then I'll kill you as a Ranger."

Cade snapped Kein's elbow and forced broken bones through the skin.

The blade fell from Kein's hand as he screamed in pain.

Cade dragged Kein to the ground and punched him in the face, throat, solar plexus, and groin. For a moment, he felt as if his victory was at hand.

Then Kein reabsorbed his two magickal avatars in a burst of light and a clap of thunder that hurled Cade to the edge of the hellmouth and left him stunned. Smoke surrounded them as the dark master straightened his savaged arm with a merciless jerk and a guttural howl.

Desperate, Cade reached for the quartz knife. Kein opened his mouth and spewed a flood of indigo light that flattened Cade to the ground and stripped him of the last of his yoked spirits.

Barely conscious, Cade watched Kein grab the quartz dagger. Drained and frozen, all he could do was watch the dark master stagger toward him and raise the blade—

Blood spattered Cade's face like a devil's baptism. He blinked, then saw Kein gag and cough blood—with the tip of an onyx dagger poking from a bloodstain on his chest.

Wind parted the curtains of smoke, revealing Anja behind Kein. She gave her stone blade a savage twist. Kein dropped his quartz dagger and sank to his knees, while his proud glare slackened into a mask of shock.

Cade scrambled away from the vortex's edge as Anja pulled her blade free of Kein's back. She seized Kein by his hair; then she stabbed him in his ribs and flanks, over and over, growling the whole time like a feral animal, her eyes wide with rage.

Kein was as limp as a marionette in Anja's hands when she spun him to face her. "For my brother," she rasped. Then she plunged her dagger into his gut.

The dark magician slumped over the edge of the fiery vortex.

Adair's hoarse cry came half a second too late: "Stop! Don't—"

Numb with pain and horror, Cade watched his nemesis surrender to gravity's embrace. Kein spread his arms, cracked a beatific smile, then said as he fell: "It is finished."

He vanished into the Pit, unleashing a crash of thunder that buried Adair's plaintive shout of "No!"

A geyser of fire and shadow shot up from the bottom of the vortex, cutting through the smoke that now crowned all of Dresden.

Anja and Cade rushed to Adair's side and helped him sit up.

"Master," Cade said, "are you all right?"

"Of course not!" He pointed at Anja. "The fuck were you thinking?"

She recoiled, offended. "I killed him. We won."

The master shook his head, furious. "You finished his spell!" He nodded at the hellfire geyser searing the sky. "Hell's rising, and there's fuck all we can do to stop it!"

Panic clouded Cade's thoughts. "There's got to be a way to close it!"

"It's too late. She locked it open when she sacrificed Kein. It would take—" He stopped in midsentence, horrified by whatever notion had occurred to him.

Anja shook Adair by his shoulders. "Take what?"

"Another sacrifice," Adair said, crestfallen. "One of equal measure."

"My mistake." Anja stood. "I will pay the price."

Adair caught her leg. "No—" He coughed up blood and gasped for breath. "Not how it works. Kein was a *nadach*. You sacrificed a man bonded to a demon. Closing the gate . . . requires an equal sacrifice. A man—" More blood-soaked coughs.

Cade finished Adair's thought: "Bonded to an angel."

Sorrow filled Adair's eyes. "Aye. . . . It's the only way."

Bombs rocked the burning city. Charred ghosts staggered in its avenues turned funeral pyres. Beside Cade, the host of Hell began its ascent.

He summoned the last of his strength and stood to face the inferno. Soul-searing heat licked at his face, promising all the pains of damnation.

It was just one step, but it would be the measure of a life. His life. To cross that threshold was to let go of everything he knew, and all that he loved.

His guts twisted with grotesque pain. He looked down, expecting to see fire. All he found was a fathomless, unnatural blackness, an uncreated womb of night.

He thought of all who had died to protect him through the years—his parents on the night of the *Athenia*'s sinking; Stefan's noble sacrifice; and all the soldiers who had been killed around him on D-day—and all those who would perish if his courage faltered now.

He smiled at Adair. "Leave a light on for me."

Tears filled Adair's eyes. "Aye, lad. That I will."

Cade nodded at Anja. She nodded back.

Then he stepped forward and surrendered himself to the Abyss.

He knew not to expect a heavenly reward, or a miraculous act of Providence. All he expected to find at the end of his fall was darkness, followed by oblivion.

Darkness was exactly what he found.

59

AUGUST

Six months to the day. If the Iron Codex was to be trusted, this would be the best time—and maybe the only time—in the next decade to attempt such a bizarre experiment.

Anja stood on the beach and watched thunderheads choke the Caribbean sky. Waves heaved and shredded themselves into foam before they landed on the white-sand beach. It was nearing high tide, so each push of surf came closer than the last to the thatched-roof bamboo shack she and Adair had shared for the past six months, since their escape from Dresden.

The house wasn't much to see. Just a few rooms and a narrow porch facing a beachside fire pit, all nestled into a clearing on the coast of British Honduras, a few hundred meters from the mouth of the Mullins River.

In the forest behind the house, palm trees swayed in the grip of worsening crosswinds. Thunder echoed over the hillsides deeper inland. To the east, lightning danced between the stormhead and the sea.

It was time. If it was going to happen, it would be now.

Trust the Codex, she told herself. *Trust yourself.*

Adair had helped her design the circles for this unprecedented work of the Art, but they both had known she would have to stand alone at the moment of truth. It was an immutable fact of the circle that it was meant for one person, three, or five—but he had been bedridden since Dresden, and time had only worsened his wounds. So he had gifted her the Iron Codex, given her access to his vast collection of lore, and guided her preparations as best he could.

Dressed in her alb and paper miter, she entered the operator's circle.

Whether she left it alive depended on whether she and Adair had read the stars correctly, as well as whether her interrogations of VERAKOS had yielded precious truth or fatal lies.

She set her sword across the toes of her white leather shoes, then drew her wand from beneath her lion-skin girdle and removed its shroud of red silk. A spark conjured by the gift of HABORYM ignited the fresh charcoal in her brazier. She lifted her hands and proclaimed:

"Exodus! Exodus! Exodus!"

White sparks vomited from the brass vessel at her feet. The howls of the tempest deepened and distorted, until Anja was enveloped by a chorus of caterwauling. She raised her voice above the din:

"I invoke thee, CADE MARTIN, karcist of karcists! And I command Hell's Infernal Descending Hierarchy to surrender you and send you forth, by the terms of my covenant with ASTAROTH, and with his master PUT SATANACHIA, and the Great Emperor LUCIFER, all by the power of the most holy names ADONAI, EL, ELOHIM, ZABAOTH, ELION, ERETHAOL, RAMAEL, TETRAGRAMMATON, and SHADDAI; and by the whole hierarchy of superior intelligences, who shall release thee to answer my summons—*venité, venité,* CADE MARTIN!"

The heavens opened and flayed the beach with rain. Hundreds of strokes of lightning landed in a matter of seconds, all striking the center of the outer magickal circle as bone-shaking cannonades of thunder shook the ground. An inhuman roar overpowered the clamor of the storm and filled Anja with terror; then she winced as a final bolt of lightning, one greater than she had ever seen, turned her world white before plunging it into pure darkness.

Then the only sound was the rain.

Anja blinked. Her eyes adjusted to the dim glow produced by smoldering patches of fire on the ground that refused to be extinguished by the summer squall.

In the other circle, his head bowed and kneeling in a pose of genuflection, was Cade. Rain sizzled and evaporated as it struck his naked body. He and the ground inside his circle's innermost ring exuded gray vapor. A wand was clutched in his right hand.

He lifted his head to let the storm wash over his bearded face, releasing more steam. With effort and evident discomfort he stood. He squinted at her. "Anja?"

Every instinct she possessed told her it was him—but Adair had warned her she might call up a demon masquerading as Cade. Until she knew for certain it was him, the only safe course was to say nothing—to stand and wait.

Cade doubled over and vomited for a few seconds. Then he wiped his face clean with help from the storm . . . and staggered out of the circle.

Anja sprinted to him and caught him just before he fell on his face. Only a man could have walked out of the bounding circle of his own free will; a demon would have needed her permission. She checked him for wounds. "Are you hurt?"

His forehead was fever-warm. "How long was I gone?"

"Six months."

"How'd you bring me back?"

"A long story. How did you survive in Hell?"

Behind his ragged beard, a teasing smile. "Long story."

She looked down at his hand. "Whose wand is that?"

"Kein's." A wider grin now. "Call it a souvenir."

They lay on the sand and let the storm drench them. When the rain no longer boiled against his flesh, Anja helped him to his feet. "Let's get you inside. Adair needs to see you."

For once, Cade sounded hopeful. "Is the war over?"

Anja sighed as she led him inside the house. "Long story."

<center>~~~</center>

It was as close to a working definition of optimism as Cade had ever seen: Anja and Adair had brought with them his clothing, Colt semiautomatic, and tools of the Art from the villa. All of his personal effects had been cleaned and put away into drawers, trunks, and wardrobes. He had expected to be handed used garments, as when he had first awoken in Scotland years earlier. Being able to put on his own clothes was a simple yet profound comfort after his Infernal ordeal.

I still can't believe I'm here.

He closed his eyes and drank in the white noise of the tropical downpour slashing across the roof and pattering on the windows. The inside of the house smelled of mildew and flowers. Lit by kerosene lamps and candles, it had the ambience of a pastoral church after dark. The furnishings looked as if they had been wrought by local craftsmen from bamboo, twine, and reeds, and the floors were weathered and grayed by years of exposure to salt air.

He emerged from the bedroom dressed and restored to a semblance of his old self. Anja was there, waiting for him. She noted the shift in his appearance. "Better."

"I still need a shave."

"Later. The master awaits." She guided him toward the house's other bedroom.

"Guess I should thank you for—"

"I did not do it for you." A stern look. "The master promised me the Iron Codex if I brought you back." They reached Adair's room. His door was ajar, but Anja paused outside and knocked on the jamb. "Master?"

"Enter." Adair's voice was hoarse, a thin shadow of its former authority. Anja nudged open the door and led Cade to the master's bedside. Candles lined the windowsills and the tops of dressers; their flames animated the walls with shadows. Lying under a threadbare sheet, Adair looked pale even in the glow of firelight. The shadows served only to accentuate how gaunt his features had become. He turned his head as Cade neared, revealing rheumy eyes. "Welcome home, lad. I wasn't sure you'd make it . . . but I'm glad you did."

Cade sat on the edge of the bed and took his master's hand. "You finally retired to the tropics, I see." The master started to laugh, but his chortle devolved into a wet, hacking cough. Troubled, Cade threw a questioning look over his shoulder at Anja.

She frowned. "It was all I could do to keep him alive." She lifted the sheet to reveal a festering wound on the master's abdomen. "The spear of SAVNOK. Its wounds never heal."

"Even worse," Adair said through gritted teeth, "is the pain. There's not enough opium on earth to take the sting from this." He beckoned Cade. "Closer." After Cade leaned in, he continued. "Don't blame Anja. Not her fault. I . . . haven't been strong enough for magick . . . since Dresden. She tried all my books. Nothing helped."

"Master, what are we doing here?"

"Lying low." Deep, lungsore coughs left Adair wiping bright blood from his lips. "The Allies tried to kill us, lad. We can't go home, or even to Spain. Soon, no place'll be safe."

Memories of Dresden left Cade confused and bitter. "Why did they betray us?"

Anja cut in, "The same reason Salem burned witches: ignorance and fear."

"She's right," Adair said. "You two don't have the luxury of friends anymore."

"What about the war? Is it over?"

His question darkened Adair's already grim mood. The master pointed at a small table in the corner of the room. "Anja . . . ?" She retrieved a newspaper and handed it to Cade. It was a copy of *The New York Times* dated Tuesday, August 7, 1945. He read its headline:

FIRST ATOMIC BOMB DROPPED ON JAPAN;
MISSILE IS EQUAL TO 20,000 TONS OF TNT;
TRUMAN WARNS FOE OF A 'RAIN OF RUIN'

He looked up from the front page. "Holy shit. They built it? And actually *used* it?"

"Welcome to the future," Adair groused.

"It can't be as bad as it says, can it?"

Anja's temper rose. "It is worse. I scried the remains of Hiroshima. The entire city is gone. Nothing but ashes, ruins, and people burned alive."

"The whole city? Leveled by *one* bomb?"

"Aye," Adair said. "A few days later, the Yanks did it again. Turned Nagasaki to fucking charcoal. . . . Man no longer needs magick to unleash Hell upon the earth."

Cade dropped the newspaper on the floor. "Jesus Christ." Staring down at it, he fixated upon another detail. "Hang on. 'Truman warns foe'? What happened to Roosevelt?"

"Died in April, about a week before Hitler blew his brains out in Berlin." A vindictive smirk. "I guess they forgot us dirty karcists were the ones safeguarding their lives." He indulged in a derisive snort, but then he started to wheeze like an asthmatic.

Anja rushed to a bedside table to retrieve a hypodermic needle with a syringe. She loaded it from a vial of clear medicine, then injected the drug into Adair's arm. His breathing slowed and came more easily.

The master's voice took on a dulcet smoothness. "My time's short, lad. And I need to know you'll carry on my work."

"I will, Master. I swear it."

"Remember our trip to the Pentagon? I sent Anja there last month, to have a look inside."

"I found a silo under the central plaza," she said. "Hundreds of feet deep. Near the bottom, a platform at the end of a long bridge. Large enough for the grandest magick circles."

Adair nodded, then interjected, "Tell him the best part."

She went on, "The walls of the silo were packed with sensing devices. All connected to floor after floor of thinking machines—"

"Computers, they call them," Adair added.

"—and many observation rooms, manned by scientists and lawyers—"

"Lawyers?" Cade asked.

"For vetting demonic pacts," Adair said. "They're trying to reduce the Art to a science so they can outwit Hell and make it do their bidding. The Midnight Front on an industrial scale."

It was chilling news, not just for its immediate implications, but for the many aspects of it that Cade knew could go disastrously wrong. "What do they mean to do with it?"

"Warfare? Espionage? Something worse?" Adair shook his head in dismay. "All I know is they never spoke to me about it, which means either they built it for nothing . . . or they found someone else to run it."

Adair's vague suspicion left Cade grasping for answers—until the worst-case scenario revealed itself. He felt his face fall as he voiced his worst fear: "Briet."

"Aye. Sounds like she deserted Kein long before Dresden."

"But how could she have ended up in America?"

"Operation Paperclip," Adair said. "A top-secret program the Americans used to recruit Nazi scientists for their aerospace program. It seems they felt Miss Segfrunsdóttir's talents were vital enough to forgive her for being a fucking fascist."

Cade felt his anger stir at the mere notion that his country would grant amnesty to any Nazi, never mind one who had helped try to kill him and possibly even destroy the world. "Are we sure she's the one running the show at the Pentagon?"

"Not yet," Anja said.

"Wherever she is," Adair said, his voice degrading to a whisper, "she can't be trusted." He struggled to draw another breath, but forced himself to go on: "Keeping her in check . . . is your problem now." He clasped Cade's hand with what little strength he had left, and he raised his other hand, signaling Anja. "Lass . . . give us a moment."

If Anja resented being sent away, she hid it well.

After she'd gone, tears welled in Adair's eyes. "You're not an apprentice anymore. You're a master karcist. Find some students, and teach them well."

"With what? I don't—"

"I'm leaving you my library. All my books."

"All except the Iron Codex, you mean."

Adair nodded. "I wanted you home. Anja wanted the Codex. Seemed a fair trade." Another cough painted the master's nightshirt with blood. "It's up to you now to keep magick alive. If you fall, the Art's light might go out forever. Don't let that happen."

The master's words struck a dark chord in Cade's memory. "Kein said almost the same thing to me, three years ago. If he was right about that—"

"A person can be right on the facts and still do the wrong thing. Kein's cure was far worse than the affliction. He had to be stopped, lad. Never doubt that. Not for a moment."

Cade nodded, then glanced again at the troubling newspaper headline. "And Briet?"

"Make peace if you can, but—" He suppressed one more hacking cough. "If the past three centuries taught me nothing else, they taught me this: *The war never ends.*"

<center>~~~</center>

It was raining again the night Adair died. Anja stood with Cade in the downpour and watched the bamboo shack go up in flames.

She and Adair had said their farewells, and she had fulfilled the master's last request, for a drink laced with all the opium he could stand, to ease him through his final passage into oblivion. Cade had asked if Adair wanted to be alone; to his surprise, the old karcist had asked them to stay. And so they had, until his breathing stopped and his cold hands went slack.

Most of the master's books and paraphernalia belonged to Cade now. The American had tasked a demonic porter to gather it all for safekeeping, along with his gear and tools of the Art. Anja had been surprised to learn Cade had returned from Hell with yoked spirits at his command, but now she realized it made sense: how else could he have suvived six months in the Abyss?

The master's tools and grimoire they had left behind to burn; they were of no use now, not to her, Cade, or anyone else.

The house blazed against the tempest, a fiery grave for the man who had been more of a father to Anja than her own sire. She had promised Adair she would not cry; it was a vow she broke now without shame or regret, because she knew the rain would mask her tears.

She and Cade watched the roof fall in, followed by the walls.

He asked, "Where will you go?"

"South. I am told many Thule dabblers fled to Argentina after the war. I plan to kill a few of them. Maybe all of them." She eyed him with grudging respect. "You could come with me."

"I have other plans."

As if summoned, the purr of an outboard motor cut through the hiss of the storm. Anja looked to sea and saw a slender boat fight its way ashore against the tide. "Your ride?"

"I believe it is."

The narrow craft scraped onto the beach. A tall man with handsome features and dark brown skin emerged from the pilothouse and braved the rain to wade ashore. His voice was deep, his accent English. "Cade! Damn your eyes, I *knew* you'd make it through the war!"

Cade met him with a fraternal embrace. "Good to see you, too, Miles." They parted, and Cade acknowledged Anja's curiosity. "Anja, this is Miles Franklin, my brother from Oxford. Miles, this is Anja Kernova, my, um . . ."

She saw he was at a loss to describe their affiliation.

"Friend," she said. "And sister-in-arms."

Miles shook her hand. "A pleasure, Miss Kernova. Will you be joining us?"

She traded a knowing look with Cade. "I have other plans."

"Splendid." To Cade, Miles added, "We need to push off, mate. Where's your gear?"

"It's just me," Cade said.

"You've finally learned to travel light. Will wonders never cease?" He gestured toward the boat. "Climb aboard, then. Time and tide, old boy."

"Just a second." Cade and Anja stood on the beach, facing each other, but neither seemed to know what to say. Anja bid him farewell with a dip of her chin, and he did the same.

Specters in the storm, they turned their backs on each other, and on the dying embers of Adair's funeral pyre. Cade got on the boat and Anja walked south along the coast, each of them embarking on a journey into a new and darker world.

The rumrunner skipped like a stone over the sea. Cade huddled with Miles inside the pilot's cabin as waves crashed over the bow and sprayed the window. Ahead, Cade saw only black clouds and dark water, and barely a distinction between them. He was at a loss to grasp how Miles could navigate by instruments alone through such chaos.

Miles glanced toward their feet. "Brought you a present."

Cade lifted a ruck from the deck. He rooted through it to find a passport with his photo attached to a new identity. "Nice. Where'd you get it?"

"Perk of my new job. I'm with SIS now."

"You mean MI-6?"

A self-deprecating shrug and smile. "In some circles."

"Fancy. Does that mean you have the ten pounds you owe me?"

Miles put on a frown. "Bit short at the moment, old boy. But my vessel is at your service. So . . . where are we headed?"

"America. I have to return a pistol to a man in Secaucus. After that, there's someone in D.C. I need to have a word with."

A wary look. "Stirring up trouble, are we?"

"Yup. And it won't be the last time. We've got a lot of work ahead of us."

"Right!" Miles grinned as he opened up the throttle and sent the boat racing headlong into another storm. "Let's get to it, then."

60

SEPTEMBER

Deep under the Pentagon's central plaza, Cade watched Briet cross the 230-foot-long steel-grate widow's walk to her conjuring stage—apparently oblivious of his presence at its center, cloaked in a sphere of silence and illusion. Whoever had built the seventy-foot-wide pentagonal platform of whitewashed concrete had demonstrated a keen eye for detail. Its edges were forty-five feet long and paralleled the walls of the five-hundred-foot-wide silo that yawned hundreds of feet into darkness above and dropped away to watery gloom far below. The platform was lit by coal-fed torchères crackling with orange flames, three along each side at regular intervals.

As the copper-haired karcist drew near, Cade saw she toted her tools of the Art over her right shoulder in a leather bag much like the one he had carried during the war. In her left hand was a satchel. He imagined it contained chalks for inscribing circles on the platform.

Three steps off the bridge, Briet passed through the intangible membrane of Cade's sphere of concealment. She froze at the sight of him standing ready with Kein's wand in his hand.

"Good morning, Briet."

She dropped her tools and satchel. "Is that Kein's wand?"

"He sends his regards. From Hell."

His implied threat seemed to amuse her. "What do you want?"

"To make sure we understand each other." He watched her eyes flit toward the silo's walls. "They can't see us or hear us. As long as you don't do anything stupid, there's no reason this conversation can't stay private."

A strange gleam in her eye. "How did you get in here?"

"Your defenses aren't impregnable. A fact I'd urge you to remember before you agree to whatever commissions the War Department might have in mind."

"So this isn't a social call." She made a slow circuit of the platform. He pivoted to keep himself facing her as she continued. "What, then? A duel? A negotiation?"

"A discussion. For now." He tried not to be inveigled by her blue eyes; he kept his focus on her hands and mouth, since those would be the likeliest to betray any magickal attack. "The world changed when the Americans dropped the atomic bomb. You understand that, yes?"

A sideways nod. "Better than most. Your point?"

"Peace is fragile. It won't take much to push the world back to war."

"War and peace. Life and death. You cling to absolutes. But there are no Platonic ideals, only a spectrum of experience. Wonder and horror, pain and pleasure—"

"Good and evil aren't a fantasy."

"Of course they are. They always have been. One man's villainy is another's heroism. One tribe's monster is another's saint. This has always been the way of the world. And it always will be, no matter how earnestly you wish it were different."

Cade's hand tightened around the wand. "Just what I'd expect of a Nazi."

"Me? A Nazi?" She shook her head. "I was never a party member. I took advantage of them, just as Kein did, but—"

"I know you helped send people to concentration camps."

She ceased her stroll of the platform's edge. Her countenance hardened. "I obeyed my master, just as you obeyed yours."

"My master never asked me to make burnt offerings of millions of lives."

"But your countrymen did exactly that in Japan. And as I recall, it was the Allies who firebombed the civilians of Dresden." She stalked toward Cade and joined him at the center of the platform. "I have work to do. If there's something you want, say it."

"Just this." He leaned close and looked her in the eye. "I didn't beat the Nazis just so they could set up shop in the U.S. of A. And I didn't spend six months in Hell just to see you start Kein's war against Science all over again."

She smirked and turned her eye toward the silo's walls. "Does it look to you like I have a grudge against Science? As for the Nazis and Kein . . . good riddance. The War Department pays a generous sum for my loyalty." A playful shrug. "What can I say? I'm a born capitalist."

"Sure you are. But know this—" Cade snapped Kein's wand in half and dropped the pieces at Briet's feet. "I'll be watching you."

As he walked away, her icy reply echoed in the silo around them.

"I'll be watching you, too."

TERMINAT HORA DIEM, TERMINAT AUTHOR OPUS

MAJOR LOCATIONS

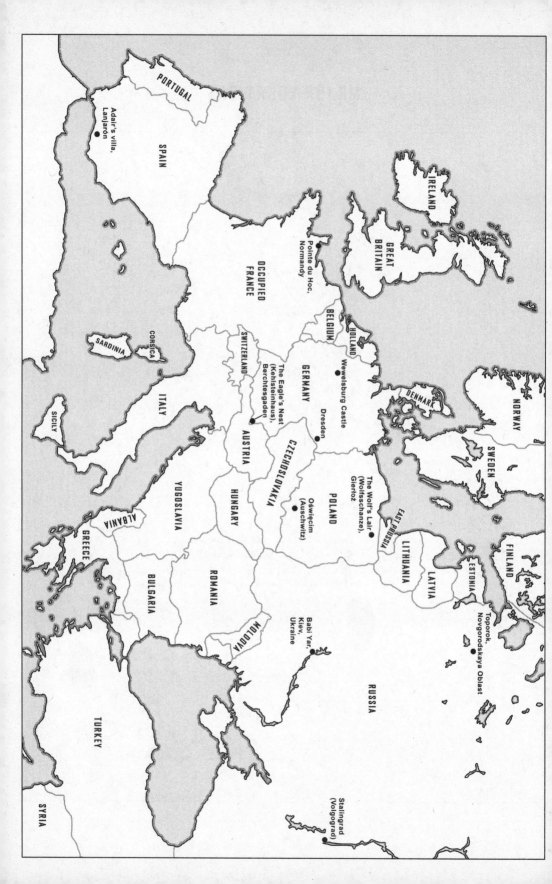

PORTUGAL

SPAIN

Adair's villa,
Lanjarón

IRELAND

GREAT
BRITAIN

Pointe du Hoc,
Normandy

OCCUPIED
FRANCE

BELGIUM

HOLLAND

NORWAY

DENMARK

SWEDEN

FINLAND

SARDINIA

CORSICA

SWITZERLAND

GERMANY

Weweisburg Castle

Dresden

The Eagle's Nest
(Kehlsteinhaus),
Berchtesgaden

ITALY

AUSTRIA

CZECHOSLOVAKIA

The Wolf's Lair
(Wolfsschanze),
Gierłoź

SICILY

YUGOSLAVIA

HUNGARY

Oświęcim
(Auschwitz)

POLAND

EAST PRUSSIA

LITHUANIA

LATVIA

ESTONIA

ALBANIA

GREECE

BULGARIA

ROMANIA

MOLDOVA

Babi Yar,
Kiev,
Ukraine

RUSSIA

Toporok,
Novgorodskaya Oblast

TURKEY

SYRIA

Stalingrad
(Volgograd)

GLOSSARY

adept—*n.*, an initiate into the Art of ceremonial magick; often used synonymously with "apprentice." The lowest level of adept in magick is a *novice;* a journeyman adept is an *acolyte;* a master-level adept is a *karcist* (see below).

Art, the—*n.*, capitalized, a shorthand term referring to Renaissance-era ceremonial magick.

athamé—*n.*, a black-handled knife with many uses in ceremonial magick.

dabbler—*n.*, karcists' pejorative for an amateur or a poorly trained adept of ceremonial magick.

demon—*n.*, a fallen angel; demons provide the overwhelming majority of magick in the Art, with the remaining small percentage coming from angels.

Enochian—*n.*, the language of angels; *adj.*, related to or originating from angels or their language.

experiment—*n.*, in ceremonial magick, technical term for a ritual involving the conjuration and control of demons or angels.

familiar—*n.*, a demonic spirit in animal form, sent to aid a karcist and amplify his or her powers.

grimoire—*n.*, a book of magickal contracts between a karcist and the demons with whom he or she has struck pacts in exchange for access to them and the powers they grant.

incubus—*n.*, a low-level (i.e., nameless) demon, a creature of pure meanness and spite, whose function is to seduce mortals or, in some cases, act as their sexual servant; an incubus can take any of a variety of masculine forms. When so desired, it can assume a feminine form; in such an event, it is referred to as a *succubus* (see below).

Kabbalah—*n.*, a system of esoteric theosophy and theurgy developed by Hebrew rabbis; it is considered a system of "White Magick," though it has a "Black Magick" component known as *Sitra Achra*.

karcist—*n.*, a master-level adept in the Art of ceremonial magick.

lamia—*n.*, a low-level (i.e., nameless) demon summoned to act as a domestic servant; though lamiae can be compelled to behave in a manner that seems docile or even friendly, they must be carefully controlled, or else they will turn against those who conjured and commanded them.

Lull Engine—*n.*, a divination tool, often consisting of overlapping wheels made from stiff paper or cardboard, that can be called upon without invoking either demons or angels.

magick—*n.*, when spelled with a terminal "k," a shorthand term for Renaissance-era ceremonial magick, also known as the Art. Not to be confused with theatrical or stage magic, which consists of sleight of hand, misdirection, and mechanical illusions. All acts of true magick are predicated on the conjuration and control of demons or, in rare cases, angels.

nadach—*n.*, a human being whose soul has been spiritually bonded prior to birth with the essence of a demon; such a union persists for life and often confers one or more special abilities.

nikraim—*n.*, a human being whose soul has been spiritually bonded prior to birth with the essence of an angel; such a union persists for life and often confers one or more special abilities.

operator—*n.*, in the Art, the adept or karcist leading or controlling an experiment.

patient—*n.*, an antiseptic term of the Art for the intended subject (often a victim) of a demonic sending (see below) resulting from an experiment.

rabble—*n.*, karcists' nickname for the world's non-magickal majority of people.

rod—*n.*, in the Art, a wand; used to impose punishments on demons and direct magickal effects.

scrying—*n.*, a term for remote viewing, or clairvoyance (i.e., witnessing events in faraway places) by means of magick.

send—*v.*, in the context of magick, to dispatch a demon by means of an experiment, with orders to perform a specified task. Such actions can include, but are not limited to, murder, assault, recovery of valued objects, and the acquisition of information.

succubus—*n.*, a low-level (i.e., nameless) demon, a creature of pure meanness and spite, whose function is to seduce mortals or, in some cases, act as their sexual servant; a succubus can take any of a variety of feminine forms. When so desired, it can assume a masculine form; in such an event, it is referred to as an *incubus* (see above).

tanist—*n.*, a karcist, adept, or other person who acts as an assistant to the operator during an experiment. Most experiments are designed to be performed either by a lone operator or by an operator with two or four tanists.

ward—*n.*, a glyph, seal, or other sigil, whether temporary or permanent, that serves to protect a person, place, or thing from demonic or magickal assault, detection, or other effect.

yoke—*v.*, to force a demon or angel into the conscious control of a karcist. Yoking a demon often incurs deleterious side effects for the karcist; such effects can include, but are not limited to, headaches, nosebleeds, nightmares, indigestion, and a variety of self-destructive obsessive-compulsive behaviors.

THE INFERNAL DESCENDING HIERARCHY

SUPERIOR SPIRITS AND MINISTERS OF HELL

Satan Mekratrig

Put Satanachia (Baphomet)			Beelzebuth		
Lucifuge Rofocale	Astaroth	Sathanas	Paimon	Asmodeus	Belial

Mortals cannot strike pacts with the Emperor of Hell (Satan Mekratrig) or the other two superior spirits (Baphomet and Beelzebuth).

A karcist makes his/her first pact with one of the six ministers (governors) of Hell; subsequently, his or her future pacts are limited to the subordinate spirits of that minister, and no others. It is possible for a minister to act as patron to many human karcists at once. None of the six ministers (aka patron spirits) can be yoked by a mortal karcist.

The ministers, ranked in terms of power and influence, from most to least, are:

> Lucifuge Rofocale (666 legions)
> Paimon (200 legions)
> Asmodeus (72 legions)
> Belial (50 legions)
> Astaroth (40 legions)
> Sathanas (38 legions)

The fortunes and influences of the spirits fluctuate as the demons vie for power in the Infernal Hierarchy. A karcist most often makes compacts with his/her patron spirit for such benefits as wealth, longevity with slowed aging, and immunity to disease.

ACKNOWLEDGMENTS

As has long been my custom, my first thanks go to my wife, Kara. She has been my sounding board, cheering section, brainstorming partner, and my rock throughout what proved to be a longer and more arduous process than I'd dared to imagine.

Next up for plaudits are the members of my Twitter-based demon-naming club: Cherie Priest, Niko Nikkilä, Chuck Wendig, Marianne Larsen (aka @danishwolf), @Xolus, John Marte, Dash Cooray, Michelle Belanger, Alana Ní Loingsigh, Luso Mnthali, James the Former (aka @AbsurdlyJames), @allyanncah, Jenifer Rosenberg, and Julianna Kuhn. My thanks also go out to Monica Valentinelli, who provided me links to pages about Enochian mythology and symbols, and to Jeff Willens, who helped enlighten me on some obscure details of Jewish demonology.

A heaping helping of gratitude is due to my friend and fellow author Ilana C. Myer and her husband, Yaakov, who helped me devise the faux-Hebrew terms *nikraim* and *nadach* to describe my humans who are spiritually bonded to, respectively, angels and demons.

I also want to acknowledge Twitter maven @GeekGirlDiva, who provided the name *Silver Sadie* for the B-17 that ferries my main character into Germany. Thanks also to all the other fine Twittizens who offered helpful suggestions I elected not to use.

Of course, this book would have suffered without the sage insights and advice of its story consultants and beta readers: Una McCormack, Aaron Rosenberg, Ilana C. Myer, Kirsten Beyer, Lucienne Diver, and Scott Pearson. I offer my deepest thanks to you all.

Last but certainly not least: I would be lost without the guidance of my editor, friend, and literary *senpai*, Marco Palmieri. Thank you for still having faith in me, brother.

ABOUT THE AUTHOR

David Mack is the *New York Times* bestselling author of over thirty novels, more than a dozen pieces of published short fiction, and two produced episodes of *Star Trek: Deep Space Nine*.

Follow him on Twitter **@DavidAlanMack** and on **www.facebook.com/TheDavidMack**, and learn more at his official website, **davidmack.pro**.

TURN THE PAGE FOR A SNEAK PEEK
AT THE NEXT CHAPTER OF THE DARK ARTS SERIES.

THE IRON CODEX

AVAILABLE WINTER 2019

1954

Anja's knee kissed gravel as she leaned her motorcycle into the turn at speed, and the demons inside her head sniggered at the thought of her imminent, sudden demise. Jagged rocks kicked up by the front tire pelted her riding leathers and bounced off her goggles. The edge of her rear tire scraped the dirt road's precipice, sending pebbles down the cliff into the fog-shrouded jungle far below. Around the bend, she straightened her stance and twisted open the throttle.

Far ahead, through drifting veils of mist, her prey accelerated and widened his lead. Anja's 1953 Vincent Black Shadow had been touted by its maker as the fastest motorcycle in the world, but that didn't matter much on Bolivia's infamous and aptly named Death Road. The one-lane dirt trail snaked along a mountainside covered in tropical forest. Waterfalls often manifested without warning and filled the road with lakes of mud, and the jungle below was said to have been blanketed with fog since before men had first set foot in South America.

Condensation clouded Anja's speedometer and tachometer. She had to trust her feel for the bike as she pushed it hard through an S-turn, and she prayed for a straightaway on the other side so that she could close the gap between her and her escaping Nazi target.

Bullets zinged past her right shoulder. Bark exploded from slender tree trunks. Stones leapt from the muddy earth and tumbled into the road behind Anja.

She glanced at her right mirror. A line of four motorcycles—souped-up BMW touring bikes, the same kind as the one she was chasing—were pursuing her.

They knew I'd go after him, Anja realized. *This is trap.*

The quartet was closing in. They were only seconds behind her now.

Anja berated herself for getting careless. She shifted her weight with the direction of the next curve and got so low that she felt the road grind against the side of her leg. More bullets ripped past above her and vanished into the mist. Swinging into the back of the S-turn, she plucked her last grenade from her bandolier. She squeezed its shoe in her left hand. "DANOCHAR," she said to her invisible demonic porter, "take the grenade's safety pin—and *only the pin*." In a blink, the safety pin vanished.

She let the grenade fall from her hand, onto the foggy road.

After she rounded the next turn she heard the explosion—coupled with the screams of riders caught in the blast or thrown from the road with their broken bikes into the haze-masked treetops far below. Men and machines crashed through the branches with cracks like gunshots. Then there was only silence on the road behind Anja.

Ahead of her, the man she had come to kill fought to open up his lead.

The roar of the wind and the growl of the Black Shadow bled together as Anja pushed the British-made motorcycle to its limits. The bike slammed through a deep puddle and parted it like Moses splitting the Reed Sea. Anja used what little mass she had to pull the bike through a close pair of perilous turns, and then she bladed through a wall of fog to see a straight patch of road with her prey in the middle of it. She twisted open the throttle and ducked low to reduce her wind resistance. Her long sable hair whipped in the wind like mad serpents.

Just have to get close enough before he makes the next turn. . . .

At last the Black Shadow lived up to its reputation. It felt like a rocket as it brought Anja to within five meters of the fleeing Nazi. She followed him through the next turn—then dodged toward the cliff wall on her right as he flung a hunting knife blindly over his shoulder. The blade soared past her head and then it was gone, out of mind.

Enough. I came for the kill, not the hunt.

Calling once more upon her yoked demonic arsenal, Anja conjured the spectral whip of VALEFOR. A flick of her wrist sent the massive bullwhip streaking ahead of her. Its barbed tip wrapped around the neck of her target, and Anja squeezed the Black Shadow's brake lever.

Her bike skidded to a halt on the dirt road, and her whip went taut. It jerked the Nazi off his ride, which launched itself off the cliff into the gray murk between the trees. As the Nazi landed on his back, his bike vanished. From the impenetrable mists came the snaps of it crashing through heavy branches, a sound that made Anja think of a hammer breaking bones.

She shifted the Black Shadow's engine into neutral, slowed its throttle to a rumbling purr, and then lowered its custom side stand. Her magickal whip remained coiled around her target's neck as she prowled forward to lord her victory over him.

A jerk of the whip focused his attention on her. "You are Herr König, yes?"

He spat at her. "And you're the Jungle Witch."

"Only by necessity." She found it amusing that the Nazis whom she had spent the better part of a decade hunting throughout South America had somehow mistaken her for a local. It was understandable, she supposed; her prolonged exposure to the sun and weather had tanned her once-pale skin, effectively masking her Russian heritage. She drew her hunting knife from its belt sheath and leaned down. "Move and I'll cut your throat."

He remained still, no doubt in part because the demon's whip was still coiled around his throat. The strap of the man's leather satchel crossed his torso on a diagonal. She sliced through it near its top, above his shoulder and close enough to his throat to keep him cowed.

"Don't move," Anja said. With a spiral motion of her hand, she commanded VALEFOR's whip to bind the German fugitive war criminal at his wrists and ankles. Certain he was restrained, she picked up his satchel and pawed through its contents. Most of it was exactly what she had expected to find: extra magazines for the man's Luger, which was still in its holster on his right hip; a few wads of cash in different currencies, all of which she pocketed. An ivory pipe and a bag of tobacco fell from the bag as she shook it upside down, along with a pencil, an assortment of nearly worthless coins, and a battered old compass. The bag appeared to be empty, but it still felt heavy to Anja. She muttered, "What are you hiding in here?"

With her hands she searched the interior of the satchel. She found a hidden pouch concealed under a large flap. Her prisoner squirmed on the ground as she untied the laces of the flap and pulled from the satchel's clandestine pocket a leather-bound journal. "Well," she said, flipping open the book to peruse its handwritten contents, "this is interesting." The few full words and sentences it contained were scribbled in German, but her yoked spirit LIOBOR made it possible for Anja to read any human language with ease. Unfortunately, the spirit was of no help when it came to parsing the acronyms and abbreviations that littered most of the pages.

She showed the open journal to her prisoner. "Care to explain your acronyms?"

"Burn in Hell, witch."

"Inevitably, yes." She flipped another page and admired its high-quality linen paper. "I know your Thule Society dabblers have reformed under the name Black Sun, as a nod to Herr Himmler. But what is Odessa? Is that your expatriate network here in South America? The one that brought you all to Argentina when the war ended?"

He maintained his silence as a faint growl of motorcycle engines echoed in the distance.

It was evident to Anja that Herr König was not going to provide any useful intelligence. At least, not in the limited time she had remaining before more of his cohorts arrived. Normally she would not have feared a confrontation with his ilk, but she had been holding yoked demons for too long. Any hour now she would need to release them, spend a week or so recovering her strength, and then yoke them or other spirits all over again. It was time for her to withdraw to her safe house in La Paz. There she could plan her next move.

But first she needed to address the problem of Herr König.

A flourish of her left hand released him from the demonic whip. Free but still on his knees, König smirked at Anja. "We'll find you, Jungle Witch."

"Your minions will try. But before I send you to Hell, I want you to know my name." She made a fist with her right hand, and the unholy talent of XENOCH racked the Nazi with torments worse than the human imagination could conceive. She raised his body off the ground with the telekinesis of BAEL and savored his contorted expression of agony. "My name is Anja. Anja Kernova." She flung him high into the air as if he weighed nothing, and as he plummeted toward the jungle she blasted him in mid-fall with a fireball courtesy of HABORYM. His burning corpse vanished through the fog and jungle canopy and was swallowed by fathomless shadows.

An eerie quiet settled over the valley. Anja took a moment to enjoy the solitude of North Yungas Road. Rugged mountains towered around her, but the jungle's misty atmosphere had imbued them all with the quality of fading memories.

Then she heard far-off motorcycles drawing ever closer.

She tucked the Odessa journal inside her jacket and got on her bike. The Black Shadow roared as she shifted it into gear, and she sped south, Hell's dark rider alone on Death's Road.

JANUARY 9

Like most gentlemen's clubs in metropolitan London, The Eddington was defined by its subdued ambience. Its interior looked as if it had been hewn from the finest mahogany and black marble, and the only things in the main hall older than the leather on its chairs were its founding members' portraits, which lined the walls and looked down with perpetual disdain on those who had been cursed with the misfortune of being born after the Industrial Revolution.

Tucked in a semiprivate anteroom, Dragan Dalca stood to greet his three smartly attired guests as they were ushered into his company by the Eddington's chief steward, Mr. Harris.

"Gentlemen." Harris gestured toward Dragan. "Your host, Mr. Dalca."

"Thank you, Harris," Dragan said. The Yugoslavian gestured toward the open seats around his table. "Please, have a seat." Noting an unspoken prompt by Harris, Dragan asked the three briefcase-toting businessmen, "You must be parched. What can we bring you?"

"Gordon's martini," said the Frenchman. "Dry as the Gobi." Harris nodded.

The American asked, "Do you have bourbon?"

Harris tried not to look put out. "I'm afraid not, sir. Can I offer you scotch whisky?"

"A double of The Macallan Twenty-five," the American said.

Harris approved the order with a nod, then looked at the Russian. "Sir?"

"The same."

Dragan caught Harris's eye. "Double Smirnoff, rocks."

In unison, the businessmen tucked their briefcases under the table.

Harris stepped back, pulled closed the anteroom's thick maroon curtain to give the men some privacy, and departed to fill the drink order, leaving Dragan alone at last with his guests. The trio greeted Dragan with faltering smiles. The Frenchman was the first to speak. "Your message implied this meeting would be private."

"I disagree," Dragan said. "And I am not responsible for your inferences." The ever-present voice nagged at him from behind his thoughts, *«Get on with it.»* Dragan ignored the criticism, settled into his high-backed chair and folded his hands together, his fingers interlaced. "I invited the three of you here to present you with a business proposition."

"Your telegram said as much," the American said, his impatience festering. The Brit and the Russian both adopted taciturn, wait-and-see façades.

«Skip the small talk,» needled the voice in Dragan's psyche.

Very well; just stay quiet and let me do this. Dragan sat forward and plastered an insincere smile onto his face. "I invited you gentlemen to meet with me because the three of you represent aircraft manufacturing companies that recently have fallen behind in the race to secure clients on the international market. And I'm sure you all know why."

"Those pricks at de Havilland," groused the American.

The Frenchman nodded. "Indeed. The Comet 1, to be precise."

"It is the only thing my clients talk about," the Russian said. "They overlook its weaknesses and see nothing but its jet engines. 'This is the future,' they tell me."

"It is," Dragan said. "Unchecked, de Havilland will dominate the market for at least another decade, if not longer. Assuming, of course, that nothing . . . *unfortunate* happens."

This time his unsubtle implication drew raised eyebrows from his guests. The Russian leaned forward. "What sort of misfortune could derail such potential?"

Dragan reached inside his jacket and pulled out a slender gold cigarette case. He opened it, plucked out a Gauloises, and lit it with a match stroked against the table's edge. Waving out the match's flame, he took a deep drag of the rich Turkish tobacco, and then he exhaled through his nostrils. "If you gentlemen are interested in reversing de Havilland's fortunes, not to mention your own, it might interest you to know that the Comet 1, despite its early success, is plagued by two fatal flaws, both of which de Havilland has worked hard to conceal."

This revelation stoked the American's interest. "What sort of flaws?"

"Let it suffice to say that one is a matter of engineering, the other of materials. Together, they could be exploited to undermine de Havilland's position in the marketplace."

Skepticism infused the Frenchman's mood. "And you know this . . . how?"

"A pair of incidents," Dragan said. "Last March, a Comet 1A crashed during takeoff from Karachi Airport. The flacks at de Havilland blamed it on pilot error—"

The Russian cut in, "The Canadian Pacific Air accident?"

"Yes," Dragan said. "Just under two months later, another Comet 1 crashed, just minutes after takeoff from Calcutta. All six crew and thirty-seven passengers were killed."

"I read that report," the American said. "It blamed the crash on a thunder squall."

Dragan shrugged. "I don't deny the storm was a factor. But it was not the cause. Sooner or later, a Comet 1 will experience an in-flight disaster that it can't blame on pilots or weather." He goaded them with a sly smirk. "Sooner, I hope, for your employers' sakes."

The Frenchman sharpened his focus, clearly intrigued. "So what has this to do—"

The curtain opened, revealing Harris. Balanced on one hand was a tray bearing the men's drinks. As he passed out the libations, he said discreetly to Dragan, "Phone call for you, sir."

"Thank you, Harris." Dragan stood and offered his guests an apologetic smile. "Forgive me, gentlemen. I shall return promptly." The others excused him with polite nods.

Dragan crossed the main hall at a quick but dignified pace. Just before he reached the concierge's desk, he caught his reflection in the glass door of a trophy case and paused to push his black hair back into place and to smooth a few rogue whiskers back into his thin mustache. Then he accepted the phone's receiver handset from the concierge, and he stretched its cord around a corner into the coatroom so that he could take his call with a modicum of privacy.

Knowing that only one person on earth knew to reach him at The Eddington, he snarled, "What is it, Müller?"

"*I apologize for the interruption*," replied Heinrich Müller, sounding nothing at all like the man who just a decade earlier had been the commandant of Hitler's feared Gestapo, "*but there's news out of Bolivia.*"

Hope swelled inside Dragan, the product of unjustified optimism. "She took the bait?"

"*Yes. Well, no. Not exactly.*" Müller's tone was heavy with shame. "*You were right, she was watching the roads to La Paz. But she didn't fall for the decoy.*"

"If she didn't go after the decoy, how do you know she—" Realization struck Dragan like a hot shower turning ice-cold without warning. "What happened? What went wrong?"

Müller breathed a leaden sigh. "*König and his guards. She took them all on the Death Road.*" After a paused gravid with shame, he added, "*And she captured his journal.*"

Profanities logjammed in Dragan's mouth, the flood of invective too great for him to give it voice. He knew not to make a spectacle of himself inside The Eddington. Instead he clenched a fist and counted to five while drawing deep breaths.

His irritating inner voice was not so considerate.

«*This is a disaster. Contain this, now!*»

Silence! I will handle it.

"Müller," he said at last, "round up everyone we can spare, and bring them to La Paz. Find the woman as soon as possible. Take her alive if you can, but your chief priority—"

"*Is to recover the book,*" Müller said. "*I remember, sir.*"

"See that you do. If you or your men kill Anja Kernova before we find that book, I'll bury your body so deep underground the Devil himself couldn't find it."

Müller was still mouthing hollow assurances as Dragan handed the receiver back to the concierge, who set it back onto the phone's cradle behind his podium.

Twenty-one steps back to the anteroom, Dragan told himself. *Breathe and put your smile back on before you step through that curtain.*

Low chatter filled the space between his guests as he sidled back into his chair. "Thank you for your patience, gentlemen. How much would it be worth to each of your employers to see your most dominant competitor suffer a very public setback? One that could ruin it, and for which it would take all the blame?"

The American turned cagy. "That's a difficult question to answer, Mr. Dalca. Depending on when such an event were to take place—"

"Assume it's happening tomorrow afternoon. In Rome."

Wary looks of conspiratorial intent were exchanged among the guests at Dragan's table. The Russian nodded. "That would be a most valuable twist of fate."

"I want you all to tell me exactly how valuable," Dragan said. "Your employers knew to send you with the authority to make a deal." He pushed a few scraps of blank paper and some pens into the middle of the table. "Write down your offer, then fold the paper and hand it back."

One by one, each man took a slip of paper and a pen.

Half a minute later, Dragan held their offers in his hands.

He smiled. "Excellent. My terms are simple. Half of your pledged amount up front, in cash. The remaining half will be due upon delivery of my promise. If I fail to deliver, your deposits will be returned in full, without question." He steepled his fingers and leaned forward. "But in case any of you might be thinking you can renege on the second half of your payment, know this: I have *never* been bilked, nor will I be. Do you all understand me?"

Fearful nods confirmed that his guests knew that his threats were not idle ones.

"Very well. Thank you for coming. I look forward to seeing you all again tomorrow."

The businessmen downed their drinks with steep tilts of their glasses, and then they rose from the table to beat a quiet retreat through the main hall and then out the front door.

Dragan stole a look through the table and inside the briefcases, using RAUM's gift of The Sight. He was gratified to see that each briefcase was packed full of cash—American dollars, French francs, and Russian rubles, respectively.

He sipped his Smirnoff, and then he beckoned the steward.

The dignified, middle-aged Englishman arrived at his table. "Sir?"

"The cases under my table," Dragan said. "Please see them to Mr. Holcombe, and tell him I want the entire sum invested in short sales of De Havilland Aviation stock."

"I shall see to it at once, Mr. Dalca."

"Thank you, Harris."

Dragan enjoyed the enveloping silence of the club while Harris and two members of his staff toted the briefcases full of cash away to the waiting hands of Dragan's broker.

Twenty-four hours from now, I'm going to be a very wealthy man, he mused. *All I need to do now is get the book back from that Russian bitch . . . and then justice will be done.*

———

Living a lie had proved a pleasant state of affairs for Briet Segfrunsdóttir.

It had been over eight years since the OSS had found her in self-imposed exile in northern Finland. When its agents had knocked on her door, she'd thought her day of reckoning was at hand, that they had come to take her to the Hague—or to put a bullet in her head—for her complicity in the Nazis' war crimes. Instead, all her sins had been redacted under the auspices of Operation Paperclip, an American secret initiative to find the scientists and engineers—and also, as it turned out, the sorcerers—of the defeated German Third Reich and recruit them into the service of the world's new master: its lone atomic superpower, the United States of America.

They'd since given her a life far better than what she deserved.

She had a nondescript bordering on meaningless job title, coupled with a generous salary and fringe benefits. A three-story brownstone in the heart of Georgetown. Immunity from international prosecution. Vast reserves of equipment, personnel, and money at her disposal, to facilitate her magickal research. The Americans had even let her keep her Icelandic citizenship despite having naturalized her as one of their own.

All they asked in return was that she be their shield, sword, and all-seeing eye. It was the best deal Briet was going to get on this earth, and she knew it.

So, she wondered as her alarm clock rang at the stroke of seven, *why is my stomach a bottomless pit of dread?* A slap of her hand silenced the alarm. As the only member of her household with a job that insisted on semi-regular hours, Briet slept on the left side of the king bed, nearest the end table and clock. Her lovers—Alton Bloch, a former accountant and aspiring Beat poet, and Park Hyun, a Korean woman who had escaped her war-torn country to come to America six months earlier as a refugee—took turns being islanded in the middle of the bed.

Today it was Hyun's turn. She snoozed on, blissfully oblivious as Briet and Alton dragged themselves out from under the covers into the unforgiving chill of a winter morning. A shrill wind rattled the bedroom windows.

Alton scratched his hirsute chest. "I'll put the kettle on."

Briet kissed his stubbled cheek. "You're the best." She slipped away to the bathroom to brush her teeth and shower.

Half an hour later she padded downstairs, dressed for work in a simple dark blue dress, her fiery red hair coiled atop her head under a towel. As she passed through the sitting room on her way to the kitchen, a jazz melody of Lester Young with the Oscar Peterson Trio spilled softly from the stereophonic speakers of the record player cabinet.

In the kitchen Alton had prepared a simple breakfast of poached eggs, rye toast, and tea. His insistence on getting up each morning to cook breakfast for Briet had been one of many tiny kindnesses that had endeared him to her. He wasn't much to look at—he was pushing forty, his brown hair was thinning, and he had exactly the physique one might expect of a longtime office worker— but Briet loved him for the art in his soul.

And for his prodigious cock. She was only human, after all.

They ate without small talk because he respected her preference for silence, especially early in the morning. Afterward while he washed the dishes, she took a few minutes to retreat upstairs to finish her hair and makeup. Then she visited her study to dote on a companion who had been by her side since before the war: her rat familiar, Trixim.

Born of magick, Trixim had outlived his mundane kin by an order of magnitude. Briet credited his longevity at least in part to the degree to which she spoiled and doted on the crimson-eyed black rodent. He stood on his hind legs and nibbled eagerly as she fed him small morsels of Gruyère, and he licked chicken-liver paté from her fingertip without nipping at her. "Good boy, Trixim," she said, scritching his head before petting him down his back. "Don't be a troublemaker—stay in your cage until I get home tonight." He affirmed her instruction by nuzzling her wrist with the side of his face.

Outside the house, a horn honked.

From the first floor Alton called out, "Your car's here!"

"Coming." She dropped a few last bits of cheese in Trixim's cage, and she locked her study's door as she hurried out.

At the bottom of the stairs she kissed Alton, who held her dove gray overcoat as she shimmied into it. "Thank you, my love," she said.

He opened the front door, admitting a wash of cold morning air. "Call me when you leave tonight. I'm making a Beef Wellington."

"I will. Tootles." She waved farewell as she bounded down the steps and across the walk to a waiting black Lincoln Continental that idled outside her brownstone's front gate, with its chauffeur standing beside the passenger door.

The driver opened the door, and Briet climbed inside the car, which was pleasantly warm. On the bench seat were copies of that morning's editions of *The New York Times* and *The Washington Post*. A creature of habit, Briet reached for *The New York Times* and skimmed the headlines to take the day's temperature.

As was typical for a Saturday paper, there was no banner headline. The most prominent item was tucked into the top left corner: U.S. STAND ON REDS AND JAPAN DRAWS SEOUL BROADSIDE. In the center column, PRESIDENT TO TAKE A STRONGER ROLE IN PUSHING POLICY. The other top stories were similarly drab: proposals for new taxes, a threat of a labor strike in the nation's ports, Thailand pushing for Indo-China to join it to form an anti-Communist bloc . . . and then, just above the fold, the buried lead:

NEW BOMB TESTS SLATED IN PACIFIC
Greatest Hydrogen Explosion May be Produced

The article's opening sentence treated the matter as if it were blasé: "The Atomic Energy Commission announced plans tonight for another series of tests for atomic and probably hydrogen weapons at the government's Pacific Proving Grounds."

Is that why they asked me to come in on a Saturday?

She dismissed the notion as quickly as she'd conjured it. Atomic weapons terrified Briet, and she frequently needed to remind herself that they and the issues they raised were explicitly beyond the scope of her duties. Fission bombs were temptations to brinksmanship in her opinion, not the sort of thing any sane person would want to see used ever again.

Two bombs on Japan was more than enough, she brooded.

At any rate, the United States had tasked Briet with managing a more personal brand of defense. One tailored to exploit her rare and dangerous talents.

She finished her cursory review of both newspapers by the time her driver stopped the car outside the North Rotary Road entrance of the Pentagon. Not a word had passed between them during the trip, making it the same as every other ride they had shared. There was, after all, no point in trying to engage a lamia in conversation. The nameless demons were creatures of low intelligence and pure spite; they were reliable for simple tasks as long as they remained under firm control, but they would never be known for having "people skills."

Briet left the newspapers behind on the seat as she left the car and breezed through the first of several security checkpoints between her and her final destination.

Officially, she was listed as a civilian research assistant to some mid-level naval officer, and that was what she had told both of her lovers. There was nothing to be gained by telling them the truth about who she really was, or the true nature of her work for the Department of Defense.

After a long walk through the Pentagon's seemingly endless corridors, almost all of which looked maddeningly alike, a lengthy and slow elevator—whose basement access point was guarded by no fewer than three armed Marines—delivered her to a sublevel not documented on any official blueprints of the Pentagon. More than six hundred feet belowground another trio of Marines with permanent frowns guarded a massive round steel door.

One Marine checked her credentials while another stood ready to shoot her dead if they failed to pass muster. When the Marine in charge cleared her to proceed, the third man opened the door and ushered her through the massive portalway, into America's best-kept secret.

The Silo.

The main space was humbling in its sheer size. The pentagonal pit measured five hundred feet across, and from its water-filled nadir to its ceiling it stood nearly a thousand feet tall. One-third of the way up from its bottom, a steel-grate widow's walk led to the conjuring stage, a platform shaped like an equilateral pentagon suspended above the pit's center. Mounted on the ceiling were industrial lights that bathed the catwalk and the stage in a white glare, and the sides of the platform were ringed by coal-fed braziers atop six-foot-tall stands.

During magickal rituals orange flames would dance from the braziers, and the overhead lights would be turned off, shrouding everything beyond the stage's edge in darkness. With the lights on, the proliferation of high-speed cameras and arcane electromagnetic sensors that festooned the walls was clearly visible. As daunting as the Silo appeared, however, Briet knew that its true marvels were hidden behind its multitude of two-way mirrored observation windows.

Dozens of sublevels surrounding the Silo were packed with thinking machines the scientists called computers. They ran on electricity and stored information on reels of magnetic tape. Inputs from the sensors and cameras were monitored by an army of technicians, physicists, engineers, and—most surprising to Briet—lawyers. While the scientists labored to quantify the exotic particles and energies of magick in order to reduce it to mere science, the lawyers concerned themselves with untangling the convoluted terms and verbiage of demonic pacts. They seemed convinced that they would find ways to exploit loopholes in Hell's contracts and by so doing trick the Devil himself into granting special advantages to the United States.

Standing alone on her conjuring stage, Briet felt a pang of nostalgia.

I miss the days when I could work magick without a fucking audience.

Footsteps on the widow's walk echoed in the cavernous space. Briet turned to see the Silo's director of operations, Frank Cioffi, crossing the bridge. Frank was the epitome of average, in Briet's opinion. Pale from decades spent indoors, a stranger to the sun. Balding and bespectacled, his face was so plain it could vanish into any crowd. He favored the pedestrian attire that had become the stereotype of engineers and scientists everywhere: black trousers, a white short-sleeve button-down shirt, narrow tie, a pocket protector loaded with pens and a folding slide rule, black socks, and dull black Oxfords.

Behind him followed two men and two women, none of whom she had never seen before. *Strangers. That doesn't bode well.*

It took the group a couple of minutes to reach the platform. Briet blamed their sloth on Frank's short legs, ill-fitting pants, and poor health. He wasn't a bad man, as far as Briet had been able to discern, but he was no paragon of integrity or courage, and she had never seen anyone who possessed his knack for making good clothes look bad.

Frank tried to preempt criticism with a jolly "Good morning, Briet!"

"Spare me the bullshit, Frank." She lifted her chin to gesture toward the four strangers at his back. "Who the fuck are they?"

"Your new tanists." He pivoted and tried to segue into introductions. "This is—"

"No," Briet interrupted. "I'm not doing this again."

His smile evaporated, leaving his jowls slack in defeat. "I have my orders."

"I don't care. This is the third time in nine years! Every time I whip a team of adepts into shape, they get transferred and some bureaucrat sends me four novices. I'm sick of it, Frank."

"You know the drill, Bree. It's all about creating redundancies in our defense plan. If Washington ever gets hit by a Russian nuke, we'll need magickal defense teams in safe locations, ready to carry on after we're gone."

She stepped around Frank to assess the latest batch of dilettantes. One of the men looked Chinese; the other was pale and blond. Both were lean and sinewy with features chiseled by deprivation. Briet singled out the quasi-albino. "You. What demon was bound by Solomon's forty-third seal?"

He looked like a rabbit about to become roadkill. "Um . . . ."

"Shut up." Briet pointed at the Chinese man. "You?"

"Sargatanas?"

"Are you asking me or telling me?"

He steeled his nerve. "Telling you. It's Sargatanas."

"Wrong. It's Sabnock. Don't speak again unless I give you permission."

Briet turned toward the two female aspirants. The taller of the pair was dark-skinned and wore her hair in a dramatic afro. "I like your hair. So will demons. Wear that to an experiment and I guarantee you some spirit will rip it out of your scalp. Cut that off, today."

As the chastised woman shrank, Briet faced the last new adept. The second woman was short, muscled, and wore her hair in a tight bun. Her fingers were callused, and her eyes were keen. She seemed to burn with the promise of competence. But Briet had to be sure.

"To speak through the flames of PARAGO, what must one sacrifice?"

"An offering of rock salt and Mercurial incense of powdered black dianthus."

It was the correct answer, provided without hesitation or equivocation. It was already clear to Briet which of her four new adepts would quickly rise to fill the group's senior role.

Still, she took Frank aside. "I don't like this."

"Neither do I. But it's not like the government gives us a choice."

"At least tell me where the latest group was sent."

Frank shook his head. "You know I can't. Even if they told me, which they don't, it'd be top-secret." He lowered his voice and put on an apologetic air. "Do us both a favor: don't rock the boat. Every time this happens, you pitch a fit. That makes the brass nervous. And trust me—you don't want that. Something scares the brass, their first instinct is always the same: kill it." He glanced at the new adepts. "Just do what they pay you for."

He patted her shoulder, as if they were conspirators who had come to an arrangement, when the reality was that Briet felt ready to erupt in violence. But she knew there was a legion of soldiers, civilians, scientists, and specialists observing her every action. If she rebelled, or cast herself in the role of a dissident here in the Silo, the Marines between her and the exit would make certain she never left the Pentagon alive.

She turned to face her adepts. Behind them, Frank waddled across the steel grate bridge, headed back into the walls of the Silo.

How long will it take me to train these bumblers? And once I do, how long until they vanish through the same revolving door that robbed me of my last twelve adepts?

Taking care not to let her face betray her anger or her mounting suspicion, she looked up at the myriad windows and cameras.

Redundancies, my ass. What are these people not telling me?

It was a question that no one in the Silo would answer, but Briet was tired of waiting for them to read her into their schemes. One way or another she was going to get the truth—whether her masters liked it or not.